THE
BLACK HILLS

THE
BLACK HILLS

Rod Thompson

BERKLEY BOOKS, NEW YORK

THE BERKLEY PUBLISHING GROUP
Published by the Penguin Group
Penguin Group (USA) Inc.
375 Hudson Street, New York, New York 10014, USA
Penguin Group (Canada), 90 Eglinton Avenue East, Suite 700, Toronto, Ontario M4P 2Y3, Canada
(a division of Pearson Penguin Canada Inc.)
Penguin Books Ltd., 80 Strand, London WC2R 0RL, England
Penguin Group Ireland, 25 St. Stephen's Green, Dublin 2, Ireland (a division of Penguin Books Ltd.)
Penguin Group (Australia), 250 Camberwell Road, Camberwell, Victoria 3124, Australia
(a division of Pearson Australia Group Pty. Ltd.)
Penguin Books India Pvt. Ltd., 11 Community Centre, Panchsheel Park, New Delhi—110 017, India
Penguin Group (NZ), 67 Apollo Drive, Rosedale, Auckland 0632, New Zealand
(a division of Pearson New Zealand Ltd.)
Penguin Books (South Africa) (Pty.) Ltd., 24 Sturdee Avenue, Rosebank, Johannesburg 2196,
South Africa

Penguin Books Ltd., Registered Offices: 80 Strand, London WC2R 0RL, England

This book is an original publication of The Berkley Publishing Group.

PRINTING HISTORY
Berkley trade paperback edition / December 2011

Library of Congress Cataloging-in-Publication Data

Thompson, Rod, (date-)
    The Black Hills / Rod Thompson.—Berkley trade paperback ed.
      p. cm.
    ISBN 978-0-425-24310-7
    1. Young men—West (U.S.)—Fiction.   2. Frontier and pioneer life—Fiction.   3. Outlaws—
Fiction.   4. Violence—Fiction.   5. Retribution—Fiction.   6. Black Hills (S.D. and Wyo.)—
Fiction.   I. Title.
    PS3620.H6875B53 2011
    813'.6—dc22
                                                        2011016474

PRINTED IN THE UNITED STATES OF AMERICA

10   9   8   7   6   5   4   3   2

ACKNOWLEDGMENTS

As this story would have never seen the light of day without the efforts of an amazing agent, Peter Riva, and the most patient editor on the planet, Faith Black of Berkley Books, I give them my heartfelt thank-you.

CHAPTER 1

The four riders coming over the hills escaped Cormac Lynch's normally acute awareness of his surroundings. His attention was on his burlap potato sack. He dragged it to the beginning of the next row, straddled it, and then hooked the top of the mouth on his belt. As he walked straddle-legged, the sack flowed between his legs while the mouth was held open by a piece of thin cord tying each side of the bag to his knees, allowing the body of the sack to drag behind him.

The briskness in the air was exhilarating and the morning sun warm as it accepted its task of chasing away the morning shadows and burning the dew from the potato plants and grasses. Bobolinks flying in and out of the lone tree standing near the field were singing and flirting with each other. It was a great day to be alive. There was a long day of work ahead, but that's what farmers did from first light till the sun went down; he was up to it.

After plowing up the potatoes and spreading them across the ground for easy pickin', his father had already ridden the mile to the cornfield on the other side of the farm buildings shortly after dawn to begin weeding. Cormac loved working beside his pa, but hated weeding and was glad his mother had wanted him to help finish picking the potatoes. Their main crops were corn, wheat, and flax, but his mother had decided to put in a small field of potatoes to sell in town for what she called pin money.

Cormac checked the progress of his mother and sister, who had started picking while he had removed the saddles and bridles and hobbled the saddle horses to allow them to graze without running off. Most farm horses were plow horses, strong, powerful, and suitable for the hard work that was expected of them: pulling heavy hay racks and wagons piled high, frequently to overflowing, with grain or corn; or pulling a plow to break up hardened soil; or pulling stone boats for relocating boulders and full water barrels for irrigation; or tearing stubborn tree stumps from the earth in which they had grown. Usually ridden bareback when used for transportation purposes while en route to the fields in full harness, but when Cormac's mother was along, his pa insisted saddles be used. Today was such a day, and the care of the horses fell to Cormac.

Four years older, his sister Becky was nigh on to eighteen and their mother only twice that. Like most western women of the time, she had married young, having Becky one year later. People frequently said they looked more like sisters than mother and daughter, which pleased them both no end. They fairly beamed every time they heard it. Becky loved being compared to her mother, whom she thought was surely the prettiest woman in the world, and her mother loved being told that she looked young enough to be Becky's sister.

Both experienced pickers, strong from many hours of hard work, they had a good head start on Cormac. He smiled as he noticed his mother glance over her shoulder to check on him and then murmur something to Becky. They had played this game before. His father was a kind but firm taskmaster; his mother, on the other hand, always found ways to turn work into fun. Now, knowing that he did not like being behind them and would want to catch up, she and Becky were going to try to prevent it.

"We'll see about that," he said softly. "We'll just see about that." He had been studying and preparing for just such an event with frequent, thoughtful practice on how to make his hands move faster and pick more potatoes in less time. He had experimented with various fingering grips on the potatoes, different strokes and alternate flips to get the potatoes into the bag. Each change produced tiny amounts of progress, and each bit of progress took him a little closer to his goal: to be the fastest potato picker in the territory.

While picking in the field, and often at night before falling asleep, he indulged himself in a fantasy. In it, he could see himself in the middle of a long line of boys lined up in contest at one end of a huge potato field, each with their own row. He watched as all bent over into tater-pickin' position and made ready, and then *bang!* A gunshot started the race to the other end of the field.

Although his competitors were always bigger, older, more experienced, and somehow always managing to get a head start and make him begin the race with the others well in front, they always proved to be no match for his intense concentration and the great swiftness with which the potatoes flew into his bag. Cormac was always the first to turn around, laughing, at the other end of the field.

Now the time was here. This was the great race of his life. This was the moment he had prepared for. His competitors had joined forces against him and were already well in the lead. "We'll see about that," he said again. "We'll just see about that." Then Cormac Lynch, the greatest potato picker of all time, bent and began to pick potatoes. He had his mother's light touch and agility with a natural quickness of movement enhanced by tater pickin' since the age of three. He hadn't accomplished much then, mostly got in the way, but his mother had assured him that his help was much appreciated and they would never have gotten done without it.

Choosing a potato with his right hand, he sent it flying between his legs and into the bag with a deft flick of his wrist while his left hand was making the next selection. Left, right, left, right, gaining speed, left-right-left-right-leftrightleftrightleftright, faster and faster, his hands found a rhythm and became but a blur. With a stream of potatoes flying into the bag, he had a strong ability to concentrate, which he now focused on the ground in front of him, blocking out all else. He did not notice his mother's and sister's frequent looks to check his progress. Nor did he see their looks of determination as they put on all the speed they possessed, or the smile of resignation they shared while shaking their heads at each other when he first caught up with, and then passed them.

With a smile and a finger on her lips to signal silence to Becky, Cormac's mother began picking in Becky's row, a few steps ahead of her. She picked half of the potatoes, leaving the other half for Becky coming up behind. With both women working the same row, Cormac was no longer pulling away from them. Catching up to him, though, was still out of the question.

Laughing, Cormac stood up and turned around when he reached the end of his row, and then threw the last potato into the bag. Only then did he see the four men riding across the potato patch toward them. Caught up in the thrill and excitement of competition, Becky and her mother remained equally unaware of the riders.

"Mother," Cormac said, nodding his head toward the approaching riders.

The women's laughter stilled as their eyes followed his nod. The freshly plowed soil had muffled the horses' hoofs, and the riders were less than fifty feet away. Their lack of concern for the damage being done to the potatoes by their horses was a clear statement of their intent and approaching trouble.

The men were dirty and unshaven, their clothes worn and disheveled, and their bedrolls sloppily tied behind beat-up and uncared-for saddles. Badly in need of rest, their horses showed the results of overuse and neglect. All were scarred with sores kept open by the frequent misuse of spurs.

Mrs. Lynch paled as their situation became evident. Her husband was a mile away, and they were unprotected. Frequently, he had warned her to keep the rifle close to her at all times.

"Hopefully you'll never need to use it," he had said. "There aren't a lot of people in these parts yet, and our farm is far off the beaten path. Even the Indians don't come around this neck of the woods since Red Cloud signed the Laramie Treaty for the Sioux and the Black Hills now belong to them. It's very peaceful out here, but the country is far from settled.

"There may come a time when you'll need a gun, and if you do, you'll need it right then and there; you'll not likely have time to fetch it." Lulled by the peacefulness that had become their life, try as she might, she just could not take the warning seriously. To appease her husband, she had learned how to use it and could shoot straight if she didn't have to shoot too far. Although she carried it around with her, it was awkward and heavy and usually left leaning against something in her vicinity: a tree, a rock, a sack of potatoes, or it remained in the rifle scabbard on her saddle. It was there now, under the tree at the far end of the field. If only she had listened to him.

A huge, filthy, fat, and ugly man with a large, jagged scar running down the side of his face from his forehead to his chin rode a few feet in front of the others. He smiled a nasty smile, showing crooked, tobacco-stained teeth. Cormac's mother knew the breath coming out of that mouth would be vile.

"This is your lucky day, lady," he snarled at her. Then, turning his head and nodding toward Becky, he told the other riders, "You can have her. This one's all mine."

"Run kids!" Amanda Lynch screamed, and broke toward the rifle. It was too far away, but she had to try. Running had always come easily for her. She had won many foot races against her girlfriends in the eastern schools she had attended, but that had not been in the soft dirt of a freshly plowed potato field.

The man's horse was too small for him and near exhaustion from carrying his weight too far and too fast with too little rest, but it was still faster than Cormac's mother, and it quickly cut her off. No matter which way she tried to run, the horse was in front of her. It had, at one time, been a good cattle-cutting horse. Like a cat toying with a caught bird, the man was toying with her, knowing he could do anything he wanted, whenever he wanted. Becky screamed behind her. A realist, she accepted the fact that she would not be allowed to get to the gun. She stopped trying to run and faced her tormentor.

"Please," she begged. "You and your men can do anything you want to me, and I'll do whatever you want if you'll leave my daughter alone."

Her tormentor reined his horse to a stop in front of her and looked down, his eyes slowly ravaging up and down her body.

"Lady," he growled, "I'm going to do anything I want to you anyway, and you'll damn well do anything I tell you. And you ain't goin' to be so damned prissy-purty when I'm done with ya. Women like you always think you're so damned special and don't want anything to do with people like me. Well, today you're going to have a lot to do with me. 'Sides, taint likely they'd stop even if I was to tell them to. They seem to be having a little fun of their own. Look at 'em."

She became aware of Becky's hysterical crying and the men's laughter; she turned to look, and her heart broke. One of the men was tearing away Becky's clothing while the other two held her, groping the bared parts of her body as they became available. Becky was struggling and trying to pull away, kicking at anything that came within reach.

"Now it's you and me," the fat man snarled.

Spurring the horse deeply reopened the dried blood on its sides and sent it leaping forward, knocking Cormac's mother to the ground. Before she could regain her feet, the man was off his horse, clamping her wrist in a steely grip with one hand and tearing at her clothes with the other.

Amanda Lynch was petite, standing but five foot one on her tiptoes, but she was agile and had the strength that comes with years of long, grueling hours in the fields. She aimed a knee between his legs and the fingernails of her free hand at his face. Not the nails of a pampered and manicured city woman, these were nails hardened by the leeching of minerals from the soil caught under them while in the fields and the rays of the strong Dakota sun beating on them hour after hour. They were the nails of a hardworking countrywoman. He was expecting her knee and side-stepped it, but with furious strength she raked her nails down hard, and like knives, they cut deeply into the flesh, sending rivers of blood gushing down his face.

"Damn you," he swore, and swung his huge fist at her face. The punch smashed in her mouth and nose, sending her near unconsciousness and leaving her hovering there, unable to move, but distantly aware of more smashing blows knocking her head back and forth, her clothes being ripped from her body, atrocious acts being done to her, and Becky's cries of pain.

Cormac did not know what to do. His was a life that had never known violence. Protected by loving parents and an older sister who thrived on caring for him, he had never known anything but love and kindness. He stood frozen as he watched his mother's vain attempt to run. But when the men grabbed Becky, he ran to help. One of the men hit him with a hard backhand, sending him reeling into darkness.

When he regained consciousness, he could see a giant of a man doing horrible things to his mother and two other men holding Becky down while a third was on top of her. Both women were naked, and he could hear their whimpering. Rising from the ground, he ran unnoticed to the pile of carefully chosen rocks he had collected yesterday while taking his rest at lunch. All smooth, all nearly round, and all about the size of an egg . . . good throwing stones.

Although his pa had taught him how to use a pistol, a rifle, and a shotgun when he was knee-high to a small Indian, he wasn't allowed to use them without his pa along, so he used rocks—and sometimes in the winter, a frozen dirt clod—to hunt rabbits and squirrels. He tracked them to their hidey-holes and waited for them to show themselves. Cormac had a good eye and rarely missed. Sometimes his mother had to ask him to please stop for a while because they were getting tired of rabbit and squirrel stew, and his pa would tan his hide if he killed an animal that wasn't for eating.

Quickly selecting three stones to hold in his right hand and one for his throwing hand, he ran, still unnoticed, to within twenty feet of the men attacking Becky. With no warning, he threw the first rock as hard as he could, hitting exactly where he had aimed, the side of the head of the man on top of Becky. The man collapsed on top of her.

"What the hell?" one of the men lying beside Becky exclaimed, his hand on her bare chest and his back to Cormac. He rolled over to face Cormac and started to his feet, but a rock square between the eyes put him back to the ground. The man lying on the other side of Becky, with his hand also on her chest, came up with a gun and fired as Cormac launched another stone. Cormac fell into a heap.

Sometime later, he heard the sound of a running horse and fought to rouse himself. He succeeded in regaining partial consciousness. Something warm was running across his face and dripping from his nose. He wiped at it, and his hand came away red with blood. With his fingers, Cormac gently traced the flow to its source and found a deep groove in his head running front to back above his left ear.

Rising on one elbow, he was thrilled to see his pa racing toward them. He must have heard the shot and come a-runnin'. Cormac took heart at the sight of the rifle in his pa's hand. A friend of his pa's stopping by to visit once had told him that his pa could shoot the eye out of a gnat at fifty paces. He would put a stop to this. But he couldn't shoot without fear of hitting his wife or Becky. Galloping to within a few feet of Cormac's mother, John Lynch hauled back on the reins and set the horse sliding to a stop on its haunches.

"Take him boys!" the fat man ordered. "I'm busy." Before the horse had come to a complete stop, John Lynch was off, his momentum carrying him a few running steps toward where the fat man was assaulting his wife.

"You bastards!" he screamed as he staggered to a halt, raising his rifle, "I'll kill y—" Rolling gunfire cut him off and echoed over the hills as three guns cut him to pieces and he collapsed to the ground.

"I'm sorry, honey," he got out weakly, with tears in his eyes. "I'm sorry, Rebecca." John Lorton Lynch, along with all of his plans, hopes, and dreams for his family, died, and fourteen-year-old Cormac Lynch gratefully sunk into the darkness of oblivion.

Silence and stillness blanketed the valley. There was no movement in the air or birds singing in the tree. With no breeze to cool its effects, the gentle, warm morning sun had risen into the sky to become a blistering ball of Dakota fire. Stubborn dew hiding in the ruts of the plowed field and on shaded blades of grass under the tree had been quickly baked away, and the freshly plowed, rich, dark soil was now scorched dry and crumbly. The only movement was the growth of the tall grass covering the valley and the surrounding hills stretching upward in its relentless quest for the sun.

In states with mountains rising to thirteen or fourteen thousand feet, they wouldn't be called hills . . . more like bumps. In Dakota, there were hills, and then there were the Black Hills. At a little more than 7,000 feet, they were inhabited by the Oglala Sioux Indians who shared hunting privileges with the Cheyenne and, occasionally, the Arikara Indians, whose home was normally at the mouth of the Cheyenne River. The many pine trees created an appearance of darkness from a distance generating the name: the Black Hills, Paha Sapa to the Indians.

The balance of the Dakota Territory remained mostly flat with small rolling hills, sometimes in groups, spasmodically straining upward out of the flatness of the Great Plains to press against the bottom side of the grass like a rock under a rug with occasional trees here and there. It was in just such terrain that John Lynch had chosen to build his farm and raise his family.

In these surroundings, Cormac slowly became aware that his eye was open. One eye was pressed downward against a potato where his head had fallen; the other was open. Open and staring at Becky's naked, twisted, and bloody body. He tried to close it. He did not want to have to look, but the eye would not do his bidding. Twice the distance away and a little to the side was his mother's body—a short distance farther, his father's. With a terrible, sickening sense of loss, Cormac knew they were all dead. Why wasn't he? He remembered the darkness encircling him and gratefully thinking he was dying. Why had he not?

Dazed and numb, Cormac slowly sat up, dizziness and excruciating pain in his head making him sick to his stomach. He closed his eyes against the waves of nausea and vomited heavily and frequently. Gently, his fingers probed the side of his head and found it covered with dried blood. He found the deep groove from the bullet, and on the ground, a dried pool of more blood. Groaning, he weakly staggered to his feet; only then did he think about the men. Where were they?

Carefully, Cormac looked around the valley, moving his head very slowly, afraid of more pain. The men were gone, only their used-up horses remained; too tired to wander, they were taking advantage of the respite from overuse to rest and graze on the rich grass the best they could while bridled with steel bits in their mouths. Cormac could see that the horses he had hobbled and his father's horse had all been taken. Strangely, he felt no relief at the men's absence. Neither had he felt any fear, he realized; neither then, nor now.

He just felt numb, like an observer looking at a photograph in one of his mother's many books, which she used to educate him. But this was a horrible, grotesque photograph at which he did not want to look; he did not want to see. He wanted to close the book and have to look no longer; but this was not a photograph, this was real, and there on the ground were his mother, his pa, and his sister, petite and pretty seventeen-year-old Rebecca May Lynch: Becky. She had loved the name Rebecca, and Cormac was the only person she tolerated calling her Becky.

How could this have happened? They had been minding their own business, working in the fields and laughing. The sunshine had been warm and friendly on the beginning of a beautiful day. He remembered hearing the birds in the tree. Tomorrow they would have been taking the potato harvest into town and picking up supplies. His mother and Becky were planning to get some material for new dresses while, as always, he looked at the new saddles in the back of the store and dreamed of someday buying his own. His pa would probably have got some store-bought candy for him and Becky. Suddenly, everything had changed. Everything was gone. Four strangers had simply ridden into their lives and taken away everything. How could this possibly have happened? Cormac Lynch did not understand. What right did they have to do that?

He resolved himself to go to Becky. Her resistance to what had been happening to her was evident in the scuffed and gouged soil surrounding her. She had fought ferociously. The more she had resisted, the more she had been beaten, yet she never stopped fighting. There were bruises covering most of her body, front and back; and her face, once so gently pretty and so quick to smile and laugh, had been smashed almost beyond recognition. Her teeth were twisted in her mouth—some were missing, and blood covered most of her upper body.

"Why?" he screamed out. "Why did you do this?"

He avoided looking at her nakedness as he covered her with

the largest pieces of her dress that he could find intact. Then, with immense dread, he went to his mother. What had been done to her was even more horrendous. Her face and body were a puffy round mass of torn flesh; there was blood over much of her body. Her eyes had swollen shut; and the sweet, soft lips that had kissed Cormac so many times, were mashed into her mouth where her teeth should have been. Her also naked body had been twisted perversely to satisfy the desires of a hideous monster.

Stunned at the violence, Cormac moved mechanically, straightening her body and covering it; he kissed her softly, as he had Becky, and moved to his father. It was almost a pleasure to see that his father, even though he was dead, still looked like his father. Stretching out on the ground beside him, Cormac laid his head on his father's massive chest. So strong his father had been, so eager to rise and begin work each day, always whistling, always happy to tease his children and their mother whenever the opportunity presented itself. Now he was dead—and cold.

Cormac remained there a long while, remembering the happy times and laughter their family had shared, along with their dreams and plans for the future. He was avoiding, he knew, what had to come next and what he had to do. He had to bury them.

The sun was getting low in the sky and the shadows lengthening when Cormac reluctantly rose. He would bury them under the tree. It would be difficult to move the bodies that far, but it had been a happy spot for them. The only tree in the valley, it had shaded them while they shared lunches, talked, and laughed during field preparation, the planting, weeding, and harvesting; and if there was no lightning, provided them shelter from the rain. His parents had treated the breaks like picnics and made them fun. Under the tree, after eating, they had stretched out for mid-day naps before returning to work, they had made plans, they had laughed and enjoyed each other's company, and under the tree the three of them would spend the rest of forever.

Cormac worked as the sun went down and a full moon rose in its place, brightly illuminating everything with a pallid softness. What his pa had called the Milky Way made a soft trail across the sky. The horses were all-in and made no effort to elude him. He caught the nearest one to help move the bodies to the burial site.

The sky was showing signs of light in the east when he tamped the last dirt onto his father's grave. All the while avoiding looking at their nakedness, he had buried his mother first, and then Becky, so they would be covered. His father would have understood. He had always told Cormac to take care of the women first.

Crawling onto his mother's grave feeling hollow and weak, his strength drained, he collapsed with the realization coming to him that he had not cried. He wondered about that. His family had been horribly, viciously murdered, leaving it up to him to bury them, and yet he had not cried. His insides felt dead, filled with a sick and terrible empty numbness. He should have cried, he thought, and the thinking made him feel guilty.

"I'm sorry," he murmured. "I love you." Cormac Lynch slept.

CHAPTER 2

After having ridden only a few miles from the Lynch place, the outlaws came upon a meandering, tree-lined creek.

"Hey, Gator." Raunchy laughed. "Let's stop and have a drink. Man, oh man, oh man, that was somethin', weren't it? Those women were sure somethin', weren't they? Right purty little things."

"For once in your life, you got yourself a good idea," the fat man responded. "I need to wash out these gouges that bitch gave me anyway. I sure taught her a thing or two. She won't be clawing anyone else like that."

Nicknamed for an alligator he had killed with his bare hands while escaping through the swamps from a Florida prison, George Milar had been on the wrong side of the law all of his life. Six inches over six feet tall, he would have tipped the scales at over three hundred pounds had he ever felt the need to get on one. He didn't care what he weighed. By the time he was ten years old, he had already decided he would do whatever the hell he wanted, and that included eating anything he wanted, as much as he wanted, when he wanted.

Gator didn't like rules and cared not one whit what other people thought. His three hundred-plus pounds of bulk concealed massive muscles that had always bulled him out of any situation. His weight was also a horse killer; he rode them until they could no longer walk. He kicked them, beat them, spurred them, and cussed at them, and when they could go no farther, he would steal another and with his huge fists, hammer anyone who complained, laughing and enjoying every minute while he did it.

He stepped down from the horse he had recently stolen, backhanding it on the side of the head when it shied away at the sudden transfer of weight from the saddle to the stirrup that twisted the cinch strap painfully around its girth.

"Pete," he ordered. "You and the Mex rustle up some grub."

The "Mex" looked at him with hate-filled eyes. The way Gator said "Mex" made it sound vulgar. Gator knew the man did not like the slur on his race and used it to put him down at every opportunity. Someday, the "Mex" was going to introduce Gator to the pointed end of the Mexican knife he wore on his belt. Until then, he would put up with the mistreatment because of the protection it afforded him.

Nobody wanted to tangle with Gator, and that provided the group with both protection and women. Their shared taste for abuse of women was the glue that held their small band together. They all liked to kill and did so for any reason, or for no reason, but their need to abuse women was their mainstay. Sometimes they kept a woman with them while they traveled, sharing her body either as a group or for their individual sadistic pleasure, until they tired of her; or until she became too ugly from the beatings, in which case they killed her and left her to rot. The

"Mex" had been hopeful of keeping the last two. He would have relished enough time to enjoy them more slowly, maybe cut them a little and watch them bleed, but Gator's woman had somehow managed to stuff enough dirt into her mouth to choke herself to death without Gator noticing until it was too late. The other went hysterical when she realized what had happened and attacked them, screaming, biting, kicking, and scratching, and wouldn't stop until she was finally beaten to death.

Too bad, he thought, shaking his head. *What a waste to lose them so soon.*

Gator removed a large bottle of whiskey from his saddlebag. "We'll have us a couple of drinks then go find where those farmers lived. If we give the horses their heads, they'll find their way home. Most farmers keep some whiskey around for medicine, and we'll be needin' some more 'fore long. And who knows, maybe we'll get lucky and find another daughter or two, wouldn't that be a kick?" They ate and drank until they passed out, talking about what they would have done to the women if they hadn't died.

———

The sun was again high in the sky when Cormac awoke to the sound of the horse stomping her feet and blowing. Tied to a low-hanging branch, the large, slate-colored grulla mare with a dark head, white-blazed face, and matching white stockings, with which he had moved the bodies had eaten all the grass in the small area within her reach and was stretching as far as the reins would allow. Grazing close by were the outlaw's other horses, so uncared for that the saddles and bridles, as badly mistreated as the horses, had not been removed.

The Lynch horses and gear had obviously been taken because they were in much better condition. Cormac's pa knew the benefits of well-bred animals and the importance of taking care

of one's property. Cormac noticed these things on some sub-
conscious level. Consciously, he was numb from the shock and
horror and the great loss of the previous day. Slowly he rose
and walked to the grulla, untied her reins, and flipped them
over her head. Nickering lowly, she extended her nose to nuzzle
his chest. A horse lover like his pa, Cormac appreciated the
gesture. It was as if she understood he was in pain and was giving support in the only way she knew how, along with her thank
you for being treated kindly.

Cormac automatically reciprocated by holding her large head
in his two hands. Leaning his forehead against her face, his nose
against her nose, the two of them breathed each other's air and
smelled each other's breath in the same manner in which Cormac had done so many times before with his pa's horse, Lop
Ear. He was reaching now for the comforting closeness he so
desperately needed. The grulla seemed to understand and nickered softly once more.

With their faces together, Cormac hugged her head for a
time and then returned to sit on his mother's grave, wanting to
remain as close to her as possible, wanting not to think, not
knowing or caring what he should do next. With his father's
grave on one side of him and Becky's on the other, he was at a
total and uncaring loss for a plan of action. Three wonderful,
happy, giving people had been horribly and painfully murdered,
his happy existence forever changed.

Cormac could not be still. His lips began to tremble and his
body began to shake; his emotion would no longer be denied.
His mind and heart wracked with pain, his body began to heave,
and his muscles convulsed uncontrollably. He curled first into
a tight fetal position and began moaning and sobbing hysterically, rocking back and forth. Then, rolling over onto his knees,
he began pounding the dirt with all of his strength, making

loud, unintelligible moans and groans and yells and whimpers like those of a large animal dying in agony. The horses watched the strange actions of the human curiously until the sounds diminished and finally ceased as Cormac, wounded, heartsick, and emotionally drained, once again passed into unconsciousness, and they returned to grazing.

The sun inched across the sky until the graves were no longer shaded. The sun was hot, and Cormac Lynch reluctantly became aware of his surroundings. He sat up to get the sun out of his face and remained there for a time in an unthinking sickly stupor, staring without seeing. Presently it occurred to him that he had not taken care of the horses' needs, and he was also becoming aware of a cold and terrible rage building in his gut, replacing the trembling sickness and sense of loss.

Cormac arose with a purpose. He was fourteen years old and had much of his height; already eight or ten inches taller than Becky and his mother had been, he was beginning to fill out like his wide-shouldered and well-muscled pa. He had been carrying the daily workload of a man for more than a year—digging, wood chopping, barn cleaning, and shoveling manure—making him far stronger than an average fourteen-year-old. His pa had taught him about guns: how to use them, how to hit what he aimed at, when and when not to use them. This was the time to use them.

You bastards! I'll kill you! The last words he heard from his pa echoed in his mind. He would keep his pa's promise. Cormac would find the bastards . . . and he would kill them.

Cormac Lynch was of the Celtic heritage of his father, a people known for their horsemanship, and Cormac's pa had taught him well about recognizing and caring for good horse-flesh. He took down the pail of water from where it had been hung in the tree to shade and protect it. He rinsed his mouth, spit, and drank a few swallows, saving the rest for the horses.

They knew what a bucket was and came easily to him. He gave each their share, talking to them and rubbing the knot between their ears while they drank. Each had been mistreated by humans and, at first, shied from his hand, but the smell of water won out. They drank eagerly and hesitantly allowed his touch.

Watching and evaluating their movements, Cormac easily selected the best of the four abandoned horses: the large and well-muscled grulla mare with which he had already made friends. He had not previously noticed her powerful hindquarters and smooth lines indicating speed and endurance, or her high-arched neck and high-held tail.

Cormac grimaced and shook his head when he examined the spur damage on their flanks. What kind of human being could treat animals like that? That was a question the answer to which he already knew all too well. He had to return to the farm for weapons and food for traveling; once there he would treat the wounds of the horses as well as his own. The sick feeling in his stomach was beginning to remind him that he had not eaten in a day and a half.

Cormac Lynch removed the bridles and unsaddled the horses, giving them time to roll in the grass while he chose the most padded saddle blanket and a saddle that appeared to be large enough to fit the grulla. Though still in poor condition, the day's rest and grazing had done all the horses good. He mounted and started the mare toward the farm; his now, he realized dully. He was not looking forward to arriving there without his family. Accustomed to traveling together, the other horses followed.

———

A few miles to the southeast, Lainey Nayle topped a hill, riding the horse of her adopted father. He had been sick for three days and was lying in the back of their covered wagon, now being driven by her mother, a couple of miles behind, while Lainey scouted ahead for the best route for the wagon. Her father had indicated the direction he wanted them to travel. They were looking for a piece of good farmland, well off by itself for safety.

He had warned her not to skyline herself when going over hilltops to reduce the risk of being seen, but she wasn't worried. Her father was very protective of her; this was simply overprotection. She was perfectly capable of making intelligent decisions on her own. After all, she was fourteen years old and looking and thinking more like a woman every day. This was beautiful, rolling green countryside with no other people around for miles.

What was the need to be so worried all the time? At the bottom of the hill was a deeply cut arroyo made years before by a fast-moving stream searching for a route to the ocean. When the source of the water had been cut off, it had simply dried up, leaving an ugly gouge in an otherwise pristine landscape. From the hilltop, Lainey could see an easy wagon passage about a quarter mile to the north, but there was no need for her to ride that far; she could cross right where she was.

She guided the horse carefully down into the arroyo, around a fallen tree, and up the other side. As she crested the top, she found herself in the center of a half circle formed by four men on horses, one of the men the largest and ugliest man she had ever seen. He took her breath away.

"Well, well, well," he snarled. "Look what we found. Don't be afraid, little missy. We are going to take right good care of you. There's no sense in you being out here all by yourself, you can travel with us. A female around the camp for a while would be a nice change. I'm tired of eating our own cookin', and we can teach you a few things you'll need to know to become a woman."

To one of the others, who had ridden up close to her side

unnoticed while she had been staring speechlessly at the big
man, he said, "Take her reins for her, Raunchy. I'd feel terrible
if her horse should get scared and run away. This nice-looking
young lady might get hurt. We'll just take her along with us to
the farm. We can rest up there a few days, and it'll give us all
time to get acquainted with her."

Cormac let the horses drink at the water tank and then rode
into the barn; the other horses followed. They knew what a barn
was: barns meant food and barns meant rest. The six stalls normally used by the farm's saddle horses and the two plow horses
now grazing in the pasture were empty, and he let the horses
select their own.

After cleaning their wounds and putting on a generous coating of healing salve, he gave each a healthy helping of grain
mixed with a little corn and climbed into the loft to kick down
some hay. The richness of the alfalfa would speed the horses'
recuperation. His pa had planned the loft with a trapdoor over
each stall's feeder to make feeding easy.

Cormac stood for a moment. He always enjoyed being in
the barn with its smell of grain and hay, horses and liniments,
and of well-oiled tack hanging on the hooks, but not this day.

All alone, now, he thought. No more Becky to laugh with
and torment, no mother to kiss him in the morning and teach
him book learnin', no pa to work beside and teach him man
stuff . . . just alone. And they weren't coming back. Never. His
insides were filled with despair and a sick feeling of emptiness
and hate. Cormac would find the men who did this, and they
would die.

He was stalling, he realized. He did not want to go into the
house alone. One of the upper barn doors was open and swing-

ing in the breeze, and he walked over to close it. Dakota rainstorms frequently came quickly, and if the hay became wet it would mold. Looking out over the farmyard, he froze in disbelief. In the distance, he could see five riders approaching. He recognized four of the horses that were coming home and their riders; on the fifth horse was a smaller and unfamiliar figure.

It was unbelievable that the outlaws would show up here. He felt no fear, only a cold, terrible hatred like he could have never imagined. He hesitated only a moment. In the darkness of the loft, Cormac felt secure that he had not been seen. He backed away quickly from the door and slid down the ladder. His pa had laid out the barn in such a way as to make it possible to move from it to the house without being seen by someone approaching from the front. "You never know when it might come in handy," he had told Cormac one day.

Running into the house, he took down the shotgun and loaded both barrels with #3 shot for a tight pattern and powerful discharge. It was a ten-gauge; his pa had wanted the most powerful shotgun available for longer range, one capable of reaching out for birds flying away. Cormac also checked the loads in the rifle and stuffed a six-gun in his belt and extra shells in his pockets.

Through the crack in the shutters, he could see the riders passing through the front gate. Riding four abreast, one was holding the reins of the fifth rider: a girl his own age. Straight and tall for her age, she was riding alertly on a small horse and looking all around, as if for a plan of escape. *Gutsy*, Cormac thought.

He had no more than had the thought when she bolted. As they passed through the gate, a slender board with which Cormac had been hitting rocks and laid down on the upper board of the gate a couple days before came within reach. While going through the gate, the outlaw leading her horse was saying something to the others and not paying attention to her when, with one quick motion, she leaned over, grabbed the board, and swung it with both hands. Connecting with his shoulder, she knocked her captor out of his saddle, grabbed up her reins, and spun her horse around into an immediate run. She was out the gate and running flat out before her captors realized what had happened.

"Well, get up and go get her, damnit, Raunchy," Gator laughed. "Don't just lay there. You lost her, now go get her."

Cormac watched as the outlaw clambered back into his saddle while holding his shoulder in pain and launched into a chase of the girl on the little horse while the other outlaws, welcoming the entertainment, laughed and hollered encouragement. Riding his pa's horse, Lop Ear, it was no contest for the outlaw; he caught up to the girl easily. Her horse was little, but it was quick, and she could ride. Every time the man called Raunchy caught up with her, she spun her horse in a different direction. The other riders laughed and shouted derisive remarks until the man threw his lasso around her horse's neck and led her back after first slapping her off her horse and then making her remount.

Cormac was tempted to knock him out of the saddle again, only using a rifle bullet instead of a board, but he wanted them all. Guns in hand, Cormac slipped quietly out the back door. Confident there was nobody to stop them; the outlaws were relaxed and conversing with no signs of fear or worry. Their line of travel to the barn would have them pass around the corner of the house.

When Cormac's father had been teaching him how to fight, he had taught him to fight fair, give the other person a fair chance, don't kick him when he's down. In this case, Cormac felt neither the need nor desire to fight fair. Outnumbered and outsized, the thought of mercy never entered his mind. They were going to die . . . today . . . now.

Carefully leaning the guns within reach against the wall, Cormac placed the lid on the rain barrel in which his mother and Becky had caught rainwater to wash and make their hair soft, and climbed up to stand on it. Already tall for his age, by standing on the barrel, he would be at an elevation equal to the riders. He picked up the double-barreled shotgun and cocked both barrels, pulled it to his shoulder, and waited, surprised at his own calmness.

The outlaws would be following a curve as they came around the corner of the house. His pa had taught Cormac to hunt doves by flushing them, whenever possible, toward a group of trees. As the doves flew away, they would have to turn to avoid the trees, and in so doing, two or three would come into alignment and could be felled with one shot. His pa had not been one to waste ammunition.

The horses' heads would come into Cormac's view no more than fifteen feet away. Standing on the rain barrel put the barrels of the shotgun in near-perfect alignment with where the outlaw's heads would appear as they came around the corner. If he held high, the buckshot spread would not hit the horses. The girl was far enough behind to be out of danger.

Around the corner they came, and Cormac waited. Their attention focused on the barn door, looking neither right nor left, they were coming neatly into line just as his pa had said. Looking down the valley between the barrels, Cormac set the sights between the centermost riders. The buckshot pattern would spread in both directions to encompass all four. He could almost hear his pa's voice: *"Wait . . . wait. . . . Hold it . . . wait."*

The doves were making the turn and coming into formation.

"Just a little longer . . . wait . . . let them get into the pocket . . . wait." The far doves came around into perfect alignment, heads all in one neat row. As their distance to the house increased, each was just a little in front of the one next to him, as if having a photograph taken, each wanting to make sure his face could be seen perfectly.

Cormac wanted them to know who and why. "Hey!" he said quietly. Their faces turned in unison, seeing him, and, in the same instant, the red rose of fire mushrooming from both barrels of the shotgun as Cormac pulled both triggers simultaneously. The gun roared, the horses bolted, and the girl—her fear and emotion so tightly held bursting loose—screamed hysterically. Cormac Lynch grabbed the corner of the house to keep from being knocked off the rain barrel as the heads of four vile human beings bounced mangled and bloody into the dirt. Vengeance was far swifter than befitted the likes of them, was far better than they deserved.

CHAPTER 3

Cormac Lynch pulled rein on the hill when they spotted her wagon. She suggested he come along and introduce himself, but she didn't really mean it, and he didn't believe that him being Cormac Lynch was going to particularly impress anybody. She obviously didn't like him anyway. Finding the wagon as it bounced its way slowly across the prairie had been no problem. Getting her calmed down had been a different story.

No matter that she had not been showing it, anyone in her situation would have been frightened, and the sudden and unexpected blast of the shotgun and spurts of blood had pushed her over the edge. As her horse bolted, she half-fell and half-scrambled off and ran away, screaming and shaking and falling and crawling and trying to stay away from the terrible person who had just blown the heads off four people.

When he caught her, she began swinging her arms and fists like a wild woman, still screaming at the top of her lungs. A few times, she connected—it hurt. She was taller than Becky had been and stronger than she looked. Once her hysteria had worn itself out, she regained her self-control and was no longer afraid.

She allowed herself to be led into the house, her eyes all the while burning holes through him and looking at him with hatred, anger, and disgust like he was some sort of monster. He had just blown the heads off four people. Eventually she told him who she was and what had happened to her.

Suddenly Cormac's stomach started sounding like a bear fresh out of hibernation, and he realized it was his second day without food. He was hungry enough to eat saddle leather if he could soak it in a little gravy for a while first. He had promised that if she let him fix her something to eat, he would see her back to her wagon.

They ate in near silence. He tried to talk her up a couple times, telling her how brave he thought she had been. Without going into detail, he explained that his family had been killed and what had just taken place was a result of that, but it made no never mind; she was having none of it. Staring at him with bitterness, she ate little. He had just saved her from horrors she could not possibly imagine, yet Cormac Lynch was a bad guy. Fine.

Theirs was a Conestoga wagon. His pa had explained to him that most folks simply used a farmer's wagon with a tarp over it to protect the goods and passengers. A Conestoga wagon was more costly but could carry a heavier load, and although it leaked a little, would float long enough to get across most streams and rivers. Usually pulled by a team of four or six oxen, with its white top flopping gently in the breeze, it was a sight. His pa had said some folks called the wagons land sailors because they resembled a ship with sails; he sure couldn't see it.

"Good luck," Cormac told her, shifting in the saddle and

gesturing toward her approaching wagon; he watched her leave. He had learned in a short period of time, as she was going to learn, that life does not always come in a sweet and pretty package all tied up with a nice ribbon. He had also learned that womenfolk looked at things differently than menfolk. He had no desire to listen to her folks being told what had happened, what a terrible person he was, and being stared at like he was Lucifer himself.

"Boy! You blow the heads off four people and right away you're a bad guy," he said to himself. Apparently, the recent events had hardened him. He could almost hear his pa. "Very funny," he would have said, just before cuffing Cormac on the back of the head. "You just killed four people, and you're trying to be funny."

Cormac didn't agree. They weren't people; they were animals and deserved to be treated as such. No, that wasn't true. Animals deserved better treatment. Watching until she reached her wagon, he started home; he had more graves to dig. He was becoming a regular mortician.

It was near dark when they rolled through Cormac's front gate. He said it aloud just to see how it sounded. "My front gate." He didn't care for it much. He liked "our front gate" much better, but offhand he could think of nobody who particularly cared what Cormac Lynch did, or did not, think. The hole was mostly dug when he first heard their wagon. Recent rains had kept the ground from packing down, but the rich Dakota soil, normally a joy to work, this time was not. It was a downright shame to contaminate it with the rot that he was putting into it. If the one hadn't been so all-fired big, the grave would have already been done.

Well, Cormac thought, *it was to be expected.* He had hoped they would just keep on going and leave him be, but apparently that was too much to ask, what with a woman's natural instinct toward mothering and all. After all, there he was, a poor child recently orphaned, miles from other people, lost, and not knowing what to do next. Poor thing. How could she possibly leave that be? At least that's how he figured she must have figured. Cormac had no such inclinations his own self.

He had worked through much of his mourning period digging the graves for his mother, pa, and Becky. Cormac's pa had taught him how to work, and he had always found it to be a good salve for his mind, a good time for thinking. Whilst his hands were busy, his mind could work out whatever was bothering it. This was going to take a lot of working out.

He had talked to his family a lot while he was burying them and asked them what he should do now. They hadn't had much to say. Cormac's pa was the most help. It had been a comfort talking to him. When the hole was mostly dug and Cormac was standing in the bottom looking out—he had dug them all plenty deep, there weren't no animals gonna get them—he felt a calmness come over him. His pa would have told him to get on with it. "You can't do anything about what's done," he had said on several occasions. "Just brush the dirt off your britches and keep a goin'."

A time or two, Cormac had just curled up into a ball in the bottom of a grave in misery, and as he packed the last dirt on each grave, he told them how much he had loved them and how much he was going to miss them.

When the chore had been completed, he had fallen asleep; but when he came out of it and had his crying binge, he had accepted the situation as much as such a situation could be accepted. He was still mighty sad and would be for a long time to come whenever he thought about them, but being sad wasn't gonna get the corn picked or the cows milked or the pigs and chickens fed. He had a farm needin' care, crops that would soon need harvestin', and the job was his for the doin'.

Digging this grave, now, was a horse of a different color. His family had been avenged and done for as much as could be. Now he had to finish getting rid of the lowlifers, as his pa would have called them, but they weren't about to get their own graves. If they liked being together so all-fired much, they could just stay together and rot into a single pile of filth, worse even than manure.

They were all goin' into the same hole. If they hadn't been lying in his front yard, he would have just left them for the critters. "His front yard" was also going to take some getting used to.

Cormac still had an unrealistic hope that if he just kept digging and ignored the newcomers in the wagon they would leave him be, but that was simply not going to happen.

"My name is Gertrude Schwartz," said the soft voice above him, heavy with an unfamiliar accent. "I'm Lainey's mother." She pronounced it *Schwartz*. He had ignored the rustle of her dress as she approached in a weak hope that she would turn back and leave. *Not going to happen*, he realized dismally.

The voice did not fit the strong face looking down at him: dark and piercing eyes over a hawk-like nose and high cheekbones with a small mouth formed with leathery skin. It would take a strong woman to wear a face like that and she pulled it off. Her body was stout and solid with no sign of soft flab, and she appeared to be comfortable inside of it. Soft eyes looked out from a craggy face. The sympathetic smile she wore was trying hard to make her face handsome and very nearly succeeded. In spite of what Cormac knew she was about to say, he found himself drawn to her.

"I'm Cormac Lynch," he answered finally

"We wanted to come and thank you for rescuing Lainey," she said, "and to apologize for her attitude. From what she told us, I am sure she treated you right poorly. She can be downright obnoxious when she puts her mind to it. She felt the way you dealt with the situation was very extreme.

"My husband and I both told her that for one boy to rescue her from four fully grown men was nothing short of amazing and would have taken extreme measures. I think she understands." She went on, "How did you do it? Lainey said you got them all with one really loud shot. We saw the bodies still lying there. What kind of gun does that much damage in one shot . . . or was she hysterical and remembering it wrong?"

"No, ma'am. She didn't remember it wrong. It was one shot, ma'am, but from both barrels of a double- barreled ten-gauge shotgun at the same time." He paused for a moment and then decided to give her both barrels, too. If she wanted to know about it, he was just the one to tell her and see how she handled it.

"I wanted them dead and didn't want no discussion about it," he said.

Her eyebrows and the corners of her mouth rose only slightly. "Well then, you sure went at it the right way. Lainey said you told her they had killed your parents. What happened?"

Cormac wasn't sure he could talk about it. He knew he didn't want to think about it, but figured when you kill somebody, or somebodies, some explainin' was in order.

"They tore the clothes off my mother and sister and treated them real bad. And when Pa came to help, they killed them all. They thought I was dead, too, but they was real wrong about that, and I made right sure they knew it."

She nodded. "I see." Her face took on an expression Cormac

couldn't read. "I believe that hole is plenty deep for the likes of them. Climb on out of there, and I'll help you drag them over here and dump them into the hole. Poppa is feelin' poorly, or he would help, too."

Cormac got a horse and towrope from the barn, and Lainey showed up and began unbuckling their gun belts. "No sense in burying perfectly good guns. You may need them sometime. You want to see if they have any money?"

"No!" Cormac Lynch was emphatic.

She pitched right in then, and with three of them working, the burial went quickly. Lainey Nayle was obviously no stranger to hard work or a shovel. It occurred to him that maybe she wasn't such a brat after all, and he realized for the first time that she sure was right pretty and had an awful lot of shiny red hair.

He helped them get Mr. Schwartz into the house and into his mother and pa's bed. Cormac's pa had never let him get away with calling his mother Ma. He said it wasn't showing her the respect she deserved. By then, it was hungry time again, and Cormac started to rustle up some dinner, but Mrs. Schwartz wouldn't hear of it. "We'll take care of this. You go light someplace," she said, and then stopped to stare at the back door. She had never seen a cabin with a back door.

A thinking man with an uncommon amount of common sense, John Lynch had designed the twenty by twenty cabin in an unusual manner. During his meticulous search for a home site on which they were going to spend a lot of years, he had made an unusual discovery. A short distance from a slow-moving creek, out of a small hill beside a large stand of cottonwood trees ran the main reason he had chosen this particular location for their home: an artesian well from which bubbled a year-round continual supply of clear, fresh, cool water from some mysterious source deep underground, pumped out of the ground by a bunch of little people called Artesians, also deep in the ground, according to his pa's story. Even as a little boy Cormac didn't believe that one. After first building a wooden trough to direct the water into a tank from which an overflow would then irrigate an area for Amanda's vegetable garden, John Lynch designed a unique cabin that was to become the envy of every woman who had the opportunity to see it.

There was a back door just five steps from the water tank, a door that would provide easy access to all the water they would need for drinking, cooking, or bathing, and when both of the doors were left open in the summer, a cooling draft of air flowed through the cabin. With the Indian wars in mind, he built into each of the four walls two one-by-one holes from which to shoot, each covered with strong, tightly fitting shutters, and then he did something very unusual—he put in a wooden floor.

In the side of the hill close to the well, he found a small cave slanting downward into the hill which he made into a root cellar by building shelves along the walls for the cool-storage of canned goods and such; finishing it by adding a secure door, enabling the cave to double as a storm cellar and refuge from the occasional tornado searching for a place to cause trouble. All told, the total home plan elicited much praise and made Amanda Lynch the envy of every woman who ever heard of it.

Mrs. Schwartz and Lainey were a well-matched team. With few words and no wasted movements, they took over the kitchen. It was amazing how they seemed to know where everything was; maybe it was a woman thing. Was it instinctive? Did all women put things in the same places? He watched briefly. He had to admit that them being there was a comfort; he had not been looking forward to being alone.

"Okay. Thank you," he answered. "While you do that, I'll empty the slop bucket. It's starting to get rank."

Taking up the bucket from its place by the counter, Cormac walked out into the night. The bucket was for collecting all of the kitchen scraps and could get to smelling real bad, but the pigs loved it and would be all grouped up in the pigpen, bumping and pushing and oinking and squealing as soon as they saw him coming cross the yard with it.

The evening was awkward and uncomfortable: the food was tasty, but unfamiliar, and the conversation was forced by Mrs. Schwartz and nonexistent with the girl. Later, sleep was evasive. It was strange to think of strangers sleeping in the bed his pa had built to please his mother, and a sullen teenaged girl sleeping in Becky's bed on the other side of the blanket, which divided the room, with her head on the pillow cover his mother had made especially for Becky. Cormac wasn't liking that much.

He missed the even breathing sounds of his pa mixed with the softer and higher pitched breaths of his mother and accented by Becky's cute little snore about which he had always teased her as being deep and obnoxious. In the darkness, he lay rigid and unseeing, staring at the ceiling, fighting back the tears and the sobbing that were struggling for release. Somewhere in the night, exhaustion overwhelmed him, his taut muscles relaxed, his tear-filled eyes closed, and his horror-saturated mind found escape. Cormac Lynch slept.

In spite of his wishes, morning came again. The rooster announced the event as the sun was rising, the chickens began scratching around the yard for food, the cows bawled to be milked, the pigs squealed to be fed, the birds sang their morning songs, and the weeds in the fields continued to grow.

"Oh, pipe down," he called at the birds, and sailed a rock at them while on the way to the barn with the milk pails. He didn't really want to hit one; he just wanted them to shut up. He was in no mood for their racket.

As hard as he knew it was going to be to return to the potato field, there were potatoes that would rot in the sun if he didn't get them picked. He had no time to lie around and feel sorry for himself. After a breakfast he ate little of, he called in the team and hitched up the wagon; the potato bags Becky, his mother, and himself had already filled were waiting to be brought in, and the remaining spuds, as his pa had called them, needed to be picked.

Within the hour, he was joined in the field by Mrs. Schwartz and the redheaded girl. They didn't say a word. They just began picking. When Cormac reached the end of a row and turned to start down the next, there they were: inexperienced and fumbling, but putting their backs into it. Cormac, his mother, and Becky had had the field mostly done, and now, with the help of Mrs. Schwartz and Lainey Nayle, all of the potatoes were in by suppertime with enough time left to do the evening chores: milk the cows, and feed the pigs and chickens. The corn and flax would be needin' to be harvested in another week or so. There was a lot of work needin' to be done . . . soon. Cormac gladly accepted when they offered to stay and help him get in the crops.

"I been doing some thinkin'," Cormac told the Schwartzes and Lainey a couple of weeks later. "Ole man winter's fixin' to come blowin' in here 'fore long, and when he sets his mind to it, he can get right ornery. Now, the way I see it, Mr. Schwartz needs a place to be still for a while, and you folks got no place to live. This is a good, paying farm, but I can't work it by myself if I work thirty hours a day. Pa did a right good job of layin' it out, and the buildings are strong and built to last. Why don't you just stay on here? If it doesn't work out, you can pack up and move on. If I decide to move on, I'll sell it to you.

The farm had been laid out in an efficient and well-ordered

manner with attention also having been given to its appearance. It was a good-looking farm. The buildings were indeed built to last and the crops located for easy rotation to leave one section to go to grass every year. When it was plowed under in the fall, it would rot and the soil would be rich and rested for spring planting. His pa always plowed all of the fields deep every fall to let more of the melting snow and spring rains soak down into the subsoil. It was an excellent piece of land and an excellent offer for the Schwartzes.

Mr. and Mrs. Schwartz didn't hesitate. They looked at each other briefly and Mr. Schwartz offered his handshake. Cormac accepted it and an amiable working relationship was created on the spot. Lainey Nayle, on the other hand, was a different story. She spoke to Cormac only when necessary and even then with thinly concealed hostility.

Mr. Schwartz mended slowly. The first week, he remained weak, and though he insisted on taking care of all of his own personal needs, Mrs. Schwartz constantly hovered close by. Cormac noticed that whenever she was away, Lainey always seemed to find something near Mr. Schwartz that needed doing. The third week saw him starting to come out of it and progressing rapidly after that point; first helping with light chores and housework as soon as he could walk, then, as his strength returned, moving outside to more strenuous tasks.

His first name was Herman, but it didn't feel right for Cormac to use it. John and Amanda Lynch's training to respect his elders ran deep; to him they would always be Mr. and Mrs. Schwartz. There was no way of knowing what had made Mr. Schwartz so weak and poorly. He had been stomach sick, very hot, and had what a lady doctor they had met on the trail called dyspepsia.

The doctor had given Mr. Schwartz some medicine that eased his stomach pains while he waited for it to go away, if it ever did. Mrs. Schwartz believed a lesser man would have probably died. Cormac Lynch was to learn that most of the people coming over from the "old country" were workers.

Herman Schwartz was not as big as John Lynch had been, but he could get a bunch of work done before the sun went down of a night. By the end of week four, he had regained his full strength and proved to be a strong and willing worker, as was Lainey, in spite of her stubborn attitude toward Cormac.

On the morning after the Schwartzes had agreed to stay, Cormac slipped out of the door with the lantern to do morning chores just before sunrise as he had so many times with his pa. By the time he reached the barn, he realized Lainey was following along behind.

He stopped walking. "Good morning," he said, surprised.

"Morning," she responded in a dull, matter-of-fact tone. "Don't let me slow you down," she told him while motioning with her hand in a dismissing manner for him to continue. "I just want to see what you are doing."

With a shoulder shrug, Cormac filled a bucket up with grain and spread it around the ground near the chicken coop repeating, "Here chick, chick, chick. Here chick, chick, chick," as he did so. After filling their shallow water trough, he threw a couple of buckets of corn on the cob into the pigpen. "Here you go, guys. Here's breakfast. Come and get it," he told them. Then he added several deep and guttural *oiyeenk, oiyeenk, oiyeenk*s. He finished that chore by emptying another bucket of corn into the sty and two five-gallon buckets of milk into their trough.

Looking at Lainey, he told her, "Be careful if you get around this building. It's called the pigsty. It's for them to get inside during the winter or whenever they feel like it. Right now there is a new mama pig in there with three suckling shoats, and she's right cantankerous. She'll know I'm no threat to her piglets, but she doesn't know you yet. She'll come after you in a hurry."

The last chore was to sit on one of the one-legged milking stools and milk their three cows. With their own two feet on the floor, the one leg of the milk stools made a secure tripod place to sit. Two of the cows were black-and-white Holsteins and one a brown Jersey but all were plentiful givers and filled several one-gallon pails that would then be emptied into the two-handled milk can. Four cats and a couple of kittens materialized from out of nowhere to sit near the edge of the lantern light to meow over and over. "Good morning, cats," he said to them cheerfully. "Who's first?" They all yowled some more. Cormac turned a teat in their direction and covered their faces with fresh milk, which quieted them long enough to clean themselves with their paws and cry for more. Out of the corner of his eye, Cormac could see Lainey smile.

While milking the Jersey last and glancing at Lainey, he told her, "If you learn to milk, be careful that this one doesn't kick over the . . ." His intended statement was demonstrated by a swift forward kick from the cow's strong hind leg that sent his milk pail flip-flopping across the dirt floor, splashing milk in every direction.

"Damn," he said simply as six balls of furry felines scampered happily to lap up as much of the spill as they could before it soaked into the ground.

For the first time Cormac heard Lainey's laugh. It was a nice sound.

The next morning, Cormac was surprised to find the lantern not hanging on it's hook or visible anywhere nearby. It was more surprising to step outside and hear Lainey calling, "Here chicky,

chicky, chickys. Time for breakfast. Here chicky, chicky, chickys."

He stopped when he had rounded the corner of the house enough to see her feeding the chickens and could see the pre-pared buckets of corn waiting by the pigpen. He took and exhaled a deep breath while shaking his head as he had seen his pa do many times, and as he had heard his pa say many times, "I will be damned. I'll never understand the female of the spe-cies."

He had one cow milked and was working on the second when Lainey grabbed a milk stool and sat down by the last Holstein.

Cormac listened in silence as she grunted, sighed, and made frustrated sounds in general until finally she had to talk to him. Disgustedly she asked, "How do you make these darn things work?"

Smiling to himself, he paused to enjoy the moment before answering. "Squeeze your fingers closed one at a time from the top down in order. It forces the milk out the bottom. Try it a few times and you'll get the hang of it."

A few minutes later, he smiled again when he heard her happy yelp immediately following the clear sound of a milk-squirt hitting the bottom of an empty pail.

They finished milking and settled the lidded milk storage cans into the tank of continually flowing cold artesian well in the special area his pa had made just for such a purpose before going in for the breakfast they knew was waiting: bacon, eggs, flapjacks in gravy or molasses, and lots of coffee. A meal prepared by Mrs. Schwartz to last hard-working people until dinnertime.

Their accent, as Cormac had previously noted and which Mrs. Schwartz now explained, was from Germany. Lainey, it turned out, was from Ireland, which explained why she spoke differently, and why her last name was Nayle instead of Schwartz.

"No, I do not have an accent," she told Cormac nastily one day. "*You* do." She described the soft manner in which she spoke as speaking with an Irish lilt.

After supper of an evening was the best time for them to talk, and it was explained to Cormac by Mrs. Schwartz during one such conversation that during a sudden severe ocean storm on the boat trip over, Lainey's parents, Connor and Jasmine Nayle, had been accidentally knocked overboard by something called a boom that had been poorly tied. She had no other family, and for some unknown reasons, although the Schwartzes wanted and were impatient to have children, it was not meant to be. As soon as they arrived in America, they eagerly adopted her and began thinking of her as their own and they as her parents. Lainey, not speaking to Cormac unless necessary, as was her habit, remained silent.

———————

In a distressing and repeating dream, Cormac had wandered, unsuccessfully searching for his family's graves. In reality, he had visited their burial site and talked to them many times, but in his dream, he could not locate them: their graves were unmarked. He would fix that. With time on his hands during a three-day rainstorm, Cormac worked in the barn and cut three crosses. With his pa's big knife to do the carving, one of his mother's books to show him appropriate letters, and Becky's favorite pencil to lay them out, he had painstakingly carved each letter with care.

Finishing Becky's last, he brushed off the final woodchips and leaned the crosses side by side against the wall of the barn while he backed away to look at his handiwork. Closing his eyes, he pictured in detail each member of his family in turn, along with the laughter and fun they had shared, as clearly in his mind as looking at a photograph. He remembered birthdays and Christmases and his mother's kisses, baked pies and taters and gravy, walking to the fields with his father in the early-morning sun, sitting out a sudden thunder shower under their tree, and laying in the grass looking up at a night full of stars with Becky beside him . . . and his mother's kisses.

Opening his eyes, he found Lainey quietly standing beside him, looking at the crosses with tears streaming down her cheeks. For a long moment, they looked silently into each other's eyes, sharing their pain. She, too, had lost her family. In silence, she took his hand and they walked out of the barn together.

It occurred to Cormac that while Lainey had also lost both of her parents, she had no place to pay her respects, or to feel close to them. Working secretly, Cormac engraved a fourth cross and placed it with the others. The next day being Sunday, he told the Schwartzes his plan and arranged for them to accompany him and Lainey, and without explaining to Lainey why, took her to their own private graveyard.

The morning sun lit the white crosses under the spreading branches of the tree as Lainey stepped down from the wagon and turned to take Cormac's hand. She disliked him and had no use for him, but she understood all too well the pain he was suffering. Inadequate as it would be, she would give him her support the best she could.

"Oh!" She gasped when she saw the fourth cross bearing the names of Connor and Jasmine Nayle. Her legs started to give out, and her body went weak. Only Cormac's strong arm quickly encircling her waist kept Lainey from collapsing, and she cried out and then wept heavily. She continued to weep throughout the service as Mr. Schwartz read from his Bible in accented and caring tones, concluding with: "Thank you for welcoming these fine people, Lord, and for bringing the four of us together as the family we each needed. And thank you for giving us Lainey to be our wonderful daughter. We ask that you watch over and protect her and Cormac from further pain. Amen."

Lainey went to her adopted parents for comfort, and then to an uncomfortable Cormac Lynch for a long embrace that ended with a gentle, soft, and warm kiss on his cheek. "Thank you so very much," she whispered raggedly.

The Schwartzes had walked some distance away to allow the two of them a degree of privacy. Presently, Cormac joined them and they went for a walk to allow Lainey the previously unavailable opportunity to release the flood of emotions they knew she was holding inside. She had thought of her parents frequently. Theirs had been a tightly knit family and she missed them terribly, but previously had no place to let it out. She fell abruptly to her knees, and then, sitting back on her heels and holding her face in her hands, a heartbroken and grief-stricken Lainey Nayle folded her head to her knees and sobbed uncontrollably.

"I would like to walk back," Lainey told them after a while. Greatly affected by her new awareness of Cormac's true nature of sensitivity and caring, she held out her hand to him. "Will you walk with me, please, Cormie?"

United by catastrophic pain and feeling the closeness neither had expected to again feel with another person, they slowly walked the worn path through the grass and wildflower-spattered pasture to home; hand in hand, each in each other's company, understanding and sharing their thoughts and emotions: no need for words.

"I feel like such a huge weight has been lifted from me," Lainey said finally. "I feel like you rescued me again. I can't even describe how I have been feeling inside. It's been horrible. I've wanted to talk to them, but we are so far from everything out here in the country, I didn't think they knew where I was. I didn't think they would hear me, but as soon as I saw their cross, they were there with me. I could feel them. I knew they could hear me, and I could finally say good-bye. It had all happened so very fast. They were trying to get me to someplace safe. One moment they were there, and then suddenly a giant wave appeared and tore them away. I can still see them for that instant, clinging to each other and yelling something to me that I was trying so hard to hear . . . but I just couldn't hear them!" she cried out jerkily. Remnants of emotion erupted suddenly and Cormac only just did catch her before she collapsed sobbing to the ground.

———————

Sunday of the next week after dinner, Lainey and Cormac walked out to the graveyard and sat sadly in thought near the crosses, both coming to grips with their losses.

"I think your parents and mine would have liked each other," Cormac said suddenly.

Lainey looked at him and smiled. "I like that. And here, they're all together. It's a nice thought."

Shortly, they arose with silent mutual consent and started back. It was a nice day. Not hot, just pleasantly warm with the friendly voices of the bobolinks ringing out and a family of ground squirrels chasing each other in play under a blue sky with a few white clouds floating lazily overhead. Things had changed between them: a bond had been formed, and for the first time, they chatted comfortably as they walked.

The path took them to a tree-shaded footbridge Cormac's father had built over the stream, which was moving slowly, full from a recent rain. "How 'bout we get a drink and soak our feet?" Cormac asked. Lainey agreed, and as they turned from the path, he snatched a handful of wildflowers from a convenient clump and handed them to her. "For you, milady," he joked, pretending she was royalty.

Lainey looked up at him and flashed a quick, happy-eyed smile, showing bright white perfect teeth and amazingly green eyes. Cormac had never looked at her from so close before. He couldn't breathe. Never before had he looked into her eyes and realized the depth and shade of their color. They were beautiful. He stumbled on a washed-up river rock he hadn't noticed. She had never before smiled at him until a week ago, and then it wasn't an all-out smile like this one. Surprised at her beauty and unprepared for the feelings it aroused, he was momentarily stunned. It felt the same as when his pa had accidentally knocked the wind out of him once when they were wrestling in fun. He tried to catch his breath while he followed Lainey down to the water, hoping she hadn't noticed.

She had . . . and loved it, realizing she was feeling happy and girlish for the first time since losing her parents. It was a good feeling.

Cormac washed his hands in the water, then gathered as much as his cupped hands would hold and poured it into her likewise cupped hands so she wouldn't have to get her dress dirty kneeling on the bank. He repeated the procedure until she was satisfied before he drank. Then, thirst satisfied, they sat together on a washed-up broken tree trunk with their feet in the cool, bubbling water and threw pebbles into the stream.

"Look," Lainey cried excitedly and pointed at a fish swimming slowly in the gentle current at the water's edge. Cormac dove for the water with outstretched hands but only succeeded in scaring away the prey.

"Good try." She laughed as he regained his seat beside her. "We had a stream like this near where we lived in Ireland, but there were no fish in it. At least none that I ever saw. A boy at the next farm was always telling me he could catch one from it anytime he wanted, but I never believed him. My father used to bring home fish he caught someplace else, and we would have a fish fry."

Cormac was amazed. "I didn't know you lived on a farm before. That explains why you're used to this work. Tell me about it."

Lainey scootched around a bit to make herself more comfortable, then began their first real conversation. "It was a lot like yours," she started, "but Irish fields are tiny compared with Dakota's wide-open spaces. We grew hay, flax, and some wheat, and lived in a small whitewashed cottage with a straw-thatch roof, stone walls, a dirt floor, and an open chimney stack. You could look up through it and see the sky, and it had a big iron hook that hung over the open hearth where my mother would hang a big iron kettle for the tea, or a big black iron pot to boil the soup or potatoes, or a large flat griddle to bake soda bread. We had one cow for milk and butter and a vegetable garden and got meat once a week from the butcher in the next town. My mother made jams from the elderberries that grew wild along the hedgerows. Hedgerows are bands of bushes, flowers, and trees, with lots of different plants that grow tightly together, and animals and insects and many birds live in them. I didn't much care for the taste of the elderberries. I like the wild-berry jam Mrs. Schwartz makes better. I wanted my mother's bread with just butter, which I spent many hours churning. That was *my* job," she added proudly.

She stopped to pick up another handful of small pebbles to arc into the water one at a time to hear them *plop*. Cormac felt privileged that she was sharing with him, and was enjoying listening to what she was saying and to the sound of her voice. This was a Lainey he hadn't seen before. This Lainey was happy, and her Irish lilt had perked up. There was a musical sound to it. It was bouncy. He thought it sounded airy. *Now, where did that word come from?* he thought as she restarted her story. It would have made his mother happy.

"The roof thatch was made with straw from the stalks of the wheat crop after it was harvested and thrashed. To bind the thatch, my father made ropes with a hook on a handle that could be turned to twist it into rope. I used to get to live with my grandparents for a while each summer until they died. I loved them very much.

"My grandfather was German, like Mr. Schwartz, and was conductor for the Belfast Philharmonic Orchestra for a spell and taught my grandmama music. She was one of ten children; my being an only child was unusual in Ireland. My grandmama's name was Mary Patricia, and I loved her name, but my grandfather, I called him Papa, called her Paddy. It's a common nickname in Ireland, especially for anybody named Patrick. I guess Papa made it work for Patricia, too. She always hoped my mother or myself would learn to love music as she did. My mother didn't, but I enjoy it. I haven't felt like singing in a long time, but I used to sing the songs Grandmama taught me a lot."

Looking upstream, she stopped talking suddenly and leaned forward. "Look," she whispered excitedly, pointing about twenty yards up stream. "Here comes a big one."

"I think it's a bass," Cormac whispered back, and quickly stepped away from the stream to run down the riverbank quietly. He stepped gently into the water with little splashing. Taking a position facing upstream, he straddled the gentle current flowing along the edge, bending at the waist to rest his elbows on his knees. He spread his fingers wide and held them, unmoving, close to the water then waited motionlessly.

They both held their breath and watched the large fish swimming lazily along the edge of the stream, grabbing insects from the surface from time to time as they presented themselves. On the alert for small creatures, it paid no attention to the shadow of a large figure bending over the water until it was suddenly scooped out of the water.

"Hey, hey, hey!" Cormac called proudly, holding up the wriggling fish as Lainey laughed, "We got supper."

Indeed they did have supper. Mrs. Schwartz offered to cook it, but Lainey expertly had it cleaned, filleted, and fried by the time Mrs. Schwartz's potato soup was ready. All agreed it was a fine meal, and with Lainey once again able to be her real self, their relationships began to grow deeper after that and their little group began the process of becoming a real family.

When the Schwartzes squabbled, they lapsed into full German, which Cormac and Lainey found amusing. Hearing it, sometimes he or Lainey would giggle, earning them dirty looks that usually turned into smiles, if not laughter. Friendship born of necessity solidified and shared respect evolved as each found their place in the workload. Nobody tried to be the boss and nobody shirked the work needing doing. They all worked well together and everyone pulled their own weight.

Cormac was pleased to see even Lainey was a hard worker, in the house as well as the fields. She showed no hesitation, even in cleaning stalls and spreading manure in the fields.

"You do that so nicely," he teased as he walked passed where she was helping them prepare a field for fall plowing.

She was a sight to see wearing an old pair of faded blue bib overalls she had altered over a red cotton blouse, standing calf-deep in a manure-filled wagon while casting one shovelful at a time in a wide arc away from the rear of the wagon. Without skipping a beat, she targeted him with the next arc and laughed at him getting out of her way.

"That'll teach you not to mess with someone who's trying to get some work done," she told him as she stood up, wiped the sweat from her forehead, and brushed back the jumble of red hair that was adding to her discomfort.

"Aw, you don't worry me," he called back over his shoulder. "You couldn't hit me if I was standing still."

"Oh, you think not, do you?"

"I know so. Heck, you couldn't hit a bull in the butt with a scoop shovel."

An evil grin spread across Lainey's face as she picked up a baseball-sized chunk of dried cow manure and bounced it off the back of his head. "Uh oh," she said as he whirled and charged back at her.

She hit the ground running and led Cormac on a merry chase around the field, jumping away and laughing at him every time he tried to grab her and missed. Finally, she ran to where Mr. Schwartz was pulling out some sunflower plants by their roots. Circling to the other side of him, she danced back and forth to keep him between them.

"Alright yoou two leettle kids," he said in an exaggerated German accent, pretending to be mad with his face all grouchy. "Yoous get away from me and go doo your nonsense some udder places. I got's vork to dooo. Yoou keep this up and I turn yoou both over my kneee. Now vhat yoou tink about that?"

Letting him win the game, they both pretended to be admonished. "Yes, sir," they said dutifully, and started back for the wagon. Four steps later, he grabbed at her, she ducked, and they ran laughing to the wagon, which she jumped into, and went back to work. He continued on the way to get the pick and shovel he was originally going for.

Springtime found them all plowing and planting from early morning until late in the day. Fall found them harvesting and plowing under the surface growth. Between times, they pulled weeds . . . so many weeds.

Cormac decided the few potatoes they needed for their own use would be grown in the vegetable garden. They planted flax. There would be no more potatoes planted there.

He and Mr. Schwartz hunted as needed for meat: sometimes together, other times alone. Pheasants, ducks, and geese—usually Canadian Honkers—were in abundance, occasionally deer wandered into the area or, more rarely, a buffalo, of which there were too few left after the buffalo hunters and which Cormac refused to shoot.

Travelers were passing by more frequently and were invited to stay for food and rest. Their company and conversation were much looked forward to for the latest news of what was happening in the world.

A traveler stopping by on his way to California gave them a well-read copy of the *Chicago Tribune*, which told them a four-square-mile section of the city had burned to the ground and hundreds of people had been killed because a cow belonging to a Mrs. O'Leary had kicked over a lantern in a small shed near the edge of town. A Bostonian wearing a sweater-vest and what he called "riding breeches" that ballooned out on both sides, along with a silly cap, spoke of Wild Bill Hickok being the marshal of Abilene and of two railroads that connected somewhere in Utah, making the railroad tracks stretch all the way across the nation.

A handsome young fellow not long out of New York who caught Lainey's eye succumbed to her flirting by giving her a nearly new two-cent piece with the words "In God We Trust" prominently displayed on one side, which he claimed was the first time the phrase had ever been used on U.S. currency. True or not, it was the first time any of them had seen such a coin. Cormac wasn't too happy about the flirting part, although he wasn't quite sure why. What did he care if she wanted to make a fool of herself? He stormed out of the house and jumped on Lop Ear bareback. With no saddle and a handful of mane, they shot into the hills like a house afire.

Another traveler, this one from Illinois, was on his way to California in search of gold and tried to talk the Schwartzes into walking away from their farm and going to find some for themselves. "They could travel together," he said.

"No tank you," Mr. Schwartz answered in his German accent. "We've found our gold right here. We go to bed at night as a family, wake up, and work this rich Dakota soil as a family. That's all the gold we need."

The travelers' stories put Cormac in mind of his mother's comments about reading, taking him places he might otherwise not go. She had been well-read and had wanted him and Becky to also be. He returned to reading her books again. Maybe one day he might be wishful of seeing some other places, but for now, he had the responsibility of the farm.

Mr. Schwartz had taken to wearing his handgun, as had most men, and taught Cormac about the powder charge, the ball and cap routine of loading it, and how to use the molds to make the necessary balls—or actual bullets if he wanted more killing power. With his pa's teachings in mind, Cormac got in some practice time shooting at targets, and his aim became better. He rarely missed with any of the guns, making

Mr. Schwartz envious. Being left-handed, Mr. Schwartz wore his holster on his left hip. Cormac always threw rocks with his left, leading him to believe he was also left-handed.

One day when Lainey had carried lunch to them in the field, Mr. Schwartz and Cormac stopped work and walked, with Mr. Schwartz on Cormac's right, to where she was spreading the lunch out on a blanket. As she bent to place a bowl down, a rattlesnake in the brush near her leg rattled his tail and struck. Cormac heard Mr. Schwartz's gun go off and saw the snake's head disappear into the brush and the snake flop to the ground before realizing that the gun was somehow in his own hand. It was he who had pulled it from Mr. Schwartz's holster with his right hand.

"Oh!" Lainey cried, running to hug him. "You're wonderful! Thank you, thank you, thank you, thank you!" Mr. Schwartz just stared at him as if he'd seen damnation. Later, when Cormac had gone to bed, he heard the Schwartzes voices as they passed outside his window.

"I never seen nutten in my life move that fast," Mr. Schwartz was saying. "The gun yust appeared in his hand and his von shot tooked the head cleand off."

It had taken Cormac as much by surprise as it had Mr. Schwartz, and he wasn't too sure what to think about it his own self. All that practicing hand movements to pick taters as fast as he could had apparently come in handy in more ways than one.

"That's the second time he has saved her life," Mrs. Schwartz responded. "She would have died if the snake had bitten her. His folks would have been mighty proud of him."

Cormac liked that thought and hoped that his parents were somewhere, somehow, proud of the man he was becoming. He hoped Becky was, too.

CHAPTER 4

Neither of the Schwartzes was much for education, but Cormac continued the study habits his mother had given him, reading and rereading her books.

"Cormie," his mother had told him one evening while selecting their next book, "you should never stop reading and learning. You are going to get an education if I have to pour it into you." She hadn't had to do much pouring. He had learned to love reading at an early age. His pa agreed with his mother and wished that he, too, had more "book larnin'," but he said there were many places from which to get an education.

"Watch how the trees and plants grow," he told Cormac one day when they were tracking a deer. "See how animals react to each other and what their trails and droppin's look like. Study people and be aware of how they move and when their mouth says one thing and their eyes another, or when the smile on their lips doesn't reach all the way to their eyes."

Lainey's mother had also been educating her, and she missed it. It only followed that she would slip into studying with Cormac. It gave them something to do on evenings and days when it was too cold to do much of anything outside other than make sure the stock had food, keep the ice broken off the stream and water tanks so the stock could get to the water, keep the cows milked, the hogs and chickens fed, and repair wagons and harnesses in preparation for spring planting. They read, talked, and argued over their opinions on what they had read.

Lainey had been after Cormac to teach her to shoot. For her fifteenth birthday present he agreed and found her to be a good student, only needing to be shown something one time. He began teaching her to shoot with his pa's pride and joy: the rifle he called GERT. Lainey was somewhat intimidated by it, but got over it quickly enough. The gun had been given to Cormac's father by a German gun-maker to repay a debt. Most of the name had been gouged off a few years earlier by a bullet that ricocheted off it instead of killing his pa. All that remained of the name was GERT, so the rifle became a she, and his pa affectionately called her GERT.

"She looks funny," his pa had told him. "But she was made slowly and with pride by the hands of a skilled craftsman taking pride in his work. It was made to use the new cartridge ammunition and will put the bullet right where you aim her at a range bordering on the unbelievable. She's one of a kind." Then his eyes lit up. He was not school educated like Cormac's mother, but he dearly loved the turn of a good phrase or yarn.

He had pulled GERT up to his shoulder and followed an imaginary moving target. "Man, man, man," he said, shaking his head with feeling. "You could scare up one of your rabbits, let him run all day and shoot him at night."

"With a pistol," Cormac reminded Lainey one Sunday morning, teaching her as his pa had taught him, "you just point it

like pointing your finger. A rifle is a whole different ball of wax;
it needs to be held very steady. If at all possible, a rifle needs to
be rested on something solid. If that's not possible, lay down.
Never shoot from a standing position if you can kneel down,
and never kneel if you can lay down." She learned quickly and
after just a few lessons, unflinching from the kick or the noise,
was hitting most things she aimed at.

Cormac had been noticing that Lainey's body was getting right
comely in a full-blown way, and with her fire-red hair, green
eyes, and an uncommonly bright-white smile, she was downright
eye-pleasin'. When they were sixteen, Cormac peeked under the
blanket dividing their room when they were getting ready for
bed one warm night, but was very nearly caught at it and doing
so made him feel guilty. He never repeated it.

He and Lainey did chores together, studied together, played
together, and had snowball fights, and once, under the pretense
of trying to wash her face in the snow, he kissed her while he was
holding her down and she couldn't resist—or so he thought.
Sometimes on Sundays when the weather was warm, they went
for horseback rides. Cormac would saddle the grulla for Lainey,
and he would ride Lop Ear bareback. Only one of the saddles was
large enough for either of the big horses, and a too-small saddle
would give them saddle sores on their backs. The grulla was a
pretty and well-behaved mare with a smooth ride, which was
good for Lainey. On those occasions, they sometimes took a lunch
and ranged far.

On one such occasion after removing a rock from Lop Ear's
shoe that left the big horse limping slightly, Lainey said he better ride behind her on the way back to rest the foot. She emptied
one stirrup and he stepped up to sit behind her saddle.

"Oh, this is scary," he said as they started back. "I might fall off." He promptly wrapped his arms tightly around her waist.

"Oh stop it, you phony!" she exclaimed, and pushed his arms back. "You behave yourself, mister, and don't get any ideas or you can just walk back." She smiled half the way home thinking maybe she had been too hasty.

———————

Then, shortly after they turned seventeen, everything went wrong, and Cormac and Lainey began fighting. It was the darndest thing. One day they were getting along just fine, and the next they were squabbling about every little thing, tormenting each other at every opportunity, and Cormac got on a first-name basis with her Irish temper.

She asked for no quarter and gave none . . . giving as good as she got. And when she had her Irish up and her green eyes were flashing, it was time to head for the hills. When he intentionally neglected to tell her how much the shotgun kicked before she fired it for the first time, the kick knocked her on her keister, and he laughed and made fun of her. Seeing the look on her face while she was getting up, he realized he had made a mistake and ran like the devil, but not fast enough. She bounced a frozen dirt clod off the back of his head, and he bled for ten minutes.

"Serves you right," she told him when he complained about it later. "Next time I'll throw harder and then turn you over to the wee people."

The "wee people," Lainey had told him, were mischievous Leprechauns that could only be seen by the Irish, but they all had a pot of gold, and if one could be caught, he was obligated to give it to the person who did the catching. She swore it was true, but to Cormac, it sounded like a pa-story.

"Dinner's ready," Lainey had called to him in the barn one day when he was cleaning stalls. Before going into the house, he washed up in a wash basin sitting on a small stand outside the door. The route to the table took him past Lainey bending to put a pan on the bottom shelf in the kitchen. Taking advantage of the situation without thinking it through, Cormac slapped her a good one across her bottom-side. Instantly her face clouded with anger and she stood up with flashing eyes, rubbing her backend.

"You nincompoop!" she screamed, and threw the pan at him, but Cormac only ducked and laughed at her, which only served to make her more angry. Yelling and screaming, she chased him out of the house with a cast-iron skillet held high with both hands. Mr. and Mrs. Schwartz exchanged looks, and the next day Mrs. Schwartz had them building Lainey her own bedroom. Cormac would have gone without dinner had Mr. Schwartz not stolen a piece of beef for him.

———————

Trips to town, though rare because of the distance, were something to which they all looked forward. Just before Lainey's eighteenth birthday on March seventeenth, Mrs. Schwartz declared it to be time to go for supplies, and then in secret reminded Cormac that it would be a good time for them to get presents for Lainey.

During their first year living as a family, Lainey had told him that her parents had been special people in Ireland and all of Ireland celebrated her birthday with the wearing of the green with her favorite shade being kelly green.

"Mrs. Schwartz," Cormac began as he sat down at the table with a cup of coffee. "What kind of special people were Mr. and Mrs. Nayle? Lainey told me that on her birthday, all the people in Ireland wear her favorite shade of green to celebrate her birthday because her parents were important, but she didn't say why they were important."

Mrs. Schwartz stopped churning the butter to look at him incredulously and then she looked at Mr. Schwartz. He was sitting straddle on a wooden bench, braiding two pieces of a broken rope together. They looked at each other for a long moment and then began to smile. The smile turned into a loud laughter and an accompanying loud guffaw by Mr. Schwartz.

Cormac could only stare at the two in confusion, but knowing something was not right and Lainey had probably been stringing him along in some way, he felt his anger rising and his face turning red. "What?" he asked. "What are you laughing about?"

They couldn't answer with other than more peals of laughter. Cormac couldn't sit still and got up from the table, knocking over the cup of coffee he had just poured for himself in the process, which only made the Schwartzes laugh harder.

He didn't understand what was going on but he was embarrassed and knew that somehow he had been made a fool of, Lainey was at the bottom of it, and he was darn well going to find out what it was all about. Cormac slammed the door on the way out, causing another round of loud laughter from the Schwartzes.

It was at that moment that Lainey came around the corner of the house not ten feet away. "Uh oh," she said, reading the look on his face in an instant and realizing she was in trouble. She had no idea what was the problem, but she knew Cormac well enough to know she had better get out of there real quick. With him hot on her heels, she ran for open spaces where the snow wasn't so deep. She being the faster and could outrun him if she could just stay out of his reach until then.

She was leading Cormac easily until snow that looked level on top was covering an eight-inch indentation in the ground below caused by a hog that had escaped the pen during the rains months earlier and had wallowed in the mud. Lainey's feet broke through the snowy crust and sank to the ground, and she fell face first into a snowbank. Before she could regain her footing, Cormac was on her, turning her over onto her back and straddling her with a firm grip on each of her arms. Other than turning her head from side to side or kicking her feet into the air, she was pinned for fair.

"All right, *Miss Nayle!*" he spit at her. "What is so dadblamed funny about Ireland wearing kelly green for you on your birthday?"

Wide-eyed, she looked up at him. "Oh no!" startled out of her, and she struggled hard not to laugh. "Oh no!" Holding in the laugh turned out to be impossible and it burst out uncontrollably.

Cormac was astounded and began babbling utterances that made no sense in furious anger. When shaking her arms proved to be a worthless effort, he grabbed the lapels of her heavy coat and bounced her up and down in the snow.

"I'm sorry," she got out through the laughter. "It was just a joke. Honest. I was going to tell you later, but I forgot to."

"So you made a fool out of me and now you think it's funny. See if this is funny." He let go of her arm, grabbed a scooping handful of snow, and began roughly pushing it down her neck and washing her face with it.

Lainey tried to turn away. "Cormie, I'm sorry. Stop, please! That's hurting me."

He paid her no attention and grabbed more snow and pushed it more roughly across her face. If he could have seen her eyes or the look on her face, he might have changed his plan. With her free hand, she made a fist and smacked the side of his head with as much force as she could muster. From the position she was in, a good swing was impossible, but it was hard enough to get his attention. He jumped to his feet, grabbed her from off the ground like a sack of flour, and pitched her into a deep snowdrift beside them.

"Don't do that again," he said angrily, and stomped off toward the barn.

Lainey Nayle was angry. Cormac had made her mad before, but never like this. Face and ears red and burning, her freckles standing our fiercely, and her green eyes flashing, she seethed as she watched him disappear into the barn. She climbed out of the snowbank, and after wiping as much of the snow as she could from the neck of her clothes, she strode purposefully into the house.

"Maybe we should head for the storm cellar," Mr. Schwartz whispered when they saw the look on her face.

Without a word, Lainey helped prepare supper and, instead of placing the food bowls on the table as usual, she set out the plates of individually dished-out food, making it obvious that she had made a plate especially for Cormac and set it before him. Making it a point of watching him all the while, she filled her own plate and ate hungrily.

Cormac had been repairing broken fence posts away from the farm buildings and missed dinner. "I'm starving," he said as they finished saying grace. But when he saw how Lainey was watching him, he was afraid to eat. He knew she had done something unusual to his food. Without touching it, with a deep sigh, he finally rose from the table and went outside, catching his coat from its hook on the way.

"Vut did yoo do tooo his food?" Mrs. Schwartz wanted to know.

"Nothing," Lainey answered sweetly. "Absolutely nothing. I don't know whatever gave you that idea."

Reaching with her fork, the self-satisfied redhead angelically took a bite of food from each of the items on his plate before happily finishing her own supper. With tiny smiles, the Schwartzes could only look at each other and shake their heads hopelessly. Cormac went to bed with no supper that night.

He was sleeping soundly and dreaming of a big plate of liver and onions and mashed potatoes and corn on the cob and still-warm fresh-made bread with a tall glass of milk to wash it down when suddenly the skies in his dream opened up and a blizzard was dumping snow in clumps on his head and something was rubbing it into his mouth and eyes. He sat bolt upright to find Lainey had been rubbing his face with snow and waiting with another bucketful. Cormac grabbed for her unsuccessfully as she emptied the bucket in his face and all over his bed before running out the front door. He climbed quickly into his pants, slid his feet into his high-topped shoes, and ran out after her. She was standing patiently waiting for him about fifty feet away.

By darn, he would show her not to mess with him, and ran to get her. When he was about halfway there, she suddenly began throwing snowballs at him. There were many, well made and hard packed, and she was throwing fast and hard. When they hit, they hurt, and most were hitting their targets. He tried to get some snow with which to return her fire but got hurt by three more painful hits in the process and quickly gave that up as a bad idea and ran for the house.

Lainey waited with a snowball in each hand for whatever he was planning but nothing happened. Happy and proud of her-self, she waited long enough to calm down before going in to go to bed, but she found the door locked. Laughing a satisfied snort at his weak response, she went to the other door, with the same results. *Very nice*, she thought, and began beating loudly on the door.

"Stop it," Cormac called through the wooden door. "You'll wake the Schwartzes."

She didn't hear the last of it because she was running for the front door. She pounded loudly until she heard the Schwartzes angry voices going into the front room from their bedroom. At that point, she ran for the barn and let him deal with them. Lainey could hear the angry German voices when they opened the door to find nobody there and the words, "the tooo of yooo" cut off by a slam of the door. By the time the voices finally quieted, Lainey had been asleep under a horse blanket in the hay for five minutes.

The next morning, Lainey woke to find Cormac making ready to milk the cow. "Hey, sleepyhead," he called to her when he realized she was awake. "Mrs. Schwartz made pancakes. You better get in there before she throws them to the pigs."

"I'm sorry," she said sheepishly.

"Yeah. Me, too," he answered good-naturedly. "That was a good one, though. The side of my head still hurts from where you hit me."

"Well, you were too rough. That'll teach you. My face is still raw."

"Here is a nice warm cow. I'll squirt some of her nice warm milk on it if you want."

She didn't.

———

They had converted the wagon to a sled by replacing its wheels with runners after the first snowfall of the year. Going into town was to be an all-day affair. They left at first light with Mr. and Mrs. Schwartz sitting on the blanket-covered bench seat, bundled in their heaviest coats against the bitter cold. Facing the rear, Lainey and Cormac piled into the back under some blankets. The ride was smooth, and the sound of the sled runners cutting through the snow relaxing. After talking a little about the backward view and what book to read next, they began to doze off and on.

A bump jostled the sled and Lainey fell against him, somewhat surprising Cormac. He hadn't believed it to be that much of a bump, but there she was, leaning against him with her head resting on his shoulder. His first reaction was to shove her away, but instead, he found himself being reminded of how nice her hair smelled and its softness against his cheek. It occurred to him that it might be fun to put his arms around her and kiss her a little bit.

The way Cormac was feeling was puzzlin', and he found himself enjoying her nearness. Why he was having the feelings he was having was a question beggin' for an answer. Although her breathing didn't quite sound like it, she must have been asleep 'cause her eyes were shut and she didn't move away. He reckoned it to be all right if she was to stay there a bit.

When they pulled into town a little after noon, the street was nearly deserted. Traffic and sunshine had worn away the snow in front of the stores. Wishful of keeping the runners in the snow, Mr. Schwartz pulled the sled around the back of the buildings to come up behind the general store.

The thick snow muffled the horses' hooves, and they slid quietly around the rear of the bank that was jutting out beyond the store. There, a girl about Lainey's age was trying hard to resist being taken to the ground by a man holding one hand over her mouth to keep her from yelling while pushing her down and tearing at her clothes with the other. He outsized her considerably, and she was losing the struggle.

Visions of his mother and Becky overcame Cormac. He was out of the wagon and nearly on the struggling duo before they realized they were no longer alone. Cormac caught the man on the turn with a fist to the middle of his face, splattering blood across the snow. The attacker fell back against the loading dock. Cormac had gained much in size and strength, and at eighteen was already larger than most men. All of the pent-up anger, hatred, and rage boiled over. Finally, here was someone he could spend it on.

No longer aware of his surroundings and holding nothing back, Cormac waded into the man with heavy blows to his mid-section as fast and hard as he could punch, alternating with more to his face, turning it into mush. The onslaught overpowered the rapist and knocked him over backward. Cormac yanked him to his feet and continued the hammering. He felt hands trying to pull him off, but he wouldn't be stopped. He broke free and continued the beating.

"Hey, Billy," came a voice from someone still in the alley beside the store but coming closer. "What's taking you so long? How about we help you with her? She should be able to handle us all."

Two men in cowhand attire rounded the corner.

"What the hell!" one exclaimed, when they saw what was happening to their cohort. They grabbed for their guns.

Not knowing he was dead, Cormac was holding the man he had been beating upright with his left hand and Mrs. Schwartz had just taken a strong grip on his right arm in an attempt to stop the beating. The dead man's gun had twisted to hang down across his belly. Cormac let the man go and as the body slipped to the ground, he grabbed the gun with his left hand and felt it pounding in his fist.

He worked the hammer fast, pulling it back again and again as rapidly as it fell. Sounding like one long peal of rolling thunder, the sound of gunshots echoed off the buildings as one man went down and the other turned to run. He didn't make it. The last two bullets opened up the back of his head. Cormac was still pulling the hammer on an empty gun when Mr. Schwartz gently took it from him.

Cormac didn't know what to do, so he did nothing. He simply stood there while men with excited voices came running. Mrs. Schwartz and Lainey were comforting the hysterical girl while Mr. Schwartz was explaining to a man with a badge why Cormac shouldn't be arrested for killing three men.

The badge belonged to Sheriff Woodrow. Sheriff Jason Woodrow was about the same age as Cormac's pa had been, a little shorter maybe, and more plump, with a round bearded face above a belly that hung over his belt. His eyes said not to let his appearance fool you; he knew what he was about, and he took his job seriously. If you strayed outside the law, you would find yourself keeping the dust off the bed in his one jail cell.

In this case, though, Mr. Schwartz needn't have worried. The Sheriff didn't make much of the incident. As it turned out, the reprobates had been swaggering around town three days, drunk much of the time, terrifying the women, and beating any men who complained. They had shot up the barbershop when the barber accidentally nicked one of them he was shaving. Since they quickly offered to pay restitution, Sheriff Woodrow hadn't been able to do anything about it other than warn them. Cormac's only reprimand came from the sheriff regarding the man being shot in the back of the head.

After having one of the women bystanders, an acquaintance of the girl, see her home, the sheriff had taken Cormac and the Schwartzes to the jail for private questioning and while doing so, poured a round of coffee from a large pot sitting on a pot-bellied stove in the corner.

"All I'm saying is, shooting someone in the back of the head looks cowardly and somehow wrong. Even though they were troublemakers and the townsfolk all wanted them to leave—some wanted them dead—a shot to the back of the head is never a good thing."

"Cowardly?" Mr. Schwartz was angry, his accent more pronounced. "Cowardly? He had pulled von of them off the girl and vas beating the stuffin's out of him. Two men comed out of the alley drawin' their guns and probably vould have killed us all, and yoouu call him cowardly?" He made an attempt to calm down. "Are yoouu charging him vith anything?"

"No, of course not. If I did, the townsfolk would have my head. No. He can leave."

"Cowardly," Mr. Schwartz mumbled, shaking his head as they stepped out of the jail onto the boardwalk.

The little group went to the general store where Mr. and Mrs. Schwartz ordered the supplies they needed. While Mrs. Schwartz, Lainey, and Cormac loaded them into the sled, Mr. Schwartz went to the bank to take care of some business. The three worked in silence; the fun was gone from the trip. Lainey and Cormac even refused an offer for some store-bought candy.

The trip home was long and silent. Mrs. Schwartz was standoffish, and Lainey only spoke to Cormac once, icily calling him by his full name, instead of Cormie, as she usually did. She huddled silently under her own blanket on the other side of the sled all the way home. When her blanket came loose and blew off her feet, he automatically reached to tuck it in. She kicked at his hand, staring at him ferociously when he looked up into her eyes. Her bitter anger and hatred was evident. She had watched him kill three more people.

So he had beaten one to death. So what? When someone commits violence against an innocent person who has done nothing to provoke the attack, the attacker has no right to complain about the severity of the response. And what the heck difference did it make which direction the bullet came from? Would the man have been any less dead if the bullet had entered his head from the front? Cormac thought Lainey would have understood, but if she wanted nothing to do with him anymore, so be it.

The townsfolk had patted him on the back, and the girl's parents couldn't thank him enough, but it was clear that the women at home thought him to be some out of control evil man, and even Mr. Schwartz, who had stood up for him in town, was somewhat reserved around him.

Unable to again bear her stony silence and unwilling to revert to the miserable existence they had once endured, that night, he left.

CHAPTER 5

The note read:

To Mr. & Mrs. Schwartz, thank you for caring about me when I needed somebody. You are very nice people. Good-bye. I like you very much.

As only heir of John and Amanda Lynch, I am giving the farm and all things I can't carry with me to Mr. and Mrs. Herman Schwartz. And to Lainey Nayle.

Cormac Lynch, March 17, 1872.

P.S. Happy birthday, Lainey. I am sorry I ruined it for you.

Another note read:

To Lainey, I do not understand your attitude. I don't know what else I could have done. It was in me. I would think you would understand because of your close experience of a similar nature. But it is your right to have whatever attitude you want. When you first came to live here, I remember how hard it was for you to deal with me being here. I won't make you go through that again. I left some books so you could keep studying. Please do. Good-bye, ~~Ho~~

Quietly he gathered up what he considered to be his most important belongings, which included a pocket knife Becky had given him, a few of his pa's papers and his big belt-knife in its leather case, a necklace-watch his pa had given to his mother when they married, and a few of his mother's books. The others he left for Lainey. He also took the six hundred dollars of moneys with him, which was his share of the crops that had been divided between the Schwartzes, he, and Lainey over four years. This was in addition to the money of his parents, which had been hidden in a secret place in their bedroom, enough food for a few days, his pa's ten-gauge scattergun, and GERT, and slipped quietly out of the house.

From the tack storage bin in the barn, he removed the gun belts, handguns, and rifles that Lainey had taken off the outlaws so long ago and which had since remained in the tack storage box . . . the guns that had killed his pa. It had been difficult, but he had cleaned and oiled them before storing them away. If somebody needed shootin', it would be because they were some type of lowlife, and using bad men's guns against other bad men and their like sounded like a fine idea to Cormac: a payback of sorts—poetic justice, his mother would have called it.

Cormac chose three revolvers with good heft that felt good in his hands. One was a cap and ball long-barreled single-action .44 caliber Army Colt with smooth wooden grips known for its range, power, and accuracy which, though in surprisingly good condition, had obviously seen much use.

A traveling gun salesman staying with them whilst waiting for the passing of a typical Dakota winter storm that had the snow piled up to the eaves, had been hoping—without success—to impress Lainey with how much he knew and had given Cormac and Mr. Schwartz a lengthy lesson on guns. Cormac had taken to it eagerly, which was no surprise to any of them. What Cormac found surprising was Lainey's interest in the subject. She had paid close attention from beginning to end. His second choice, a rotating-cylinder revolver with similar wooden grips that appeared near-new, carried the name of Smith & Wesson imprinted on the body and used the same .44 caliber cartridge as his pa's rifle. Although the past owners of these guns had held their other belongings in total disregard, Cormac was forced to grudgingly give them credit for taking good care of their weapons. A third gun, taken as a spare, was also a Smith & Wesson and used a like ammunition, but hadn't been as well maintained, causing the action to be stiff and needing work.

Putting the spare gun in his saddlebag, Cormac made sure the guns were loaded and strapped on to the two holsters. They slid nicely into place, but wearing two guns made him feel flashy, like a tinhorn gambler. He decided wearing the right-hand gun by itself would be adequate.

Until the snake incident, he had always considered himself to be left-handed, but it didn't seem that his hands much cared which one did the shooting. His right had blown the head off a snake, and the left had dispatched two of the three would-be rapists easily enough. Although he had begun noticing that most things could be done as easily with one hand as the other, wearing the gun on his right side felt a bit more natural. His pa's being the only rifle of any interest, he returned the others to the storage bin.

Securing the Army Colt and the scattergun to the gear on the packhorse in such a way that either could be gotten quickly for an easy grab in an emergency, Cormac concealed them under a loose canvas cover. Experience told him that prepared was the sensible thing to be.

The best horse on the place, or any other place, as far as Cormac's pa had been concerned, was his large gray gelding that he'd had since Cormac was thirteen. The horse had been given him as a yearling by a colonel in the Union army, whose life his pa had saved twice during the war. According to the colonel, the gray was special because its sire had been from some Arabian country. Cormac's pa had affectionately named him Lop Ear. Partially for his one ear, which perpetually hung down after being bitten half off in a fight with another stallion before he had been gelded and had his manhood stripped away, thus removing his fighting tendencies. And partially so he wouldn't be gettin' highfalutin ideas and wantin' to be treated like royalty just because of his proud-walkin', high-steppin' and long, slender legs and arched neck, and carrying his tail so high and fancy.

Cormac led Lop Ear out of his stall and threw his pa's saddle on his back. It was not only the saddle in the best condition, but it was the only one large enough to fit the big horses and Cormac, who was now six foot four.

Wanting a second saddle horse that could double as a packhorse, he chose the outlaw's grulla of which he had become quite fond. A beautiful and long-legged dark slate-gray mare with mustang lines that looked to be about the same age and size as Lop Ear, she was well mannered and friendly with a smooth gait that made her easy to sit. They had become friends and, for lack of a better name, Cormac had simply called her Horse in the beginning and had never felt the need to change it.

A gift that Lainey had made for him came to mind, and just before leaving, he tiptoed back into the house to get it: an arrowhead she had found and made into a neck-charm with a strip of rawhide she had braided. Cormac had taken it off while getting cleaned up to go into town that morning and forgotten to put it back on. Pausing for one last look, he sighed, and silently closed the door.

"Our guiding star," as his pa had called it, was high in the sky when Cormac stopped on the hilltop overlooking their valley. Cormac had a moment of hesitation.

"It's not ours anymore," he said aloud. *It's not mine anymore either . . . It's theirs. Oh, the heck with it*, he thought. He was eighteen years old. Maybe now was the time to go see some of the sights travelers had been telling them about.

"Well, Lop Ear, that's about enough dramatics," he said. "Let's us go say good-bye to Mother, Pa, and Becky, and point our noses west and go see what it's all about anyway." The grulla followed willingly to the gravesites on her hackamore.

The crosses didn't seem to be enough. The names he had so carefully inscribed on them now seemed so inadequate. It had seemed like enough at the time. But no longer. There should be something telling what wonderful people they were, telling how his pa had always worked so hard to love and take care of his family, and how his mother had worked in the fields by his side all day, cooked their favorite meals, made them clothes, and sewn special gifts for each of them of an evening, and how Becky had always taken the time to play with him when he was little and tell him stories. Three crosses with just their names wasn't enough, but there was nothing he could do about it now.

The horses stood quietly beside him somehow knowing something was wrong. Horse blew and Lop Ear shook his head. Cormac mounted, and they set out at an easy lope. Lop Ear could keep that up all day and put a lot of miles behind them, and Cormac wanted some miles behind them by morning. The events of the day had left him keyed up, and he wasn't the least bit tired. It would catch up with him, no doubt, but for the time being he was enjoying the night ride. There was a strange mixture of sadness for the life he was leaving behind. He would miss the Schwartzes. After a bit he added silently *and Lainey*. But at the same time, he felt an excitement for what lay ahead. The fate and shaping of Cormac Lynch was now in his own hands. His mother and pa had laid the groundwork, teaching him to be honest and God fearin', and they gave him a strong work ethic.

His pa had said, "The foundation of a good life is hard work." His mother had taught him to read and to learn. Mr. and Mrs. Schwartz had continued to teach him by example, and he had to admit that he had learned a lot from Lainey. She was a fine person, mighty notional, but a fine person. She believed the people of the world could be divided into two groups, those who were Irish, and those who wanted to be. Yes, he would most definitely miss Lainey. They had become very close, until they had begun to fight. Cormac could not understand it and regretted the fighting and arguing. The feelings he had been having while her head lay on his shoulder were something to ponder. *I wish*, he thought. A lot of good wishing would do. What was it that the gravelly old traveler had said a couple of years ago when Cormac had told him he wished his parents were still alive? "If wishes were horses, all beggars would ride. If cow turds were doughnuts, I'd eat till I died."

The air was crisp and bitterly cold with a full moon looking down from above. His pa had made up stories for Cormac about the face on the moon, and he had never been quite sure when his pa was truth-tellin', or when he was making things up. His pa had once told him that people sometimes acted strange when there was a full moon. Pa had also teased Cormac's mother by tellin' him, when she was within ear shot, that that was the reason women liked to get men out during a full moon, because the men would become crazy and propose marriage.

That night, the big old full moon was shining brightly on the snow, reflecting from it and adding a special quality to the night, making it more like a soft day. Many a night, as a small boy, Cormac had played outside in just such light until being called in by his mother. It was soothing, something familiar to travel with. Not wanting to be sky-lighted, he skirted the hill-tops, and it allowed him to see into the surrounding valleys. He doubted anyone else was out at this hour, but if he was, others also might be.

The part of the country he was leaving behind was dotted with occasional lakes and rolling hills that one of his mother's books had explained were the result of glaciers passing through about a zillion years ago. Cormac could never quite grasp the concept of where all that ice had come from in the first place, but the book said it had totally changed the landscape—cut the tops off hills and used them to fill in valleys, moved around giant boulders and deposited them elsewhere, and created lakes—making him wonder what the country had looked like before.

Somewhere in front of him was the two-day-ride-wide Rocking R cattle ranch, after that, he needed to drop south to get around the badlands, and then go west through a couple of other large ranches. That would take him through a corner of Nebraska, then a turn right through Wyoming, and he would be on his way "out West."

The dawn was long in coming, but slowly the sky began to lighten in the east; it was going to be another blue-sky day. He never tired of the vastness of a big sky over the rolling hills, no matter if the hills were covered with snow or grass. To Cormac, the sight was always tremendous.

Horse apples on the trail had called his attention to the tracks of another horse that had passed through earlier, and now they were joined by a third following the same route. The moonlight was reflecting from a thin coating of ice in the bottom of the tracks, indicating that the sun had melted the blown-in surface snow and it had refrozen. He figured the other riders to be about a day in front of him.

His stomach had been doing its bear-in-the-woods imitation for some time and was becoming more insistent, and the countryside had been changing, with the hills becoming larger with more trees. A little ahead and off to the side ran a stream with a thick grove of birch trees, looking like a good place to grab a bite and bed down a while.

He had been up for more than twenty-four hours, eight of which had been spent in the saddle. He had killed three men, alienated the only people who meant anything to him, and given away the family homestead. That seemed like more than enough for one day. A little food and sleep was sounding almighty good.

Judging by the tracks, yet another rider coming from the south had joined the others. The area was beginning to get downright crowded. Cormac had only ridden about twenty-five miles and already there were four people in the neighborhood. What would anyone be doing riding in this weather if it wasn't necessary? The other riders had also veered off toward these trees. Well, there was nothing unusual about that. Most good campsites were frequented frequently, or should it be frequently frequented? What would his mother think about using those two like words together? Likely, it was some kind of a double-grammar somethin' or 'nother.

The stand of birch was fair in size and too thick to see into. Cormac pulled off his heavy mittens, flexed his fingers a few times to limber them up, and unbuttoned his sheepskin coat. He worked the action of his pistol to make sure it hadn't frozen and there was a cartridge in the chamber of his rifle before laying it across the saddle in front of him. He believed the other riders to be at least a day ahead of him but had no wish to find out by surprise that he had been mistaken.

Wary of trouble and riding loose in the saddle, Cormac Lynch watched Lop Ear's ears as they followed the tracks into the grove. If the horses smelled company, their ears would perk up to listen for accompanying sounds. The tracks led him to a campsite with a ring of fire-blackened stones below a forked branch propped up to hang the handle of a bucket to heat water or a coffee pot. His bet was on the coffee pot, but it may have been wishful thinking. A cup of horseshoe coffee was sounding pretty darn good.

His pa used to tell him, "The way to make a good cup of coffee is to throw a handful of coffee into some water and boil it a good while, and then throw in a horseshoe. If the horseshoe sinks, add more coffee, and boil it longer."

He missed his pa, he surely did. His mother and Becky, too. John Lynch had loved to make up poems with which to tease Cormac's mother and also loved to make up stories. A poem came to mind that his pa had made up while petting one of the cats that hung around during milking, waiting to get sprayed in the face with a stream of fresh, warm milk.

Without slowing his petting, he had just come out with it:

Poor little tittin tat
Sittin on the titten toe

Hit him with the bitty bat
Dod damn it.

Cormac hadn't known what it meant, doubted his pa had, but it was fun to listen to. His pa had been a man worth remembering. He wasn't book-read, but his brain was mighty quick.

Cormac was careful to not mess up the signs until he had a chance to study them. According to the droppings, trash, cigarette butts, and the like, two people had waited here for two days. One was a heavy man of medium height with well-worn boot heels making deep tracks, and the other, a man not much on wide but his mother had done a good job for him on tall, walking with large strides. His boots did not sink deeply into the snow, and according to the yellow letters in the snowdrift, his initials were C.S. Cormac could still think of no good reason for this many people to be out in this kind of cold.

Recent travelers had spoken of rustlers becoming more prevalent as more folks moved west. There would always be people too lazy to work, living off the efforts of others. He felt sure the riders he was following were up to no good, and rustling was the only thing that fit. Well and good. It didn't affect him, wasn't anything for him to worry about. It was someone else's problem. Just keep him out of it. He had seen all he wanted of bad guys.

His pa always told him, "Take care of your horse first." He removed the saddle and gear from the horses, and then, with a cut-off shovel brought along for just such a purpose, broke the ice from the stream and cleared an area of snow down to the brown frozen grass underneath for the horses to eat. After they had time to roll and drink, he slipped hackamores on them with ropes long enough to let them graze, gave them a quick brushing, and checked their shoes for stones. A small stone lodged in a shoe could cripple a horse and lay it up for days, if not weeks.

That chore finished, he built a double-handful-sized fire and had two large cups of coffee to wash down some thick-sliced bacon along with some biscuits Lainey had made. Mrs. Schwartz had taught her well, although Cormac liked to tease her that she couldn't cook. He rubbed the back of his head while he remembered the previous Christmas. She and Mrs. Schwartz had split up kitchen duties and Lainey's job was to cook the goose Mr. Schwartz had shot the day before.

"Loooks like we both ready to put on the feed bag," he remembered Mr. Schwartz saying when the two of them had sat down at the table while the women were still setting it. "Which you like betta? The white meat or dark meat."

Knowing Lainey had just left the kitchen area and would be walking behind him close enough to hear, Cormac had answered, "It don't much matter. If Lainey's cookin' it, it's all gonna be dark meat."

She had made his ears ring with a smack to the back of his head. But both women could cook up a storm, and he was going to miss that. He was not looking forward to living off his own cooking. He had woefully little experience in that department, and he would miss picking on Lainey.

Using his slicker as a ground cloth, Cormac spread his bedroll and crawled in. Lop Ear would sound the alarm if they had visitors. The ground was icy cold and hard beneath him. His pa had taught him how to deal with that, but he did not want to spend time building a wide fire, letting it burn down, and then scraping it away to the warm earth on which to put his bedroll. He was tired enough that he didn't think the cold was going to bother him much. It didn't.

Using his saddle for a pillow, he pulled the blanket over his head, allowing his warm breath to act as a heater, and was asleep immediately, only to wake right up again thinking he had forgotten something. Actually it was two somethings. After getting Lop Ear's bridle and stuffing it into the front of his coat to warm the steel bit for the morning, he pulled his gun, and with it in hand, let the lights go out again.

It was the latter part of dusk when Lop Ear snorted Cormac awake. He came out of his bedroll in a hurry. It scared him to realize he had slept so sound and heard nothing all day. His pa had taught him to sleep light on the trail.

Some brush popped. The light was poor, but he could just make out a horse coming through the trees. He drew back behind four trees growing closely together, his gun still in his hand. The horse turned out to be a large deer. The winter had been very cold with an overabundance of snow, forcing animals to range far from their home territories for food. His camp was downwind from the deer, and the deer had not yet caught their scent.

Some fresh meat to begin his trip would be good. He cocked the pistol inside his heavy coat to muffle the sound and braced his arm against the tree, aiming for where the deer's head was going to be.

The unsuspecting deer moseyed out of the heavy brush into the clearing to stop there, standing dead still, suddenly suspicious, with its head held high, smelling the breeze. It was a beautiful eight-point buck, bigger than Cormac had expected, and his gun-sight was pointing dead center at the white blaze on its forehead. All that was necessary was to let the hammer fall. The deer was magnificent.

Cormac stepped out from behind the trees. "Go on, big boy," he said. "Be on your way." Before the words were out of his mouth, the deer was gone. His muscles were like tightly coiled springs suddenly released. His first leap was every bit as magnificent as he. Cormac listened to it crashing through the brush. He really didn't need meat as badly as he thought.

He rode through the night. Although the moon came up less full than the night before, there was still plenty of light with which to see well. They startled a few night creatures out scavenging for supper, and a couple of beavers waddling toward a stream scurried for cover, scolding him as he passed for disturbing them.

The sun came up right on time, its warm rays more than welcome. The saying, "It's always darkest before the dawn," could also be said as, "It's always coldest before the dawn." He decided riding at night is only fun for a short time. He would have to get through the day with a couple of catnaps so he would sleep when night came. Cormac stopped for breakfast and coffee—lots of coffee—in a hilltop grove of trees. Sitting on the sunny side of one of the trees after finishing his breakfast, leaning back and enjoying the sun with no particular place to go and no particular time to get there, Cormac let himself drift off to sleep.

Lop Ear woke him with a soft whinny. If they were going to be traveling companions, they were going to have to have a talk about Lop Ear waking him up all the time. Checking the position of the sun, he realized that sleeping so long had killed the morning and scared the heck out of noon. He finished off the coffee cold, left some bread for the camp-robbing jays, and they got on their way. He guided Lop Ear into the arroyo at the bottom of the hill and followed it all the way around the next hill before finding a way out. Skirting a rock outcropping, they topped out into a campsite with a small herd of cattle being held by three riders. A fourth rider was throwing a loop around a calf. Resting in the fire was an instrument Cormac had heard described as being used by rustlers to change brands. It was called a running iron. He could see at a glance that these men were changing a double P-Bar brand to a double R-Bar.

"Oh, for Pete's sake," he told Lop Ear and Horse. "I don't care what they're doin', but the least they could do is keep an eye open for travelers. How dumb can they be?" He started the big gray back into the arroyo.

"Hold it right there!" A man in a sheepskin coat almost identical to his own stepped out of some thick bushes next to the camp, holding up his pants with one hand and covering Cormac with a gun in his other. Nope, not too bright, doing what he had obviously been doing not twenty-five feet from where they would be eating.

"We'll just see who's dumb here. You sit right still and just maybe I won't shoot you. And that's a big maybe." He was long getting along in years, as was the pistol in his hand, but the steady manner in which he held that pistol spoke of more than a casual relationship.

"Look," Cormac said, "I really don't give a hoot what's going on here. I'm not interested in other people's problems. I'm just traveling through. I have no idea who the Double P-Bar belongs to, and I don't care to. I have no interest in you or your friends or those cattle. So I'll just go on my way, and you can keep right on doin' what you're doin'."

Cormac nudged his heels into Lop Ear, and the horse obliged by stepping forward.

"If your horse takes another step, he'll be missing a rider."

The tone in the man's voice suggested Cormac would do well to pay it attention. They stopped.

"Hey, boys!" the gunman yelled out, and the other three came on the run to rein in beside him. "He just rode up out of the arroyo while I was doing my business in the bushes. One of you boys keep him covered while I fasten my britches."

"Damnit, Willard," said a cowboy in a black ten-gallon hat. "Use your head for something besides a hat rack, will ya? I told you not to do that so close to camp. I don't want to smell that while I'm eating."

To Cormac, he said, "What are you doin' here, boy?"

"Mostly wishin' I was someplace else," Cormac answered. "I was just trying to explain to your friend that I'm just passin' through. I couldn't care less what you fellows are doing. I don't know anybody around here—don't care to. Now, if you'll just holster that hog leg, I'll slip back into that arroyo and move on outta here, and you fellows can finish up what you're doin'."

"I'm afraid it's not that simple, young friend," Black Hat answered. "You stumbled in here, and now you've seen us. We'll have to deal with that."

A long, tall drink of water with a beard to match said, "You're goin' to have to kill him, Luke. We can't be leavin' no witnesses behind us."

The last rustler to join the group was about Cormac's age.

"I didn't agree to any killin'," he said, angrily. "You said we was just gonna run off a few cattle. You said nobody was gonna get hurt. He already told us he ain't gonna tell anybody. Let's just let him go. We can finish the brandin' and go on our way."

Black Hat had already made up his mind. "We can't trust him. He'll say anything now just to get away from here, but once he's away it'll be a different story."

Cormac's pa had told him about Indians who controlled their horses through signals with their heels, and he had spent a good deal of time training Lop Ear to do the same. He would pull his reins to the left and nudge his right flank with his heel. Lop Ear eventually got the idea and would let himself be guided in this manner. With a nudge on his right side, he stepped left. A nudge on his left moved him to the right.

Cormac nudged the horse's left side, and he obliged by stepping right, bumping into Horse, who had come up to stand beside them. "Whoa, Lop Ear," Cormac said, making a show of pulling up on the reins he was holding in his left hand while his right was reaching under the canvas flap covering the pack that Horse was carrying and coming out with the scattergun. He neck-reined Lop Ear to the left and swung the scattergun around, cocking both barrels in the same motion.

If it hadn't been such a serious moment, Cormac would have laughed at the looks on their faces when those double barrels came around at them, but the trick was chancy and anything could happen. He was ready.

"Now, you fellows just take it easy. I would hate to have this thing go off accidentally. If you all will just lay your guns down carefully, I'll just point ole Lop Ear out of here and we'll part company."

"Well, that's not likely gonna happen," said Black Hat. "There's four of usn's and only one of you, and you're just a pipsqueak kid."

"Well," Cormac mimicked him, "that may very well be, and I can certainly see where you might be inclined to think that way, but it would be a mistake on your part. You see, I believe I'm holdin' the difference right here. It's a ten-gauge loaded with double-ought buck and don't care a whit how old I am. If I pull these triggers, it'll take two of you, maybe even three of you, right out of them there saddles. In addition to that, there is a pistol here that I can get into action as quick as I did this scattergun. I just might get all of you."

Cormac paused to let them chew on that before going on. "Now, this is your game," he said slowly and clearly. "If you shoot me, this scattergun is goin' to go off, but you all just call it as you see it. If you want, you fellows just go ahead and cut loose, and I'll do the same; when we're done, we'll count score."

Well, they were not what one would call happy rustlers.

Truth be told, they were looking kinda down in the mouth, but there was Black Hat, still considering it—he made the wrong decision. The wrinkles around his eyes shifted, and Cormac started taking up the tension on the triggers.

"Wait!" cried the young one, who had wanted to let Cormac leave in the first place. He was on one of the middle horses and sure to get hit if Cormac fired. "Just wait a damn minute! That's the kid I was telling you about. I was in River City when he killed three men attacking a girl, and I heard the sheriff say he had blown the heads plumb off four men who had killed his family. The Sheriff also said he did it with one shot from a ten-gauge shotgun, and unless I miss my guess, it's that one right there he's got pointed at us right now."

Black Hat paled, and the wrinkles around his eyes changed again.

"Okay, friend." His voice was strained, and Cormac noticed he had dropped the "young" from the title. "You made a believer out of me. Now, how do we get out of this?"

Cormac let them wait a long minute without speaking. Gray Beard, who had an end position, started edging his horse to the side.

Keeping his gun leveled where it was, Cormac nodded at him and told Black Hat, "That horse movin' makes me a bit nervous. If he takes one more step, ole Betsy here is going to start talking to y'all, and I doubt you'll care much for the conversation."

"For God's sake, Fuller, sit still! Those scatter barrels are pointed right beside my face!" Black Hat exclaimed, without turning his head.

Then Cormac told them, "I know I'm not going to shoot you, unless you make me. If I wanted to do that, it woulda already been done. However, I'm not so sure of y'all. So if you fellows will just drop your guns on the snow, get off your horses, and stand over by the fire with your hands in the air, I'll be able to watch you as I ride away, and that's just what I'll do."

The young one spoke up again, "Let's do it, Blackie. He don't look to me like the type who would shoot an unarmed man. Besides, if we shoot him, that there gun of his is gonna go off, and I don't want to be anywhere in the same territory in front of it when it does."

"All right, all right," agreed Blackie, "I'm puttin' down my gun. You just keep your finger light on that trigger." He stuffed his gun into its holster and took the big black hat off to wipe the sweatband. From the moment he had heard about the four heads blown to bits, the rustler had lost interest in this situation and was just waiting for someone to give him an out.

When they were all standing by the fire, Cormac told them to open their coats so he could see if there were any belt guns: there were not. Keeping "Betsy" covering them, he searched their saddlebags and found a couple more guns and then took their rifles from their scabbards. They kept standing still like good fellows. They had a lot of respect for Betsy. Betsy hadn't been Betsy until that minute, but he thought she would remain Betsy from then on; he kinda liked the way it sounded. Betsy and GERT. Quite a pair, they were.

Once he was certain he had all their guns, Cormac exchanged the scattergun for his rifle and nudged Lop Ear away from Horse. Lop Ear was gun trained, he knew, and would stand still for what Cormac was about to do; he had no such confidence in Horse.

"I want to show you boys somethin'," he told them. "Look off over there. You see that big ole jack?" He pointed about seventy-five yards out at a jackrabbit sitting up looking around. "I'm going to fire twice. The first time is to get him movin'; the second will be to stop him again."

Black Hat snorted.

"Ain't never been no man alive could hit a runnin' jack with a rifle."

Cormac snapped a quick shot, kicking up snow a few feet to the right of the rabbit, so he would run to the left, away from the herd, and the jackrabbit took off like he had a sudden urge to go see Texas. A rabbit's hind legs are long, strong, and made for jumping. With his first leap, he sailed about ten feet and hit the ground runnin'. There are few things as fast as a fully grown jackrabbit, especially if he is frightened, and watching one in motion is worth seeing. A rabbit just running to get somewhere will mix in a jump or hop up in the air every now and again to look around. That's the reason a rabbit is said to hop. They will run a few steps and hop, covering six or eight feet in a single leap, then run some more.

When hunting them, just for the fun of it, Cormac would sometimes try to hit one in mid-leap. The first time he had tried, he missed, and the second time, he hit it again in the same place. His pa had heard the shots, and when he asked Cormac what he had shot, Cormac had to apologize for wasting ammunition, and told him what he had been attempting to do, promising not to do it again.

His pa wasn't one for wasting ammunition, but he had a way of surprising Cormac from time to time, and he surprised Cormac that day when he told him to keep trying. He said his eyes weren't good enough anymore to do it, but Cormac might be able to, and he would be proud to see it. Cormac had eventually gotten where he could hit them in the air maybe eight or nine times out of ten. His pa had smiled big the first time he had seen it happen, said he was proud as a peacock. Cormac didn't know what a peacock was, but he liked the sound of it.

Mostly, though, Cormac would just put them in his sights,

lead them a little, pull the trigger, and that was that, or, if he had to make absolutely sure of the shot, he would put two fingers against his tongue and let out a shrill whistle. Most rabbits will sit up and look around to see where the noise is comin' from, making an easy shot, but the object of this demonstration was not to kill a rabbit; it was to make a point.

Cormac sight-tracked this jackrabbit until he got up to speed, all the while keeping track of his new acquaintances out of the corner of his eye. A western man had a lot of respect for anyone who shoots well, and many shooting contests happen around camps when things got boring. Boys will be boys, his mother would have said; these men were just such boys. Their attention divided between the rabbit and his rifle, they were not about to do anything to ruin the shot.

When a rabbit is afraid of something, it doesn't fool around none, and this one wasn't fooling around one bit. No hopping was this one doing. He was running flat out on his way to someplace else. Just when Cormac was about to pull the trigger, the rabbit saw something ahead not to its liking and veered sharply. Cormac compensated; then pulled his sight out a little in front of it. "Squeeze softly," his pa's voice was saying, "don't jerk the trigger, squeeze it gently." Cormac squeezed it gently, and the rabbit rolled sideways, ass-end over appetite, coming to rest motionless in a snowbank.

"Well, I'll be damned," Black Hat burst out. "I wouldn't a believed that if I hadn't seen it, but why the hell did you do it?"

"Because I want you fellows to realize that what I shoot at, I hit. Now we're all going to mount up and herd those cattle back to where they belong. I'll bring up the rear where I can keep an eye on you, and should any of you develop a sudden taste for far-off places, you're just not going to make it.

"It's your responsibility to stay within my range. If I see any of you getting anywhere near the outer limits of the range of this rifle, I'm just going to figure that you are making a run for it, and ole GERT here is just gonna reach out and knock you right out of that saddle."

"What the hell is going on? You said if we put down our guns, you were going to ride away and leave us be. You said you didn't care what we were doing."

"Ah, now you believe me. Before, you wouldn't, but now that the tables are turned, all of a sudden you want to believe me. Well, when I first came out of the arroyo, I didn't, and if you would have let me be, I would have done the same for you, but you didn't. You had to be tough guys and were going to kill me. That sort of thing has a tendency to change a fella's perspective, so now we're just going to take these cattle home and let the folks they belong to decide what to do with you. Now, that's enough talking. Get on your horses and let's get started."

"What about our stuff here in camp?" asked Gray Beard.

"You'll just have to come back and get it, if you're able. If you're not, it won't much matter. Now, let's get going."

"How are we supposed to know what the range is on your rifle?"

"Now that there is a dilemma, ain't it?"

CHAPTER 6

———◆◆◆———

The double P-Bar belonged to one Paul Putnam, Cormac learned. They pulled within sight of the spread just before dusk. The ranch buildings were sitting on a rise in the center of a large flat land, giving a view of the surroundings several miles out. A well-kept white ranch house with a well-kept white outhouse, a well-kept white barn with a well-kept white corral, a well-kept white bunkhouse with its own well-kept white outhouse, all surrounded by a well-kept white rail fence; all in all, a well-kept spread.

The drive had been uneventful, nearly. After being on the trail a couple of hours, the young cowhand had suddenly turned his horse and took off running. Cormac pulled up GERT and put the sight in the center of his back. Before Cormac could squeeze off the shot, he saw a calf running out in front of the young rustler. How the calf had gotten that far out without him having seen it sooner didn't figure. Cormac kept the sights on the young man until he turned the calf and started back. The young cowhand looked across the herd at Cormac and waved.

Three or four miles later, it happened again. It was only after the young rustler neared some trees that would lead over a hill and out of sight that Cormac realized there was no calf in front of him this time. He was leaving the country. However, the young man had misjudged GERT's range; Cormac still had plenty of time to stop him. Cormac put the sight once more in the center of his back, and then raised it a few inches to allow for the distance.

He was a thinking man; Cormac had to give him that. He had set it up nicely, and now here he was, making a run for it. Cormac remembered that he had tried to talk the others out of killing him and held the shot.

"Ah, the hell with it, Lop Ear," he said aloud. "I can't shoot everybody."

As the runner entered the grove of trees, he looked back and waved his hat. With the drama having played out behind them, the other rustlers hadn't seen it. They didn't realize one of their group was missing until they arrived at the ranch and several riders rushed out to meet them. With puzzled expressions, the rustlers looked around the distance surrounding them, then at each other, and finally at Cormac, but they said nothing. Cormac pretended not to notice. *Let them wonder,* he thought.

He stuffed GERT back into its scabbard. When the P-Bar riders encircled them, he wanted no mistakes made about his intentions. Mr. Putnam readily accepted the facts, and to show his gratitude, invited Cormac to stay the night. Cormac was about to refuse when two of the riders rode up to sandwich Mr. Putnam, and he introduced Cormac to his daughters. They were both about Cormac's age, pretty and shapely with brown hair and matching eyes. They had a ways to go to match up with

Lainey, most likely would never make it, but they were pretty nonetheless.

Well kept, he thought. When it come to girl makin', Mr. Putnam had it all figured out. Maybe Cormac could stay one night after all. That he thought of Lainey before accepting puzzled him a mite.

After Mr. Putnam made the rustlers help re-brand the cattle, he intended to take them into town and turn them over to the sheriff. However, with the rustlers in easy hearing distance, he and his riders made big talk of having a hanging, but they were just funnin' at the rustler's expense.

The Putnams were a nice family. Mrs. Putnam was excited to have a guest to cook for and graciously accepted the rabbit he brought for the pot. A friendly woman who moved around her kitchen gracefully, it was easy to see from whom the daughters got their looks. The girls helped her some with the cooking and later with the cleanup, but were not as at home in the kitchen as their mother.

Outdoor girls both, they sat their saddles with the same grace and ease as their mother evidenced in the kitchen. Mrs. Putnam set a good table on a red-and-white checkered tablecloth. The dinner conversation was easy and listening to Mrs. Putnam's southern accent pleasant.

Although Cormac didn't believe it to be their normal seating arrangement, his eyes were very happy the girls were seated directly across the table from him. They were right easy to look at.

The Putnam girls were even friendlier than their parents: laughing, joking, teasing, and flirting with him while serving and clearing supper dishes. Both had dressed up nicely and were working hard to be friendly.

A little too hard, he thought when they laughed long at

something he said that wasn't all that funny. From the look on Mr. Putnam's face, he had found the incident amusing. Their spread was miles from town and Cormac was of a mind that the girls lacked much male company for whom to show off. It occurred to Cormac that the hands were all a generation or two older, possibly an intentional act by Mr. Putnam. The girls had watched him like two cats about to catch one bird, and Cormac didn't figure that bird ought be him. The sun rose the next morning to find Cormac already on the trail an hour.

————————

Before getting "out West," Cormac first had to get across the Missouri River, a wide expanse of prairie, and around the Black Hills and the Badlands. Cormac had heard that the Missouri River ran wide, fast, and deep. Coming out of a thick grouping of spruce trees at the top of a hill, it was a thrilling sight to a country boy who had seen very little but the farm and the small town where they did their trading.

To date, the most exciting thing in his life had been the times they had been in town when the stagecoach came rolling in and sliding to a stop in front of the hotel with its whoops, whoas, and howdies. The arrival was followed by the hostler's changing of the team, while the passengers went next door to "Mom's Café," usually for some of the stew or beans and cornbread for which "Mom" was famous.

Usually, by the time the team was changed and the traces that connected the horses to the stagecoach re-hooked, the passengers had finished eating, made their trips to the outhouse behind the hotel, and were filing out onto the walk, ready to board. It was a well-coordinated procedure, normally going off without a hitch. The townsfolk were used to it, but Cormac always found it exciting and fun to watch. Becky had shared it with him a time or two, but after that spent her time shopping with her mother.

"What do you think about that, guys?" Cormac asked the horses as they neared the river. "Quite a sight, don't ya think? I don't know how in the world we're goin' to get over it, though. It's so wide I doubt I could throw a rock to the other side, and look at how fast that log out there is movin'. Lord! That's a challenge, it surely is, but for now, it's near suppertime."

"How about we camp here overnight and in the mornin' we head on downriver and see can we find some way to get to the other side? All in favor? Not talkin', huh? Okay then, I say we stop; you had your chance to vote. But let's back up away from this big ole river a bit. It's cold enough already, and I 'spect it's gonna get breezier and colder here by the water."

It turned out to be a correct guess, though Cormac would rather have been wrong. By dark, the breeze was getting downright frigid. He chose a campsite beside a large boulder in a grove of tall, mature white spruce trees relatively free of snow. The boulder was as tall as he and six or eight feet wide, with a slight overhang on a flat side facing the down-river direction. Good sense told him any breeze would be moving downstream with the river, and the boulder would serve as a windbreak. He scraped together a bed of pine needles on which to put his bedroll and built a stone fire-ring in which he built a fire between his bed and the flat side of the boulder. The heat from the fire would reflect off the rock and back at his bedroll giving him a near doubled amount of heat.

There was plenty of deadfall wood to stack up on the far side of his bedroll that would allow him to feed the fire all through the night without getting out of bed. At the head side of his bedroll, he rolled a log on which to sit in front of the fire that extended all the way from his bedroll to the boulder. He warmed himself by the flames while smoking a couple cigarettes before slipping into his bedroll for the night.

Near on to get-up time, Cormac heard a noise he could not identify coming from the river. After slipping on his high-top farmer shoes, he made his way to the water. It was quite a sight in the waning moonlight. With massive amounts of water flowing silently passed, the river was unsettling to a non-swimmer, such as Cormac. It was awesome looking, yet powerful and deadly, and more than a little scary. Definitely not to be taken lightly.

The sounds he had heard were emanating from a very large shape coming down the middle of the river with a giant revolving wheel of some kind on one side and a big smokestack belching smoke into the sky. Some travelers a few months back had told them about riverboats, but he had never seen one. He guessed that's what this was, and the noise of whatever was driving it sounded strange in the middle of an otherwise quiet wilderness night.

The wind close to the water had a bite to it, making Cormac turn up his sheepskin collar and put his back to the breeze. He had picked up smoking cigarettes and dipping snuff from Mr. Schwartz. Although the trees in the area were mostly spruces, there were others bare of leaves for the winter, one of which he chose for a little wind protection, leaning his back against it while he smoked.

The flare of his match must have been observed by whoever was driving the boat as it was answered immediately by a tiny bleep of the whistle acknowledging that somebody knew he was there. Cormac quickly took a hard pull on his cigarette and made a circle in the darkness with the glow and got another tiny bleep: a friendly sound and response between two strangers on a dark night letting each know they weren't alone.

The big boat passing in the moonlight proved an impressive sight. Comin' all the way from Ireland, Lainey had traveled much more than he and told him there were many things "out there" that he hadn't seen. This was definitely one such thing. After a breakfast of bacon, biscuits, and coffee, he was having another smoke and watching the fire consume a large, dry chunk of wood before packing up. It had just fired a pocket of pitch and flared brightly when Lop Ear blew a warning. The horse was looking toward the river in the downstream direction.

"Thanks, boy," Cormac called to him quietly, throwing his smoke into the fire and melting into the trees. Waiting for his eyes to clear from staring into the fire, he removed the hammer thong from his gun, loosened it in its holster, and unbuttoned his coat.

"Hello the camp."

Cormac remained silent and looked hard in the direction from which the voice had come. He could just make out two shapes in the early graying light. The smaller of the two slipped off to the side, and the voice called again.

"Hello the camp. Anyone there? There are two of us, and we mean you no harm. Your coffee smells almighty good. We could sure use some; we been walking most of the night and getting mighty hungry and really cold. A little coffee would be a life-saver."

Cormac still made no reply; he couldn't tell where the other shape had gone.

"Okay, we'll move on, but can you please let my wife come in and get warm? She's very cold." The other shape returned, doing something at belt level that appeared to be, maybe, fastening its pants. "Can't say as I blame you," the voice continued. "It's dangerous traveling now days. You never know who, or what, you're going to run into. My wife and I had a spell of bad luck, and we had to run. My wife's got relatives upstream a ways and we're trying to get there. We'll move on now."

The shapes moved toward the river in the upstream direction. The larger shape appeared to have his arm around the smaller one.

"Okay, wait," Cormac called. "You can come in. Just both of you keep your hands where I can see them."

A man and woman came hesitantly into the light. They were not dressed to be traveling in this weather. Their coats were too light, and they had no mittens or gloves and only the woman had a head covering. The man was of average size with no hat, although he was protected some from the cold by his heavy hair and beard, but the too-thin coat he was wearing was much too small to button. The large, thick, and heavy coat she was wearing and the big hat pulled down around her ears could only have belonged to him, which spoke well of him.

She was of average size, with dark hair and cheeks blushed red from the cold. Cormac wondered if there were any others with them that were still hiding in the woods, but a glance at Lop Ear and Horse showed them paying no attention to anything other than the approaching couple.

"Go ahead and sit down on that log by the fire," he told them. "I'll get you some coffee and fix you something to eat."

"That would be greatly appreciated, sir." The man helped his wife around the fire to the log, only to huddle and stand as closely as possible to the heat, holding out their hands and turning first their backs and then their fronts to the fire. The man turned back with his hand out to Cormac. "My name is Ferguson, sir. John Ferguson. They call me Jack, and this is my wife, Rebecca. May we know your name?"

Unspeaking, Cormac shook the hand and stared a long moment at the only person other than his sister he had ever met named Rebecca.

"Good morning, my name is Cormac Lynch. Welcome to my fire. One of you will have to drink from a bowl; I only have one cup."

"Mister, if you're willing to give us coffee, I'll drink it out of my shoe if I have to."

Cormac fried more bacon and potatoes, giving them the last two biscuits with more coffee with which to wash it all down. The food quickly disappeared.

"Thank you, mister," the woman said finally, smiling widely, the first words she had spoken. "Do you mind if I call you, Mack? Cormac sounds so formal and not at all as friendly as you really are."

"You're welcome," he answered. "I'm glad I was here, and yes you can." Cormac rolled a smoke and offered the makings to his man-guest.

"No, thank you, but my wife might like some. She's from the hills of Tennessee and most of the people in that neck of the woods smoke or chew, or both."

Speechless, Cormac offered it to the woman who eagerly accepted. Making a paper trough with her thumb, forefinger, and middle finger of her left hand, she filled it with tobacco, and then rolled it expertly with the same hand, licking the sticky side of the paper. She finished the roll with one hand while she handed the tobacco bag back to Cormac with the other. Cormac had never seen it done better. He watched in amazement as she lit it and took her first long drag.

"I can do that with one hand, but not as gracefully as you," he told her. "I've never seen a woman smoke before."

"It does surprise some people, but I enjoy it," she said while she gave the big hat back to her husband and shook out her long dark hair. The hot food and fire were doing their jobs, and with the fire close in front, Rebecca Ferguson unbuttoned the big coat. "It reminds me of home. I learned how to roll cigarettes making them for my daddy. I haven't got to have one lately, so it tastes very good." Unwrapped, she was a woman of average looks made more attractive by her smile.

"Tell me what's happened that's got you travelin' half dressed in the dark on a cold night like this," instructed Cormac.

"Curse me for a fool," began the man named John, shaking his head sorrowfully. "I lost her in a crooked poker game. I can't believe I was so stupid. By the time I realized what was going on, it was too late, and I was in serious trouble.

"On second thought, could I change my mind and have that smoke you offered? I only smoke but rarely."

Cormac handed him the Bull Durham bag and waited while he got his smoke going with none of the experience and grace shown by his wife. The day was getting off to a hazy start, but it was light enough to see through the trees to the river running fast and deep and looking very cold.

Cormac was anxious to get on his way; he didn't like the ominous look of the clouds; they were in for some weather. But at the same time, he couldn't just leave them to fend for themselves. They had neither the clothes nor the experience to deal with the storm that was coming, and he was curious to learn how a man could lose a wife he obviously cared for in a game of poker.

"Right after we married five years ago in New York, we moved to Southern Missoura. We both wanted to raise our children in the country, but had no idea how hard the life of a farmer was, and we knew nothing about farming. We hadn't thought it out. I had some money saved, so we bought an existing farm to save the time and effort of building our own. We couldn't wait to start planting our own crops.

"That's when we first began realizing there was more to it

than we thought. We didn't know how much water it would take, and there was only a small well near the buildings that ran dry anytime we tried to take out too much. There was enough rain to get us through the first year, and we sold our crops for enough money for food and seed to get us through the next, but that year brought very little rain. We got a very poor crop, but figured the upcoming year would be better. It wasn't.

"Rebecca's sister in Pierre wrote us that her husband could give me a job in his general store, so we jumped at it. We couldn't find a buyer for a farm with no water, but we sold our furniture and personal effects and left with one hundred and twenty-five dollars. Travel expenses and food took us down to one hundred and five, but that was still plenty enough money to live on and buy space on the riverboat to Pierre. I think it's about another thirty miles upriver from here."

John Ferguson halted his story to ask for another cup of coffee. Cormac poured it for him while he continued.

"We planned on staying the night in a small village on the river about fifteen miles south of here and catching the boat in the morning. We were told there's one coming through on a weekly basis, and the next one was due tomorrow morning; that's this morning now. While we were waiting, Rebecca wanted to get a bath, and while she was taking care of that, I went next door to the local saloon for a beer. That was my first mistake.

"There were some fellas playing poker for matchsticks back in one corner. Now, I am not a poker player, but I do enjoy it. There was a lot of laughing and joking from the table. They were having a lot of fun teasing a big guy about always trying to bluff them and always losing. One went to the outhouse and stopped to talk with the bartender on his way back. They were laughing and having fun, and I found myself drawn into the conversation;

he invited me to join the game. So I said sure, it's just match-sticks, it's a good way to kill time waiting for Rebecca.

"I was lucky and started winning right off. One of them makes a joke after I'd won a few hands that it was too bad for me we weren't playing for money. The big guy that was always losing his bluffs agreed. He had better luck playing for money, he said. He couldn't take matchstick-playing seriously, so he talked the others into playing for two-bits and four-bits.

"I was still winning more than I was losing so I stayed in the game. I couldn't believe my good fortune. I had never done so well. Somehow the bets had increased to five and ten dollars, and I was still winning. I couldn't wait until Rebecca returned so I could show her how much money I had won.

"By then, the big guy was pretty drunk, I thought. I realized later he was just acting and they were all in on it. Then I got dealt four aces, and he was raising. First thing you know, I had all of my money on the table, and he took out a big wad of bills and threw it in the pot and said I had to match it or he would win all the money without even showing his hand.

"I told him I didn't have any more, so we should just show our hands; I knew he was bluffing again. He said no. I had to match his bet or forfeit the pot. Just then, Rebecca knocked on the window, all sparkly clean and pretty and smiling at me, to let me know she was there.

"The big guy said he would accept a voucher that she would clean his house for him as a matching bet because he was terrible at house cleaning and was tired of living in a pigsty. It was either agree or lose all of our money, so I agreed. It was just to clean his house, and I would help her if I lost, but I knew my four aces wouldn't lose.

"When he dealt the last card, he fumbled a little and it was easy to see he was bottom dealing. When I called him on it, he became furious and pulled out his gun and said I better realize real quick that I had been mistaken, or he was going to kill me right then and there, right in front of Rebecca. I'm no good with a gun. In fact, I don't seem to be much good at anything."

Rebecca's hand found his and squeezed. "Mine was still in my holster with the thong on the hammer," he continued. "I wasn't anticipating any gunplay.

"I asked the other players if they hadn't seen it, too, and they all said no, they hadn't seen anything. It was too obvious for them not to have seen it. I knew then I had been set up, and they would kill me for the money if I gave them the chance. So after agreeing that I must have been mistaken, I let him take the pot with a royal flush he had dealt himself.

"He said if she wasn't at his house the first thing this morning, he would come looking for us. He said there was no place to hide, and the boat wouldn't be coming until around the dinner hour. He was making jokes to his friends that made it clear he had more than house cleaning in mind for her once he got her there.

"I had no choice. I took the directions to his house and promised we would be there early. When I walked out, I let them hear me tell Rebecca that we should go get something to eat before turning in, and then we started walking and just kept going. We just left our things. I had to get her out of that village."

Horse and Lop Ear came to attention, staring downstream a few seconds before the sounds of riders came to them.

"Someone's comin'," Cormac told them. "Quick, hand me your dishes and get behind the boulder and stay quiet." He unbuttoned his coat and loosened the Smith & Wesson in its holster as seven riders came into sight through the woods.

"Hello the camp, we're comin' in," came the voice as the

newcomers rode in without waiting for an invitation. Cormac had just gotten out of one situation with rustlers, now he was in another one with who knows what. If this was what the world was like off the farm, maybe he better just go back and spend the rest of his life pickin' taters, shootin' rabbits, and teasin' Lainey. Well, at least pickin' taters and shootin' rabbits. The Lainey door was closed. No, that whole situation was closed. Time to pretend like he was a big boy and play the hand life was dealing him. At least he knew God wasn't stacking the deck.

Although appearing to be holding a cup of coffee with both hands, Cormac faced the newcomers with the weight of his coffee cup supported by his left hand, leaving the right free for gunplay, if such became necessary.

"Mornin' boys," Cormac said easily. "If you're wantin' coffee, I can make you some if you got cups. I only got this one."

"We ain't lookin' for coffee. We're lookin' for a man and a woman who's got something that belongs to me. You seen anything of them?" The man doing the talking must have been the bluffer; he was runnin' the show, and he was big. All were dressed for cold weather in heavy sheepskin coats with big collars and warm gloves, if there was such a thing—Cormac's fingers were always cold when he was wearing gloves, mittens were much warmer. Most were wearing the ten-gallon hat that was getting so popular.

"Nope, sorry," he answered. "But I just got up. If they came this way, they passed on by without me hearin', but I'm surprised my horses didn't hear their horses and let me know." That was a nice touch, he thought.

"They aren't riding, they're walking."

"Why in the world would anybody be walking as cold as it is? They smokin' loco weed?"

"You're right about that, but he's not the smartest one around these parts. It's hard to track them in this cold. The ground is frozen solid, and we lost their trail about an hour ago. Maybe they went inland. I reckon we'll go back and circle the area and see if we can pick up any sign."

Cormac Lynch watched them leave and immediately started packing up.

"I'm guessin' they'll be back; we gotta get you outta here, and we gotta find some shelter. There's a norther a comin'."

"Mister, it's not fair you getting dragged into this, but if you're willing to help, I have to let you. I don't know how to protect Rebecca on my own."

As always, Cormac packed the scattergun and his extra pistol last, each tied separately for quick access if needed, as the scattergun already had been once.

They needed to make time, and the fastest way was for Cormac to walk and let them ride on Horse. Mrs. Ferguson needed to ride and Cormac couldn't ride with her while making her husband walk. It was Lop Ear's turn to carry the pack. Cormac had the husband wear his own coat and hat and let Mrs. Ferguson wrap herself in his slicker around the blanket from his bedroll.

They were packed and on the trail within ten minutes. He didn't bother to put out the fire. As cold as it was, that fire wasn't going anywhere.

"We'll head upriver for a ways to get some distance between us and them, and then we'll swing inland to find shelter. I think this storm is gonna be a norther, and they can get rough. I would imagine if we can stay out of their way until it starts, there'll be no tracks to follow and they'll head for home and that'll be the end of it."

Cormac Lynch stepped out smartly. There was no mistaking the weather was quickly getting colder. They came upon some hills after what Cormac thought to be about two miles and turned inland as snow flurries began. The temperature continued to drop rapidly, and the snow got heavier. Luckily, with no wind to push it, it was falling straight down. If it had not been for the circumstances, it would have been a very pleasant walk.

Away from the river, the land was no longer flat, and the going became harder. Cormac had the Fergusons walk a ways to get warmed up, but the doing of it slowed them down, and he re-mounted them at the first sign of her getting warm and loosening her blanket wrapping.

The snow was deepening, and the wind had started blowing, dropping the temperature even more and putting a bite in the air. Cormac knew the signs of a Dakota blizzard in the making. Birds, rabbits, and squirrels were nowhere to be seen; they were already holed up in their lairs. Cormac needed to find a hidey-hole for them, too, and soon.

They came upon a stream flowing out of a tree-filled canyon with hills eventually climbing to four or five hundred feet and followed it upward. Somewhere in the canyon would be shelter. On a flat plain in the middle of a blizzard was no place for anyone with a choice and a lick of common sense. Sitting in the saddle, Mrs. Ferguson pulled the blanket up around her head, like a tent held together from the inside, and Mr. Ferguson had his arms wrapped around her from behind with his own head down, letting his hat be his windbreak.

God was done fooling around and was getting serious; he'd given all the warning he was intending on. The piercing icy wind that penetrated the marrow was bitter cold and lashing out brutally with the driven snow turning to sleet and being driven nearly horizontal, dropping the visibility to less than ten feet. Walking into the wind, the icy sleet covered the faces of Cormac and John Ferguson and found its way down their necks and under their collars. They were getting wet through and through.

The blanket wrapping Mrs. Ferguson's upper body had become sleet-coated over the slicker and had frozen solid into a private shelter. Her wisely holding it away from her body as much as possible kept an air space around her to be warmed by her breath, with her husband's body to protect her back. Her legs, however, were not so lucky and became soaked, and were probably beginning to freeze. Her blanket-tent was showing signs of cold-chill shakes making it clear that her body temperature was dropping too far and too fast.

Although Cormac had waterproofed his shoes with melted tallow, the coating of ice forming on the outside was beginning to freeze his feet, and they were becoming painful and throbbing with every step. Frostbite would not be far behind. The Fergusons' feet would be wet, and lack of use would make them even colder than his own. Forced to keep looking around for shelter, Cormac couldn't hide his face, and it was an open target upon which ice was forming into a mask. It was a freezing, bitter cold.

Cormac knew he could wait no longer; if there was to be a shelter, he would have to build it. As they traveled up the canyon with the river on their left, the wind suddenly dropped as they followed the river around a left-hand corner. They found themselves facing a tight stand of twenty or thirty spruce trees on their right, about twenty feet from the river and close to an embankment. Cormac guessed the embankment would measure out to be about twenty-five feet high with the bottom having been hollowed out to leave a large overhang, which had been cut out by previous flash floods racing around the corner many times a year for many years: a cave with a roof, but no sidewalls. Deadfall wood for fires was abundant. They had found their windbreak. "Thank you," Cormac said, looking upward into the freezing fury of the storm as he helped Mrs. Ferguson into the shelter. "Thank you very much."

In a matter of minutes, Cormac and John Ferguson had a large fire radiating heat into their makeshift home. Whatever he was or was not, John Ferguson was no slacker; he pitched in without being told. He was a worker, and they worked well together.

After removing the pack and saddle, Cormac dried the horses with an empty gunnysack, and then, with fallen logs, the two men built a three-foot-high reflecting wall on the opposite side of the fire from the hollow to direct the heat inward. With an axe from Cormac's pack, they cut and stacked enough firewood under the overhang to last a few days. An abundant amount was still there for the taking, but Cormac wanted to get in a goodly supply before it became snow-covered and wetter than it already was.

While they were busy, Mrs. Ferguson had taken charge and set up a kitchen close to the fire with items from Cormac's pack. Using melted snow, she had made a pot of stew from his supply of jerked beef, potatoes, and his last wild onion as well as had a batch of pan-bread nearly done baking on some embers she had pulled from the fire.

If they were careful, they had enough food for three or four days, plenty of water, and a better-than-expected shelter. There was enough of a shallow overhang leading off to one side to give them a path around the corner from the living area to allow them a place to take care of private concerns.

It would be necessary to ration the horses' grain a bit, but there was a decent amount of tall dead grass somewhat protected by the trees, most likely not needing too much effort to keep open. They'd get by.

Cormac surveyed their situation while he quickly got on the

outside of Mrs. Ferguson's more-than-welcome vittles. She had rationed their portions to make what food they had stretch as far as possible. That woman had a head on her shoulders, she did. All in all, their little group was in pretty good shape; they were going to be just fine. And, for a few days at least, Cormac was going to have food that actually tasted good.

CHAPTER 7

Although Mrs. Ferguson's coffee wouldn't float any horseshoes, it did hit the spot, and she did right well on the stew, especially considering the few ingredients with which she had to work. Cormac allowed as how it was far better than anything he would have made. He was more than happy to turn the cooking over to her.

They had themselves a real, old-fashioned blizzard kicking up a fuss. Outside of the area protected by their overhang, visibility was down to five or six feet. The stream twenty feet away was invisible in the whiteness, obliterated by the primeval force driving the sleet and snow nearly parallel with the ground. Forecasting outward in his mind, Cormac knew from experience that nothing was moving for miles around except that icy-cold, powerful Missouri River.

The fancy riverboat would be tied up someplace, people and animals large and small would be hunkered down and tucked into houses, holes, barns, or anyplace they could find to hide from the ferocity of the storm. He knew they were in better shape than most. The people and animals in the open and exposed to the full onslaught of the storm would huddle and group together; only the strongest would survive. This was nature in the raw—every bit as terrible as it was awesome.

"Shortly after we were married, I received an appointment as a professor of history at Harvard College," said John Ferguson in answer to Cormac's question about his previous occupation. "I had applied for it nearly two years before. It was almost like a wedding present. We had to move there, but the extra money came in handy." Once they had everything arranged the way they wanted, they had settled in for a chat by the fire, and the talk had turned to frontiers. "The frontier was one of the subjects I included in some of my history lessons," he said. "Having found history interesting since I was a pup, it's easy for me to talk about it.

"Since the beginning of time, people have always pushed out new frontiers; that's what they do. The definition of a frontier is the part of a country next to an unexplored region. It was taken from a French word meaning borderland. In the very beginning of America, the frontiers were on the fringe of the settlements on the far eastern coast, and any exploration was, of necessity, to the west. Hence the frontier, in this country, has always meant the Western Frontier, and the people moving there were said to be moving 'out West' and were changed by the doing.

"The frontiersmen shed their restraints, made bold decisions, and considered themselves to be more 'American' than their eastern counterparts because they were taking great risks and helping in the expansion and growth of our country."

A particularly hard gust of icy wind was redirected into their hollow, flaring up their fire and sending a thick trail of fiery sparks harmlessly out into the storm and causing them to hold shut their unbuttoned coats until it passed.

"There was the Appalachian frontier west of Connecticut that instigated the French and Indian wars in 1760, and the western part of Georgia was a frontier before heavy population pushed the frontier farther westward. Kentucky and Tennessee were frontiers with heroes like Daniel Boone and Davy Crockett, and in turn, the Dakota Territory became a frontier, and then on to Wyoming and Montana. Piece by piece, frontiers swept the nation, and now it's populated coast to coast, with a lot of open spaces in the middle of course.

"Someday the oceans will be considered a frontier, and who knows, it's outlandish to think of, but maybe someday a thousand years from now, maybe even the stars and the heavens will be a frontier. Looking up at the stars from our farm on a warm summer night, Rebecca and I often talked about what it might be like to look down at the earth from the stars, from God's point of view. It must be really beautiful. I'll bet he's proud of his work.

"It sounds silly now, in light of all that has happened, but I guess the romance of the whole frontier idea was part of our decision to move west. We wanted to be involved in that expansion. We wanted to do our part to help shape America. I know it sounds foolish now, but we didn't realize the depth of the risk we would be facing.

"In retrospect, whatever possessed us to think we could become farmers with no experience to back us up is totally inconceivable. The accounts we read in periodicals and fiction stories made western life out to be appealing and romantic, but we were totally unprepared."

Mrs. Ferguson listened intently to her husband, nodding her agreement from time to time. "Lest you somehow think otherwise," she interjected, "we would do it over again. We would just have prepared more thoroughly. I was in complete agreement with my husband's decisions."

"Even his poker bet?"

She smiled wryly. "Especially his poker bet. He had no choice; the situation had gone too far. He had been sold a bill of goods by some very experienced con men who led him like a lamb to the slaughter. I'm from the hills but I met John on a shopping trip to town and for the last ten years before moving to Missoura, we had been living in cities under police control, letting somebody else protect us, and again, we have no experience or knowledge of this sort of thing.

"Now, we're going to Pierre so he can take the job working for my sister's husband, and I will take in laundry until we get enough money to buy another farm, a place to raise our children and teach them the things that we have learned. We know more about it now, and we won't make the same mistakes. But he was just trying to salvage our money the best he could and take care of me.

"He found himself in a stressful situation, and people don't always make the right decisions under those conditions. One can only do what one can do based upon the experience they have, and in this case, he had no experience to draw from. But considering the facts, I think he did quite well. I'm very proud of him."

She smiled at her husband, and he mouthed the words, "I'm sorry."

She squeezed his hand again, total absolution in her smile. "But he did get us out of there."

They would make the best they could of a bad situation and die together holding hands if that was meant to be. Their life had taken a bad turn, but they weren't complaining, they were dealing with the situation as it sat. They were westerners now.

The transition had been made; they were learning and growing. They may have made some bad decisions, but they were good people, strong people. The kind of people America needed to keep up the expansion. They would raise their children—two boys and two girls if they got their wish—their crops and their horses, and they would help raise their grandchildren. They would work hard, and they would face many challenges, but they would face them together, hand in hand, and they would make it. They didn't deserve to get treated the way they had been and have their money taken from them. Maybe after he got them to Pierre, Cormac would have to go see about that.

———

On the morning of the second day, the snow was a foot deep with a coating of frozen ice covering the top of everything between them and the creek, which was also ice coated along with all of the tree limbs and branches. With the shovel from his pack, crunching through the frozen surface of the snow with every step, Cormac expanded the area of open grass in the trees and broke the ice from the stream enough to get some water for cooking, fill his canteens, and allow the horses to drink.

Cormac hadn't tied the horses, but they weren't going anywhere. He spent a great deal of time petting them and running his hands over their bodies and their long legs, cleaning their hooves, and using a special comb for their manes and tails and a brush for their coats. In warm months he would use a curry-comb, but he did not want to thin out their hair, especially during weather as cold as this. He brushed the air two inches in front of their faces repeatedly, "accidentally" brushing their faces from time to time until they moved forward enough to feel the brush. After that, when he again began brushing the air in front of them, they would automatically step forward to meet the brush. They were learning to analyze situations and react accordingly. They were learning to learn.

On day two, the sleet turned again to snow and was now beginning to drift. With a general depth of more than three feet, the drifts were becoming substantial and creeping into their area. Cormac and John Ferguson had to work harder to keep the horses' grass and a trail to the stream open.

By day five, they knew everything about each other that they wanted to share, the food was running low, and Cormac was becoming concerned about his ability to get them out once the storm stopped. *If* the storm stopped. Cormac was remembering being told about the rain having once fallen for forty days and forty nights, but that was highly unlikely so he would just worry about people-sized problems. As his pa had taught him, and as he related to the Fergusons, the first two priorities of survival were shelter and water, in that order. As long as they had those two things, they could live several days without food. He would worry about getting out when the time come.

Professor Ferguson was impressed that Cormac's mother had been giving him schooling and teaching him to scribe. He shared some of his learning about poetry, the arts, and music. A favorite of Mrs. Ferguson's was a little ditty written by a doctor around 1750 titled "Little Bess, the Ballad Singer." She sang the only verse she knew in her best accented voice:

When first a babe upon the knee
My mother us'd to sing to me.

I caught the accents from her tongue
And e'er I talk'd, I lisp'd in song

With nothing to do but talk, they discussed many topics, and Cormac was envious of the vast amount of knowledge they held between them. Knowledge they would pass on to their children and grandchildren as a basis from which to continue their educations.

After learning Cormac had been raised close to the Black Hills yet knew next to nothing about them, Professor Ferguson was expounding upon a subject for which he obviously felt great passion.

"Great poets," Professor Ferguson was saying while he rearranged the burning logs and added more wood to the fire, "write thousands of words in their lifetimes. They read and study and ponder and experiment with the various meanings and sounds of word combinations, striving to give just the right emphasis and implications that will allow readers of the works to make the desired inferences, and sometimes, just sometimes mind you, everything comes together perfectly, and the result is exquisite perfection." He paused and repeated himself for emphasis. "I like the sound of those two words. *Exquisite perfection*, only two words, but what magnificent words they are. Two words that can be applied to only a very few things in this world, but for those certain things, they are the only two words that accurately do them justice.

"A French artist named Leonardo di ser Piero Da Vinci painted a great many pictures in his lifetime, but in 1519, after working on it for seven years, he completed a half-length portrait depicting a seated woman with an enigmatic smile that has been called by some the greatest portrait ever painted: a masterpiece. That's what the Black Hills are: one of God's greatest masterpieces, exquisite perfection."

"God at her very best," broke in Mrs. Ferguson with a private-joke smile to her husband.

"Yes, yes, dear." He smiled back, nodding. "I know. I know."

"I've only seen photographs," he continued, still looking into Mrs. Ferguson's eyes and returning her smile, "but would dearly love to take Rebecca to see them sometime. The Fort Laramie peace treaty gave the Black Hills to the Sioux Indians forever," he explained, "on the condition they remain there, and quit scalping white people. The government also promised white people would stay off their land, but an army general named Custer claims to have found gold there, and now more and more people have been breaking the treaty and begging the government to reclaim the land. However, even before that happened, some Indians were coming out of the hills to attack white travelers and settlers and then running back to the hills to escape, so they were themselves breaking the treaty.

"The government has been refusing to give permission to go into the Black Hills or to protect any people that do. On the Indians' side, the war parties are conducted by individuals, and not necessarily condoned by the Indian chiefs. Anytime some young buck with a few loyal followers gets to feeling his oats or wanting to prove something, they go out on their own to do some raiding. Our government can't control all of our citizens, and the Indian government can't control all of theirs. It's a recipe for disaster, that's what it is, and I think it's going to happen. It's just a matter of when."

That night the storm broke, and they awoke to sunshine-blanketed snowdrifts, where snow backed up as high as their heads against some restraint. Lainey would have loved this view.

"We got our work cut out for us," he told the Fergusons. "Pushing a trail through that snow is going to be hard work; it'll be too soft to walk on top of without snowshoes. But we got to do it; we're out of food. We can't be any more'n a mile and a half from the river, and once there, according to you, it's probably about thirty miles as the crow flies to Pierre, but following the winding river, who the heck knows."

After washing down the last few bites of jerky with some coffee Mrs. Ferguson made by re-boiling the grounds she had been wisely saving, and giving the horses the last of the grain, they packed up and headed out. Away from the snowdrifts, the snow depth averaged between three and four feet. With Mrs. Ferguson riding Lop Ear, and Horse carrying the pack, Cormac and John Ferguson, each leading a horse, alternated breaking the way in ten-minute intervals.

They were both strong and John proved to be no slacker and up to the task, as was the sunshine. The day was pleasantly warm and when they weren't leading, the men walked with their coats unbuttoned and held open to allow more ventilation.

Progress was slow but steady, and dinnertime came around to find them nearing the water with their stomachs wishing there was something coming down the chute. A rabbit or other varmint would make a fine lunch, and Cormac unhooked the hammer thong and loosened the gun in his holster in preparation of an animal or bird suddenly flushing from a snowbank or the brush. As a group, they broke though the last of a tightly grown grove of green spruce trees not far from the water.

"Well, well. Look what popped out of the woods. Good to see you folks. I was worried about you." There were all seven riders with the bluffer, still the apparent leader, sitting comfortably on his horse with a gun in his hand, pointing at John Ferguson, who had promptly thrown his hands into the air. With no more warning than that, the man pulled the trigger, and Professor Ferguson staggered backward and fell unmoving to the ground. Cormac was stunned.

"What was that for?" he asked numbly as Mrs. Ferguson ran to her husband.

"I couldn't have him running around the country with his lies about crooked poker games and such, now could I?" As he was swinging his gun toward Cormac, Cormac palmed his and put two .44 caliber bullets into the middle of the big man's chest. He was slammed backward off his horse with his eyes and mouth open wide in surprise. As shocked as Cormac had been at the senseless killing of Professor Ferguson, so were the big man's friends, and that may have contributed to their next mistake.

Grabbing for their guns, three of them cleared leather before Cormac, shooting quickly but not hastily, placed his bullets exactly where he wanted them, and they joined their friend on the ground in the same condition as he: dead. Being killed quickly was more'n they deserved. Cormac would do it again more slowly if it were possible.

Cormac turned his attention to the last three. Their hands were as high as they could reach. They were suddenly decidedly lacking of enthusiasm in their venture.

"Take it easy, mister, please! Just take it easy! We ain't doin' nothin', really. We didn't even want to come, but it's not healthy to cross Luther. He was mad at the guy for crossin' him and wanted to teach him a lesson, and he had his eye on the woman. But we didn't want any part of it, mister. Honest."

"Well, let's us consider the situation," Cormac said seriously. "My friend had his hands up, and your friend shot him anyway while you three sat there and watched. Now you have your hands up, and I have a gun pointed at you. Kinda funny how attitudes can change dependin' on your point of view, ain't it?" Cormac clicked the hammer of his pistol for effect and the men started. He had their undivided attention.

"Mister, wait, please!"

"Oh, shut up! Thank God I'm not cut from the same lowlife crud as you and your friends. I'm not going to shoot you for no reason. Just make sure you don't give me one. Keep your hands right where they are, and you might leave here in one piece."

Cormac looked at the Fergusons. The whole story was told in a glance. Mrs. Ferguson was holding and rocking her husband, crying uncontrollably. What a waste, Cormac thought. What a damn shame and a waste. A peaceful man, John Ferguson had willingly complied with the implied contract. The man had pointed a gun at him without shooting, indicating that if he didn't resist, he would not be shot. Mr. Ferguson acknowledged acceptance of the agreement by raising his hands in the air away from his gun, and the son of a bitch killed him anyway.

All of the Fergusons' plans for buying another farm, having children and grandchildren to hold and to love and give Christmas and birthday gifts to, grandchildren to whom to pass all of the valuable knowledge they had spent a lifetime acquiring, vaporized in an instant of cruel stupidity.

Returning his attention to the three with their hands up: "You damn well better keep your hands up . . . and get off your horses," Cormac said nastily, motioning with his pistol and not wasting any foolish words about what would happen to them if they didn't follow directions. They damn well knew. They had the idea, but it was a bluff. Like most people, he carried but five bullets in his six-shot revolver for safety. His gun was now empty, but they didn't know that.

Once they were standing, he had them remove each other's guns and throw them in the snowbank. Casually he picked one of the guns out of the snow and checked the load before holstering his own empty pistol.

"Now take off your coats."

"Mister, what are you goin' to do to us? It's cold as hell."

"Just do it, or you'll be in a place considerably warmer than you would like."

Unhappy about the turn of events, they just did it.

He could see they weren't carrying any belt guns.

"Okay, you can put your coats back on again. Now, you . . ." He pointed at the man who had been doing the talking. "There's the matter of some money. Go empty all of their pockets and put it on their chests."

Cormac clicked the hammer on his pistol as the man started to move and the man quickly stopped again.

"Get my point?" he asked.

The man nodded. "I get it. I won't try anything. Believe you me, mister. You got the Indian sign on us. We believe you."

Cormac had the man bring him the money. The big man called Luther had more than five hundred dollars; the other three had a total of one hundred and fifty.

"Mister, the little guy on the end has a . . . had a wife and two kids."

"For a married man, he made some pretty stupid choices now didn't he?"

The man nodded his agreement.

"Now yours."

The three hesitated.

"Trust me. You do not want to make me any madder at you than I already am."

Between them, they come up with another two hundred and seventeen dollars.

"Is there any law where you come from?" Cormac asked.

"There is a judge that comes through every month. He's due back in another week."

"You take these guys back and tell the judge what happened and take these hundred and fifty dollars to the wife. The rest of the money is going to the wife of the man you guys just killed."

"Hey, mister. We didn't kill him. That was Luther's doin'."

"You didn't stop him. You were as much to blame as him. You'll probably tell the judge some cockamamie story to keep from getting any of the blame, but I'm not a lawman so it's no skin off my nose. If it was up to me, I'd just shoot ya now and be done with it. In fact I'm still sorely tempted. You and your kind are too damn worthless to live. Now you load up them mangy bodies and git while I'm still feelin' generous."

"What do we tell the judge? What's your name?"

"What are *your* names?"

After they had told him, he repeated the names out loud, and then, liking the sound of his new nickname, he answered. "I'm Mack Lynch, but if I hear any stories about myself or Mrs. Ferguson being blamed for any of this, I will come and find each one of you, wherever you are, and I'll finish what I probably should finish right now. *Do you understand me?*" They all were nodding they understood.

Cormac didn't realize that his action of drawing on and shooting down four men with five shots while being covered by one of them at the time, had just made him a legend. The would-be hard cases wouldn't have lied about that for nothing. It was too good a story, and it had happened right in front of them. In fact, they were a part of it.

They would each tell it many times, telling and retelling the event in detail every time they found someone willing to listen to them, anywhere, anytime: Mack Lynch, the fastest gun they had ever not seen. He was so fast, they would say, they never even seen his hand move.

He refused their request to give them back their guns, and

after he followed them far enough to make sure they were gone, he returned to Mrs. Ferguson. She was no longer rocking. She had lain down beside her husband with her head upon his chest and pulled his arm around her shoulders, as they must have lain a thousand times before. Rebecca Ferguson was silently crying with the numb empty-sickness that can only be recognized by someone who has experienced the same great personal loss. Cormac remembered all too well; his heart was breaking for her and his own tears were freezing on his cheeks.

If there was anything with which Cormac had experience besides farming, it was death. He knew when losing someone deeply loved, the best thing to keep from going crazy was to have something needing doing. Additionally, he needed to get Mrs. Ferguson up from the frozen ground and get them both someplace where he could get some food into her, but he also knew she would not be interested in doing anything for herself, but she would do anything for her dead husband.

"Mrs. Ferguson, I lost my sister and both of my parents in much the same way. I truly understand the deep pain and numbness you are going through, but we have to get him into town for a proper burial." He reached for her hand. "Please let me help you up."

In all-engrossing agonized shock, she moved automatically, doing whatever she was told, standing head down with arms motionless at her sides, her tears frozen unnoticed on her cheeks. Cormac removed Mr. Ferguson's heavy coat and hat and put them on her, over her objections. After that he tied the body to the nearly empty pack rack and lifted Mrs. Ferguson up onto Lop Ear. She was of very little help.

With the snow deep in many places, the travel was agonizingly slow until they were passed by a steamboat chugging upriver that announced to the world with a few blasts of its steam whistle that it was going to put in at the next wharf, which was just coming into view around the next bend in the river. Cormac hurried to catch it.

One dollar for each of them and fifty cents for each of the horses bought them passage on deck to Ft. Pierre where her sister lived; four-bits bought two beef sandwiches and two cups of weak but hot coffee. Rebecca Ferguson sipped a little coffee, but refused food. They docked in Pierre just before five p.m. Under other circumstances, the boat ride would have been a fun experience.

With Mrs. Ferguson still riding in unexpressive silence, they took Mr. Ferguson's body to the funeral home. At the suggestion of the funeral director, they then went out to buy John Ferguson a new suit and make arrangements for the barber to come and give him a bath, a shave, and a haircut before the funeral director dressed him and made him ready for his funeral on the morrow. With a wave of her hand, Rebecca still refused all offers of food.

A saddle needing to be looked at in a store window display next to the barbershop conveniently located next to the "Men's Haberdashery" gave Cormac the excuse he needed to make her do the shopping and take care of the arrangements by herself. He wanted her to have something to occupy her mind, and taking care of the man she loved was something she was accustomed to, and would have wanted it no other way.

"Here, Mrs. Ferguson," he offered. "Here's the money back they cheated your husband out of and a bit more. There's a new saddle in the window next door I want to look at," he told her awkwardly. "I know nothing about suits anyway. I've never had one. So you go in and make the arrangements with this barber here and then go next door and pick out a nice suit for John. I should be back by then."

Unmoving, she stared numbly at the money in her hand for a long moment, and then silently nodded her head and, still holding the money, entered the barbershop. Cormac walked across the street to a point from which he could easily keep an eye on her through the store window.

The winter sun had already set, making it dark and easy to watch her in the well-lighted shop. The man just finished by the barber was a gentleman who stopped before leaving to brush himself off and to watch Mrs. Ferguson while she paid the barber from the sheaf of bills she was still holding before opening the door for her. Cormac thought that was a nice gesture. He would have never thought of that. There was a lot he didn't know about social graces that he would have to learn or he would stick out like a country goof. The man watched her walk next door to the men's apparel shop before following her, without going in. Through the window, he watched her briefly before stepping to the corner of the alley, which ran beside the men's store. Looking furtively in all directions without seeing Cormac, who had slipped into a shadowed doorway, he stepped into the dark alley, which Mrs. Ferguson would have to pass by on her way to the funeral home.

"Oh, for Pete's sake," Cormac said to nobody. He window-shopped past a few stores in the direction of the funeral home, crossed the street, and walked slowly back up the other side to stop in front of the alley entrance and roll a smoke. The toe of a scuffed and worn boot protruded from the darkness near the wall not three feet away.

"If you want some advice, friend," Cormac said lowly, "I would let this one go by. I saw her and her husband in the village downriver and followed them out of town. But before I could make my move, another hombre came out of the bushes and shot the husband and told her to put up her hands.

"Instead, she came out with a two-shot derringer from some-place I couldn't see 'cause it came out so fast. She put one bullet right between his eyes. I decided it would be healthier for me just to help her get her husband into town and wait for the next one. You might want to do the same."

Cormac took a step before stopping once more to light his quirlie and chuckle in the darkness to the sound of running feet moving down the alley. Maybe that fella would think twice before trying to rob someone else . . . probably not.

The funeral director, having recently handled the funeral for the mother-in-law of Mrs. Ferguson's sister, gave Cormac directions to the sister's house, and Cormac took Mrs. Ferguson there next. When the door opened and Mrs. Ferguson saw her sister, she again burst into unrestrained sobbing. To Cormac's relief, her sister rose immediately to the occasion. The brittle expression on the face of the tall and stern-looking woman softened instantly, and she held her younger sister in silence, letting her cry while looking over her shoulder at Cormac in questioning confusion.

Cormac explained to her what had happened and that Mrs. Ferguson had had no food to speak of all day, gently extracting himself from the situation against Mrs. Ferguson's protests. She had quickly become accustomed to him doing for her.

"Your sister will take care of you now," he explained gently. "I have to locate a stable for Horse and Lop Ear, but I will see you tomorrow at the funeral." He kissed her cheek, and she allowed herself to be held for a long moment until he gently pulled away. Remembering all too well what she was going through, his heart again went out to her, but he had to get shut of her; his own loss was not that far in the past.

The funeral director knew his job. The next day he asked Mrs. Ferguson's sister to hold her husband and five sons in the parlor to allow Mrs. Ferguson a few minutes of private time with her husband. After patiently waiting for her to come out on her own, the director loaded Mr. Ferguson into the black horse-drawn hearse with the help of Cormac and the brother-in-law, a spindly, hawk-nosed man who looked like he should have been an undertaker himself.

Although the sun was warm, the weather was crisp and cold. The sad little family managed to fit into one buggy. Cormac followed them and the hearse the half-mile to the cemetery and one of the six graves the funeral director had previously paid the town drunk and his half-breed Indian friend to dig before the winter cold froze the ground solid.

"Yea, though we walk through the valley of the shadow of death, we will fear no evil, for Thou art with us. And now, we return a good man and loving husband, John Bartlow Ferguson to your hands, oh God. We know you will welcome him home, and we pray that you assist his family and friends to get through this terrible ordeal." With that, he shook the hands of all present, told the grieving widow sincerely how sorry he was for her loss, and drove the black hearse once more down the hill.

So that's how it's done, Cormac thought. He had buried seven people, but this was his first real funeral. It wasn't any more fun.

"Mother, Pa, Becky," he mouthed with his face turned upward and his eyes closed. "I love you, and I'll always miss you."

The family misunderstood, but appreciated his tears. He wiped his eyes, and said his good-byes, agreeing to come by for dinner the next time he was in the area, and rode Horse down the hill. He had to restock his pack before catching the "Missouri Belle" that would take him back downriver.

Of the three mercantile stores available, he settled on the store with the saddle in the window: Benson's Supplies. The saddle was of beautiful black leather with intricate stitching, and Cormac wondered if he would ever be able to afford such a saddle. It didn't matter; it was neither the right size for Lop Ear nor Horse anyway.

Due west were the Black Hills, a land he had heard was of uncommon beauty, where gold was rumored, angry Indians guaranteed. No thanks, when for just a few dollars he could enjoy an easy boat ride far enough south to detour around the volatile Black Hills and the Badlands that stretched all the way into Wyoming Territory and then continue his western journey.

Coming into town, he and Mrs. Ferguson had crossed the first railroad tracks he had ever seen. He crossed them again on his way back to the river, but this time, the first train he had ever seen was sitting on them, making very strange sounds, emitting steam from various locations and smoke from its stack as had the riverboat. The painted words on the side proclaimed it to belong to the Chicago and Northwestern Line. Lop Ear and Horse didn't like it a bit and Cormac dismounted to stand between them, holding their bridles and talking to them.

It was still some distance away but close enough to frighten them when the whistle blew. They reared up, nearly taking Cormac off the ground before he calmed them down. He could see the engineer looking straight at them when he blew the whistle again, laughing when it frightened the horses, making them jump and rear. "Numb-skulled dimwit," said Cormac. Talking continually, he calmed them again and turned them to face the other direction while thinking he would like to talk to that engineer by hand.

CHAPTER 8

Eventually the train moved on as they heard the whistle of the riverboat. They made it onboard with no further incident, where Cormac refused a cabin in favor of staying with the horses below in what he had learned was called "the hold." He didn't think they were going to like being down there when the boat began to move, and he was right.

They were all right once the boat was in motion, giving Cormac time the next day to go up on deck and watch the riverbanks and trees go by. Some people on the shore waved, and he waved back. After that, he sometimes was the first to wave at the shore people or those in small boats, and they waved back, mostly.

The sun was shining, creating an unusually warm day. Riding a paddle wheeler, as it was called, was a fun experience, somewhat like a party atmosphere with a lot of people standing and sitting wherever they found comfortable. A few people held glasses of different kinds of liquids, and a small group of musicians wearing red-and-white striped clothing had gathered on the deck near the front of the boat around a piano in transit, playing a fast-paced music some called Ragtime. He overheard a cheerful and smiling, happy-faced woman obviously having a good time, explaining to her frumpy husband, who obviously wasn't, that it was a fast-march tempo mixed with a syncopated work-song melody. From the look on her husband's face and his manner of treating her, he was a husband wishful of being her wasband.

A group of Indians camping on the bank backed away from the water as the boat drew closer. The captain had apparently caught sight of them first as he had the boat much closer to the opposite bank than previously, returning to the center of the river when the Indians were out of range. One of the Indians shot an arrow at them in protest, or just to see how close he could come. Cormac waved with exaggerated enthusiasm. No one waved back.

"Not a very friendly people, are they?" said a voice beside him. Cormac turned to see a middle-aged gentleman with gray mutton-chop sideburns reaching almost to his gray handlebar mustache above a gray goatee. He was dressed all in gray as well with a gray top hat and three-piece suit over a white shirt and gray bowtie. Cormac's eyes merely skimmed over him on the way to his companion. Holding his arm was an attractive, younger woman. Pretty and also well dressed in an elegant green dress with matching jacket over a frilly white blouse sporting an amulet on a black neckband and carrying a parasol, she was enjoying the attention she was receiving. She was quite attractive, Cormac thought, as long as she didn't have to compete with Lainey, especially if Lainey would have been wearing that green dress.

Cormac returned his attention to the speaker. "Nope," he

answered the man. "They don't seem to be. I think the captain purposely steered us away from them, but they didn't give me the feeling of wanting to be too close anyway. They probably heard of the Sultana."

"What's the Sultana?"

"Steamboats have become pretty reliable," the man answered as he lit a cigar, "but several have exploded, usually killing two or three hundred people. One working the Mississippi back in '65, the Sultana, killed more than eighteen hundred people when it exploded. Most were Union soldiers returning home after the war. Downright pity. They lived through the horrors of war only to get killed on their way home during peacetime. Now me, I fought for the Confederacy, but I still think it was a shame. Yes, sir. Damned shame, it was a right damned shame."

Cormac allowed as how riding the riverboat had been every bit the fun experience he had thought it was going to be, and it had certainly solved his problem of how to get across the Missouri river, but it was time to get off. At the next stop, in Omaha, they did just that. Now, being south of both the Badlands and the Black Hills, according to the ticket agent, they could continue westward on a mostly straight line to the next city on his journey: Cheyenne, in Wyoming Territory.

———

"Those are right nice-looking horses you got there. What'll you take for them?"

The man speaking was standing beside a gracious carriage with a finely matched team and a driver sitting high on the seat waiting for the word to leave. Having just disembarked, a word he had heard used in the process seeming to mean getting off the boat, Cormac was leading the horses and walking to stretch his legs.

"No, thanks," Cormac answered without slowing down. "Not for sale."

"Everything is for sale," the man called. "Name your price."

"Not for sale," Cormac reiterated.

"Hey! Wait a minute. Let's talk."

Cormac did not want to wait a minute and continued walking. He heard the carriage before he saw it pull past and stop, blocking his way.

"Mister, I told you, these horses are not for sale. Now, would you please move your carriage so I can move along?"

"Everything is for sale. Now name your price. I want to buy your horses, and I'm offering to pay your price. Now don't be a dummkopf. Tell me how much I am going to have to pay."

As tall as Cormac, with about ten years on him, broadshouldered and accustomed to getting his way, the man looked fit and capable.

"Mister, look. This lop-eared gray horse belonged to my father. My father set store by this horse, and my father is dead now. This horse is not for sale for any amount of money. He and the grulla are friends, and she's not for sale either."

Cormac turned to walk past him only to have the man grab his coat sleeves. "Look, Bucko. I'm not used to being put off. I make it a habit of getting what I want, and I want those horses."

Eye to eye, they stared silently at each other.

"Well, you're not going to get 'em," Cormac said finally, yanking his arm free and turning to leave. The man would not be shaken and again grabbed his arm. Pulling Cormac back, he smashed him hard in the face, just missing his nose. Cormac fell backward and staggered to his feet, rubbing his cheek. He pulled back to swing a roundhouse to the side of the man's head, but found himself instead on the ground again before he could swing. Cormac had no fighting experience; he had never been in a fight in his life. He kept getting up and getting knocked down, but he continued getting up anyway.

Presently, he remembered a wrestling move his pa had taught him. As he once again regained an upright position, the man had become overconfident and swung again, expecting the same results. Cormac sidestepped and grabbed the man's arm as it passed, turning to go with the punch and using his attacker's own momentum, he threw him head-first into the side of a passing carriage. As the man staggered back toward Cormac, Cormac realized he might not get another opportunity and put everything he had into a punch that snapped the man's head back and laid him out cold. Shaking his hand and flexing his fingers, he realized his thick mittens were pretty good for hitting.

"When he wakes up, tell him the horses are not for sale," Cormac told the driver, an old black man grinning from ear to ear as he climbed down from his seat.

"Ya, suh, I surely will. May I shake ya hand, suh? I been hopin' for that for a long time. He runs over everybody. Thank you, suh. Thank ya very much."

Cormac took his hand. "So this is civilization and that was a gentleman," he answered. "Not the way my pa described it. I'd be obliged if you didn't tell him which way I went." Cormac didn't want the episode to turn into gunplay, but there was not enough money in the world to buy those two horses.

"No, suh, I won't. Which way are you goin'?"

Cormac considered lying, but thought better of it in favor of trusting the old black gentleman. "West," he answered.

"Ya, suh." The old man beamed. "Thank you, suh, east it is."

Cormac smiled his thanks. "You'll do, sir," he told him. "You'll do."

They left west out of town. Cormac had heard that traveling

through the territory of the Omaha Indians was a risky business at best. It being so cold should keep them in their lodges, but they still had to hunt from time to time. He didn't know what kind of Indians had been on the riverbank, but if they were out and about, so would others be.

Winter lasted long that year, luckily, with no sign of Indians. Storms came and storms went with Cormac sharing caves or self-made shelters with Lop Ear and Horse, and moving slowly westward in between, not really bothered by the storms and sometimes playing in them. They spent one day camping on a plateau on the wind-protected side of a pretty valley just to watch it snow. He and the horses were accustomed to cold, sometimes going weeks without seeing another living person.

On one occasion, supplies dwindling and snow-locked in a large cave, the three of them went without food for three days, other than a soup made with the last of Cormac's flour and sugar water to put something in their stomachs. When they had food, they all ate, when they didn't, they all went hungry. They shared. He found the horses loved the sugary mixture and would do anything to get it. Cormac suspected that them being hungry helped. Under those conditions, teaching them to come at a call or motion of a hand-sign happened easily enough.

Next he taught them to kneel and lie down. By the time the storm let up, both horses would kneel at the "Kneel" command, or lie down on "Down." While they were in that position, he took to crawling on them, over them, or beside them, using them for a pillow, or just lying on the cave floor in front of them while looking into their eyes and petting their heads. The last night in the cave, he slept between them for warmth. Sometimes he just talked to them about anything and everything, or nothing, and they heard more than they ever wanted to hear about women in general, redheaded women in particular.

Later, he would change the kneel and down commands to "kneel, please," and "lie down, please," or for more fun, an offhand "oh, go lie down someplace," which was much appreciated by whoever was watching when the command was actually carried out.

They found their first green grass of spring peeking through melting snow around the base of a travel sign: an upward-pointing arrow-shaped sign indicating that Crow Creek Crossing was fifteen miles ahead. The words CROW CREEK CROSSING were lined-out and CAMP CHEYENNE was written in smaller letters. The word CAMP had later been also struck out, leaving simply CHEYENNE. Cormac allowed as how folks in them parts had trouble making up their minds. Cormac and company camped that night beside the sign, and after traveling a short distance the next morning, come across a train track going the same direction.

"Ain't that great, guys? Looks like we coulda been riding all this time, and didn't even know it." However, Cormac didn't begrudge the time. Had they taken the train, he would have missed spending the time and training with Horse and Lop Ear. Their friendship had grown; it had been a fun few months.

They followed the train track until it crossed a bridge made with railroad ties over an arroyo; the ties made it too difficult for the horses to walk across and necessary for them to ride a quarter mile to find a crossing. As they neared Cheyenne, they also neared the track again in time to see a Union Pacific train passing about fifty yards away.

Not forgetting the last train they had seen, the horses started getting a case of restless. As the train neared, the engineer spotted them and blew the whistle. Cormac could see him laughing when the frightened horses began rearing and crow-hopping, wanting to run away. The engineer kept laughing and blowing

his whistle. Cormac, tired of these engineers and their shenanigans, slid down from Lop Ear for solid footing and bounced
three bullets off various places around the cab of the train. The
laughing and the whistling stopped. The engineer no longer
thought it funny and was yelling something as they pulled away.
Cormac made a big show of pretend laughter. Idiot!

———————

Cormac was wishful of seeing a real city. Being only a few years
old, Cheyenne was still one step above a railroad camp and of
little interest. "Denver," said the stable hostler when Cormac
put up the horses, "is a few years older and thriving."

A pile of potatoes and gravy and three thick pieces of fresh
bread filled Cormac's stomach right up . . . mostly. A piece of
pie and three cups of coffee took care of any corners that had
been missed. Maybe Cheyenne was a glorified railroad camp,
but they knew how to feed a hungry man. Next stop . . . Denver.

"Four days, if you're pokey and only make about twenty-five
miles a day, three if you're in a hurry and watch the sun rise and
set from the saddle," said the hostler when Cormac claimed the
horses the next morning and asked how long it would take to
ride to Denver.

Four days later found Cormac riding Lop Ear into Smith's
Livery & Blacksmith Shop in Denver, Colorado, with Horse
trotting freely alongside. Her not wanting to be anyplace where
he and Lop Ear wasn't made keeping her on a lead rope as point-
less as it was for Lop Ear to be led when Cormac was riding
Horse.

Although Denver was more city-like than Pierre or Cheyenne, it didn't quite live up to his expectations. There were the
stables, churches, general mercantile stores, saloons, clothing
stores, a blacksmith shop, a red-light district, and banks, just

more of them, but they were all busy; he had to give 'em that. And there were a lot of people, all going and doing.

A passerby said Denver was only about ten or twelve years old, give or take, but was growing by leaps and bounds, what with the railroad bringing in more people every day and all. People were buying and selling and investing, and money was being made.

In answer to his question, one of the saloon's three bartenders directed Cormac to the First National Bank on Fifteenth Street, while he drank his first beer ever. "The bank's existence was pretty iffy," said the bartender, "but they put a guy named Moffat in charge, and he's turned it around. They got a safe now as big as a house they claim is impossible to break into, but nobody has tried nitro yet, so time will tell."

Cormac had been getting nervous about the money he was carrying since the incident with the horses in Omaha; six hundred dollars was a lot of money. He found the place easy enough and twenty minutes later he had a piece of paper stating that Cormac Lynch had a bank account with five hundred dollars he could withdraw upon demand. It felt pretty darned good. Now he just had to figure a way to start earning more before it ran out.

Having no idea how to even go about looking for a job, he returned to the barkeep at the Trailhead Saloon and had his second beer ever. He could get to like this stuff, he thought. When Cormac had been in the first time, he had seen Chinese and Irish, Scandinavians, blacks, and whites, businessmen in suits, miners and farmers wearing the same bib overalls as he, cowboys and railroad workers and all dressed in more different styles of clothing than Cormac had ever before seen, most of them wearing guns, either out in the open or concealed about their person as he could tell from lumps under their clothes and pieces of guns protruding in various places.

Some were standing at the bar, others leaning against upright columns; some tables had card games in progress, and still others had two, or three, or six people in serious discussions, likely conducting business of some sort. The saloon seemed to be the town meeting place. He figured if anybody knew of a job available, the barkeep would be the one to ask what was going on around town.

According to Patch, the bartender, The Trailhead Saloon had once been only a tent at what had been the track end of the Denver & Santa Fe Railroad. The railroad had sold the site to Patch's boss, Doc Mason, for a share of the action. The location turned out to be centrally located and an excellent place for a saloon, and as the city grew, so grew Trailhead's business. Inside of five years, Doc Mason bought them out for an ungodly sum of money. The railroad didn't want to let it go, but Doc Mason had been smart enough to get an option to buy out their share put in the contract.

The barkeep was called Patch because of the patch on his left eye, which had been poked out in a fight as a kid. The other kid had been bigger and stronger, he said, and always picked on him. The barkeep told Cormac the eye-poke was deliberate and made him furious. He said he had whupped the bigger kid within an inch of his life, and only stopped when some people pulled him off. After that, he beat on him again anytime he seen him and could catch him, all the while knowing full well his own ole man was going to give him what for for doing it. The other kid's family finally accepted nothing was going to make him quit and moved out of town.

The patch put Cormac in mind of Baldy, the old swaybacked plow horse his pa had let him use when he was first learning to ride at five years old. With her being blind in her left eye and shy in her good right eye, Cormac, riding bareback, had learned to quickly grab a handful of mane to stay on top of her. Whenever anything moved unexpectedly on her right side, she was just naturally goin' to shy left every time, and that's just all there was to it.

"Can ya use that hog leg?" the bartender wanted to know.

"I do okay," Cormac answered. "Why?"

"Well, most stagecoaches got replaced by trains, riverboats, and the like, but Butterfield still makes a spanker run back and forth between here and Boulder and sometimes they pick up gold for the bank. The only way to get to Boulder is a horseback or the stage, and they need someone to ride shotgun. It pays mighty good—twenty-five dollars a trip, if you're interested. Their local manager just left here so I know the job is still open. If you tell him I sent ya, he'll probably hire you on the spot."

"What's a spanker, and what's it mean to ride shotgun?"

"Boy! In those bib overalls and farmer shoes, I thought you looked like you just left the farm, but you really did, didn't you?"

Six rough-looking cowboy toughs had bellied up to the bar to stand with one foot on the rail, and stare impatiently at Patch. In a voice intended to intimidate, one of the toughs called, "You gonna wait on us or what?" He stared first at Patch, then at Cormac.

Cormac met his gaze.

Unperturbed, Patch ignored the tone of voice. "Hold your horses, friend. I'll be there when I get there. Wait a minute while I wait on these tough guys before they have a fit," he told Cormac.

After serving Cormac another beer upon his return, Patch told him, "Riding topside on a stage is no picnic to begin with, but a spanker is a rough ride over rough roads." The beer had Cormac beginning to feel more cheerful than he had been. "They have to make the trip up and back in one day. The road is rough, and the driver hits it hard. It'll relocate your intestines for you."

He stepped away to give an amiable newcomer in new-looking duds a double shot of whiskey and came back.

"Riding shotgun means you're along for protection. Your job is to sit up on the seat beside the driver with a shotgun and keep the outlaws and road agents from holding up the stage. It's a rough ride, and it's dangerous; that's why it pays so good." Cormac ignored the tough who was still glaring at him and looking for trouble.

"My object is to make some money," Cormac said, feeling his beer. "I guess I can handle a little danger. Where's the stage office?"

Cormac drank the last of his beer and stared back at the tough. If he wanted trouble, he sure as hell came to the right place. One more beer and Cormac Lynch just might take it to him. But he opted against it and set out in search of a job.

Patch was right and the Butterfield Stage Line manager, a plump, well-fed individual, did little more than ask his name after hearing Patch had sent him before giving him the job. After putting up Lop Ear and Horse in the Butterfield stable, Cormac took a room at Mrs. Colwell's Board and Room, a freshly painted two-story house with a new roof, a new front door, and new furniture in the parlor; business must be good. Money was in evidence everywhere in the city of Denver, Colorado.

The Butterfield hostler was doing his job; the next morning, Lop Ear and Horse were munching contentedly on a generous helping of grain in their feed bags. Cormac petted and talked to them for a few minutes before digging out and strapping the .44 long-barreled Colt on his left side and climbing up onto the stage carrying their double-ought-buck-loaded double-barreled shotgun. He was loaded for bear, his pa woulda said. The driver looked at the Colt as Cormac settled down onto the seat beside him. "Can you hit anything with that thing?"

"Nah! Probably not," Cormac answered. "But just the seein' of it should scare off the boogers."

In the event of his demise, he made out a paper to carry in his pocket tightly wrapped in oilcloth stating that the reader would receive fifty dollars from the First National Bank of Denver for notifying them of the event. Upon receipt of such news, the bank was to honor the reward from his funds and then have somebody go find Lainey Nayle in the Dakota Territory northeast of Pierre and give her whatever was left of his money, if she would take it. If not, they were to give it to the newly formed Red Cross of which he had recently heard. Lainey was also to be given the opportunity to buy his horses and other possessions for two hundred dollars from the deliverer. Failing that, they would become the possessions of the deliverer. It was signed: *Cormac Lorton Lynch 1875.* Slapping the long reins across the team's rumps, the buckskin-clothed, grizzled old driver called Cactus spit out a strong stream of tobacco juice, wiped off his chin, and let out a war whoop that would wake the dead. The team laid into their harnesses with enthusiasm, taking them out of there on high.

Cormac remembered the excitement he felt watching the stage as a kid, and now he was part of the action. At a time when many were content to make fifteen dollars a week, Cormac Lynch had a job making twenty-five dollars a day, three days a week. His life was off to a good start. Feeling the excitement, he couldn't restrain the urge to yell and promptly did so . . . at the top of his lungs.

The stage bounced, the three passengers complained loudly, and Cormac held on for dear life. The road was just two wagon ruts, but Cactus knew it well and managed to hit every rut and every bump—the big ones he hit twice, thought Cormac. It was easy to understand why it was called a spanker. His rear end was taking a beating, and his intestines did feel like they were getting relocated, as did his spine. The bouncing had him wishing he had visited the outhouse one more time before they left.

The driver alternated the horses walking with running to rest them from time to time, but they kept moving nonstop until mid-morning when the driver suddenly hauled back on the reins and called, "Whoa!" The stage came to a stop.

"We'll take a ten minute break for the horses," called out the driver. "Men to the right, lady to the left. Be back on the stage in ten minutes or get left here, and I ain't foolin'." Then to Cormac, "You go use the bushes if ya got to, then come back and I'll go. I don't want to leave the stage alone." Then in a lowered voice while climbing down, he said, "You don't have to be too watchful on this trip. If anybody has holdup ideas, it will be on the back leg, but today we won't be carrying any gold."

The men made it back on time, but they had to wait for the lady. "Lady, we'll pick you up on the way back," the driver called, and gave a half-hearted holler at the horses. "Hiyah."

She came running out of the bushes, straightening her skirts. Cormac noticed the driver had his foot solidly on the brake and the reins taut. They weren't going anywhere. As her door clicked shut, Cactus took his foot off the brake, loosed the reins, and yelled for real, "Hiyah!" The horses knew the routine and were ready. They hit the end of the traces that connected them to the stage running. Thinking back on it, Cormac realized the horses had been expectant of stopping and had already begun to slow down just before the driver had yelled whoa. Cormac figured it to be their regular stop.

The country they were traveling through was thick with

bushes and pine trees of which he was ignorant of the names, but it was a beautiful ride and the smell of pine was springtime-strong. Cactus slowed for a particularly bad bump, and Cormac glanced up at the mountain on his left in time to see a person on foot disappearing over the top. Why a person was on foot in the wilderness, coincidentally right above a bad place in the road severe enough to force the stage to slow was a question that rode suspicious on his mind. Since his job was to guard the stage, Cormac looked for a holdup man behind every bush.

In Boulder, they left the stage at the livery for a fresh team and went next door to the Stage-Stop Café, where they had the strangest-tasting liver and liver gravy he had ever eaten, and he loved liver. Becky used to make liver for him, but his mother wouldn't. It was the only thing she drew the line at. She had helped in the breech birth of a calf while his pa had been helping a neighbor, but she thought liver was slimy.

They returned to the livery as the traces were being reconnected. Remembering the man on foot, Cormac rechecked the loads in the scattergun and loaded the normally empty cylinders on both pistols. Cactus looked at him questionably with his eyebrows raised. "Just playin' it safe," Cormac told him. Cactus shrugged and climbed up into his seat.

The midday shadows were short when they walked the stage to pick up two men and two women from the hotel. One of the women was a not unattractive blonde about Cormac's own age, who was making eyes at him while he put down the step and held the door open. Cormac smiled politely and climbed back up to his roost. He had no time today for nonsense; he had a job to do, and he was getting twenty-five dollars a day to do it.

Cormac was wary as they neared the suspiciously deep, possibly intentionally made rut where the man had been walking high above. Cactus regripped the reins in preparation for slowing down. Cormac saw something move higher on the mountain and yelled at him, "Let 'em hear the whip, straddle the rut, and take 'em through on hell!" Cactus reacted unquestioningly.

"Hiyah!" he yelled, and slapped the horses' rumps with the reins with one hand while he pulled the whip from its bracket with the other, cracking it over their heads. The stage leaped forward as a rifle shot echoed from the mountain and a bullet ricocheted off the metal handrail behind Cormac. Holding the scattergun with his left hand, he pulled it down by his side with the butt back against the stage behind him and his Smith & Wesson in his right hand as four riders with kerchiefs over their faces burst out of the bushes in front of them, their hands full of guns.

Cactus had the stage already into the middle of them, and their attempt to block the road failed; they were forced to split apart with one on the left and three on the right side. Cormac cross-fired, hitting the single on the left center chest with his right-hand pistol, and taking out two on the right when he pulled both triggers of the shotgun at the same time, firing with his left hand.

The remaining rider on the right got off one shot, which missed, before Cormac swung his right-hand pistol back to put an end to that holdup business. The holdup man's body jerked twice from Cormac's three shots before falling backward from the out-of-control horse rearing wildly.

Cactus kept the horses all-out, bumps be damned, for at least a mile, finally slowing to a trot, a walk, and then to a stop when they come to an open space from which it was easy to see there were no outlaws around. "By thee Gods, man! That was some shootin'. Where'd a farm boy learn to shoot like that?"

Cormac shrugged. "I dunno," he said as he reloaded. "I just did what had ta be done."

"I'd like to shake your hand," said the undertaker-like passenger stepping down from the stage with his hand out when they stopped later at Cactus' normal resting place for a bush break and to ease the horses. "What's your name, boy?"

"Mack Lynch, sir," he said, accepting the handshake from him and others, all of whom were standing in a group. "From Dakota Territory."

"Well, Mr. Mack Lynch, I thank you. That could have been real bad." In the excitement, no one had noticed another holdup man stepping out of the shrubbery with his gun pointed at Cormac. He was calm, obviously experienced, and fully expectant of cooperation.

"If everyone stands real still and puts their hands in the air, no one is going to get hurt."

"Oh for Pete's sake," said Cormac. The girl, standing beside him still trying to make eyes at him, fainted, and Cormac, remembering the man shooting Mr. Ferguson although his hands were up, palmed his freshly re-loaded Smith & Wesson and put two bullets into the middle of the holdup man's chest.

Looking down at him, Cactus shook his head. "I don't understand. I been held up before, but it's unusual for this many to be involved. Usually, it's just some cowboy with an empty poke that wants to celebrate a little, or take a girl upstairs, and they don't really want to hurt anybody, but these guys were dead serious. That rifle shot was meant to put you in the ground, boy!" The other male passenger, an affable man of confident strength and stature, studying him with analytic eyes, shook his hand in silence.

"If you keep walkin' in rattlesnake country you're gonna get bit," Cormac told the Butterfield manager when they returned to Denver. "I figure if I keep ridin' shotgun, I'm gonna get dead. That rifle bullet was aimed at me, and I can only thank God it missed; the next one might not. I'm not gonna push my luck for no amount of money. I can't spend it if I'm dead, so thanks, but no thanks. You're gonna have to find somebody else."

Cormac went back to the Trailhead to see if Patch knew of any other jobs available. Cactus was already there and telling everybody within earshot of Cormac's prowess with his guns. He was still wearing both with the thongs off.

When he bellied up to the bar, Patch brought him a beer without being asked. "You made a name for yourself today, boy."

"A name for himself? That pip-squeaked hick from the sticks? He couldn't draw a deuce in a stacked deck, let alone draw them guns a his." The tough guy who had been staring at him the day before was back with one of his friends. Other patrons quickly slid out of the way.

"Look at him, with two guns and farmer-boy bib overalls, acting like he's so tough. Hell, he's still a wet-behind-the-ears kid. He don't know what tough is. Hell, down Texas way, we swat the likes of him like flies. For two bits, I'd take him apart."

His friend threw a quarter on the bar. "He ain't dry behind the ears yet, but the kid looks to me like he's got sand, and I think that would take some doin'. There's your two bits; I think I'd like to see that."

"You guys got something stuck in your craw or what?" asked Cormac. "Fun's fun, but I just came in here to talk to Patch and have a beer. Now why don't you guys just leave me alone, and we'll forget all this nonsense."

With a ten-gallon hat on his head, a red kerchief around his thick neck, a plain red shirt and brown vest over blue jeans with brand-new boots, the tough guy was a typical-looking cowboy who had had too much good food. His face was round and flabby, and when he stepped away from the bar, his belly hung well over his belt, but it wasn't all flab. He moved well.

He swaggered over to Cormac. "Come on, farm boy, just 'cause you're big, don't mean you're tough. Come get your lickin'."

Cormac easily ducked a roundhouse left but stepped into a wicked right hook that had him seeing stars. Groggy, he fell back against the bar. "How's that, boy? Come on. We ain't done here."

Cormac wasn't going to let that happen again and walked in on him swinging only to get caught by a straight jab to his nose that started a river of blood gushing down. He managed to duck the next one and landed a stiff uppercut to the chin that knocked the cowboy on his backend.

Backing up, Cormac gave him time to regain his feet as he had been taught, and they came together again, both a little wiser. Cormac dodged a left hook and took a powerful right to his midriff that doubled him over. The cowboy clubbed down on the back of his head with his two fists held together, and Cormac went to his knees.

Before he could regain his feet, the cowboy kicked him once in the stomach, missed a kick to the head, and landed one on the hip, knocking him to the floor. They both hurt like the devil. *Prize fighting is another job I don't want*, he thought, pulling back from the next kick and rolling to his feet, right-stepping away from a powerhouse right to grab it as he had his attacker in Omaha. It worked the same way. Cormac grabbed the arm and pulled hard with the swing, using the cowboy's weight as leverage to pull him off his feet and slam him head first into the bar. That took the fight out of him, and he crumbled into a heap on the floor.

"Can I use one of your wet towels to wipe this blood off me?" Cormac asked Patch. The blood was all down his front and soaked into his shirt and overalls. It was going to take more than a wet towel to clean it up. He would take care of it later. He used the towel on his face.

"Back to our conversation, do you know anyone else needin' help around here Patch?"

"Only a feed store, but I don't think you'd like standing around in a store all day, waiting on people. But I can ask around."

Cormac ordered another beer and went to use the outhouse. There was paper on the floor, and the seat was wet. Swell. Men are slobs. His pa woulda talked to him loudly about leaving their toilet in that condition for the women. Returning to the beer waiting for him, Cormac looked into the mirror to see the two cowboys at a table, drinking whiskey and glaring at him. Sweller. It would be better if he just left before there was more trouble.

Patch promised he would ask around about a job for him and Cormac turned to leave.

"What's the matter, farm boy? You gotta run home to mommy?" Cormac ignored him and kept walking.

"Hey! Farmer boy! I think you're a damn yellow-bellied coward."

Cormac turned to see the loud mouth standing in front of his table, his legs spread and his hand over his gun. "Okay loud mouth, you win. You've been trying to get my goat, and you've succeeded. You can find out right now if I know how to use these toys of mine, if you want. If this is the hill you want to die on, pull your gun, if you're that damned stupid. But if you do, I'm gonna kill ya."

The loud mouth was just that stupid. He batted his eyes a couple times and realized he had misjudged the kid altogether. But he had made his brag and couldn't back down now. He went for his gun. Cormac waited while his hand gripped his gun and pulled it out of his holster so all could see that Cormac had not drawn first, and then shot him dead center with one bullet. There were plenty of witnesses to vouch that it was a fair shoot. In the telling of it later, it was said that no one had actually seen his hand move. The gun was just suddenly in his hand . . . and the legend grew.

"Thanks for your help, Patch. I guess I better move on. I don't want anymore of this."

"You never told me your name."

"Mack Lynch, from Dakota Territory. Thanks for your help. Will you tell your law what happened, please, so it doesn't get distorted?"

"Sure. Good luck wherever you end up, but that draw of yours is the damndest thing I ever seen, or never seen. I was watching you and wondering why you weren't going for your gun, then all the sudden it was in your hand. I never saw the likes of that, and in this saloon, I've seen plenty. I think, my young friend, you're going to find that fast draw to be a blessing and a curse all wrapped up in one package."

Since spring had arrived to start melting the snow, traveling would be getting easier. Maybe he would go see what was so all-fired special about the Texas that everyone went to see when they left after putting up their GTT sign that was always left behind tacked to their door. GTT: GONE TO TEXAS.

CHAPTER 9

Not wanting to draw any more attention, he bought himself some jeans and western boots that the clerk explained had high heels to keep his feet from slipping through the stirrups, getting hung up and helping to get him drug to death. He was on his way to get Lop Ear and Horse when he was stopped by a gravely, down-in-the-cellar voice, with a face to match.

"Excuse me, young man. I would like to speak with you, if I may." Elderly, with the rough-textured, weather-beaten skin of many hours in the saddle, he spoke with certainty and toughness he felt no need to demonstrate. He knew who he was and didn't give a hang if anyone else did or not. Cormac recognized him as having been on the stage returning from Boulder.

"Yes, sir. What can I do for you?"

"Ah, manners. I like that. Your parents raised you well. I was on the stage today."

"Yes, sir. I remember you. I noticed your gun out in case I needed help. I thank you for that."

"You did a good job out there today."

"I'd rather not have had to; it was a surprise. We weren't expecting to have any trouble. We weren't carrying any money or gold."

"That was my fault, I'm afraid. I was carrying $30,000. I was just picking up the money for a herd of cattle I sold last month and wanted to get it to the First National Bank. I've heard they have a very strong safe."

"You're right about that. It's nearly as big as a house. They showed me the inside. I don't see how anyone could break into that thing; it's massive. Everyone is waiting for someone to try to rob it just to see how strong it really is."

"Well, you're right, it certainly looks strong, but if they let you see the inside, that means you have some money in there, too. They wouldn't have let you see it otherwise. That makes you different than most young men your age, if you're saving your money instead of drinking and girlin' till it's gone."

"Well," he went on, "my money is their problem now, and I have a banknote instead of cash, thanks to you. I understand you quit your job when you got back in town, but you obviously weren't afraid. I think that shows a lot of common sense. I stopped you to offer you a job. I got a spread up in Montana just outside of Virginia City called the Flying H where I run a little beef, and I could use a good man."

"Thanks for the offer, but I don't know anything about cattle, and I won't hire out my gun. But thanks anyway." Cormac turned to leave.

"Wait. I don't want to hire your gun. Oh, I can't guarantee that you might not have to use it sometime, but it's not why I am offering you a job. I already have about twenty riders, but good help is hard to find. I can pay twenty-five a month and found. The bunkhouse is clean, you'll love our cook, and Montana's got the biggest, bluest skies you'll ever see. Whadaya say?"

He held out his hand. Cormac hesitated and then took it. "I been wantin' to see Montana anyway, and I guess it's another chance like this I'll not be gettin'."

Cormac's new boss looked at him more thoughtfully. "That sounded a mite Irish. Is one of your parents Irish?"

"No, sir," Cormac answered, a little surprised himself. "I used to have an Irish friend that would sometimes lay the Irish on thick for the fun of it or to tease me. I guess some of it stuck to me." Then, to change the subject, "I don't even know your name, sir. I'm Mack Lynch, from Dakota Territory."

Cormac's new boss was J. B. Haplander, from Texas by way of Montana. They settled their arrangements and agreed that Cormac would meet him at the ranch in a few days.

The trip to Montana was pleasurable and uneventful other than a horse race when Cormac learned that Lop Ear and Horse knew something about running. He had always thought they probably did, but never had the need to call on it. Their high-arched necks and tails, and long-legged fancy stepping were somethin' to see, but he had never run them. He'd just never had the need.

Crossing Laramie Plains in eastern Wyoming, the weather was warm and Horse's gait smooth and easy riding. The spring grasses were making everything green and there were plenty of wildflowers blooming. It was a soft and lazy day, and a pleasant ride. He had told Mr. Haplander he wanted to take his time and see the sights on the way and was doing just that.

Around mid-day, he was plodding along on Horse, dozing off and on in the warm sun, when a dream of Lainey smiling at him was rudely interrupted by a group of what he had been told to watch out for but hadn't: Cheyenne Indians. About five or six suddenly swooped down off a grassy hill on his right, whooping and hollering at the tops of their lungs.

He turned Horse left, and there came another bunch of about the same size.

"Okay guys!" he hollered, and bounced his spurless boots off Horse's flanks. "Get us outta here!" That was very nearly his undoing. Horse's acceleration darn near left him sitting in mid-air. He barely managed to grab the saddle horn to pull hisself back on top. Lop Ear was right beside them, runnin' free and easy, and Cormac learned right quick an important fact of life: he had himself a couple of horses that took their runnin' seriously.

By the time he got his balance back and his bottom side back in the saddle, he was wide-awake and leaning teary-eyed into the wind with his hat following behind and the wind filling his mouth; he yelled with excitement. Those Indians liked to yell—let them hear what a real yell sounded like. A Johnny Reb stopping at the farm for supper and an overnight rest had taught him the Rebel yell that had put the fear of God into many hearts. He reared back and let one rip. Horse liked it: Cormac felt her muscles surge as she briefly pulled ahead of Lop Ear.

Cormac hollered at Lop Ear, "You gonna let her get ahead of you like this? Come on, get up here!" Lop Ear was up for it, and get up there he did. Inch by inch, until they were again neck and neck, matching stride for stride and muscle for muscle; they were running low to the ground with grass-muffled hoof beats pounding, steel-like muscles straining, and loud breaths of exertion exhaling huge amounts of air with every stride to make room for the enormous amounts of oxygen their great bodies were consuming as they reached for every possible inch of ground. The three of them fairly flew over the fresh and new prairie grass. The excitement refused to be contained, and he yelled again just for the pure hell of it! He almost forgot the Indians were even back there.

Cormac looked back to find his pursuers dropping farther and farther behind. He caught up his hat from where it was flopping in the wind behind his head and waved it at the Indians with another Rebel yell. This horse race wasn't even close, and they damn well knew it. They knew it, and were pulling up, giving it up as a bad job.

He had heard that Indians had a healthy respect for good horseflesh, and one of them waved back at him. Cormac returned the wave and let the horses run; they were having a good time and enjoying themselves. So was he. "Good job, guys!" he yelled into the wind. "I guess we showed them a thing or three."

Cormac Lynch was having a very, very good time. The sky was wide open, clear, and blue without a cloud in it, and there was an equal amount of rich green grass beneath it; the sun was bright and warm, new spring flowers and grasses were pushing their way into the world, and the occasional bird and a couple of flocks were flushing up in front of them. He was eighteen years old with money in the bank and not a care in the world, no responsibilities, and—as long as he kept some things pushed out of his mind—no cares or concerns. He didn't know how far they had run, but it was far and the horses were still running easily, just beginning to sweat; it was time to start slowing them down. A covey of partridges flushed from the grass around them, and he was right in the middle of the bunch. The fast little birds were all around and under them with their wings fluttering in his ears, so close he coulda reached out and grabbed one. Again the excitement was too much to contain, and he turned loose another Rebel yell.

————————

First he found Virginia City, and then he found the Flying H. The sign over the front gate said he was in the right place. In large, handwriting style letters, it read FLYING H, with a wing on each side of the *H*. The Flying H was a big spread, cleanly maintained and busy. The ranch house was a large and sprawling two story with windows on all sides of the first as well as second stories, and a porch all the way across the front sporting a porch rail.

A little behind and to the left sat the largest barn Cormac had ever seen. It had been easily visible for the last two miles. Also two stories, strangely enough with two small windows on all four sides at the second-story level, large double doors in the front and back with a third double door on the side opening into an oversize corral. The corral was partitioned in half with a cowboy in one of the halves doing his best to stay in the middle of a horse with other ideas, while another cowboy was roping a second horse out of a small herd in the remaining half.

It was later explained by Mr. Haplander that the windows in the loft of the barn were for fighting off Indians, if needed. Although it hadn't happened a second time, the Indians had attacked when he and his wife and oldest son, Lucas, had first started the spread. Mr. Haplander reckoned it was never tried a second time due to the high losses suffered by the Indians, what with Lucas shooting from the upper windows in the barn, and he and Mrs. Haplander from the second-story windows of the house.

A bunkhouse was located between the barn and the house with its own outhouse behind. Everything was painted white, and a cowboy was just putting the finishing touches on a fresh coat of new paint on a shed behind the main living quarters.

Over a slight rise on a trail coming into the ranch appeared a frustrated cowboy yelling at his dapple-gray horse to run faster in an attempt to catch a girl flying in on a black-and-white Paint staying easily in front of him. His dapple-gray was making a good effort, but in the end, just didn't have what it took. Laughing, the girl slid her Paint to a stop at the corral and dismounted, as did the cowboy, but he wasn't laughing.

"I tried to tell you, Mark, but you wouldn't listen," called the cowboy with the rope. "What'd she get you for this time?"

"None of your business," snapped the loser, picking up the reins to the Paint and leading both horses into the barn. Cormac walked Horse up to the corral and stepped off as Lop Ear joined them.

The girl was a year or two younger than Cormac, cute, with a pert nose in the middle of a round face framed by thick yellow hair. With a full, well-rounded body clothed in close-fitting jeans and a close-fitting checked shirt, she was an eyeful. *Dressed like that on a ranch full of men*, thought Cormac. *I'll bet she gives her pa fits.*

She had a pleasant smile and used it easily. "Hi. Can I help you?"

Cormac snatched off his hat. "Yes, ma'am. I'm looking for Mr. Haplander. He hired me down Colorado way." She was eyeing Horse and Lop Ear.

She walked around them, running her hands over their skin and legs. "Nice horses. Can they run?"

Cormac resisted the urge to tell her they had just outrun a gang of scalp-happy Indians. "They're okay. I haven't run them much."

"They both look like a lot of horse. Maybe we'll have to try them out. Are you Mack Lynch?"

"Yes, ma'am. May I know who you are?"

"You're the most polite cowboy I've ever met." She smiled. "I'm Laurie Haplander. My daddy and mother built this spread from the ground up. Daddy told us that you would be coming soon. You seem to have impressed him in some way. What did you do?"

If her daddy hadn't told her, maybe he shouldn't. "I don't rightly know, ma'am. We met and talked a bit, we got along, and he knew I was needin' a job and told me to come on up." The cowboy who took the horses to the barn was returning, his face as grouchy as a tree full of owls. "Is Mr. Haplander here?" Cormac asked.

"Sure," she answered, "but let me introduce you to my kid brother first. Marcus, this is the Mack Lynch Daddy told us about. Mack, this is my brother Marcus. I'm the nice one; he's the pain in the . . . Well, you know how teenage boys are."

Marcus shot her a dirty look as Cormac held out his hand, but it was refused. "Just what we need, another hotshot cowboy of some kind. What did you do to impress our father?"

"I was just explaining to your sister that I don't know. We met and got along. I needed a job, and he hired me, but I'm no hotshot cowboy. Fact a the matter is, I'm no kinda cowboy. I was raised on a farm and don't know a thing about cattle ranchin'. Mr. Haplander said y'all would teach me."

"Oh that's wonderful. A greenhorn." Marcus Haplander spun on the ball of one foot and strode toward the house.

"Don't forget," Laurie called after him, "you're doing dinner dishes next week."

"Don't mind him," Laurie told Cormac. "He's a numbskull sometimes. Like I said, he's a teenage boy; he doesn't accomplish much. In fact, he's been known to spend an hour trying to figure out how to do a twenty-minute job in ten. Come on. Let's go find Daddy and let him know you're here."

The inside of the house was equally clean and fresh painted, with pieces of large cowhide-covered furniture nicely arranged. Having never seen luxury, Cormac was duly impressed.

Mrs. Haplander was an older version of Laurie, grown past cuteness and pretty and into handsome, worn gracefully. Mr. and Mrs. Haplander were cordial and polite before telling him to pick out a bunk in the bunkhouse and look around until their son, Josh, returned. Josh was the ranch foreman and their son, Lucas, was the foreman at the silver mine they owned in the Rockies, on the northwest corner of their property. Although their other hands worked for one or the other, Cormac was told he would be splitting his time between the two, depending on where he was needed at the time.

To say that Cormac was impressed was an understatement; he was awed. Mr. Haplander had said they had fifty thousand acres, and his idea of running a little beef was five thousand head. The Lynch farm had been thirty acres with two cows, five pigs, a few pullet chickens, and a couple of Rhode Island Reds.

Josh had been out with the other men starting the spring roundup for counting and branding. He was nothing like Marcus. He held out his hand with a big smile. "My dad said he had hired a farmer, but warned me not to sell you short. He said you would probably be running the place in a couple weeks. I told him good. I'm tired of doing all the work around here." Josh introduced him to the cook, an old Irishman that answered to the name of Duffy. Cormac would find out that the men affectionately called him King Duffy. His kingdom was the kitchen between the two dining rooms, and he ruled it with an iron hand. He put up with no cowboy nonsense, such as food stealing, or sneaking into the kitchen for snacks.

There was a dining room for the Haplanders in the main house, and one that had been added onto the side of the house for the hands at some later date with the kitchen located between the two. Duffy served the Haplanders; the men served themselves from large bowls and plates of food placed on a wide shelf separating the kitchen from their dining room, and they were expected to keep their dining room clean. Duffy wasn't gonna be their mother. From time to time, men were assigned to help him for the day or a week.

It was decided that Cormac would start out working for Josh until the roundup was over, and he was warned that they started early. It was still dark when the ringing of the breakfast bell found Cormac taking care of Lop Ear and Horse. Breakfast was plenty of beans, beef, gravy, and all the bread they wanted. Duffy had started as their trail cook with his own chuck wagon. After his first trail drive, the house cook had been given a generous severance pay, and Duffy took over the kitchens, sleeping in the bunkhouse with the men.

"The fastest way to learn," Josh told Cormac as they were riding out to the branding corrals, "was just to start doing it. I'll show you how." Lop Ear wanted to be ridden that morning and Cormac obliged. Josh was amazed that Horse trotted freely alongside. "Your horses are beautiful and a lot of horse, but for the roundup, you need a cowpony. One that is small and fast and can turn on the spot for herding cattle.

"They'll be spinning and balking and doing everything they can to get away from you. I'll loan you a pair of chaps until you can get into town and get your own. Otherwise the brush down in the washes and ravines will cut you to pieces, and you better take a last look at how pretty those new boots of yours are. By tonight, they'll look ten years old. The most important thing to remember is this, when the dinner bell sounds, hightail it in here right quick, or you're liable to find yourself suckin' hind tit."

Lop Ear and Horse didn't care for the idea, but Josh picked

out a little brown mustang mare for him. Cormac soon learned what Josh had been talking about. "Your job," Josh explained, "is to ride up and down the draws, in and out of the brush and anywhere else you might find any cattle. Run them into the pens and somebody else will take it from there for the branding. Try to keep a rough count of how many you bring in so we can double-check the cowboy's counts with the final tally every day.

The need for a quick cowpony soon became obvious. The first group Cormac found was five back in a draw. As he rode around to get behind them, they scattered in five different directions, and his horse took in after the closest one. Only a quick grab at the saddle horn and a lot of luck kept him on top of the horse as it went sideways, spun around, and burst forward; he was into top speed almost instantaneously.

The horse was little compared to Lop Ear and Horse but she was a lot of horse. She seemed to read the cattle's minds as they chased one after another to the pens, sometimes in singles and sometimes in groups. Groups were a lot of fun. That little horse ran her heart out. Two or three in a group would invariably try to go in two or three different directions at the same time. Cormac got in the habit of counting them when he first saw them. Once they started moving he would be far too busy, and sometimes just plain forgot about it.

Duffy had rolled his chuck wagon out to the branding site and by the time Josh had called break-time on the first day, Cormac was an experienced cowhand, at least at running reasonable cattle. He didn't know about a loco long-horned steer the men called old Mossy, a mean old son, they would tell him later.

He was glad when the dinner bell rang. He had just spotted a small group of cattle in a wash, and decided to run them in with him. Wrong idea. By the time he got them to the pen, there was nobody at the gate, and he had to open it and try to get his bunch in without letting the others out. It was a challenge, but he got it done and went eagerly to the chuck wagon. All that was left was a half plate of beans and a little coffee. He stood looking at his plate in dismay. That round-up stuff was making an appetite. And he was hungry. Dismally, he turned to locate a place to sit when everyone began laughing at him, and the cook called him back. "Here you go, boy," he said. "We was just havin' some fun with ya. Here's your plate." He handed Cormac a plate piled high with beans and beef. After eating, they relaxed, napped, or smoked, and were back in the saddle within the hour.

King Duffy's chuck wagon was designed and built by Duffy himself. On each side of the exterior rode a fifty-gallon water barrel while inside were two five-gallon water buckets for back-up, and storage cabinets with doors, drawers, and storage bins for potatoes and such laid out horseshoe-shaped around the front and sides leaving room for movement in the center or as a bed area for an injured cowboy on the trail, or for himself during the cold or rainy season.

Opening the tailgate would give him a kitchen counter with daily-usage cabinet and storage for his beloved Dutch ovens from which he produced delicious stews, sourdough biscuits and bread from his working base-stock, and occasionally a cake or some pies. All under the wagon hung a large drooping tarp into which he gathered firewood or dried cow-chips as they became available when on the trail. A shaving cabinet with mirror and needed shaving items was planned that would hang outside when on the trail for cowboys who wished to make use of it.

Cormac had been looking forward to an easy job of just riding a horse all day. By the end of the day, he had used up three horses and rounded up nearly three hundred head of cattle, and he was one tired farm boy. He was glad to climb back on his big, smooth-riding horse for the ride back to the ranch. So much for thinking a cowboy's life was an easy life.

He spent time with Lop Ear and Horse every morning and rode them back and forth to the ranch. The hands weren't expected to work late on Saturday night and not at all on Sunday, unless there was a need. Cormac took his horse-duo for long rides every Sunday morning that almost always turned into runs. Having learned that not only could they run, but loved doing it, was like found money.

Any little excuse found them flying over the flat prairie or sloping hills, jumping streams or logs, cutting up like the youngsters they all were. He kept working with them on kneeling and lying down on command and began teaching them to play hide-and-seek by following his scent. Whenever they found him, he gave them a carrot or an apple if he had one, sugar water if he didn't.

Within four days' time, Cormac was in and out of the brush like he had been born to it and hitting most rope throws successfully. He had been knocked off his horse twice, had his horse knocked down once with him on it, and had his hand mashed between the rope and the saddle horn. He never complained about any of it.

He got made fun of regularly, but only because someone else was usually around to see his tumbles and mistakes, and the fun-making was just that: all in fun. Cowboys worked hard and appreciated a good joke. As was his nature, Cormac jumped right in and was the first one in the saddle in the morning, and the last one to give it up of a night. The job was a good fit, and Cormac had made friends by the end of the second day.

The branding corrals were portable and had to be moved every three or four days. Cormac took his turn at roping and branding, getting the bumps, bruises, cuts, and rope burns that went with the territory—Josh had lost two fingers on his left hand and walked with a limp. Cormac twisted his leg throwing a large calf, burned the hip of his other leg when a steer bounced the iron out of his hands and it fell against his hip, with the red-hot iron sticking to his skin.

He learned to top off an unruly bronc feeling his oats on a cold morning. Some did love to buck first thing in the morning. Often they would stand half asleep while paying no attention to the saddling process, and as soon as a cowboy's bottom hit the saddle, they would stick their nose in the dirt and go to bucking. Cormac thought it a hell of way to start the morning. On day four, there were more cowboys than usual getting ready to go out, but Cormac didn't notice. Maddy, a young wrangler from Colorado, had Cormac's horse already saddled for him and tied outside of the corral. "She looks so much like mine, I had her roped and haltered before I realized she wasn't my horse and as long as I had her, I figured I would throw your saddle on for you."

"Well, that's mighty nice of you, Maddy," Cormac answered him as he swung into the saddle. He and the little brown mare had gotten used to each other, and a couple of crow-hops of a morning and she would settle right down. This morning, he wasn't really paying attention. "What part of Colorado you from?" he asked. "I was through Denver and Boulder a while . . ."

All hell broke loose when he hit the saddle. That little brown filly exploded into an untamed piece of wild bronc moving all directions at the same time, with a strong itch to dump him and head out for the wild places. Getting almost perpendicular on the first buck, she followed it up by going sideways, sunfished a few times with her belly to the sky, and hit perpendicular with her second try. Unexpecting and inexperienced, Cormac lost one stirrup on the first jump, his quick-grabbed grip on the saddle horn with the sunfishing, and the other stirrup and all contact with the saddle when she hit perpendicular. He hit the dirt upside down and hard about ten feet away with all the breath knocked out of him while the horse took off hell bent for leather.

Peals of laughter confused him as he fought for his breath and staggered to his feet. He stumbled to the rail-fence to sit down as the cowboys, still laughing, began mounting and moving out. "You all right?" asked Josh, walking up to him while choking back laughter.

"I reckon so, but what the hell is so all-fired funny about me getting bucked off? And I wonder what's wrong with my little mare? She and I was getting along right well, at least I thought so."

"Before you try again, you better check under your saddle first. Somebody probably put a burr under your saddle blanket."

"Why in the hell would they do that? I coulda broke my damn fool neck."

"They were just having some fun with the new guy. Don't be too mad, you'll get your turn later with some other new guy." Cormac looked up as Maddy rode by laughing at him. Cormac had to smile when he pictured himself sailing through the air upside down. "All right, Maddy," he called. "You got me this time."

When he got his breath back, catching his mare took some doing. She didn't want to go through that again. Sure enough, when he raised up the back of the saddle blanket, he found a big ole sharp cockle-burr. "You better rest her for a couple days," Josh called to him. "Her back is going to be sore, and we don't want to make it worse."

Josh taught him how to splice a broken rope or braid a new one. To Cormac, Josh seemed to be taking care to teach him about everything, and he was a willing student. He learned fast.

A month later, on the last day of the roundup, Josh figured most of the stock had been rounded up and had all the punchers looking harder and deeper back into the brush for any last holdouts. Cormac followed the tracks of fifteen or twenty head of cattle until they disappeared into a stream and he lost their sign. He figured they probably had already been brought back as there were horse tracks following them, brought to his attention by one having an odd-shaped hoof.

That was the day he met Old Mossy. Old Mossy was five years old, the biggest steer in the bunch, and had never been branded. He had been spotted a few years back, but escaped into the brush after knocking down a rider and managed to stay hidden for a couple of years.

On two other years' roundup, he was able to dodge the rope and again escape into the brush. Another year, Josh had gotten a rope on him, but the wiley old steer went sideways, pulling the horse over and pinning Josh's leg. Old Mossy spun back and only another rider turning him had saved Josh from getting gored, and probably killed.

Cormac had made it a habit of counting the cattle when he found them before running them in. On the last day of the roundup, after counting the thirty-six cattle he found in an arroyo, he left them to ride around and get behind them. While riding through another narrow boulder-strewn arroyo with nearly vertical sides of steep sand and broken rock with occasional young Ponderosa Pines and a few outcroppings, he came face-to-face with the elusive steer.

With murder in his heart, wild-eyed Old Mossy dropped one horn to a lance position and charged with about fifty feet between them and no room to turn around. Cormac's only chance was to try to make the impossible climb up the side. He turned the cowpony into the hill and used his reins as whip on her rump and, for the only time in his life, wished he were wearing spurs.

The little mustang was game and gave it her all, but the slope was impossible. Her hooves were digging a groove into the hill, causing a chain of events with a most unlikely conclusion. The dirt being pulled away caused a minor landslide that, in turn, caused some dirt and a rock on the lip of the ravine five feet above the ravine floor to fall. A rock that was lodged under the front of a twelve-inch boulder slipped, causing that boulder to then roll off the edge of the arroyo upon which it had been sitting and under which the steer was just passing. The boulder bounced off Old Mossy's head, knocking him colder than a Dakota icicle, as Cormac would tell it in later years.

"Well I'll be damned," Cormac said to his pony. He could see from the steer's sides swelling regularly that it was still breathing. An idea for a little fun occurred to him. The steer had fallen to his side, leaving a small amount of room between itself and the arroyo wall.

Cormac urged the little pony forward to step over the steer's front legs, and then his back legs where the arroyo was slightly wider, just wide enough to get the horse turned around. Keeping a close eye on the steer, Cormac put his noose over the steer's horns and snugged it down tightly around their base, tied the other end of the rope to his saddle horn, picked up a handful of rocks and a large stick, poured some water from his canteen onto the steer's face, and waited behind Old Mossy for him to come out of it, which didn't take long.

The steer regained consciousness and staggered to its feet, standing head down and spraddle-legged until he regained his balance. Once he began showing signs that his mind was back in the game, Cormac hit it across the rump with the stick, yelled "Hiyah!" and then ran for his horse. The steer lunged forward and hit the end of the forty-foot rope as Cormac hit the saddle, and they all charged forward simultaneously.

Standing in the stirrups, Cormac yelled and kept yelling while throwing rocks at Mossy's rump, and they shot up and out of the arroyo at full speed. Running flat out, the steer was hightailing it straight at the branding corral where the men were working the irons in and out of the blazing fire.

Cormac let out his Rebel yell to get their attention, then as the steer saw the fire and swung to the right side to go around it and the pen, Cormac hauled back on the reins and slid the pony to a stop on his haunches just as the steer hit the end of the rope. It was like snapping the end of a whip with the steer swapping ends, going tail end forward, and spinning around in a half circle toward the fire and the men with the branding irons.

Unfortunately for Old Mossy, running the lead end of the rope forty feet in front of Cormac, when he spun, he was going too fast to keep his balance and his feet got tangled up, falling him onto his side not ten feet from the branding fire. Before he figured out what had happened to him and reacted to the situation, four cowboys were all over him and their combined weight made it impossible for him to get up. A fifth cowboy, carrying the branding iron, was right behind them and laid it into him. Old Mossy bawled as the smoke and stench of burning hide filled the air, and the cowboy holding down the front grabbed the rope off his horns and rolled aside. The others followed, letting old Mossy get to his feet. He bawled some more, and took off for the bushes, making a running pass at a cowboy on the way.

"How the hell did you do that?" Josh wanted to know as the

others gathered around when Cormac rode in. Everyone had agreed to not tell him about the loco steer just to watch the fun.

"What do you mean? I found that old boy and didn't think you boys would be able to get him down and keep him down long enough to brand him, so I reckoned I'd just run him in and drop him by the fire for you. I just threw my rope around his big ole horns and drug him out of the bushes, pointed him in the right direction, and hit him with a stick a few times to get him moving, and just run him on in. Was that all right?" he asked with feigned wide-eyed little boy innocence. "Did I do something wrong boss?"

"No! Hell no! But you're lucky that crazy old steer didn't take in after you. He coulda killed you like he tried to kill me."

"Him? Nah! He tried gettin' ornery at first, and him and me, we had us little talk, and I told him he shouldn't oughta be actin' that way and showed him the error of his ways, and he just came on along like a good fellow. Like I said, I had to hit him with a stick a time or two, but he weren't no real trouble." It occurred to Cormac that the others had known about the steer and intentionally not told him, like they hadn't told him about the burr under his saddle, and now Maddy was standing right there, ready to listen to every word he was saying. *Okay, fun's fun, and turnabout's fair play.*

"Back in Dakota," Cormac went on, "my pa taught me how to handle situations like that. He said when you run across a feisty old bull or mean horse, you just walk right up in front of him and look him in the eye and say 'now look here, you old steer. You ain't as mean as you think you are. If you don't settle down I'm just going kick you in the butt a few times until you do.' Once they know you ain't skeered of them, nine times outta ten, they'll just settle right down."

Let 'em try that on some loco steer and see what happens to them, he thought with an unsmiled smile. *What do you think of that, Pa?*

Josh said it was time to start wrapping up for the day, but Cormac told him that just before finding old Mossy, he had found some other cattle in a wash he wanted to bring in. "I'll ride with you," Josh offered. When they found the wash and looked down at the cattle bunched in the bottom, Josh said, "Good find. Looks like about twenty-five, maybe thirty head."

"No . . . it's, ahh," said Cormac, remembering he had already counted them and hesitating slightly for show. In storytellin', his pa had told him once, timing was everything. "There is . . . ah . . . thirty-six, actually."

"Okay smart-guy. We'll see," answered Josh.

As they drove the cattle out of the dry riverbed and confirmed the count was exactly thirty-six, Josh looked at Cormac strangely. "How in the hell did you count them so fast?"

"Oh, I didn't count them," Cormac answered seriously, shaking his head. "I just counted their feet and divided by four."

"Oh, to hell with you," Josh said as he spurred his horse away from Cormac. He knew he had been joked. *Maybe I'm turning into Pa,* thought Cormac happily as he watched Josh ride away.

CHAPTER 10

Stepping outside after helping clean up their dining room after supper, Cormac made himself a smoke. He heard a chuckle from the shadows of the night behind him. "Had a little fun with my boys today, did you?" Mr. Haplander came out of the night smoking a cigar.

"I just did what I was told, sir. Josh told me to bring in all the cattle I could find, and that's just what I did."

"It's all right, boy, I know my hands, and I'm sure there was more to the story, but a stick? You hit Old Mossy with a stick?"

"Yes, sir. I surely did."

Mr. Haplander chuckled again.

"Glad to hear you're making a place for yourself, son. I figured you would when I hired you. Sounds like everything is going all right for you, then?"

"Yes, sir. I think I can safely say that to be true. Thank you very much for the job."

"I noticed when you got here you were only wearing one gun."

"Yes, sir. I had only worn the other one because I was riding shotgun on the stage. Wearing both of them makes me feel like I'm showing off like a tinhorn gambler."

"Very wise, young man, very wise indeed. I'm proud of you. I haven't told anyone about what happened in Colorado, and I won't."

"Thank you, sir."

Mr. Haplander put out his cigar in the dirt. "Good night, boy," he said, and walked into the house.

"Good night, sir."

Mr. Haplander went into the house smiling. Laurie had been out of the room when Josh had told the story of Old Mossy earlier during dinner, and after she returned and could overhear, Mr. Haplander asked Josh to repeat it for him. Anytime there were good things that could be said about Cormac, he always made sure she overheard them. "He's quite a man," he added to Josh at the conclusion, for Laurie's benefit.

Mr. Haplander was hoping she would take an interest in Cormac instead of some of the other men with whom she was always flirting, before she got herself in trouble. She was too damned good looking for her own good, the spitting image of her mother when he first met her. He smiled at the thought. Oh yes, he definitely had to find her somebody worthwhile and be quick about it.

Cormac Lynch filled the bill nicely. He was a strong, hard-working, fine young man with courage, convictions, and principles that reminded him of himself when he was younger. He just had to be very careful and not get caught. Laurie was every bit as stubborn as her mother and had the same temper. If she suspected anything at all, it would be all over: so far, so good.

With the roundup completed, the next morning Josh sent Cormac to work in the mine. Horse and Lop Ear were happy he didn't have to leave them in the corral again. The other miners lived in Virginia City or the surrounding area. Other than Lucas, Cormac was the only one working both the ranch and the mine. He didn't understand why, but it made him feel kinda special. Lucas wasn't a talker. It was a quiet, but pleasant ride with little conversation other than as they were leaving.

"Why you taking her for?" Lucas wanted to know when Horse followed them out of the corral.

"She don't much like bein' left behind."

"What difference does that make? She's just a horse."

"Horses have rights, too. I can throw a saddle on her any time of the day or night. I can ride her up the side of a mountain, or into a raging river or a freezing blizzard, or ask her to run her heart out for me, and she will. She'll literally run herself to death for me if I ask her to. Whatever I want her to do, she'll do, as will Lop Ear. I think that has earned them a few rights to how they want to be treated. We three gottin' kinda used to travelin' together."

"Well, it's certainly fun to watch."

The Flying H silver mine was an intimidating sight. The big hole in the ground held up by some wood beams was not a place into which Cormac looked forward to going.

"It's not so bad once you get used to it," Lucas Haplander told him when he hesitated. Family resemblance ran strong in the Haplander family. The boys had the same bulbous noses and wide-set dark eyes of their father, and Laurie's face was a younger mirror-reflection of her mother. The men were tall, wide-shouldered, and strongly built, hard-working ranchers and miners, while Laurie and her mother were medium-tall with abundantly filled-out figures, although Mrs. Haplander was becoming somewhat pear-shaped with age. The teenage boy, Marcus, threw the whole plan off-kilter. He was short like his mother and sister, strong-chested and thick-necked like his father with a strong purposeful walk, for all intents and purposes like Old Mossy, with an attitude to match. If something didn't get out of his way, he would walk through it or over it and didn't much care which. He seemed to have no assigned responsibility and popped up here and there as he, or someone, deemed fitting.

In Cormac's mind, Marcus just didn't seem to fit the Haplander mold, but then Cormac didn't understand all he knew about the man/woman having children thing, and what he did know wasn't much. Living on an isolated farm with no contact with the other kids his age, his sexual knowledge was limited. Peeking under the blanket at Lainey had got him to wondering about it with some unfamiliar thoughts and feelings, but he wasn't making much progress on figuring it out. Watching Laurie bounce around the ranch kept bringing it to mind.

Stopping at the miner's shack, Lucas came out with a cap with a metal piece attached to the brim and a tin box.

"This is a miner's cap you can use until you get your own. The metal piece is for the candleholder when we get inside." Holding up a tin box with the soot-blackened bottom, and a tin cup affixed to the top; he removed the lid to show two trays inside, one on top of the other. "This is a miner's lunch pail I'll loan you.

"Duffy will put up a lunch for you. The bottom layer will be filled with coffee that you can heat in the cup over a candle, and the trays will usually hold sandwiches or some kind of Irish stew. Duffy makes an Irish stew to write home about.

"The men aren't due here for another thirty minutes. While we're waiting, let me show you the mine." With an uneasy feeling of trepidation, Cormac followed him into the blackness. The floor took a downward slant as soon as they entered, and they walked around a cart that Lucas explained was for bringing ore to the surface.

As they left the influence of the light flowing in from the entrance, Lucas took down some candles from a box on a shelf carved into the wall. He gave Cormac one new candle and two stubs to put in his pocket for emergencies.

He showed Cormac how to fasten the bent-spike candle-holder to his cap-bracket. "The spike can be driven into one of the timbers to hold the candle when needed." Lucas led the way into the mine.

"A mine is a passageway to the pitch-black bowels of the earth where absolutely no light of the sun ever reaches. If we want light in a mine, we have to create it.

"There are shelves with candles every hundred feet, but always, and I mean always, carry two stubs in your pocket as spares and some matches to get you to the next shelf and more candles. There will also be a box of matches on each shelf. If you smoke, you don't down here, only outside in the fresh air. Gases can build up and explode. You'll be working with me today and I will explain the twelve unbreakable safety rules as they apply. I repeat: they are unbreakable. You get no warnings. If you break any of them you are fired on the spot; draw your time and leave.

"Mining is completely different from punching cows. No horseplay down here. It's much more serious, and it's dangerous. There have been some accidents, but nothing serious, and we have had no fatalities. We want to keep it that way. A mine has to be taken seriously and understood. You can't just walk in and take out a big piece of the hill and walk out. If you try, it'll all come down on your head.

"You have to learn how she looks, and how she feels through the soles of your shoe, or when you put your hand on the wall, and you have to learn to recognize the sounds, rather its ground movement, or the Tommy Knockers."

"What're Tommy Knockers? Are you fixin' to pull my leg? I thought everything down here was supposed to be serious."

The flickering candle made shadows flit back and forth on the ceiling and walls as they passed under the equally spaced massive wood beams. Lucas had explained on the ride over that they were part of the timbering that had been learned from Cornish miners coming to America after the turn of the century in ought-two or three, when the minerals in their own mines had petered out.

"Tommy Knockers are hard to explain. They're kinda like the little people the Irish like to talk about. They can't be seen, but can sometimes be heard knocking in the walls or under your feet or up in the ceiling. Some miners have claimed to have been warned of a cave-in or led from one by following the sounds of a Tommy Knocker. Top-siders who aren't miners say they don't exist, so believe in them or don't, but do not ignore them."

On the way to the working, they passed several short tunnels that Lucas explained were drifts where they had drifted the tunnel a few feet one way or the other in search of the vein. After a short distance, it was abandoned if it didn't prove out. Two had been hollowed out into small rooms that had given them some rich ore but petered out, leaving a cave to be used for storage.

Presently, they rounded a corner into the main drift with a vein of rich silver ore, the value of which was kept secret, but it assayed high. They had been working it for three years. A portion of one wall near where the shaft entered appeared to be damp.

"It would be easy digging," Lucas agreed, "but it is just too unstable and too risky when it's wet, and that's most of the time. After every rain storm, or when the snow melts in the spring, we have to stay away from that wall for three or four weeks to let it dry out, before we can mine it, and even after that. There is no way of knowing if it's dried out back into the hill, so we just leave it alone." There were several ore carts, some sledgehammers, and more picks and shovels. Cormac correctly assumed he was going to become closely acquainted with all.

The high-topped farmer shoes he had saved came in handy. He wasn't afraid of hard work, had an eager mind, and learned quickly. He learned how to put his weight behind the swing of a double-jack or a pick for maximum penetration, and how to knock off the mud that built up on the steel. He learned how to set a charge and the correct amount of nitro to control penetration without bringing down the wrath of God.

But still, Cormac didn't take to the mining. He didn't like every part of his body being covered with dust every day and having it creeping into his ears and up his nose. It disturbed him that after carefully washing and scrubbing every part of himself thoroughly in the river, if he sneezed, what he blew out would be part dust.

For a short time, he tried wearing a full mustache like most of the other miners seemed to favor, but it felt funny, tickled his nose, was always full of dust, and he laughed at himself when he looked in the mirror. He recalled his pa having grown one, only to shave it off again after his mother said she wasn't going to kiss that thing. The thought made him smile wide.

Not being able to smoke when he worked in the mine, he took up tobacco chewing and didn't like that every time he spit, it was half dust. And he did not like being cooped up. He preferred being out under the blue sky as had been promised. And he didn't like the total darkness when the candle went out . . . total . . . complete . . . all enveloping blackness. When deep in the mine, he yearned for the view over his horses' heads as they crested a hill, swam a river, or flew across a grass-covered prairie.

He frequently reviewed his surroundings to place things in his mind, thinking of the possibility of a sudden cave-in that blew out all of the candles and blocked the entrance. What would he do? He had no idea. Lucas said it would depend on the circumstances. Not a fun thought.

The pick and shovel work and swinging a double-jack sledge-hammer or carrying timbers filled out his chest and shoulders, taking him up two shirt sizes and one belt size due to washboard-like stomach muscles. Overall, he had taken on some heft. Laurie had also done some filling out and enjoyed showing it around. When he was given chores to do around the buildings, she always found an excuse to come around and chat. She was right fun to watch and talk with but their meetings always left him with unexplained reactions with which he knew not what to do, but had begun thinking it would be fun to find out.

Most Saturday nights the hands got cleaned up and went into Virginia City to shop, if they had it to do, but mostly to get liquored up, play poker, spend their money on dance hall girls, or meet up with friends from other ranches and mines. Virginia City was a clean little town with two saloons, a few shops, a church and a school, one red-light house with six girls—two of whom were good looking—a livery, and a bank that was always closed whenever he was in town. He would usually have a few drinks with his friends, but mostly just enough to be sociable; he had never been drunk. After watching his friends sober up every Sunday morning, he allowed as how he would pass on that part.

Scott's General Store had a nice saddle that had caught his eye that looked to be about the right size for Horse and Lop Ear. When he had a little more money saved, maybe he would buy it if it hadn't been sold by then. When his pocket money reached a hundred and fifty dollars, he asked Mr. Haplander if he could take it to the bank for him and have them transfer it to his bank in Denver, and then do the same with fifteen dollars of his pay every month. Mr. Haplander smiled his approval and quickly agreed.

Every couple of months they let him work the ranch again, but inevitably, he always ended up underground again, two months up and two months down. He asked Josh once if he couldn't stay on the ranch, but was told the "old man" wanted him to alternate and learn the whole operation.

Saturday night in a small town was different than in the city. Farmers and ranchers and miners, who had worked all week from sunup to sundown, came to town to kick up their heels, or buy supplies, meet friends, socialize, get drunk, or to chase girls who came to town to be chased. They didn't want to go home with nobody having flirted with them, or made an outrageous comment to them.

"Hey, Mack," yelled a local in the corner. "My sister is still waiting for you to come see her."

Cormac just waved and headed for the bar. He remembered the sister. Beatrice. Cute as a button, schooled at an all-girls school in Boston, nineteen years old, looking for a husband, and protected by four older brothers, all as big as a house. Cormac had met her once in the town square for a picnic lunch. Apparently, she had gotten more of an education in Boston than her parents had supposed. She made it abundantly clear that she would rather be having a few drinks with Cormac at a secluded swimming hole outside of town. With four older brothers and an ornery pa, that looked like a sure way to end up married whether he wanted to be or not.

He ordered a beer at the bar just as a tall redheaded woman disappeared outside the window into the night. He forgot about his beer and ran out to the street to see a lady twice his age disappearing into a carriage. What was Lainey doing tonight, he wondered. In a foul mood, he returned to the bar as a cowboy from the Slash 7 Ranch entered the swinging doors at the same time. Cormac pushed him aside and stomped through the door. He had just put his foot on the railing and took a drink of his beer when he was yanked backward and thrown across the floor.

He looked up from the floor to see a muscular, blond, Swedish cowboy. He knew he was a Swede because the swede told him so his own self.

"Yoouu may tink I'm dumb juust 'cause I am Sveedish, but dat don't meen I am, and yoouu can push mee around."

"Well, you may think I am dumb because somehow you found out I am a farmer but that doesn't mean you can push me around," Cormac answered him as he got to his feet, and hit him, or meant to. When his fist got to where the Swede was, the Swede wasn't.

Cormac's second mistake had been when he got up off the floor. While he was getting up, the big fellow of Swedish extraction grabbed his arm and yanked him up across his massive shoulders, carried him out the door, and dropped him in the street.

"What the hell are you doin'?" Cormac wanted to know.

"Ever time soamebody vants to take a sving at the big Swede, I end up payin for a vindow or a meirror or some tables and chairs. I don't do thet enymore. If yoouu have to fight, it vill be outside." And then he proceeded to teach Cormac something about boxing.

Cormac got up confidently from the street and swung at the big Swede, and it was all downhill after that. That swing was the closest that he came to making contact. He had never seen so many fists in his life. Cormac finished the fight being pulled out of a horse trough in front of the saloon by his friends.

Later, Cormac got teased about it pretty good, too. He took the ribbing and let it pass . . . until the next Saturday night. The next Saturday night Cormac was waiting for the Swede, and they went at it again with the same results. It wasn't until the third fight that he got to hit the Swede, but it was a good one. Cormac had learned about the feint and was watching for it. The Swede was always dancing while jabbing with his left and holding back his right, cocked and loaded. Suddenly, he would feint a left jab and send a hard right cross down the chute that would have Cormac seeing stars and shaking his head, if he wasn't knocked down, or out. This time, Cormac had practiced and was prepared for it.

He began the fight with his same awkward footwork as usual, but when the Swede feinted with the left jab, instead of ducking left and leaving himself wide open for the coming right, he quickly changed his stance for more power in his left arm, brushed off the feint with his right hand, ducked right, and introduced the Swede to his left going in over the Swede's right that found only air. Cormac's left caught the off-balance Swede on the side of his head and knocked him ass-end over appetite. Cormac welcomed the moment to catch his breath while helping the Swede get back to his feet.

"Ah! Yooou've been practicing," said the smiling Swede with his accent. "Now ve haf better fight. Yaah, shure." The fight didn't last long after that. Cormac managed to duck and weave and block some of the incoming punches while improving his footwork, but the Swede didn't repeat his previous mistake, nor did he let anymore of Cormac's punches get through. They sparred for a couple minutes with the Swede enjoying himself, and then Cormac saw the look on his face change. "Uh oh," he thought, just as the Swede uncorked a left that staggered Cormac, and followed with a right brought up from the ground . . . or from the next county. It didn't matter where it came from. Either way, it put Cormac upside down into the water trough again. The Swede helped him out of it with an offer to buy him a beer.

Every Saturday night for the next seven weeks, Cormac was waiting for him, and every Saturday night for the next seven weeks Cormac got upended, but he continued to learn. He studied his opponent and practiced open handed with his friends what he had learned: how to duck and weave and slip punches; he learned footwork from watching his opponent's feet and went to wearing his flat-bottomed farmer-shoes for the fights after realizing the Swede had begun wearing his flat-bottomed boxer shoes for faster footwork and greater balance. He learned to keep his chin down and his guard up while using his elbows to protect his solar plexus and his fists to protect his face. He also learned how to block punches with his forearms and punch through his opponent.

The "Swede" turned out to be an ex-boxer from St. Louis working on the Slash 7 Ranch. Oftentimes the fight would last thirty to forty-five minutes: once it was over in three when Cormac got careless and let his guard down, quickly learning the folly therein. It became a joke in town with locals and cowboys coming miles to watch. All of the Flying H ranch hands and miners were there to cheer on Cormac with all of the Slash 7 riders there supporting his opponent. Some were making bets and some had standing bets on the eventual winner overall, and some just wanted to see if Cormac would finally give it up as a bad job, something at which he was just no darn good. It became regular Saturday night fare.

The saloons and sporting ladies did a booming business and some of the stores stayed open late. Everyone had a good time except the fighters. They tired of getting hit and walking around bruised and battered all week just to start all over again on Saturday night. Cormac's opponent was named Sven Arnbjorg, big, blond, strong as an ox, and he punched like a locomotive. He had boxed under the name of the "Big Swede."

Then one night, Cormac had a plan. He got in the first punch. Prepared for a long fight as usual, Sven led out with a half-hearted jab and Cormac was ready, he had gotten quickly into position, standing flat-footed and loaded for bear. When the Swede jabbed, Cormac put everything he had into a straight-out, right smash to his chin. Sven staggered back and back until finally his feet couldn't keep up with his body and he tipped over. Feeling proud of himself, Cormac watched the big man fall into the dirt.

"Come on, big guy. Get up here and take your lickin' like a man," Cormac teased. "Yaah, shuur," Cormac mimicked. "Yoouu ged up her and I knock sum mor stuffin's outta yoouu." He was surprised to see the Swede do just that. Sven stumbled a little, but he got to his feet and looked at Cormac wearing a look Cormac had not seen before. The fun was over. The big Swede with years of boxing and many fights to his credit with only two losses, the fighter who had only quit fighting because he had badly hurt another fighter and did not want to do it again was mad to the core.

Until then, he had been holding back just a bit, taking a little off his punches, not moving in quite as quickly as he would have in a real match, he had just been having fun. No more. All bets were off now. One bystander heard Cormac mumble "Oh, damn!" and they went at it for real. The Big Swede against a big Celt with no holds barred.

With his chin neatly tucked in behind two huge fists, a newly determined Sven Arnbjorg came in raining punches, hooks, and crosses all over Cormac. The ferocity of the attack took Cormac by surprise, and a well-aimed right blurred his vision.

With his forearms and shoulders, Cormac managed to cover up, but Sven caught him with a couple of good ones that jumbled his thinking, but he staved off the onslaught long enough to get his wits back and launched a counter-attack. Though the Swede kept his face well protected, Cormac snuck one through from time to time and peppered him with body shots, all the while alternately taking and getting slammed by big Swedish fists coming from every direction. Both fighters sometimes got knocked on their nether ends, and both waited for the other to regain their feet.

It was a tit for tat slugfest for over an hour; Cormac's legs were getting wobbly, his arms were feeling like lead weights, and his breath was burning his lungs, but he could see Sven also weakening, and when Sven slipped and went to one knee, Cormac backed away and stood gasping for air, with his fists hanging at his sides, waiting for Sven to get up.

From those positions, they looked at each other, and without a word between them, agreed. It was all over but the shoutin'. The crowd had gathered larger than ever. Cowboys, miners, store owners, bartenders, sporting girls, men and women alike all watched in utter silence as Cormac walked unsteadily forward and Sven got to his feet. With their hands and faces a bloody mess, both fighters stood face-to-face with still not a word between them until Cormac asked raggedly with his Swedish impression, "Yoou redy for some beer?"

"Yah, shuure," the big Swede answered.

"Yah, shuure," Cormac answered.

And then came the shoutin' as the crowd came to life whooping and hollering and yelling and hat throwing and even a few guns fired into the air. This fight would long be remembered and long be hashed and re-hashed. Some had heard of professional bare-knuckle fights lasting fifty or sixty rounds, but this had been a no-round fight: no chance for either participant to rest. It had been a slugfest, plain and simple. Holding each other up, but under their own power, they led the crowd into the saloon for the first of many drinks. First a double shot of whiskey from the special bottle like every bartender kept under every bar, washed down with a lot of beer.

In appreciation for attracting so much business, the saloons gave them free drinks and offered to pay them to make it a regular Saturday night attraction.

"Either yoouu got ta be nuts or yoouu tink I yam if yoouu tink I fight him again," Sven told the group of owners that approached them.

"Even if you offered me a whole saloon," Cormac agreed, "I wouldn't fight him again for it."

Mooney's Café gave them free steak suppers; Scott's General Store offered them discounts on new saddles, and the red-light ladies offered them free samplings of their pleasures. Together they had the drinks and steaks, and Cormac said thank you very much, maybe later, to the other offers. He had heard of the health problems resulting from spending time with some of the sporting girls.

Now the saddle was a horse of a different color. That was mighty tempting. He had wanted one for a long time, and wanted to make sure he got the right one, but he just couldn't make up his mind. The brown leather of the saddles had a special gleam to it sometimes and seemed to feel smoother, but black saddles had a charm of their own. He remembered seeing a Mexican saddle with special stitching in a small leather shop in

Denver that was beautifully made, but had an oversize saddle horn. *Just too many decisions to make right now*, he thought. *Better wait a bit until I've had a chance to look at a few more.* He told them he would let them know later. Sven made arrangements to go by the next day for a saddle and was being escorted up the stairs of a side-street house by two lovely admiring ladies as Cormac rode out for home. Sven happened to look out at the street as he rode by and waved with a goofy smile on his face.

––––––––

There were a few more fights after that. Cowboys being what they are, some couldn't resist a good challenge, and he was a challenge for them. But mostly, it was good clean fun until an oversize, drunken Mexican half-breed going by the name of Ghago, with the help of two cronies, decided they were going to take Cormac apart and see what made him tick. As Cormac walked through the swinging doors into the bar, Ghago hit him and knocked him backward into the street and the three of them charged after him.

As he staggered and stumbled backward down the two steps to the dirt street, knowing he couldn't regain his balance in time to meet the fast advancing threat, he let himself fall backward and rolled over to his feet in time to double over the closest attacker with a kick squarely between the legs. By their rules, fair play was out of the question.

Expecting to find him down and helpless, the second attacker had done a running dive from the top step leading to the wooden boardwalk. Cormac grabbed his outstretched arms and, using the attacker's own weight, swung him in a half circle, launching him into the horse trough just as Ghago slid to a stop in front of him. Cormac let loose his best punch, which staggered the

Mexican backward against the side of the nearest horse at the tie-rail. Slender and wiry, Ghago was fast on his feet.

When he bumped into the horse, his hand went up to the back of his neck, and as he caught his balance and stepped forward, a throwing knife appeared in his hand and flashed downward. Cormac was slowed by the thong still holding his gun from falling out of his holster, but his first shot was still fast enough to stop Ghago's throw with a bullet in the middle of his chest.

The second shot took the survivor of the kick, a hearty soul hunched over holding himself with one hand while gritting his teeth and coming up with a gun in the other. Cormac then turned toward the third gunman rising out of the horse trough with a gun in his hand, causing an instantaneous change of heart. The eyes of the would-be attacker opened wide in shock, and he threw his gun into the street. "No! Please!" he cried with both hands stretched out in front as if to stop the bullet he knew was coming.

Cormac's gun was already aimed at his chest with the hammer back and his thumb just beginning the slide off. All that would have been necessary was to let his thumb slide off the edge. He let it go, but stopped it. It was a temptation, but he remembered telling Lop Ear a long time ago that he couldn't shoot everyone, and the man had dropped his gun. He hesitated. His life had come down to this. From a happy family pickin' potatoes to this: Cormac Lynch, killer of men.

Awe, Lainey, what happened? What did I do that was so terrible?

"Oh, hell!" he said finally. Cormac adjusted his aim a bit and let the hammer fall, putting a hole in the shoulder of the gunmen's gun arm. It spun him around, and he stood holding his wound, expecting another bullet.

"While that's healin'," Cormac told him, "think about what happened here every time it hurts. The next time you're inclined to pull that gun on somebody, remember how you felt looking down the bore of a forty-four when it was doing business."

A boy of maybe fourteen or fifteen was one of the onlookers who had quickly gathered when the fight began.

"Are you Mack Lynch?" he called.

Cormac allowed as how he was.

"Thought so. I've heard about that draw. It's even faster than they said." His voice was loaded with admiration. His words called Cormac's attention to the fact that the speaker was wearing two guns. He raised his eyes to look into the excited eyes of a kid. Cormac started to say something to him and then remembered that he himself had killed four men by that age. The thought was sobering; having a fun evening no longer interested him. Lop Ear and Horse had come up to sandwich him and share his sober reflections.

"How 'bout we go home, guys." It was an easy step into Lop Ear's saddle, and as a threesome they plodded sadly out of town with him wondering if wherever his family was, were they still proud of the man he had become.

CHAPTER 11

Winters were cold and Cormac found a benefit to working in the mine deep beneath the earth; the temperature never varied more than a few degrees. After Christmas, he was sent out to the northern line shack with Wolfgang Hartzman, a stocky German ex-wrestler, another refugee from "the old country."

Mr. Haplander didn't like fences, but a valley on the north side of the Flying H led to a deep arroyo over which he had lost many head of cattle when, drifting with the wind, they fell over the edge to their deaths in a blizzard. A fence had been put up across the three-mile wide valley entrance and it needed to be monitored and kept in good repair from cattle knocking it down by leaning against the posts to scratch their backs. Two or three broken posts could easily lay down a fifty-foot section of fence.

Their job was to ride the gap and make repairs as often as necessary, blizzard or no. The amount of work didn't call for two men, one was plenty but the danger of a man being injured with no help for miles was real, and the men complained of being alone for long periods of time with nothing to do. Cabin fever was also real. Loneliness and being cooped up could get to a man. As a way of passing time, Wolfgang taught Cormac some wrestling moves, and Cormac reciprocated by teaching Wolfgang how to accurately hit what he aimed at.

Wanting to continue his mother's teaching, Cormac always carried a book in his saddlebag for spare-time reading, oftentimes just a dictionary from which he had learned things like *didactic* being an instructional way of speaking like a teacher might use, and *incommodious* meant inconvenient, but this time he had forgotten to bring one, and that, he thought, was downright incommodious. And didactic. How on earth would somebody come up with a word like didactic? Was someone sitting around one day thinking, "We need a word for instructional speaking. I know. Let's call it didactic and have faith that someone has a dictionary so they can find out what it means."

Also incommodious was climbing into a really cold bed at night that sat next to a really cold and thin cabin wall. "What you do," Wolfgang told him, "is get into bed and roll up into as small of a ball as you can, then as you get warm, you straighten out by degrees."

"Sure," Cormac answered. "But by the time you get straightened out all the way, I still got thirty degrees to go."

Cormac Lynch and Wolfgang Hartzman took turns starting the morning fire. A fire would be burning when they went to bed, which meant the next morning coldness would necessitate the sudden throwing-off of blankets, running to the potbellied stove, throwing in wood shavings pre-whittled for fire-starting, lighting a match to it, stacking increasingly larger wood pieces on the young flames, sitting the already prepared, and usually frozen, coffee pot on the flat stove top, and jumping back into bed until they could smell the coffee and hear it boiling and the cabin had warmed enough to get out of bed.

Other than the catalog in the outhouse, the only thing in the cabin to read was a dime novel left on the table by some past cowboy, written by an author back East named Buntline with stories purportedly about the "Real Western Frontier." Most western people thought it was mostly just real silly and figured Mr. Buntline had never been outside the city limits of his own town, let alone "out West."

They were happy when finally their time was up and their relief showed up on the horizon. By the time the relief riders arrived, Wolfgang and Cormac were packed, mounted, and saying good-bye.

Winter was replaced by a beautiful spring with wide Montana skies, so big and so very blue. Restlessness was settling in for Cormac. Working for twenty-five dollars a month for the rest of his life, half of it in a black hole in the ground, was becoming less and less appealing. He had been there nigh on a year, and for him it was work in the mine, work on the ranch, and go into town for drinks on Saturday night. He was getting fidgety, and the horizon was garnering his attention more and more as time went by more and more slowly. The novelty of a new job was wearing off and being replaced by boredom.

Mr. Haplander seemed to be continually requesting him for painting buildings and repairs or driving Laurie into town with the buggy for supplies. Running Lop Ear and Horse across the prairie was the only exciting thing in his life. The three of them looked forward to their Sunday-morning rides exploring the Rockies or flying across the prairies and over the gently rolling hills of the Flying H. They made it a point of always stopping by the patch of sweet clover growing on the afternoon-shady side of a close-by hill. The horses loved it, and Cormac sometimes even nibbled a few bites just to be sharing something with them. It wasn't bad. Over the years, he had eaten worse things. Lainey's cooking, for example. No, that wasn't true. It was just his old habit of teasing her that was kicking in.

He and Laurie were becoming close, and she was exciting to be around. She sat close to him on the buggy seat while on the way to town, touched his arms or hands frequently while talking to him, always had a smile for him, and gave him an excited kiss on his birthday. She had finished filling out, making it necessary for her and her mother to make all of her dresses and blouses. Store-boughts just didn't have enough room in certain places, and even then, some didn't seem to have come out right. They fit her more than a little bit close, and the buttons on her blouse were frequently straining to do their job. But her blue jeans fit just fine.

On one Sunday, Laurie was waiting for him at the corral with her Paint saddled and ready.

"Good morning," she said with a smile. "It's a beautiful morning and an early ride sounded great. I thought I would tag along with you, if that's alright."

"Sure. Let me throw a saddle on Horse, and we'll get going."

As he was finishing the task, she called to him as he was stepping into the stirrup. "I'll race you to the river." Taking off before he was in the saddle, she went out of the corral at a gallop and turned east. The river was two miles from the ranch buildings and served as their eastern property line. Horse was on the move while Cormac was still mounting, and Lop Ear was right behind.

Her Paint, Dandy, was fast. Cormac had seen her handily beat her brother's horse the first day he had arrived, but he was sure the Paint was no match for his duo. His early Sunday morning running rides had gone unnoticed with the other hands usually sleeping off their Saturday night trip to town.

Laurie was proud of her horse, and Cormac, not wanting to show her up and make her feel bad, held Horse back; besides, it was more fun to have her in front of him where he could watch her. Horse didn't care for that even a little bit, and kept trying to grab the bit in her teeth. She wanted to show that black-and-white horse what running was all about. Every time Lop Ear started to get ahead, Cormac called him back. He wanted to keep the race close. Of course Laurie was the first to the river where she pulled up, laughing.

"Those big ole fancy horses of yours aren't so much. I knew Dandy could beat them."

"She is a good runner; I gotta give her that," he told her. He wasn't lying. She probably would outrun most other horses, just not his.

Laurie stepped down and led Dandy along the river to cool her down. Cormac walked beside her, and Lop Ear and Horse followed along behind. Laurie kept looking back at them.

"I've watched them follow you all over the ranch, and I can't get over it. They're like puppies. How do you get them to do that?"

"I had nothing to do with it. It's their own idea."

The river had narrowed with water rippling over the rocks near the shore, and the sun was shining warmly on the grass. The only sounds were from the chuckling water and a few birds singing in the branches of the Ponderosa Pines that were filling the air with the sweet pine scent of sap running in the warmth of the morning sun.

"Let's stop for a while to enjoy the sunshine," Laurie suggested, while tying Dandy to a lower tree branch in such a way as to allow her to graze. Laurie walked down and stretched out on her back on the grass by the river with her hands behind her head. The blue jeans and long-sleeved blouses she normally wore fit her especially well, but Cormac couldn't remember having previously seen the ones she was wearing today. They were tighter even than normal, her blouse only just managing to stay together.

Cormac sat down beside her. "How long have you had Dandy?"

She smiled up at him for a long moment, her eyes sparkling with excitement and her face flushed. The strength of the thread holding the buttons onto her blouse and the very fabric itself were being severely tested as her bosom swelled with every accelerated breath. She asked him softly, "Do you really want to talk about horses?"

Cormac knew what she meant, and no, he really didn't want to talk about horses. She had grown into an extremely attractive woman with an abundant body made to please any man; the thought of unbuttoning those buttons had been full on his mind for some time.

He had frequently heard the hands discussing her looks and shape, and they all agreed that she and her parents had their caps set for Cormac. They figured her pa's wedding present would be a section of the Flying H upon which they could build a ranch. Cormac was glad he had some money in the bank with which to do it.

Cormac had always made little of their talk and laughed off the suggestion with a wave of his hand, but here it was. She was offering herself to him on a soft carpet of green grass under a clear blue Montana sky, with the soft lighting of the early-morning sun, a sweet pine fragrance in the air, and the music of the chuckling river nearby, almost as if the location had been carefully preselected. Her full lips looked mighty soft and inviting.

From time to time, a hand or a cowboy in town had tried to capitalize on the freeness of her spirit, only to find her flirty ways a charade. She was merely having fun, and like learning the range of a new rifle, after being a slender flat-chested adolescent who had suddenly developed abundantly overnight, she was experimenting with the range, power, and effects of her recently acquired figure. She would, however, not be lain down until she found her life's mate. Now she had made her choice and was going after him, all guns firing.

Cormac had fantasized about such a moment. He wasn't sure exactly how to do what was obviously expected of him, but he was certain he was going figure it out. Apparently it was something that comes natural. He had refused such offers before, but never from a woman such as Laurie Haplander. With Laurie, he realized, it was more than a physical attraction; he liked her a lot. They laughed a lot and enjoyed each other's company. She was an exciting, vibrant, and desirable woman, yet he was hesitant.

He recalled overhearing a conversation between his mother and Becky late one night when they had thought him to be asleep. His mother had revealed that she and their father had never gotten personal until they married. Cormac felt that to be a value worth honoring; it shouldn't just be recreational, he thought, but between two people with special feelings for each other; he believed that. But he and Laurie did have special feelings toward each other. But even that wasn't the main gist of it. So what was his problem? What was his hesitance? Why wasn't he already claiming his moment instead of thinking it to death?

Looking down at her smiling eager face surrounded by thick golden-blonde hair and wearing the look that had driven men insanely out of their minds for centuries, he found himself wondering why not. Wondering what in the world was wrong with him. Wondering if somehow, something in his violent past had affected him in some strange way. Wondering how she would look with red hair, or maybe a handful of freckles sprinkled across her face? . . . or if she was taller and her smile was a little brighter white? Wondering if . . . Damn! . . . Damnit, damnit, damnit! . . . Lainey! . . . Lainey Damn Nayle! . . . Damn that woman! She didn't want him anyway. Why couldn't she just get out of his mind and leave him the hell alone?

But, he had to stop this; he couldn't let it go any further: it wasn't fair to Laurie. She wasn't just offering the obvious, she was offering a lifetime with a home and kids, and arguing and making-up, getting up before dawn, working until long after dark, taking care of him when he was sick, crying with him when he failed, and a white picket fence with flowers in the yard and a vegetable garden. She was planning forever. The other hands were right; her father would most probably give them land for a ranch as part of the package. By agreeing to what she was offering today, he would be agreeing to the rest. But, he wasn't ready to do that, and he couldn't not tell her. He turned away.

"I'm sorry, Laurie," he said simply. "Any man in his right mind would jump at what you are offering me, but it wouldn't be fair to you. I like you a lot and think about you a lot, sometimes in the middle of the night in ways I can't tell you about. And I've thought of this moment, but now that it's here, I can't do it."

"What?" Surprise registered across Laurie's face. "What's the matter, Mack? What's wrong with me?"

Cormac couldn't look at her. "Absolutely nothing, Laurie," he answered, shaking his head. "Not one single thing. In fact, I can tell you a great many things that are wonderful about you and not one single thing bad. But to go with you to where this is leading us, you deserve someone who loves you, and I was just this moment forced to realize that I am not that someone."

"My pa loved one woman in his whole life, and I guess it's going to be the same with me."

Cormac took in a deep breath and exhaled slowly.

"Unfortunately for me, my 'one woman' can't stand the sight of me. I like you a lot, but I'm not in love with you in the way you want me to be, and it wouldn't be fair to you to let you go on thinking I am. There's a woman back in the Dakota Territory that I just can't seem get out of my mind. I'm sorry."

First she stared at him in disbelief, and then she sat staring into the river with tears flowing freely down her cheeks as her body shook with silent sobbing. Presently, she numbly stumbled her way to Dandy, and they rode back to the ranch in dismal silence.

Feeling nearly as miserable as she, Cormac could think of nothing to say that she would want to hear, and accordingly, said nothing. When they got to the ranch, still without speaking, she slapped his hands away as he tried to unsaddle Dandy for her. He remembered Lainey kicking his hands away from tucking in her blanket. He seemed to have that effect on women.

Going to the bunkhouse, Cormac rolled up his belongings and left.

"Tell your family good-bye for me, and I'm sorry. I didn't mean to hurt her," he told a surprised Josh on the way out the door to where Horse and Lop Ear were waiting.

Josh bristled, "Did you touch her? She doesn't do much around here but flirt with the hands, but she doesn't need you taking advantage of her. If you laid a hand on her, I'll . . ."

"No," Cormac cut in, "I did not take advantage of her."

He strapped the pack on Horse, and with his bedroll behind the saddle and a quick look at the house, rode out of the ranch yard. Laurie was simply standing forlornly on the porch between her parents with her arms hanging by her sides, as he rode away. Any money he had coming, Mr. Haplander would deposit into the bank—or he wouldn't.

If what he had done, or not done, in not taking advantage of her vulnerability was the right thing, why did he feel so terrible? Life was complicated and not for the weak.

With no destination in mind, he turned east. He had been hearing more talk of gold in the Black Hills. Maybe he could dodge the Indians and go hit a strike of some kind and get rich. Mid-day, he made a dinner camp with a small smokeless fire hidden from unwanted guests a short distance from a stream. There wasn't much in his pack; he should have gone into Virginia City for supplies, although there was still a mite of coffee, sugar, salt, and some flapjack makin's, and he knew how to hunt. He would have to make do. He did not want to explain why he was leaving.

With Horse and Lop Ear leisurely grazing their way to the stream, Cormac came out of his thinking-about-Laurie induced trance when the coffee boiled over and sizzled on the fire. As he reached across the fire to retrieve the pot, a voice came from behind him.

"You hold right still now, so I don't miss. I'm going to be the man who killed Mack Lynch, the Dakota gunfighter."

Cormac faked a quick right step, spun left, drew, and fired three times in quick succession. With no time to aim, he had to fire on the spin as soon as the gunman came into view. Not being able to depend on just one shot, he spread three and hoped for the best. Two of his shots hit their mark. It was the kid that had watched him shoot Ghago and his men in Virginia City.

Cormac walked to where the body lay. A kid, most likely with a father and mother waiting at home for him. A mother who had held him and loved him and had dreams for him. And now she would cry for him. Cormac sat down on a nearby log and stared at the dead boy. He was responsible for that. Cormac Lynch. Cormac Lynch had killed a teenage boy. He dug out his makin's and rolled a smoke.

When suppertime came, Cormac was still sitting on the log. His eyes burned and his throat was raw from too many cigarettes and his lungs hurt. How could this have happened? A young man had died at his hand because some worthless people had ridden out of the hills and taken Cormac's life from him, and his father's life, and his mother's life, and his sister Rebecca's life, and the children she might have had.

No more plans did they get to make. No children did Becky get to have or teach how to tie their shoes, or kiss their owies, or make breakfast for and celebrate birthdays with. No times did she get to lay in her husband's arms in bed late at night and look out the window at the stars. And his parents did not get to hold Becky's children, and kiss them goodnight and see them excited when their grandparents came to visit. Death was very final. And now Cormac Lynch had taken another life. Maybe Lainey's attitude was right after all. Maybe she was right to not want him around.

The kid must have somehow learned where he worked and waited for him to leave the Flying H. So now Cormac Lynch was a gunfighter, not a reputation he wanted. He could change his name, he reckoned, but it would just happen again under the new name, making a name change again necessary. Times were changing with most of the country relying on judges, juries, and executioners, but frequently on the frontier, the gun was still the final word.

Cormac briefly considered changing his name but decided against it. He was and would always be, the son of John and

Amanda Lynch, brother to Rebecca Lynch, and that's just the way it was going to be. Mr. Cormac Lorton Lynch and the rest of the world were just going to damn well have to deal with it. This kind of thing was apparently going to be a condition of life, and he would just have to deal with that, too; he would have to be ready.

"Well you might, boy," his pa would have said. "Well you might."

When his tobacco was gone, Cormac tied the kid across his horse and took him to the sheriff in Virginia City. The kid's one shot had burned Cormac's right forearm wrist to elbow, proving that it had been self-defense. Cormac got a bath and a room at the Virginia City hotel. That night he dreamed of lying next to Lainey on the grass beside a creek and woke up wishing he had dreamed just a few minutes longer. It had been looking like it was going to have a completely different ending. The next day he bought plenty of supplies and headed south; he had to go someplace and east was Black Hills chock-full of Indians, west was a whole range of mountains, and north was Canada. That only left south.

———

And so began the training of a gunfighter. From then on, he would practice every day but Sunday. Practicing on Sunday to kill somebody just seemed wrong. That very day Cormac began the one-hour daily practice routine, drawing from every conceivable position with one or both guns, right- or left-handed. He drew while standing, sitting, lying down, riding on a horse, drawing while rolling and shooting, or diving left or right into a mid-air, roll-over-to-face-backward position.

After that day, without fail, he worked on one-handed draws from either side, the cross draw, drawing a gun from his belt, drawing a right-hand gun with his left hand, and his left hand gun with his right hand. He practiced the border shift, the road agents spin, and any other way he could think of, and he practiced daily. If he was going to stay alive, he would have to be prepared for anything.

Traveling all day was just that: traveling. His mind was dwelling unhappily on events of the last few days. That night he slept restlessly and woke up to the sound of a gun battle in the distant east.

He sighed. "I guess we better go see what's goin' on, guys. Better put on your runnin' legs today, we may need 'em." Hurriedly, Cormac packed, checked the loads in his guns, filled all the cylinders, and strapped on the Colt. The scattergun was tied on the pack in its normal quick-release fashion, and GERT was comfortably under his right leg. He held the duo to a comfortable gallop a little below full out. He didn't want them worn out in case he found more than he was bargaining for.

The reports were from several different calibers in spasmodic bursts. A sudden burst of multiple gun voices sounding like single-shot rifles, judging by the rapidity of the shots, would be joined by what sounded like two repeating rifles. Many Indians had gotten their hands on repeating rifles, but not all. The battle sounded like two persons with Winchesters, or maybe Henrys, which had been Winchesters before there were Winchesters, holed up and fighting off a war party of Indians with single-shot rifles.

Unhappily, it was just that. Cormac was correct.

With his long-glass, he could see into a shallow valley from behind a group of hilltop boulders. Two buckskin-clad white men were pinned down in a boulder group encircled by a red-skinned welcoming party. Outnumbered in an indefensible position, it was only a matter of time. Out in the open, the boulders had been easily surrounded. The attackers could draw the fire from one direction and attack from another. Cormac could make out four Indian bodies and one Indian pony carcass sprawled motionless on the ground. The trapped men were not going down easily, but they would eventually go down. Unless they got some help.

"Hang on, boys. Here comes the cavalry." Dropping back, Cormac made his way around the hill to a stand of Ponderosas on a slight rise and unlimbered GERT. After laying out a few cartridges for rapid access and removing the thongs holding his six-guns in their holsters, he rested the rifle on a branch for support, quickly realizing there was another with a better height. Unnoticed by him, on the first resting site was a puddle of freshly dripped sap from a higher branch making GERT's front stock a sticky mess. Nuts!

While the two were busy holding the attackers at bay, three sneakers on the side were inching unnoticed toward them flat on their stomachs. From his viewpoint, Cormac could see the buckskin-clad men were being manipulated. Indians on the south side would suddenly fake an attack to draw their fire, dropping at the first shots to avoid any more losses, but while the white men were shooting, the Indians crawling up on the north side would advance a few feet, and then the attack would reverse. Each attack put them six or eight feet closer and kept attention away from the sneak attack coming up from the side.

Cormac set GERT's adjustable sights to compensate for the approximately two hundred-yard distance, lined them up on the lead sneaker, inhaled, exhaled slowly, and held the exhale while gently squeezing the trigger until GERT bellowed. The forward Indian's body jerked noticeably followed a half instant later by the accompanying report. Cormac quickly pulled back the bolt to eject the spent cartridge, reloaded, and caught another ex-sneaker running away.

Two shots were enough to give away Cormac's location, and the mounted Indians sped toward him. He missed a running target with another shot from GERT, quickly bringing both pistols into the fray for a couple of shots each before doing a fast reload and firing of GERT and the scattergun that was followed by more pistols shots. The range was too great for pistols, but Cormac was hoping to give the appearance of more than one defender.

The Smith & Wesson was a good little gun, but it had a long ways to go to compare with the Colt for range and accuracy. The Colt picked another of the charging Indians off his horse, and that was enough for them. The front-most Indian yelled something in his own tongue and pointed at Horse and Lop Ear standing a ways off from Cormac, and the Indians headed for parts unknown. Cormac picked off one more with a long shot from GERT as they went over the next hill, foolishly riding straight away from him. They should have known better.

By the time Cormac had reloaded his guns, the buckskin-clad men were riding up the hill to thank him. With one tall and broad, at least two or three inches taller than Cormac, and the other tall and haggard in appearance, they were a sight.

Looking around quizzically, the skinny one spoke.

"Man. Wit all tha firpower and all, I thot the Cavry was here or sumthin. Whatcha got up heres anyways?"

"A couple pistols, a rifle, and a shotgun. I was hopin' they would think there were several men here. I guess it worked. Where you boys headed?"

"The Rockies. We been trappin' the Black Hills, but all the fuss bout gold's got the Injuns all het up. We've had a couple close calls lately from sum of the young bucks and reckened it might be a good idee to have a look at the Rockies." He looked at the pack riding on Lop Ear.

"Any chance you got sum coffee in thet ther pac? We relized them thar ainjuns was comin' and had to leave our outfit behind and hightail it outta camp yestday morn'. Didn't mattr ta Abe any, but me, I had a knife I set store by in thet pak. We just ben stayin' a half jump heda them eva since. Some coffee wuld go down rite good."

"Sure. If one of you will go check on your friends to see if they're stayin' gone like good fellows, I'll fix us some breakfast. I had to skip out on mine when I heard your commotion."

"Wal, we sure thank y'all for com'n. They kinda had us ovr a barel." Tall and broad turned to tall and skinny. "You wanna chek out their direction and I'll go hav a luk at our bak tral and mak sur we got no cumpny com'n up from behind."

Knowing his own appetite and guessing at theirs, Cormac had a couple plates filled to overflowing with thick bacon and flapjacks along with a can of molasses warming by the fire in jig time. The horseshoe coffee was hot and strong.

"I only got one cup. You'll have to fight over it between ya."

"Nah, we drunk outta tha saim cup bunchs a times," answered the broad one. "Sum tims it cain't be he'pd." The three of them fell to it. This was eating time; talking time would come later.

"So tell me about the Black Hills," Cormac said after the food was gone and the coffee cup was full again. Cormac was using his metal plate from which to drink coffee. It worked, but cooled the coffee too fast.

"Well, sir. First let me thank you for the grub. My back bone was getting sore from rubbing on my belt buckle." Then he laughed at the look on Cormac's face. "I'm from Ohio. Cuz there is from the Ozark's Mountain country, that's why we speak differently. He's my cousin, I just call him Cuz, cause it's easier than saying Bartholomew all the time and shorter than cousin.

He doesn't like being called Bart. My name is Abe Langston. Abe, for Abraham, after Abraham Lincoln. My pop was a friend of his when they were kids. What's your handle?"

Cormac told him, and they shook hands all around.

"I speak more better, y'see, cause I had the chance to go to school and get some eddication? He didn't. He's just *dumb*." He exaggerated the improper accent and the word *dumb*, and ducked the empty tin cup thrown at his head.

"You asked about the Black Hills; they're magnificent. That's them yonder stickin' up in the distance. See how dark they look?" Cormac nodded, they were truly magnificent. Abraham went on. "That's the Ponderosa Pines makin' 'em look black. It's where God lives, a mountain man's heaven. The first time we went in, we were speechless. There was an over-abundance of goats, deer, elk, bear, buffalo, beaver, a couple jillion birds, and streams full of the largest trout you ever saw. I tell you, it's a woodsman's paradise. We thought we'd found the Garden of Eden. It's a heaven right here on this earth, and the Indians want to keep it that way. They don't over-hunt an area. If white men get in, they'll ruin it."

He hesitated and then nodded at the yellow Bull Durham tag hanging out of Cormac's pocket. "Y'all saved our lives and fed us, so I hate to ask for more, but you reckon we can have some of that? It's been a long time since I had a smoke of real tobacco instead of dried leaves and it's looking almighty good— if you can spare some."

Cormac threw him the bag. "Keep it. How about you, Cuz? You want one? I got plenty." With no hesitation, Cuz nodded eagerly, and Cormac got two more bags out of his pack and tossed one to each of them, taking back his own half-empty bag. "It's worth it to hear what you're telling me. I was born and raised not far from the Black Hills and have heard stories about them all my life, but never from anyone who had actually been there. Go on, please."

"The Indians call them Paha Sapa, which is Sioux for the Black Hills. Newspapers have called them mysterious and unexplored. They claim no white man had ever entered them and that there have been no maps of the area until an army general, I think his name is Custer, went in there last year, but mountain men have been through there for years. Jedediah Smith took fifteen trappers there a long time back, and Cuz and I have been there nigh on to five years, and we've met a few others going and coming. Some weren't too smart and lost their hair for it.

"The Indians knew we were there but left us alone as long as we didn't flaunt it in their faces because we provided a lot of food for them the first year. It was a hard winter, and they were struggling to survive, only having mostly bows and arrows and the snow being so deep they couldn't get around. With our rifles, we dropped several deer and elk and one bear close to their villages in places where they could easily get to them and left them to be found. They didn't spoil because of the cold.

"The Indians been there forever. It's the religious center of their world. First one tribe takes over until they get pushed out by another. The Arikara were run out by the Arapaho who got pushed out by Cheyenne, who got pushed out by the Kiowa, who was then run out by the Lakota Sioux. The Sioux came to the Black Hills to purify themselves, they say, and to seek visions. I think the Lakota Sioux are pretty much firmly entrenched there now. They've proven to be one of the strongest and most moral tribes, although some of them do believe in polygamy. One wife takes one side of the teepee, leaving the other side for the newcomer, and they share the wifely duties and chores.

"Their Wichasa Wakan, that's their word for medicine man, or holy man, believe their medicine is stronger in the Black Hills, and they have healed people that had been given up for dead. In fact, some rumors claim that some dead have even been brought back to life."

"Do you believe it?"

"I don't know what to believe. They say Crazy Horse is a mystic who spent three days on Bear Butte in the Black Hills searching for a vision. They say in his vision, he saw himself leading his warriors to great victories while riding out in front of them with many bullets flying around him, but none of them actually hitting him. Since then he has led every attack from out in front, and to this day has never been hit." He paused to build another smoke to replace the one he had let burn out. "And now we have the Helawees," he added.

"Who are the Helawees?" Cormac asked when Abe's cousin got over a sudden choking spell.

"They're just a small tribe of Indians come down from the north," Abraham explained. "A very brave bunch; the only thing keeping them from being great warriors and hunters is their poor sense of direction. They spend a lot of time climbing tall trees, looking around, and calling out, "Where the helawee?"

"Okay, yeah, yeah," laughed Cormac, waving his hand. "I've been hearing talk about gold in the Black Hills."

"If you're thinkin' 'bout goin' in after it, *I* wouldn't. According to the newspaper article, the Laramie Treaty gave the Black Hills to the Sioux for their absolute and undisturbed use and occupation forever, and now, according to the new paper, Custer claims to have found gold there, and people are beginning to want it back, and the Indians are understandably disturbed with the Wasichus, that's Sioux for white men."

"Two aus!" interjected Cuz excitedly, pointing at Lop Ear and Horse. "Two aus!"

"Well, I'll be," answered Abraham. "I think you're right, Cuz."

"Now what's that all about?" asked Cormac.

"He just realized that you are the one the Indians call Two Horse."

"What?"

"We been hearing about you. Two Horse. They speak of a white man who rides with two mighty horses faster than the wind, and they call him Two Horse."

"That explains it. They have tried to catch us a time or two," responded Cormac. "The leader of the group that just left pointed at my horses and yelled something to the others on their way out. Well, that's wonderful. That's what that is. That's just damned wonderful. We better get out of here in case they return with a bunch of their friends."

"After today they'll probably call you Two Horse with Long Rifle. It'll be big medicine if any of them can kill you and take your horses. You're a challenge for them, so watch yourself. It would be a great honor to hang your scalp on their lodge pole and have your horses. Quite a coup."

With the help of Cuz and Abe, they were packed and moving within five minutes. After riding back to Virginia City, the three got what they needed and were saying good-bye at the edge of town when a rider came tearing into town, hell-bent for leather. "Cave-in! Cave-in!" he yelled. "The Flying H had a cave-in!"

CHAPTER 12

D amn!" erupted Cormac. "I gotta go. That's where I worked until a few days ago. If you guys wanna come help, we'll be needin' all the help we can get."

An unselfish lot, western people were prone to helping each other. The mountain men easily agreed.

"Okay. Thanks," Cormac said. "Go north and bear just a little west for about fifteen miles, and I'll meet you there."

"Where are you going? They'll be needing help right away."

"I know," Cormac answered. "That's why I can't wait for you. I'll go on ahead."

"I don't know what you mean. We are ready to leave with you right now," Abe said with a look of confusion on his face.

"It's quicker to show you than explain," Cormac answered, loosening Lop Ear's reins. "Let's go, boy!" he called. Lop Ear sensed the urgency in his voice and leaped forward, full out within steps; Horse was right with them.

In amazement, the mountain men watched them ride away. "So that's what the Indians are talking about," Abraham told Cuz as he put the spurs to his Appaloosa.

With both horses white with sweat, Cormac crested the hill faced by the mine entrance. Unloading before Lop Ear had come to a stop, he handed his reins to a woman in a crowd of flustered onlookers. "Walk him until he cools off."

"What about your other horse?"

"She'll follow," Cormac told her, and ran to the mine. A flurry of activity was happening at the entrance. A man Cormac did not recognize was walking quickly into the mine with a bottle of explosive. Cormac grabbed his arm to stop him.

"Wait! What are you doing with that?"

"The shaft collapsed. We gotta get it open again quick before they run out of air, if they are even still alive." He tried to pull away from Cormac.

"No!" said Cormac. "An explosion could make it worse. We have to dig them out."

"I'm a miner," said the other. "This is the only way."

"I worked in this mine until a couple of days ago," Cormac told him. "I know what I'm talking about. We can't use explosives."

"You must be new then. I've been doing this for years." He yanked his arm free. "We are going to blow a way in to them," he said as he started walking away. Cormac grabbed him again with his right hand and the bottle of explosive with the left. Letting go of the man's arm, Cormac ended the argument with a hard right to the jaw. Turning while the man was still falling; he returned the explosive to the shack as Laurie rode up with a group of ranch hands, and the man trying to blow up the mine was hightailing it over the hill.

"Where's your dad and brothers?" he asked her as she ran up to him.

"They went to Denver to do some business. I'm in charge of the ranch. Lucas is down in the mine."

"I just took a bottle of blow-up juice away from some guy heading into the mine. This is a hard rock mine and an explosion might cause more harm than good. Dalton!" he called to the closest man he seen. "Guard the explosive and don't let anybody get to it. Shoot 'em if you have to. Laurie! I want to look in the mine. Get your men here and wait for me. Don't let anybody do anything. There are two mountain men who will be along shortly. Have them wait with you." Without waiting for her response, he rushed into the shack for a cap to hold a candle and then into the mine where he grabbed a handful of candles before continuing down to the blockage.

About half the way down to the working, the shaft was filled high with broken rocks. Something didn't look right to Cormac, but he couldn't put his finger on it or take the time to worry about it. The last timbers visible were lying cracked, broken, and splintered on the floor, half covered with rocks, dirt, and boulders. They would have to start digging by hand.

Laurie did not think it strange at all to be regarding the men as her men. She had been left in charge, and that's the way it was. She waited with Dalton by the miners' shack as her men surrounded her. "Mack is back. He went to look at the mine to decide what to do. Everybody wait right here until he does."

Most heads were nodding. "Why are you letting him say what we should do? I thought he walked away yesterday?" asked a cowhand called Tex.

"That don't matter," she answered. "He's back, and I'm glad. He's the best man for the job."

"But who gave him any authority to do anything? He don't even work here anymore."

Laurie looked him in the eye. And then with an edge in her

voice, "He came back to help, and that is how it's going to be. You say one more word about it you won't be working here anymore. Now shut up!"

Cormac called from the entrance, "Laurie! Have the men get miner's hats and candles from the shack and bring them in. The guy I took the nitro away from is gone. Have somebody keep an eye out for him. He's a wiry little guy with long blond hair."

"I know him. He worked here for a few days when you were out at the line shack. Lucas fired him for stealing a little silver out in his pockets every day. He thought nobody would notice, but we all grew up with this mine; we're not pilgrims. We'll watch for him."

Laurie was wearing a miner's cap and comfortable work clothes. There was no time for silly schoolgirl nonsense; there was work to be done. She brought the miners in to Cormac.

"I want to go outside to check something out," he told her. "You line up the men to start digging here in a fire brigade line to the outside. Have two in front with picks to loosen up rocks and pass them back to the next in line and so on until they can be dropped outside. Use buckets for the dirt and small rubble. Pick a couple strong people to use a double-jack on the big rocks and throw them into an ore cart to push out. Then have a second ore cart and someone standing by to push out the full ones and empty them. If you have to make any adjustments to that plan, do what you think is best. I'll be back as soon as I can. Pull in as many of the people from outside as you can get a hold of, and above all else, do not let *anybody* get in here with explosives." He repeated himself. *"Anybody."*

Cormac ran up the shaft to the outside as Abe and Cuz arrived. He commandeered two people to cool their horses. To some bystanders, he ordered, "Go in the shaft to Laurie

Haplander and ask her what she needs you to do." A few of them weren't moving. "Now!" he ordered. "I said now! There are people's lives at stake, and we don't have much time." He got behind them and began pushing them into the mine. Grumbling, they went.

Turning to the mountain men, he said, "Grab any horse and come with me." He ran to where the woman was walking his horses. "Thanks," he told her, and stepped up onto Lop Ear. With Horse following, he ran them around the entrance and straight back about fifty yards.

Cormac explained to the mountain men, "One wall of the mine gets saturated after every rain and makes working it too dangerous. There has to be something corralling that rainwater and spreading it out into the hill. We're looking for a varmint hole up here somewhere: a skunk or coyote den, or maybe a prairie dog hole. Those things will spread out underneath the ground like a miniature mine and go on forever. I tried to dig one up that was ruining my mother's vegetable garden back in Dakota, but gave up right quick when the hole got too deep. Then I tried to drown him out.

"I dug a trench from an Artesian well that we had and let water run into the hole all day and all night, but it never did fill up. I don't know where in the hell all that water went. Back down to the Artesians, I guess. I think that's what's happening here. I think if we can find it, the dirt will be softer, and we can dig quicker. Spread out about fifteen feet on each side of me and lets all stay even," he instructed the mountaineers. After guiding Lop Ear to a point that he thought was approximately a straight line from the entrance, he waited for Abe and Cuz to get in position.

As a unit, they dismounted and searched slowly forward. About two hundred feet later, Cormac turned right to make a pass back in the opposite direction. It was on the third pass that Abe called him. "I think I got it, Mack."

Somebody had made a small dam with rocks to catch rainwater and direct it into a prairie dog hole.

"Well, I'll be damned," Cormac said in amazement. "What the hell do you suppose that was for?"

Abe responded, "Don't know. Makes no sense that I can see."

"Me neither," echoed Cuz.

"Whatever it's here for, it's probably the reason one wall of the mine stays damp all the time," answered Cormac, shaking his head. "Makes no sense to me either, but I'm not going to worry about it now. We gotta get to those guys below before they run out of air, and I figured the soft dirt would be the fastest. Let's go get some help and tools and we're going to need some timbers. This dirt is going to crumble easy." Beside Lop Ear's left front foot were a horse's hoof prints with one being made by a deformed hoof.

Cormac dismounted to study on it. There were old and new tracks made by the same horse making a clear statement that the horse making the tracks had been there many times. He recalled seeing that print before during his first roundup.

While getting more men and tools, Cormac checked on Laurie. The rocks and dirt were flowing in a steady stream. One of the two men, dirt covered, sweating, and swinging picks and double-jacks with force and regularity and really putting his back into it, was familiar. Cormac was surprised to recognize Laurie's antagonistic brother, Marcus.

Other neighbors and townsfolk had come to help. There was only room for so many people in the shaft, and Laurie was alternating the volunteers in and out to keep fresh workers and the material flow moving as quickly as possible.

Cormac explained that he was going to put together a crew

and start another shaft from the other end where it was damp and soft. If one shaft didn't pan out, maybe the other would. He had Cuz and Abraham hitch a team to the wagon of new timbers sitting by the shaft while he rounded up workers and tools to start digging. Abe and Cuz were right in the thick of it. Tough mountain men accustomed to living and surviving in the out-of-doors, they were well muscled and outworked any four other men.

Being damp, the soil was soft, making the dirt and rock removal go quickly, but they were slowed down by the necessity of having to timber the walls frequently to keep them from collapsing; they were digging straight down. Following Laurie's lead, Cormac alternated workers, taking his own turns, keeping fresh workers in the hole. A portable hand-crane on a movable base was put into play to haul out the bigger boulders, or if they were too large to deal with, the shaft was dug around them. More townsfolk and neighbors were arriving steadily.

During a break, Cormac went to check on Laurie and found her tired and dirty. She was working right in the line with the others. He was proud of her. She noticed him watching and smiled. Cormac smiled back and returned to his crew; obviously, she had hers well under control. With torches, they worked through the night.

While Laurie's crew was making steady progress, Cormac had ever-increasing trouble keeping the walls from collapsing. The sun came up to a bright day, and Cormac's hole had narrowed in width to a size big enough for only two men to work at a time. The workers in both crews were tiring faster and needed relief more often, but little by little, the holes continued to deepen.

By late afternoon, out of necessity, the hole size was narrowed to being only wide enough for one worker, leaving Cormac alone in the hole, working on loosening out of the soft dirt the heavy boulders that no one else had the strength to move. His arm and leg muscles were screaming, his back was aching, his lungs hurt with every breath, and he had a pounding headache when he heard a welcome voice from above him.

"Vaught yooouu doin' down dere, friend Carrmac? Keepin' all da fun for youself, I tink. Cummed up from outta dere und I sho yoouu ow it's dunn, I tink. Yaah, shuur." "Carrmac" was quite happy to let the big Swede "sho 'em ow it vas dunn."

He rested for quite some time, until he could see Sven beginning to labor.

"Okay, you big Swede," he called down. "YOOUU cummed up oughta dere und let me hav turn now. Yaah shuur!"

They rotated twice more before Cormac broke through. He was moving mechanically, without thinking. Dig out a boulder and hold it up for someone to take from him, and then do it again, until a boulder he was trying to pull from the side of his mini-shaft fell away and disappeared. It confused his exhausted mind. He didn't understand where it went, until he heard a cheer coming out of the hole that had been left by the boulder.

Happy voices were calling and hollering. He had broken through the ceiling of the main chamber. He recognized the voice of Lucas calling out that they were all right, and that he was just in time. They had run out of air, one had already died, and three passed out. A few more minutes would have seen them all dead.

Cormac was afraid that his shaft was going to collapse at any time and stopped digging. He explained that Laurie was bringing another crew in through the original shaft.

"Laurie? Did you say, Laurie? I thought I heard you say Laurie." Lucas was having a hard time believing what he had heard. Cormac assured him that yes indeed; his baby sister was coming to his rescue.

Having removed his shirt that kept getting hung up on sharp-edged boulders, Cormac acquired rope burns while being pulled out with the help of a rope hooked to the hand-crane. He took his crew around to the main shaft, and after directing food and water to be lowered down to the miners, he went to help Laurie.

He was dirty and black from working in what was now being called the air shaft, he took his place in line and helped pass the boulders and buckets of dirt outside. Laurie walked by on the way out on some mission without recognizing him covered in dirt and sweat-made mud, only to return shortly, nearly passing him a second time. She glanced at him, and then looked again.

"Mack!" she exclaimed, rushing to him. "You're exhausted. Get out of here. Go lay down before you fall down."

He pushed her hands away. "I'm fine, I'm fine," he said, and kept passing whatever was handed him down the line. The more workers they had in the line, the faster the shaft would be reopened.

They dug the rest of the day and through another night. Cormac was no longer aware of his surroundings. His movements were completely automated. Take what was handed him on the right and pass it to the left, and repeat.

At some point he heard cheers, and people quit handing him buckets and boulders. He thought himself dreaming when he heard Mr. Haplander's voice and felt hands guiding him to somewhere. He knew he was dreaming when he realized he was lying on the grass next to Laurie again.

"I'm sorry," he told her. "I'm sorry. I never wanted to hurt you. I'm sorry." He mumbled the words over and over until his aches and pains disappeared as he fell into exhausted sleep.

Still on the grass, Cormac awakened seventeen hours later with a pillow under his head and covered with a blanket. The sky was a deep, deep blue with a few puffy white clouds. Laurie was sitting in a chair nearby with her parents and family. Every muscle he had was stiff, and he moaned when he moved.

He had lots of immediate attention, all wearing smiles.

"They didn't want to move us and just let us sleep on the grass where we passed out," Laurie told him. "I've been awake about an hour. How do you feel?"

Cormac stretched one limb at a time. "Everything still works, how are the miners?"

"We only lost one. If you hadn't come back, we would have lost all twelve."

"It was a joint effort," he answered. "You were terrific."

Her mother and father came to put their arms around her.

"We are very grateful to you and extremely proud of our daughter," said her dad. "Look at her. When the chips were down, our little girl came through with flying colors. We couldn't be more proud of her . . . and Marcus," he added.

"Markie was right at the front of the line, swinging that double-jack sledgehammer and pick longer than anybody," Laurie told Cormac proudly as Marcus exited the mine with Lucas and came to stand beside her.

"My baby brother moved more rock than anybody else in my crew," she said as she put her arm around him. Pausing momentarily, she looked at Cormac. "You're right, it was a joint effort. We work well together."

"No, no, no," she added quickly at the look on his face. "That's not what I meant. I know you and I can't be together. I understand, and I'm okay with it. Unhappy with it, but okay with it. Whoever she is, she's a very lucky woman. I hope I can find someone to feel that way about me. I just meant that we all did really well."

Cormac breathed a sigh of relief.

He took the Haplanders to the beginning of the cave-in rubble and showed them the marks on the wall that he had noticed previously. "I've had time to think about it and those are scratch marks from the driven steel to set an explosion. If you want to look hard enough, you'll find matching rocks torn out of the walls. This cave-in was no accident, and he was fixin' to do it again when I got here. If Lop Ear and Horse wouldn't have gotten me here so fast, he would have succeeded."

Taking them to the air shaft, he described how the makeshift dam had been directing the water into the hole and about the tracks of the deformed hoof. He told them of the first time he had found the tracks following some cattle into a stream during the branding roundup.

"The same hoof tracks are all over the corral right now. Most of them are clear tracks, meaning that the others had left before him."

"That horse belongs to Tex," Lucas broke in. "I've seen it often enough. He lives in town. We can find him easy enough if he hasn't left."

"Good," Cormac said. "Now, let's go back to the front shaft. I have one more thing to show you."

Removing a white quartz rock from his saddlebag, he broke it into pieces with a nearby pick. The inside was bright white with a vein of lead thickly laced with silver.

"I took this out of the air shaft. I don't know what all the rest of this stuff I been telling you means, I reckoned you could figure it out, but I think I know what this means," he said, handing each of them a piece of the silver-filled quartz. "Doesn't that mean that maybe you have a very thick vein of silver in that damp wall where you couldn't dig because of it being so damp? I'm thinking someone else found it and wanted to keep you from doing the same."

"Well I'll be damned, Mack!" exclaimed Mr. Haplander. "You just saved us from making one hell of a mistake. The assays have been dropping, and we thought the mine was petering out. The reason we had gone to Denver was to complete the arrangements for the sale of the mine to some investors from San Francisco who said they knew the strike was about dead, but they wanted to keep working it to see if they could find something by going deeper. Now I see why. They had some inside information from somebody here, and with those tracks, he won't be hard to find. I still have time to stop the sale. Tomorrow would have been too late.

"This also explains our cattle count. It was much lower than expected this year, and now I know why. Whoever the traitor is has been rustling, too. But he's gotten too confident. Thanks to you, Mack, we can follow his tracks right to him. Now that Laurie has a handle on the situation, we sure wish you would stick around."

"How 'bout it?" Lucas asked him. "You're too good a man to lose."

"Come on, Mack. I'll be okay, I promise," coaxed Laurie, smiling.

"Thanks, but no. I've been getting a bad case of trail-itch for some time now; it's time to scratch it and get back on the trail. But thanks for the offer."

Mrs. Haplander put her hand out to shake. "Laurie told us what happened between you two; I want to thank you for not taking advantage of our daughter. You're a good man. It would have been a pleasure to have you in our family." Cormac shook her offered hand.

"By the way," said Mr. Haplander, "we still owe you some wages. I'll put it in your account, along with a good-sized bonus by way of a thank you."

"Thank you," he answered, and started for the corral to get Lop Ear and Horse, then stopped.

"Say," he said. "What happened to my two mountain friends? I kinda lost track."

Mr. Haplander smiled. "Laurie said those two big ole boys put in a heap a work."

"They stuck it out until we broke through," Laurie said, "and then they lit out. They said to tell you thanks, and they still owe you a big favor that they'll return anytime you need it. They said for you to just send up a smoke signal in a breeze headed for the Rockies, and they'll come a runnin'."

"They also told us," Mr. Haplander cut in, "that you unlimbered some big ole cannon and chased off some woolies that was fixin' to take their hair. Looks like you've had a busy few days."

Nothing in his experience had prepared Cormac Lynch for such compliments and accolades. He had found it to be extremely embarrassing and quickly changed the subject to how well Marcus and Laurie had done until someone handed him a large bowl of Duffy's Irish stew. The stew got first priority until it was gone. And then the first lapse in the conversation gave him the chance to say his good-byes and get back on the trail. He took it gladly.

———

Cormac wondered at the bloodlines of Horse and Lop Ear. They were holding a ground-eating pace, easy to sit with the miles steadily disappearing behind them. The two appeared capable of loping almost endlessly. In reality, they had to have breaks, and he alternated their pace between a lope and a walk, removing all the gear from them for an hour break at lunchtime, and allowing them the opportunity to rest and roll in the grass. It was November month with Indian summer all around. Snow had not yet fallen, and the weather was still warm. The leaves had already traded their shades of green for more beautiful shades of golden browns. God was redecorating.

Montana's mining country was shrinking behind him, the miles melting away. Skirting hilltops rather than cresting them to avoid sky lighting themselves, Cormac remained constantly alert in all directions for other riders or anything that might be a danger. In dry country, dust in the air signaled other movement, but the Great Plains were covered in tall grass as far as the eye could see, with ravines formed by thousands of years of heavy rains cutting into the earth.

A trickle of water running along the ground making a slight indentation on the surface was followed by more water, which, like most humans, follows the path of least resistance. Over time, the indentation became a rut, then a trench, and finally an arroyo invisible from a distance and deep enough to allow a large war party to lie in wait for unsuspecting travelers. This was the same Indian country as when he had first learned his horses were runners. That and his realization that the fate of Lop Ear and Horse lay in his hands were making him more cautious now.

Cormac had seen a good bit of country with his legs wrapped around one horse or the other while looking out between their bobbing-up-and-down ears; the trio enjoyed being on the trail. They enjoyed each other's company, and the horses seemed to enjoy learning what was on the other side of the next hill every bit as much as Cormac.

Frequently, he checked their back trail for other riders and to be aware of the route they were taking. His pa had taught him that the trail looked different looking back than looking ahead. Looking back painted it into his mind so he could find his way back should it became necessary.

Although, his thoughts were frequently on Laurie and Lainey, he was continually evaluating the front trail for ambush possibilities and mentally rehearsing various reactions to different danger situations. He had learned well the importance of a planned response.

His daily drawing practice had become a habit. The next time something threatened him, he wanted to be prepared. He wanted his reactions automatic and unthinking, mentally prepared for the unusual things that usually happen. Sometimes these things happened real sudden-like, and in the seconds or fraction of a second it took to think about what to do, it was too late: death sometimes comes very fast and is very final.

Take that large, dark, inverted *C* that looked like a shadow on the ground in the distance, for instance. Early-morning and late-afternoon shadows set off the highs and lows of uneven ground making the usually unseen seen. If it were actually an arroyo, it could hold several horses or a couple war parties of Indians below the surface of the surrounding countryside, making them invisible to coming travelers such as him.

Knowing the Indians wanted Two Horse dead and his scalp on a lodge pole was unsettling, and that they wanted his horses was disturbing. Two Horse for Christ's sake—utter nonsense, except it wasn't funny. The Indians also wanted Lop Ear and Horse, and he had heard stories of how some Indians mistreated their horses by riding them to death or eating them. He couldn't let that happen. Their lives were in his hands. There would be no more lazy-dozing in the saddle. He would remain vigilant and treat each possible threat as seriously as if it were his last.

For example, if there was a trap planned using the C-shaped arroyo coming up, how might it be planned? He knew Indians took advantage of every opportunity, such as laying in wait for travelers by hiding in the woods and ravines. Were they smart enough to split up into two or more groups with the first group exposing themselves, shooing their prey into the arms of another group maybe?

Since leaving Dakota, Cormac knew he had been lucky on several occasions. To date, he had only had one altercation with Indians. He couldn't count on always being so lucky; as his pa had told him, luck was elusive. Something flashed in the late-afternoon sun from the center of the *C*—something metal? Cormac had altered his course so as to pass on one side of the *C* and not to get trapped in the center if it proved to be more than an indentation in the ground. The flash had come from about two hundred yards out and a little to his right. Was it intentional? Was it a trap? Were there Indians waiting there? Did they want him to turn into the hands of others?

These thoughts flashed through his mind along with thoughts of what to do about it if he was being laid for. The answer was simple: get the hell out of there.

"We're off to the races, guys. Let's get us outta here."

With the arroyo on their left, Cormac sharp-turned Lop Ear to the right and, in one motion, loosened the reins and slapped his heels against the horse's flanks while leaning forward to avoid being left sitting in mid-air when Lop Ear's hindquarters exploded. They shot forward and were off in an instant, narrowly avoiding Horse trotting beside them.

They got maybe fifty feet before a group of Indians waiting in the gulch directly in front of them, along with those waiting in the gulch farther ahead and to the left who had been expecting him to shy into their midst, rushed out to give chase. Had he turned left as expected, there would have been no escape. Now he had a chance. The land was mostly flat with no obstructions, and he was riding Lop Ear.

What kinds of Indians were chasing him was of no consequence, any kind would make him just as dead. But Cormac found the thought in his head. From what he had learned from the Flying H riders, traveling south across Wyoming made them most likely Cheyenne, Arapahoe, or possibly Lakota Sioux from the eastern part of Nebraska and Dakota, although it wasn't totally out of the question that good ole Geronimo might have gotten bored and brought some of his Apache buddies up from Texas to create a little mischief. Geronimo had a way of not staying nailed down anywhere. Most likely though, they were homegrown Cheyennes, for which the city had been named. Didn't really matter which variety they were though, if Lop Ear stubbed his toe, they were gonna be in a lotta hot water.

Both horses realized this was trouble and settled into the act of getting somewhere else. Being grain-fed that morning in addition to their standard diet of the rich and moist plain's grass to increase their stamina for just such an incident, they were prepared for the challenge.

Had he the time to enjoy the sight, Cormac would have appreciated the smooth movement of the strong muscles rippling under their shiny coats. He loved to watch them run and frisk when they were playing with each other. It was a sight second only to Lainey's smile; he thought them to be majestic. Right now, though, he had other things on his mind.

Cormac Lynch bent low against Lop Ear's neck to reduce wind resistance. His hat, loosely riding on his head, had, as always, blown back to hang by the neck strap, and his eyes began to blur from the wind hitting his face. Luckily, being so confident in the trap they had set for him, there probably were no others lying in wait for him, but he needed to avoid being trapped by contours of the land and the ravines and gulches like the C behind him.

No dummies and good judges of horseflesh, the Indians

knew full well the quality of the horses they were pursuing. Each wanted the horses for their own. Other than a few quick shots in the beginning that let Cormac know they had the new repeating rifles, they held their fire, not wanting to risk hitting the magnificent animals they were chasing. Cormac knew the futility of trying to hit anything at this pace and concentrated on helping Lop Ear win the race for his life. If they wanted Lop Ear and Horse, they were damn well going to have to catch them. An interesting dilemma for them and one for which his mother would probably have had a word. They wanted to chase and catch horses that they wanted because the horses were so fast they couldn't be caught.

Miles melted away, and an occasional look over his shoulder showed Cormac that most of the Indians were falling away, unable to maintain the pace. Warmed to their task, Lop Ear and Horse were running easy and loose and enjoying themselves, but realizing the sense of urgency.

Looking far back, Cormac could see the fifty or sixty Indian group had shrunk to one and that one had somehow come up with a spare horse that ran beside him on a long halter rope. This Indian was being easily out-distanced by Lop Ear and Horse but Cormac sensed him to be serious. As one fighting man to another, something flowed between them. Cormac knew the Indian had no intention of giving up and, somehow, he knew that the Indian knew that he knew.

As he looked back, Cormac could see the Indian jump from one horse to the other, still clinging to the rope of his first mount. By alternating horses, he could maintain a greater speed for a longer distance than the others. Cormac tightened the reins ever so slightly so as to slow Lop Ear just a bit and conserve his strength as much as possible. This was going to be a long race, and the prize to the winner was his life.

———————

Although no longer effortlessly, the horses were still running easily and were far from drained. Cormac could no longer see their pursuer, but he knew the chase was still on. That was one determined redskin. A group of boulders on the horizon was growing larger and looked to be out of place on the otherwise flat prairie of this part of Wyoming: an anomaly.

———————

The word reminded him of his mother's teaching at every opportunity. He remembered a particular lesson that had come immediately after she and his pa had quarreled over some trivial concern, and his pa had sheepishly conceded her to be right.

"Anomaly," Cormac remembered her saying. "Anything inconsistent or odd." Then with a sly glance at the husband she dearly loved, "Like your father thinking he is ever going to win an argument with me." Remembering them was such a sad sweetness.

"All right, Lynch, quit daydreaming and figure out what you're going to do about the Injun on your trail," he said aloud. And then, louder, "Hey, Lop Ear, you gettin' tired yet?" Over his right shoulder he watched Horse running happily beside and just a little behind them. "How 'bout you? You ready to take a rest or you want to go another hundred miles or so?"

The boulders were of varying sizes and appeared to have been dropped from the sky, some large, some small, and some huge that had landed on top of each other looking as if Mrs. God was cleaning house and just swept them out the doors of heaven. Some looked like God was showing off by delicately balancing one on top of the other, two or three or four high. A few appeared to have split in two from the force of the fall. Over all, an interesting display of workmanship.

"Good job," he said, looking up into the sky. "I'm impressed. You mind if I use them for a while?"

Then, to the horses, "Okay guys. Enough is enough. Lets us find us a comfortable rock to sit down on and wait for the fellow that's trying so hard to catch up. He's been wantin' to catch up, so let's let him. You did your job, now let's let GERT do hers."

The boulders appeared to have fallen in a roughly laid out circle about a couple hundred yards in diameter with boulders ranging from bucket size of thirty or forty pounds to some large enough to hide Horse and Lop Ear behind.

"Wow, guys, look at the size of these things. They must weigh about a gazillion pounds."

Removing GERT from her scabbard riding under his right leg, Cormac stood on Horse's saddle to climb up the back side of a huge boulder that had broken in half and rolled apart, leaving an exposed stone tabletop large enough and flat enough to lay upon with a slight rise on the front side high enough for concealment. On hands and knees he crawled across to the other side to lie down to wait.

He found several empty cartridges scattered about along with quirlie tobacco, burnt and un-burnt, showing the remains of partially smoked cigarettes, the papers long since blown away. He smiled grimly and shook his head at the meaning. Others had also used this to ambush some unsuspecting traveler. Now he was about to do the same. The thought stuck in his craw.

CHAPTER 13

———◆———

Cormac stood up and waited until he could make out his pursuer. Most would have called it a lost cause, but the Indian had not given up. Obviously, he was a fighting man, and as such deserved respect, although Cormac knew the same treatment would not have been given him if the situation were reversed.

Cormac watched as the Indian grew closer and began to slow and knew he had been seen. About a hundred yards out, the Indian came to a complete stop, considering the situation. A hundred yards was kid's play to GERT, but Cormac stood unmoving. Each alone, they faced off, silent in the stillness; no birds in the sky, no movement of the tall prairie grasses, just standing with the heat of the sun reflecting from the boulders and a lone fly buzzing some feet away.

Cormac held GERT high above his head before gently placing her on the stone tabletop, doing the same with each of his gun belts. Removing his pa's knife from its sheath, Cormac demonstrated his intentions by using the shiny blade to reflect bursts of sunlight in the direction of the Indian. He was fully aware that when he laid down his guns, he had given up his strength in favor of the Indian's.

It was common knowledge that beginning as children, Indians were trained in hand-to-hand combat and the use of sharp instruments as weapons. Cormac was being a fool to give up the advantage of his guns and a perfect point of ambush, but his pa had once told him, "Right or wrong, son, what others would do or not do matters not in the least; a man has to stand for something or he is of little worth."

Cormac watched as the Indian dismounted and made a show of also placing his rifle on the ground, followed by his lance, his bow, and his quiver of arrows. Holding his knife at arm's length above his head, he accepted Cormac's challenge. He, too, would fight with only a knife. *What was it John Ferguson had said? Curse myself for a fool?* That's probably the way it would end up. Calling himself a fool, Cormac took a deep breath and dropped to the ground to begin walking toward his warrior foe.

Cormac stumbled once on a prairie dog hole concealed by the tall grass, caught his balance, and walked on. He could see the strong copper-skinned features of the Indian walking toward him. As tall as Cormac, the Indian was broad shouldered, strong, and well muscled, and moved with an easy smoothness and grace that bespoke confidence. Most assuredly the victor of many such battles as evidenced by large and small scars, he approached Cormac fearlessly. Created by the Wakan Tanka, their Indian name for the Great Spirit, he was a product of many generations of free-spirited fighting warriors: a warrior in every sense of the word—born, bred, and trained to kill from birth, unhampered by conscience, or social or private idealism. When in battle, he would have but one thought—to kill. His long black hair was tied back and a single feather pointed upward behind his head; a necklace of one large—probably eagle—claw hung around his neck. The war-painted red-and-white stripes under his eyes were bright.

"I wonder if I could get him to add a blue stripe under them," Cormac wondered. "Oh, for cryin' out loud. This is no time for nonsense; pay attention. This guy is serious. Look at the size of that knife, for Christ's sake . . . big as a Bowie knife. I picked a hell of a time to get noble . . ." He glanced upward. "God, if I'm not up to this, would you please let Lop Ear and Horse somehow find their way to Lainey?"

Cormac was jarred out of his silly-side when, about twenty feet away and stabbing his knife high into the air with his right hand, the Indian suddenly screamed *"Hoka Hey!"* and charged wildly.

"Oh, damn! . . . Uh . . . *Chicago!*" Cormac yelled, and charged forward.

The gap between them closed. As they were about to come together, Cormac suddenly threw himself into a block at the Indian's feet. With too short of a distance remaining to stop, the Indian warrior fell over him, hitting the ground and rolling again to his feet. He rushed back at Cormac, who was also rolling to his feet and spinning to meet the charge.

With a wild lunge, the Indian sliced at Cormac's face, and when Cormac parried with his knife, quickly grabbed the front of Cormac's shirt and fell back, taking Cormac with him. With the knee of the Indian in his chest as the Indian fell backward, Cormac found himself flying through the air and over the Indian. Twisting like a cat in the air in a wrestling move taught him by the ex-wrestler, Wolfgang, Cormac landed on all fours, facing the Indian. He slammed the toes of his boots into the ground and catapulted himself forward into a headlong dive into the midriff of the still-rising Indian, who blocked his knife thrust with his own knife.

They fell again, both quickly coming to their feet in the protective stance commonly used by knife fighters, slightly bent at the waist, both hands out in front with one hand holding the knife at the ready. Circling each other, reassessing each other, the first clash was over, and they were both still unharmed.

"Indian zero, white man zero," said Cormac aloud with a grin, remembering the description he had heard of a ball game. A puzzled look flashed over the Indian's face, and Cormac leaped forward, slashing up and to the left. A red welt appeared above the waist of the Indian on his left side, traveling upward and across to his right chest.

"White man one, Indian zero," he said again.

"Ahhh!" the Indian growled angrily, waving his free hand as if to say "stop it."

Much like sword fighters, they circled. Parry and thrust, circle and parry, slice and parry and thrust, feint, move in, move out, slash. A scratch here, a shallow cut there. Grunting at each other, evenly matched and each trying to intimidate the other. Both fighters cautious, but the force of their thrusts would be deadly if they connected. Engage and disengage, some hits, some kicks, some bites.

"Damn Injun bites like a bear."

Cormac narrowly avoided being thrown through the air again, and did manage to throw the Indian over his hip, but the Indian recovered to his feet and before Cormac could take advantage of it, they came together, and the Indian tripped Cormac with a foot behind his leg. They went down with the Indian on the top and only Cormac's quickness saved him as he deflected the big knife into the dirt.

He tried, and failed, to get his own big knife into the neck of the Indian before the Indian broke off and rolled quickly to his feet. The warrior spun, hoping to find Cormac exposed, but was disappointed to find him also upright and prepared. This Wasichu was indeed quick.

Evenly matched for strength and courage, they were both tiring. One of them would soon make a mistake, a fatal mistake.

It's going to be you if you keep this up, dummy, thought Cormac. *You're playing his game. You're not a knife fighter; he is. You're only alive by dumb luck; he's trained in this. I wonder if he'd let me stop for a minute and go get my gun. Probably not.*

Cormac pretended to again trip on a prairie dog hole and stumbled backward. Eagerly, the Indian warrior rushed to take advantage and was met by a left hook and a hard right that smashed his nose into his face and started blood gushing down his chest. Surprised and not accustomed to fist fighting, the Indian fell back. Punching rapidly with left jabs and right hooks, Cormac pursued.

Trying desperately to get away from the blows, the Indian continued to back away. Advancing and unable to get set while hitting at a target that was falling away, Cormac was unable to get any real power into his punches. The Indian came under another attempt at a left hook with a right-handed knife thrust that missed the mark but stuck deeply into Cormac's side.

Cormac clamped down forcefully with his elbow against the hand holding the knife to lock it against him. Yanking his own hand that was holding his knife back, away from the Indian's grasp, he let it continue up, around, and down in a full back-circle only to complete the circle, come back up, and plunge deeply under the Indian's ribcage and up into his heart. Cormac pulled his knife from the instantly dead Indian and let him collapse to the ground.

Bleeding badly from his wound, Cormac staggered back and stood looking down at the body, exhaustedly gasping for air. Twisted in death, the once powerful arms and legs of a once prideful warrior were ungracefully pointing at odd angles.

"It's too bad. What a waste," Cormac said out loud, shaking his head. "Why can't human beings just get along with other human beings?"

Holding his wound together to slow the bleeding with one hand, Cormac Lynch wiped the blood from his knife onto the grass and then, with the other hand, rearranged the body into a more respectful position as he remembered all too well doing for his family so long ago, crossed the well-muscled arms across the warrior's chest, and placed the Indian's big knife into the lifeless hands. He followed that by kneeling on one knee and looking into the sky to say a brief prayer for the dead Indian's family.

Cormac wiped his knife on some grass again and put it back in its sheath, turning to return to Lop Ear. Not thirty feet away, sitting stiffly upright, stone-still and watching him closely, was a another Indian, with a rifle in one hand, a lance in the other, a bow and arrow-quiver over his shoulder, and a large silver amulet around his neck.

"Damn," said Cormac simply.

For a long moment, they stared at each other, unmoving, giving Cormac the impression somehow, that the Indian had been there watching for some time. Watching him kill. Watching him arrange the body. Watching him pray. Still holding his wound closed as best he could with one hand, Cormac collected Kahatama's weapons and took them to the mounted Indian. Motioning that he should also take Kahatama's ponies, Cormac backed a few steps away.

Stone-faced, the Indian accepted the weapons. With no out-

ward signs of a signal, as if on its own, the Indian pony took
him to collect the dead warrior's horses.

The Indian wrestled the dead body onto the closest horse
and remounted with an easy grace. After allowing another long
moment during which the Indian and Cormac once more stared
intently into each other's eyes, the Indian rode back to Cormac
and handed him the dead Indian's feather, and spoke.

"Kahatama."

Cormac didn't understand. The Indian repeated it. "Kahatama."

Cormac could only shrug his shoulders and shake his head.
"Kahatama!" the Indian repeated more firmly, pointing to the
lifeless body.

"Oh, his name. Okay, Kahatama," Cormac responded, nodding. "Thank you."

With Cormac watching regretfully, the Indian rode away
leading Kahatama's horses. *A strange people,* he thought, *with
their own customs and beliefs. And honor,* he added, nodding to
no one, *definitely some kind of honor system that probably went
back many generations, if not centuries.* Cormac felt it would be
interesting to understand, and surprisingly, the not understanding of it he felt to be his own loss. The Indian never looked back.

Cormac walked slowly back to the horses. He had a wound
to repair. Like most westerners not living in town with ready
medical treatment available, he would have to fix himself and
hope for the best. Be stoic, just like in the Buntline book.

Yup, that's me, he thought as he gritted his teeth. *Stoic.*

First he had to get his guns. Without them, he felt naked.

———

Cormac built a small fire for coffee and hot water to clean his
knife wound and sewed it together with a needle and thread

from his saddlebag. He finished his repair by dousing the wound with whiskey. Not a fun time, but it could have been worse. He could have lost the fight. The wound didn't yet appear inflamed, so maybe he was going to be lucky and not get infected. After reclaiming his weapons, he made his way to the trees he could see sticking up in the distance and found a secluded water pond in the center of the boulder patch.

Plenty of deadfall firewood was strewn about, but to avoid the bending, carrying, and gathering process, Cormac opted to draw from a supply of wood left by previous campers tucked into a small cave that appeared created for the purpose. After some strong coffee and a cup of boiled beef-jerky soup, he felt better. He could rest up here for a day, maybe two. He rolled out his bedroll and made camp back away from the water to leave open access for the animals that relied on it as their water supply. When rain came during the night, he found the cave was large enough for the wood, his gear, and one sleeping body, if that body were curled up.

Cormac awoke to a cloudy day, but the rain had passed. After a coffee and bacon breakfast, he packed up and headed out . . . to go where? They were pointed in the general direction of Denver, and that was as good as any. There was no urgency; he had supplies, eighty-five dollars in his poke, and more money in the bank in Denver. Mr. Haplander had been depositing part of his wages for the last several months and had said he would put a bonus in Cormac's account for his help in saving the mine. Maybe he should wander down there and see how much he had accumulated. He had to go someplace.

The trip was uneventful, and he walked into the Denver Bank three weeks later just before closing on a Friday afternoon. "Yes, sir, Mr. Lynch. I took that deposit myself. It was five thousand dollars, giving you a total of five thousand, seven hundred and twelve dollars and thirty-seven cents. He had started to deposit twenty-five hundred, but his daughter told him it wasn't enough and suggested he double it. Mr. Haplander resisted until the daughter threatened to go get his wife. I guess he knew he was outnumbered. He just laughed and went along with it. I think he was okay with the five thousand all along though and was just having fun with the daughter. Mr. Haplander said you had earned it. May I ask you please, sir, if I'm not being to bold, what you did that was worth five thousand dollars?"

"Yes, you may, and thank you for the information," Cormac answered, and started for the door.

"But you didn't answer my question, sir."

"I didn't say I would answer it. I just said you could ask it."

Cormac could feel the clerk's eyes on the back of his head as he walked out the door. Let him figure it out.

A five-thousand-dollar bonus. Wow! And a total of five thousand, seven hundred, and twelve dollars and thirty-seven cents. More wow! That was enough money to buy a small ranch. Now, that was worth thinkin' about. Patch seemed to have good connections, maybe he would know of one for sale. Cormac changed his mind about going into the Trailhead Saloon before he got there. He had ridden all day and just wanted to relax. That saloon seemed to be a bit livelier than he really needed at the time, and after thinking it through, he had no business buying a ranch anyway. He had been getting restless at the Flying H and had only been there a few months. There was a lot of country he had yet to see. He might as well stick around for a couple days, maybe say hello to Cactus and Patch and have a look at how city folks lived before heading out.

―――――

After that, Cormac wandered, not staying nailed down anywhere and took to wearing both guns all the time instead of just the one. His life was turning out to be more dangerous than he had intended. He wasn't looking for trouble. He just wanted to be left alone, but God seemed to be telling him to "Go ahead. Live a peaceful life, but keep the thong unhooked."

Staying on the move, Cormac worked some ranches and stayed away from mines; he had no liking to be underground so much of the time. He outran a couple of Indian war parties, one of which nearly had him surrounded until Lop Ear pulled a burst of speed from somewhere deep inside and led them out of the trap.

Cowhands being nomadic by nature, and Lop Ear, Horse, and himself liking to see the greener grass on the other side of the next hill made working ranches an easy way to see some country. Riding the grub line, they stopped at whatever ranch or campfire they found handy, most always welcomed and rewarded with free food for the conversation and news.

Some of the ranchers were skilled cattlemen; others were just getting along. Some knew cattle but didn't know business; some were just the opposite. Cormac learned about grazing and grasses and the importance of not overgrazing an area, and he learned about locoweed, poisonous gymson weed, and a thousand other trivial facts necessary to cattlemen, like handling stampedes, going without sleep, long night watches, riding point, the taste of eating dust while riding drag position, saddle sores on his hind-end from a sweat-covered saddle, branding, and always carried with him the memory of a cantankerous old steer named Old Mossy. And he also learned how the unexpected sound of a rattlesnake behind him in the bushes in which he was in the process of squatting to do some morning business can quickly solve the problem of constipation.

The B-B in western Kansas was a nice spread on some good land with natural irrigation, a clean bunkhouse, and a cook that knew how to make bear-sign. Another wandering puncher working for the Flying H had said they were the best doughnuts in three states, and Cormac couldn't disagree. He was hired on as ramrod, but they called it Segundo, and as such, he was drawing forty dollars a month. He got along well with the men, and they were good workers. They knew what needed doing and got it done with very little guidance. Then why was he getting restless after only eight months? More and more, he found himself looking at the hills and wondering what lay over that way and getting up in the night to go outside for a smoke and look at the stars. Sometimes he wondered if Lainey was looking at the same stars at the same time.

A young wrangler not yet eighteen years old going by the name of Jingles for the jingling Mexican spurs he wore coming back from town one Saturday night a lot faster than he went in, kicked up a lot of dust coming into the ranch yard and woke everybody up by firing his gun into the air as he got near the gate. Having been rousted out of bed early that morning, Cormac wasn't too interested in getting up again after just having gotten to sleep. He put on his hat and guns before going out to investigate.

"All we did was kiss one time," Jingles was telling a group of riders in front of the main house with their guns out. He was surrounded by the other hands and their boss, Con Wellington.

"That was one kiss too many. The rules in this town have been set long ago," answered a suited man in a bowler hat appearing to be the leader, as Cormac walked across the yard toward them. "Cattle people are not allowed east of the tracks. Everyone in town knows that, and you should have. You boys are welcome to come into town to buy supplies, or have a drink, or raise a little hell, but you do it west of the tracks. East of the tracks is the nicer side of town. If you don't know it by now, you sure as hell will by the time we get done with you. I'll not have my daughters associating with the likes of you. Take him, boys," he said to the others.

"Nobody is taking anybody," Con Wellington said calmly. "Who are you?"

"*We* are the business men that own all those businesses in town, and we make the rules."

"Well, those are pretty stupid rules, because *we* are the ones who spend the money in those businesses in town," responded Con Wellington calmly, "but if they are the town rules and the other citizens have agreed to them, so be it. Cab City is about the same distance; if that's the way it is, we'll just start going there. We'll have to check with your storekeepers and see if that's what they want, but for tonight, you folks go on home and if we find out that's the town rules, we'll abide by them, won't we, Jingles—"

"It don't matter what he says," the bowler-hat leader interrupted. "There are more of us than you, and we have the guns, as you can plainly see . . . they're pointing at you. We are taking him with us, and we are going to teach him a lesson. Take him boys."

"If you try, your group is suddenly going to get a lot smaller," Cormac told them as he walked up to the group, coming from the side, "but if that's what you want, you go ahead and see if you can ride that bronc."

As one, the rider's heads turned to look at the voice, and the guns began to swing toward him. "Wait everybody, freeze!" exclaimed one of the riders. "For God's sake, don't make him go for those guns! I saw him shoot a guy in Dodge City. That's Mack Lynch!"

In an instant, the brushing sounds of guns going back into their holsters was heard throughout the group. "We'll be going now, Mr. Wellington," said the suddenly polite and soft-spoken leader. As one, the group turned without another word and rode out of the yard, leaving those remaining to stare at Cormac.

"Is that true Cormac?" asked Con Wellington. "I thought your name was Cormac Lynch, but I guess Mack is short for Cormac. I never made the connection."

"Yes, sir," said Cormac. "It's true. I'm sorry. I'll leave in the morning."

"That's not necessary, Cormac. This would have gotten ugly if you hadn't been here. You're more than welcome to stay."

"Thank you, sir, but no thank you. If I stay, sooner or later, sure as shootin' someone with a gun will come looking for me, and somebody else is liable to get hurt in the ruckus. I'll leave in the morning." The next day, he drew his pay and did just that.

———————

He was headed southwest, riding down a hill into a two-bit town three days into Southern Colorado after leaving Kansas, when Cormac realized it was his birthday and decided to wet his whistle and tie on the feed bag at the local saloon to celebrate. That was a decision he later wished he'd thought better of. He first registered at the hotel and then rode over to the saloon. He figured that a couple drinks and food that he hadn't cooked his own self and a good night's sleep in a real bed would be celebration enough. He later thought the sign over the door of the saloon should have prepared him. It proclaimed A SALOON WITH NO NAME.

"What do you think?" He was riding Horse with Lop Ear carrying the pack beside them as they stopped in the street and looked up at the sign. Horse nickered her approval. Cormac shifted his weight and swung his leg over the saddle horn to slide off but instead, he swung it back over and sat down.

"You know what, guys? Sorry, Horse. I know you're not a guy. I think it's time you two had a birthday. As Lord and master, I do hereby proclaim forthwith this thirtieth day of June to be your birthdays and therefore cause for celebration."

Cormac backed Horse away from the hitching rail and turned up the street. "Let's go buy you some new shoes for your birthday and get you a room in the stable, and just maybe, if you don't kick the blacksmith, I'll get you a rub down and some grain or corn in your feed bag."

After making arrangements for the blacksmith, who also owned the stable, to re-shoe both horses and give them a good brushing and combing, Cormac walked to the saloon. It was of the large size, with the expected long bar along one wall and a door at one end leading to the storage and living quarters, and that was where they ran out of normal.

There were oddly shaped tables of various types of wood and style, some large enough for eight or ten people, some only for two. There were large and small soft chairs, hard chairs, and small straight chairs in various locations ringing tables and lining walls. In one corner, a large red umbrella with dangling white fringe hovered over a table that had been built using multiple types of beautiful woods by an obviously skilled craftsman.

Another corner was arranged like a parlor; with pictures, a table with surrounding chairs upholstered in red, and a rug on the floor. Most of the pictures were nice to look at, some weren't, and one was just plain ugly. If it had belonged to his pa, his pa would have probably said he was gonna trade it to an Indian for a broken watch and then throw away the watch.

The rug made Cormac think of his dirty boots, and Lainey warning him about his dirty high-topped farmer shoes after chores late one night.

"Cormac Lorton Lynch! Don't you dare come into this house

and walk on my fresh-mopped floor with those dirty old clod-hopper shoes! Either clean them off, take them off, or go without supper and sleep in the barn tonight!" Cormac remembered looking in the door for support from Mr. Schwartz sitting at the table; he had been working hard all day in the Dakota-hot fields, and he was tired and certainly not in the mood to be pushed around.

Mr. Schwartz only wiggled his toes with one pushing out through a hole in his sock to call attention to the fact that he had no shoes on either, and with a smile, pointed to them sitting on the porch outside the door and shrugged his shoulders. What's a man to do? Later, when Cormac had been morose and brooding about it, she teased him as she walked by.

"Oh, boo hoo! Boo hoo!" she cried, pretending to rub her eyes. Unfortunately for Cormac, he had been holding a towel at the time and snapped the south end of her when she was going north. He was instantly in real trouble then. Lainey had grabbed the broom and put the run on him in no uncertain terms.

There were floor-length curtains on the windows of a thick material unknown to Cormac and more pictures large and small of mountains and lakes, pastures and streams, flowers and trees, a person riding a funny-looking two-wheeled contraption with one really big wheel in front and a tiny wheel in the rear, and a multitude of other subjects placed on the walls at various heights. One was large and hand painted of an attractive lady with long black hair and a captivating smile on a wall all by itself. Most bars were made for standing only, however, along the far end of this one were five tall stools for sitting that reminded him of the one-legged milk stools they had used on the farm for milking.

Like the other patrons, he shied away from the stools and found a spot at the opposite end of the bar, behind which were several exotic-looking bottles of alcohol. Cormac rolled and lit a cigarette while waiting for a double shot from a bottle that looked to be soundly built, and when it came, sipped it slowly as he took it all in.

A pretty waitress in a high-necked dress that fit her well from the waist up, but loose enough from the waist down to swish the floor when she walked, moved gracefully in and around the tables delivering drinks and food, and somehow managing to stay just out of reach of searching hands.

"Sort of takes your breath away, don't it?"

A cowhand leaning against the bar beside him and looking at the oddities, made a motion with an empty glass that took in the room. Cormac looked around the room again, seeing a splotch of red stain by his feet and smelling the remnants of gun smoke, the tracked-in mixture of dirt, hay, and manure on the floor, the whiskey and the sweat, and hearing the saloon sounds: the tin-penny piano along the back wall playing a song about a girl named Clementine with an old-timer, a couple of farmers, a businessman in a three-piece suit, and a couple of teamsters— all drunk, or near enough to it—making up new verses that had her living an interesting life:

> *He said he loved her*
> *Said he wanted her*
> *But the next day*
> *He was gone*
>
> *She went searchin'*
> *Cross the river*
> *All they found*
> *Was his dead bones.*

And there was the unintelligible chatter of voices: a too-loud laugh of a sporting dance hall girl helping an overeager drunk cowboy up the stairs, a poker player loudly asking for three cards, and the excited voices of two cowboys coming in the swinging door already feeling their oats.

"That it does, pardner," Cormac answered, nodding. "That it does. I wonder how a place like this come to be."

"The story goes that the owner had once been a wealthy rancher with a wife who collected furniture from different parts of the country, even imported some from other countries. When she died from some kind of fever, he lost interest in ranchin' and bought this saloon, then furnished it from his home because it reminded him of her." Cormac signaled for a drink refill and motioned at the cowhand's empty glass.

"You want a refill on that?"

The cowboy grinned at him. "If that's an offer, I surely would. I'm huntin' a job, but my poke's a bit on the empty side lately."

Cormac smiled back. "Been in that boat a time or two myself. I'll buy you a couple and when you get the chance, you can pass it on to someone else like us. How long since your stomach's seen any food?"

"You a mind reader? I stopped at a ranch that set a mighty fine spread, and when I left, the lady gave me a couple sandwiches to take with me, but I polished them off two days ago."

"Been through that, too. I was just wondering what an establishment like this would have to offer in the way of food; I'm almost afraid to ask. It's my birthday, and I just got paid three months wages. I figure to have me a good dinner and a good night's bed sleep in a real bed at the hotel. How 'bout we have another drink, and then see can we scare us up something to eat, on me?"

His new friend showed no hesitation, and they selected a beautifully made table with colored inlays that, upon closer inspection, was marred by initials carved in two places. What a shame. Three cowhands walked in the door, looking around with the same astounded look that Cormac probably was wearing when he had walked in. It came to him that he didn't know pardner's name, and that was fine. It was likely they would never see each other again anyway, for tonight he could just be pardner.

The three newcomers passed by them and went to one of the larger tables, sitting down facing the door as if awaiting something, or somebody. Likewise, Cormac had chosen a chair with his back to a partition allowing him to watch the door and keep the rest of the room under surveillance.

The three newcomers hadn't long to wait. Their ordered drinks hadn't had time to arrive yet when four men and three ladies entered and joined them. The new group must have been there before; they walked past Cormac's table, looking neither right nor left, going straight to the first group's table.

They were all dressed in the style of the day, the men in three-piece woolen suits with ties and bowler hats, the women with high-neck long-skirted dark dresses with hats to match. All three carrying matching handbags, one had a parasol over her arm. Obviously ladies and gentlemen looking somewhat out of place in such an establishment, looking more like they just stepped off the pages of a magazine advertisement.

It occurred to Cormac that all of the patrons were playing the same game. Whenever anyone walked in the door, all eyes watched expectantly for their reaction. A few more people straggled in singly or in pairs while Cormac and pardner were eating. Most reacted in the same manner.

The food was mighty tasty. After eating his own trail cooking, most anything prepared in a real pan would have been a treat, but the steak was thick, tender, done to a tee and served under a layer of cooked onions along with a large helping of beans with a south-of-the-border taste on man-sized plates: the cook knew something of cowboys' appetites. They took their first bites suspiciously, smiled at each other, then relaxed and settled down to do some eatin'.

No words passed; they concentrated on the task at hand. When the last bite of beef and the last bean had been swallowed, they both wiped their plates clean with the last of the fresh-made bread they had been given and cleaned up the crumbs. If it had been a food-eating race, they would have finished in a dead heat, washing down the last bites with the last of their whiskey. Cormac motioned for a couple of cups of coffee. He thought they had both had enough alcohol for the night.

"This is what I call living high on the hog." The cowboy sighed contentedly.

"Sure is," Cormac agreed. "That is, without doubt, the best eatin' I've had in a long time," Cormac told him. "I used to know a couple women up in Dakota Territory that could cook like this. They coulda made boot-leather soup taste good, and then serve it with biscuits smothered in some kind of German gravy and doughnuts in case you weren't already stuffed like a plump chicken. Man, could they cook."

Pardner nodded agreeably. "I've a met one or two like that over the years, but they usually leave a lot to be desired in the looks or attitude department."

"Well, you're part right," Cormac agreed. "These two were mother and daughter. The mother didn't look so great but once you got to know her, you didn't notice. The other was her adopted daughter and one look at her causes most men to start thinkin' maybe being married ain't such a bad idea; that is if they can get their brains to start working again."

They leaned back and dug out their makin's and just as they finished rolling their quirlies, all hell broke loose.

"Wait, please!"

One of the first cowboys to sit at the larger table had knocked his chair over backward getting up and was backing, unarmed, away from the table with his two hands held up in front of him, palms outward. Two of the men in the group that had joined them, along with one of the women whom Cormac had considered to be ladies, were rising and all three began shooting into him. Cormac would have to adjust his thinking on the definition of a lady.

Three armed shooters against one unarmed man wasn't Cormac's idea of a fair fight, but it was no real concern of his as long as their guns didn't start pointin' in his direction. The thought gave him a sense of guilt. Why? Who said he had to be his brother's keeper, as he once heard a preacher say? Had there been any warning, he might have felt the need to try to stop it, but it was over and done before anyone realized what was happening so why was it any of his concern? Keeping an eye on the shooters, he lit his cigarette and held the match over for pardner. Cormac was startled at his expression. Pardner's eyes were wide and panicked.

The two friends of the recently deceased had done nothing, and were still doing it. They moved only their hands, placing them palm down on the table at arm's length. The men shooters holstered their guns; the woman returned hers to her bag, and then the four men and three women turned to leave. Cormac downgraded his opinion from three ladies to three women. Ladies that he had known didn't go around shooting unarmed men, or armed men either, for that matter.

Although pardner was tensed, as if expecting something, he was keeping his head down and his hands were nowhere near his gun; Cormac didn't like it. This thing wasn't over, not by a damned sight, and the group would have to pass by their table on the way out. They had almost made it when one, slightly in the lead, suddenly pointed at pardner.

"That's another one!" he exclaimed. "Get him!" They all turned and started to draw, the woman shooter jamming her hand into her bag.

Cormac swore, "Ah, hell!"

Why couldn't they just leave? He had already removed the hammer thongs from his guns and hooked his foot under the rungs of the chair next to him. His quirlie still dangling from his mouth and his flat-topped black hat back on his head, he kicked the chair into them while unloading up and out of his chair to begin firing with both guns as he stood up. He didn't like using the Colt for close work indoors because the large amount of smoke from the magnesium, saltpeter, and sulphur gunpowder mix made visibility difficult and the sulphur would leave a long-lasting stench, but he had no time to be choosy. The woman was the quicker; her hand was coming out of the bag with a pistol in it and turning. She was looking cruelly into his eyes, thoroughly enjoying what she was about to do.

Cormac shot her first. Her eyes widened and her soft, lovely shaped mouth uttered a surprised, "Oh!" She looked down at the two holes in the center of her chest, then again into his eyes as it sunk in that she was dying. "You . . ." she started in a bitter accusing tone as her legs gave up the ghost, and she was left with nothing to support her and collapsed.

Well, if she could go around shooting people, people could sure as hell shoot back.

Both guns hammering, Cormac had already picked his target order. After the "lady," the little one looked to be the fastest, and was; the big one looked to be a very close second, and was. Cormac took them in order and the other two last as their guns were clearing leather. The big one and the little one had surprised looks on their faces too, as if they never thought it could happen to them. Hell, it could happen to anybody, even Cormac, and would if he got careless. He knew he would meet somebody faster someday and he would go down in some dusty dirty street or some saloon, to nobody's surprise.

What difference would it make to anybody, anyway? He had a few friends and acquaintances who would admit to their friends and their acquaintances that they knew it was going to happen someday, and then what? When the Denver bank got the news, someone would take his money and his horses and property to Lainey, who would probably refuse them. And that would be the end of Cormac Lynch and the John Lynch chain of descendants.

Turning to the two remaining ladies, he decided to give them the benefit of the doubt and continue to think of them as ladies since they weren't shootin' at him and wouldn't. They were statues with eyes wide as saucers.

"My God!" pardner exclaimed finally, staring at Cormac in disbelief. "My good God!"

There was a whole saloon full of witnesses to keep the sheriff happy, and staying overnight in this town no longer held the appeal it once had. After accepting an abundant amount of thanks from pardner and an offer to explain what had happened to cause the incident—an offer Cormac declined, it was more than he needed to know. He hadn't known pardner's name, didn't need to. It was suppose to be his birthday celebration. He had just wanted to relax with a drink and a good steak. He wasn't looking for trouble. He wasn't making any trouble, and then, all at once, strangers were ready to kill him. For what? Just because he was sitting there? And then he had to shoot them just to keep himself from getting shot. He had never seen them before, didn't know anything about them, and didn't want to know anything about them. To hell with them. If they didn't want to die, they should have just left him the hell alone.

Cormac gave pardner a few dollars to tide him over, left enough money on the table to cover the food, drinks, and the chair that he had broken, and rode out. He had seen some interesting sights, had a few good drinks, and his belly was full of a great steak.

"I guess that's it for our celebration," he told the horses disgustedly. "Happy Birthday." Leaving town was the order of the day.

Realizing they had never introduced themselves, pardner watched Cormac ride away from the livery. He didn't even know his savior's name. Wanting to know to whom he was indebted and remembering being told that his benefactor had registered at the hotel, he went there and explained to the clerk what had happened and asked to see the register.

Cormac Lynch, known to many as Mack, had signed-in simply as Mack L. A bystander, listening when pardner explained to the sheriff what had happened, heard the name as Mackle. The name would be repeated frequently in other saloons and around campfires as the many witnesses told and re-told their stories of the Mackle guns. They were unbelievably fast and deadly . . . and they didn't miss.

It would also be told that he had shot a woman. The fact that she had just finished helping to kill an unarmed man and was pulling a gun out of her purse with which to kill yet another, not to mention Cormac, would be dropped from the story as it was passed around, but the message went out: "Stay the hell away from the Mackle guns."

CHAPTER 14

Too upset at the turn of events to sleep, Cormac pointed their little group at a high peak silhouetted by the distant moon and rode half the night before calling it a day. Some coyotes yapping on the other side of a nearby hill woke him mid-morning. Strangely, he wasn't hungry and settled on some coffee and cigarettes for breakfast while he thought about the previous day. It was unsettling.

Sitting on a flat-top stone, he removed both six-guns from their holsters and placed them on the stone beside him, staring at them while he lit yet another smoke. Maybe Lainey's attitude was right. She didn't like the killing. But what else could he have done? He had killed men, but only in self-defense, or the defense of others. Would it be better to live in some city where everybody is protected by law officers? No more galloping over the prairies with Horse and Lop Ear? No more searching for whatever was on the other side of the hill? No. He wouldn't be fenced in. He and Horse and Lop Ear needed room to breathe.

Cormac poured himself another cup of horseshoe coffee and slowly and methodically dismantled, cleaned, and oiled each gun. He wished they weren't needed but he did enjoy the feel of them in his hands. The smooth, hand-worn, wooden grips were comforting in his hands. Belatedly, he realized that they had left town traveling west when previously they had been going in a southerly direction. No matter. One direction was as good as another. What was to the west? Utah . . . or Idaho, maybe? No matter either. He had never been to either of them.

Still in Colorado, he stopped in Leadville. The sign wasn't much and neither was the town, but it had a lot going on. Having found himself on a trail going through the mountains, Cormac hadn't expected much, but the place was bustling with people. Turned out there was a traveling judge in town and a fellow named Sanderson was being tried for shooting a guy in the back.

Under a sign bragging that the crossing streets were named Third Street and Harrison Avenue was a cheerful fella being called Soapy making bets with passersby as to whether they could tell which of three shells was hiding a little pea after he had moved them. While the game was being demonstrated to new prospective players, Cormac noticed finding the pea was an easy feat, but somehow, once someone had placed a bet, the pea was nowhere to be found. He elected not to wager. His pa had warned him to never play the other man's game.

The trial was being conducted in a saloon with entertaining lawyers striding around the "courtroom" waving their arms and quoting the bible. It was claimed that Sanderson, a tall, gruff, and cocky gunslinger with the unshaven look of a thug, had killed somebody by shooting them in the back.

It was claimed that Sanderson was a cold-blooded killer who would just as soon shoot someone from ambush, or in the back. That gave Cormac something to consider. Although he wouldn't deliberately sneak up and shoot someone in the back to avoid the possibility of getting shot himself, if a person needed killin', he couldn't see as how it made a whole bunch of difference which direction he—or she, Cormac remembered—happened to be facin'. He pondered on that a spell.

It was bad for a bad guy to shoot a good guy in the back. If Cormac was a good guy—some would dispute that—was it okay for him to shoot a bad guy in the back? Who, then, decides who are the bad guys and who are the good guys? More and more of these decisions were being made in courts, but many were still being decided out on the range when there was no law to be had for many miles. People couldn't be bothered taking a rustler all the way to town and spending two or three days there to be a witness, or making a second trip when the traveling judge got around to coming to town. Consequently, a rustler was simply shot, or hanged, and it was over and done with.

In this case, Sanderson was released when the only witness turned up dead on his way to testify. Cormac took the last room in the hotel and left the next morning. Fixing a broken wagon wheel for a lady farmer he met on a road a little farther down the line got him invited home for supper and to meet her husband. They offered him a job, and he stayed six months. They were nice enough people, over their heads when it comes to farming and planning to return to the east after the upcoming harvest. They offered him if he would stay and help out until then, they would give the farm to him. He told them thank you, but no thank you. He had lost his interest in farming. Apparently, he had become a full-fledged cowboy.

Then a friendly cowboy that Cormac met on the trail and

rode with for a couple of days convinced him to go back to Northern Colorado. "Why don't you ride along?" he asked. "You and I get along pretty good, and they've got a good-sized spread. Big spreads can usually use another hand. If they don't, wait a couple days, somebody will quit, and if no one quits, I'll shoot somebody."

Cormac knew he was joking, but he turned out to be right. It was a good job with a nicely kept ranch, good food, and a decent foreman. Cormac was known there simply as Mack until one night at the local saloon, a gunslinger wearing two tied-down guns recognized him in town and remembered seeing the shoot-out at the "No Name Saloon."

"Mackle!" he cried out, and went for his guns. Cormac had heard talk around campfires that the fast gun at the "No Name Saloon" was someone called Mackle. He had no idea how that had come to be, but when he heard the call, he knew it was meant for him. Cormac had taken to keeping his hammer thongs off whenever in town or around other people. Catching Cormac in the middle of a sentence and turned half away from him toward the bartender had given the gunslinger an advantage that was almost enough.

Cormac's dedicated practicing had taught him it was a fraction of an instant faster, when reacting to sudden threats, to draw from whatever position he happened to be in. Accordingly, he wasted no time in turning to face the threat. Turning only his head and moving nothing but his right arm, his Smith & Wesson came up firing.

Cormac's first bullet spun the gunfighter into a pole as his guns were leveling on Cormac. Leaning against the pole and dropping to one knee, the gunfighter was again bringing his guns to bear. Cormac's first shot had been a practiced reflex action. Now his mind was also in the game. He put two fast-rolling shots into the gunman's chest, and the contest was over.

"Jesus!" exclaimed the bartender. "While I was thinking you were a goner, you were already firing . . . So you're Mackle. I would not have believed it if I hadn't seen it with my own eyes. What they say is right. You just may very well be the fastest gun alive."

"Mackle" met the eyes of the bartender for a contemplative moment before sighing a long and sad sigh, silently shaking his head, and walking out into the night. He had accepted the necessity of defending himself, but killing a man was not fun. When he drew his pay, the foreman told him about a neighboring rancher looking to hire a horse wrangler to ride herd on a hundred head of horses to Texas for two dollars a head to fill an order placed by the Texas Rangers. Cormac took the job. It had sounded like easy money, but horses are more spirited than cattle and keeping them in a group was sometimes a task; shooing off rustlers was a nuisance.

On one such occasion, while the helper he had been given by the rancher had gone into a nearby town for supplies, three cowboys with bandanas over their faces rode out of a gulch he was passing.

"We wanted to thank you for bringing your herd to us, so thank you very much. We'll take them from here."

Cormac could see by their eyes behind their bandanas that they were all young fellas. Neither their clothes nor their horses were anything special. They had most likely been going someplace, seen his helper leave, and decided to take advantage of the situation "You have to be the most polite horse thieves around, but what makes you think I'm just going to give them to you? Your guns are still in your holsters."

"Because there are three of us and one of you. You can't hope to outgun us all, so if you will just turn around and ride away, we'll just take these horses off your hands."

Cormac answered amiably, "You look like intelligent fellas.

Why don't you forget this nonsense and go on your way? I don't have to outgun all of you. I'll just shoot you."

"Where will that get you? If you do, my friends will shoot you. Are those horses worth your life?"

"Are they worth yours?" Cormac asked him.

"No, I guess not." The wanter-of-horses-without-paying-for-them reined his horse as if to leave and went for his gun. He saw only the fire-bloom spurting out the bore of Cormac's gun and felt himself falling backward off his horse.

The others remembered they had immediate business elsewhere.

———————

"I count one hundred and one," said the ranger as he shut the gate behind the last horse. "Did I count wrong? I was told to expect an even hundred."

"No, your count is fine. Three fellas wanted to take the herd, but didn't have what it took. I let the starch out of one, and the other two lit out for parts unknown. We picked up an extra horse in the deal and my helper got himself a new saddle."

The ranger smiled. "We're glad you made it. The last herd didn't get through, and we're running short of horses. Come on up to the house . . . we'll settle up. I was told you was to get two hundred dollars, and we're to wire the rest to your boss."

On the way to the house, Cormac answered his questions about the drive. Inside were eleven other rangers, celebrating

"No, it's not a celebration," answered the ranger when asked. "We're just having a drink to the boys at the Alamo." There were sturdy chairs and a few benches, a long kitchen table, western desert horse and gun pictures, gun cabinets and racks, an ammunition cabinet, two saddles on racks, gun belts on hooks, paths worn into the wooden floor: it was a house for men.

The speaker was a wiry man of normal height with a large mustache and sun-wrinkled skin, brown from many hours under the Texas sun. The newness of a large red bandana around his neck contrasted with his aged and worn clothes. His boots were obviously comfortable, but had, also obviously, been in need of replacement for several months; his gun belt and pistol were well cleaned and well oiled, and the pistol grip appeared smooth and well worn.

"This is March the sixth. Just forty-one years ago today it was, in 1836, that the Alamo was lost, along with Jim Bowie, Davy Crockett, and William Travis; but it was one hell of a fight. One hundred and eighty-two volunteers, most of them Texans, held off twenty-six hundred Mexican troops for ten days. We think they deserve a drink in their honor. Care to join us?"

"Absolutely," Cormac answered. "Other than maybe mountain men that never come down from the hills, I 'spect most everyone has heard of them, but I understand Santa Anna lived to regret it."

"You damned betcha he did. He learned right well the folly of messin' with Texans. Forty-six days later, Sam Houston run him to the ground, blocked off his escape, and cut his troops into mincemeat. Ole Santy Anna tried to escape by mixin' in and trying to pretend to be one of his peons until one of Houston's boys heard him called El Presidente by one of the real peons and that was that. He just signed over the rights to Texas just as big as you please."

"I didn't know all that. I'd be proud to have a drink in their name."

"Speaking of names, what might be yours?"

"Lynch," Cormac told him, a smile on his face and his hand out. "Mack Lynch."

The ranger, a knowing and capable-looking individual, shook the offered hand. "I'm John Ford. The boys call me cap'n, most others call me Jack. I've heard of you."

A large, cold, and dangerous-looking ranger handed Cormac a tin cup half filled with an unidentified brown liquid.

"You might wanna sneak up on that," he growled. "The cap'n was over Kentucky way a while back and brought that back with him. It's homemade. It'll likely grow hair where you don't have any and burn off what you do have, but it'll get your attention."

Cormac clicked his cup with a couple of the closest rangers and took a swallow. The ranger wasn't wrong. His first swallow burned its way to his stomach and set it on fire. He thought it a wonder there was anything strong enough to keep it in. The others were watching expectantly. The look on his face didn't disappoint them; they all laughed.

A ranger at the table spoke up, "I've heard you're pretty quick with that gun of yours. Are you?"

"I'm okay. I do the best I can, but I'm just an ole tater picker, trying to get along," Cormac answered. It wasn't somethin' he liked to discuss.

"I've heard you're 'most as fast as Mackle," said another.

"Nobody's as fast as Mackle," offered the ranger who had given him the drink. He held up the jug, questioning if Cormac wanted more. With a smile and a headshake, Cormac declined. He would finish what he had, but if he had any intention of leaving under his own steam, what he had was more than enough.

The ranger Ford came back with Cormac's money and counted it into his hand. Cormac folded and buttoned it into his shirt pocket. The fast-gun conversation was still on.

Jack Ford said to the others, "I've heard stories about both of them." Then to Cormac, "I wouldn't bet a nickel either way, but if you were to meet, I'd give a month's wages to be there. How would you like to be a Ranger? We could use another good man."

Not one to pass up an opportunity for a little fun, Cormac said, "I've heard Mackle is almighty fast. You should recruit him."

"Not likely. I've never heard of you shooting anyone when it wasn't self-defense; Mackle shot a woman."

It wasn't funny anymore.

"I heard that, too, but I got it from someone who was there, she had just finished helping to shoot an unarmed man and was getting ready to shoot him next." Cormac's voice had taken on a bite.

The ranger cocked his head and looked at Cormac from the corner of his eyes. "Calm down. Your tone of voice sounds like you're defending him."

Cormac shrugged his shoulders. "I've ended up on the wrong end of the stick a time or two because someone didn't understand something I did."

"If what you say is true, I probably owe Mackle an apology for helping to spread the myth. Let's change the subject. What about you becomin' a ranger? I could have used someone like you a few years ago when I was chasing an outlaw named Cortina."

"I think I'll pass on that," Cormac replied. "I don't seem to be too hot on staying put anywhere, but I'm right flattered at the offer. I know the Texas Rangers are a tough group. Too bad there weren't a few of you boys at the Alamo. Santa Anna might have gotten a surprise."

Cormac stayed overnight in their camp and went to sleep chuckling about a shootout between Mackle and him—such a thing.

Remaining in Texas, he drifted from ranch to ranch, learning more about cattle and western folks as he went. Westerners were an odd mix of transplanted easterners and immigrants come west to make their fortunes. Some were looking for new starts, some were running from something—family, debt, the law— others, usually young men, just wanted to see the "Wild West" they had read and heard about.

They came from all walks of life and trades: lawyers and doctors, storekeeps and barbers, tradespeople skilled at working with their hands, and any number of other professions. Many, although they hid it to fit in, were well educated and opinion- ated, generating interesting and sometimes heated conversations around campfires and in homes. Some were women looking for husbands, or excitement, and they sometimes settled on land by themselves, or found work as teachers, seamstresses, and waitresses or, frequently, ended up working on the shady side of town, or upstairs over a saloon. But all were looking for a change of lifestyle; all found one.

Sometimes people took new names or were given new names because of where they were from, some action they had taken, or something that happened to them—names like Buckshot, Roper, One-Eye, Peg-Leg, Lucky, Digger, Jingles, and many others. A few had tried calling him Dakota, but it didn't stick. The foreman of the Bar-M in Montana liked to hang nicknames on hands and tried calling Cormac the Dakota Kid. That was silly, Cormac thought, but at the same time, kind of fun; but it didn't stick, and he was relieved when it stopped. What people called themselves, or what their past had been, was unimportant. People were judged and accepted, or avoided, by what proved to be their integrity, or lack thereof.

Most were decent, hardworking folks, though some were troublemakers: lazy and trying to ride on the backs of others, doing as little as possible. Some couldn't get along with the

people "back East" and moved "out West" to find a better grade
of people, only to find that it wasn't the other people that were
the problem. Wherever they went, their problems traveled right
along with them, and then there were always the crooks, outlaws,
and con artists looking for folks gullible enough to be scammed.

The western movement had created a new language, a new
dialect his mother would have called it. Like most westerners,
Cormac's vocabulary and speech patterns had changed dra-
matically from his mother's teachings. He had taken on the
western dialect of y'alls, howdies, and the like. It was hard not
to, and most people coming west flowed into the new language
quick enough. A New York lady's "she is such a sweet little girl,"
and an ex-Ozarkian's "at ole gurl is a sweetern," would become
a cowboy's "she's a right sweet little thing."

Some of his job changes followed gunplay. Most of the time,
however, the changes were due to restlessness, a desire to see more
country maybe, or in hopes of finding a place where he would be
contented for more than a month or two. He was tired of moving
around, but he just didn't know how to stay put or why he couldn't
stay happy anywhere. He had had some good jobs and some good
bosses, and made some good friends, yet every time, after a few
months, he always began to realize that he wasn't really happy
wherever it was that he was and he would leave.

A couple times friends had suggested he just needed to meet
a good woman, and he had had several chances. He had spent
time with some pretty girls on rides and picnics and such, and
once, in a town in which he had briefly stopped, he bought a
box lunch at an auction sale primarily because the girl that had
made it was rather plain looking and her lunch wasn't attracting
any decent bids. He bid two dollars, the highest of all the bids
that day, and made a big show of taking her arm and leading
her to find a nice place to eat it.

Her lunch was very good, he spent the entire afternoon with her and enjoyed her company more than most, but there was no special spark between them.

He continued to traipse from place to place. Unfortunately, at the same time, Cormac Lynch was gaining a reputation as a man to fight shy of as word got around that he was that gunfighter from the Dakota Territory. And on a few occasions, he had been called out as Mackle. In either case, it wasn't a label he wanted, it just sort of settled on him, like a heavy blanket.

Hard labor had filled out his arms and shoulders and he refused to be put down or disrespected for any reason. If someone wanted trouble, they got it; he backed down from no man. He had learned about fighting from the Swede and he learned how the first punch in many fights is the winning punch.

If it was gunplay they wanted, they got that too. Coming out the winner in two or three gunfights was all it took to earn the name of gunfighter. Some glory-seekers, like the fool kid from Virginia City, search out gunfighters with the dimwitted scheme of making themselves a name. Most merely end up learning what the underside of grass looks like.

Cormac left Texas as ramrod on a cattle drive to Kansas for the Ocean 3, a ranch started by three ex-sailors who had pooled their money to buy a herd of cattle and a little land, then claimed grazing rights to four times as much as they had purchased, and like most large ranchers in their day, claimed any unbranded cattle that came their way. They knew nothing about ranching but weren't afraid of hard work and had been smart enough to hire people who did. Their brand was a long wavy line followed by a number three.

"The long line makes the brand more difficult to be worked

over by a runnin' iron," they told Cormac. It had proven to be a good idea. Their losses to rustlers being fewer than most, their herd had tripled in size quickly, and it was time to take some profit. Their foreman at the time, it had fallen to Cormac to take a herd to the cattle buyers in Kansas to be shipped by train to eastern markets. Cormac's bosses were Kalen Brockmore, Jedediah McLeary, and Tom Bossen. Tom had been a bosn's mate on their last ship. Cormac had no idea what a bosn's mate's responsibilities were, but he thought it a fine play on words. His pa would have made something up about a Bossen bein' a bosn' but he wasn't his pa and didn't have his gift of gab, or his way with words. They were all good men: strong men. Cormac got along best with Tom, so it just sort of worked out natural like, that most orders were directed through him. They were all there on this morning.

"There have been reports of a large band of outlaws about thirty or forty strong stealing herds and selling them in Mexico. The last was about a month ago." Tom Bossen paused. *Come on, out with it,* Cormac thought. He knew there was more. "Mack, they always kill all the riders."

Tom was doing the talking. Under cover of stopping for a dip of snuff, he paused to let that sink in. "There's also an Indian raiding party scalping and raping their way this direction that you'll need to keep an eye out for. You will likely have trouble before you get to Kansas, but we're counting on you to get the herd through."

Cormac looked at Kalen; he was itchin' to say something. He looked at Jedediah, and Jedediah nodded for him to speak his mind.

"We've waited as long as we could to give the beef a chance to fatten up. We have also been hoping to get word that the outlaws had been stopped, but we can't afford to wait any longer.

Keep it under your hat, but we need the money. As you well know, this is our first profit herd, and we're stretched almighty thin. If we lose this herd, we'll be back to starting over."

Because of his height, it wasn't necessary for Cormac to look up to many men, but Kalen was such a man. Standing three or four inches above Cormac's six foot four, it was necessary.

"We're going to pay a bonus; we want the boys one hundred percent behind you. One dollar per head will be put into a pot for you and the boys to split when you get through. That should get their attention."

He was certainly right about that.

"A dollar a head?" Red exploded when Cormac told them around the supper fire the first night out. "Good God, man! That's three thousand dollars."

Red was Cormac's unofficial second-in-command. A skinny, freckle-faced Irishman, he had to wear suspenders to keep his pants up. His accent made Cormac think of Lainey. He was older than the others but would never say by how much. He was generally thought to be around fifty, old for a puncher. Slender, older, and he had a taste for Irish whiskey, but he was like a little banty rooster; he'd fight at the drop of a hat . . . and sometimes be the one to drop the hat, or knock the chip off some shoulder. Everybody took to him.

"The bosses don't have to worry none," Red added, "for three thousand dollars, we'd run the devil out of hell and take this herd right through the middle, flames and all."

Everybody yelled in agreement.

Cormac looked around at the group. They were eighteen strong and, other than himself, Red, and Cookie, none were over twenty-two; half had a year or two to go before they would see twenty, and two were even younger. That was the normal lot for cowboys. Boys became men quickly, wanting to pull their own weight. Most were working alongside their parents on farms and ranches before their sixteenth birthday, as he had, or out on their own if they had no parents, or couldn't get along with the ones they did have. Boys back east were still going to school, rolling hoops and wearing knickers, but in the West, kids did a full day's work for a full day's pay.

"Three thousand dollars! 'Land a Goshen,' my pa would have said," spouted Mickey, their wrangler, another Irishman. "There are eighteen of us, counting Mack. How much is that? Anybody know how to figure it?"

Cormac's mother had been teaching him numbers and what to do with them, but sometimes they just refused to cooperate. Cormac had just started to work it out when the kid came up with it. Every ranch had one they called the kid. In this case, Indians had wiped out his family, along with forty-seven other people on the same wagon train. He had survived because, just before the attack, he had walked away from the train to take a bush-break. He had heard the shots and yelling and recognized it for what it was, and being no dunderhead and knowing there was nothing he could do about it, he hid. Now, just a half a year over thirteen, he was big for his age and trying to prove himself. He was the first one about whenever there was work needing doin'.

"That's a hundred and sixty-six dollars each," he gushed. "Man, oh man, oh man, oh man, Mack! That's over a year's wages." Ten dollars a month and found was the usual wage for a cowhand. As segundo, Cormac made twenty.

Their Scandinavian, Oley, usually spoke little. In a voice heavy with accent, he said "Yah, idt souns goodt. Vhen I get mine I'm heading for Denver. There is this leetle gorl vorking there that's so purty it hurts your eyes yuust to loook at her, 'specially vhen she's all gussied up. I tin' she need soambody like me."

"You Scandihoovian Yahoo," called Mickey, imitating Oley's accent from the other side of the fire. "You're full of prune juice. You tink all the pretty girls need soambody like yoooh."

They all laughed, and the rest of the night passed with stories of how the money would be spent—if they made it. If they did, Cormac might break down and buy the new saddle he had his eye on in Denver, but the rest of his share would go to the bank there. The frugal habits of his farmer-parents were a comfortable fit and a fond memory.

He didn't much keep track of how much he had, but it should be sneaking up on a tidy sum. What with gunslingers looking for him as Mack Lynch, or Mackle, and Indians trying to catch Two Horse, Lainey would probably end up with it anyway. Sometimes, when he awoke in the night, he would start thinking about her and not be able to get back to sleep, wondering how she was, or if she married. That she was pretty was a given, but she was also a warm and nice person. He didn't know the words to describe her voice but he remembered enjoying the musical sound of her Irish lilt, and their ride to town in the back of the sled with blankets over them . . . and how he had felt with her head on his shoulder. The smell of her hair was strong in his mind.

He thought of the time when he was sixteen and had used a mirror to peek under the blanket dividing their bedroom one warm summer night when they were getting ready for bed. She had just finished getting undressed but hadn't yet got her night-gown on, and he remembered how guilty it had made him feel. He never repeated the incident. He remembered feeling guilty, but remembering the way she looked made him smile in the darkness. He also remembered it had been well worth it. He could live with the guilt. Unhappily, those kinds of thoughts always led to the memories of the hatred in her eyes, and the disgust in her voice. Damn it to hell!

Occasionally, Cormac couldn't help thinking about how things might have been if what had happened hadn't, but that was wishful, wasteful thinkin'. He had since met a few girls who smiled a little too wide, laughed at his jokes a little too loudly, or put a little extra swing in their hips; a couple even made a bold suggestion or two—girls that were easy on the eyes and fun to talk to, but of no real interest. He never sampled any of their pleasures. He just wasn't interested in them. Laurie Haplander had generated the most interest, but even she had come out on the short end of the stick when compared to Lainey.

Just as well, he had gotten too rough around the edges to be any good to a woman. The ones who had set their cap for him and flirted with him would have lost interest soon enough. When he had left the farm, he had realized the making of himself was to be in his own hands. What had he made of himself? He drank some, smoked some, sometimes chewed tobacco or dipped snuff, and backed away from no man.

All in all, Cormac felt safe in saying that he was not husband material, but he was satisfied with the type of man he had made of himself. He felt himself to be honest, hard workin', and God fearin', but he couldn't say he had accomplished much to speak of. Others his age had started ranches, farms, or a business in town by his age. It seemed that he was just wandering.

No, there was no use in him thinking settling-down thoughts about Lainey, or any woman—especially Lainey. Although, he had heard it said that you can't make a silk purse out of a sow's ear, he never really understood it. All of a sudden, it made sense.

Cormac listened to his men's plans to spend their windfall and laughed along with them and cleaned his guns. He would wear a third gun tucked in his waist until they got to Kansas. He hoped they would not be needed, but he believed what his pa had tried to get his mother to accept and which she so tragically found out too late: one must be prepared. Sometimes when a gun is needed, it is needed right then, and five seconds later is just too darned late.

He remained motionless as his mind went back to that terrible day. The mental pictures formed in his mind and tears welled up in his eyes, and the inside of his nose took on a strange crinkling sensation until he realized the voices around him were silent and the men were watching him. He still couldn't think about it and, as always, pushed it down and shook it off.

"Just daydreamin' what I'm goin' to do with my share," he told them.

They all laughed at his guns and belts, with one being brown and one being black and one pistol longer than the other, but when Cormac stood up and strapped them both on, the laughter stopped. He had told the men about the rustlers; the guns brought it home. They knew the damage he could do with those guns, and if he was taking the threat seriously, they would do well to follow his lead. It finally sunk in . . . some of them might not get to Kansas.

They would be following the same Goodnight-Loving Trail upon which Oliver Loving had been killed by Comanches in '67. It ran across the arid and lonely untamed vastness of sun-blasted Texas, up through Colorado and into Wyoming. They would follow it across an unpeopled portion of Texas before cutting off for Dodge City on a route that had been described to Cormac by a puncher using lines drawn in the dirt beside a campfire. It might skirt the area the rustlers seemed to favor.

––––––––

The first day they made but ten miles. Three thousand head of cattle stretched out to nearly a mile. Looking down at them from a hilltop, they looked for all like a giant snake weaving its way through the irregular countryside.

Oley was working point and Mickey running drag with their remuda. The bosses had made sure there were plenty of spare horses—they were going to be needed. Red alone would go through five or six a day; he was everywhere, checking on point and drag, directing the others and running back cattle that tried to head out on their own. Cormac intended on doing all the scouting; if there was skullduggery afoot, he was going to find it.

Buntline's book was silly, but it did have a few entertaining moments and only cost a dime, which, in Cormac's opinion, was eleven cents more than it was worth, but it had added a few words to his vocabulary, skullduggery being one of them. The word was probably made up by some inventive writer somewhere that didn't get out much. But, was there any skullduggin' to be done, he would be the one doing it.

They suffered the heat and longed for the coolness of the evenings. To give Lop Ear and Horse some rest, Cormac would use another mount here and there, but he wanted his own horses for scouting. If it became necessary to get someplace—or away from someplace—in a hurry, Cormac wanted a horse between his legs with plenty of speed and bottom. In simple terms, when the chips were down and hell was exploding, he wanted to be sittin' right smack in the middle of either Lop Ear or Horse.

By the end of the week, they had settled into a routine and were making twelve to fourteen miles per day, and by the end of the fifth week were on the verge of passing out of Texas, when it began to rain. Most days were real scorchers; the rain was more than welcome. They had been a day and a half without water, and Cormac thought his mouth was so dry he coulda spit cotton. A few days break from the heat would be enjoyed.

Whenever possible, he stopped the herd at night in flat areas with surrounding hills to help hold it, and to make watching easier from one of the hilltops on nights with enough moonlight. On one such night with a full and bright moon overhead and too many things on his mind to sleep, he elected to take advantage of the good weather to carefully clean his saddle and holsters with his pa's leather balm and finished by cleaning his guns. Although he had just cleaned them a couple days earlier, too often was better than too seldom. He began scouting early the next morning, and just before dawn found a few cigarette butts and the tracks of two riders.

They were being scouted . . . from then on no more cowponies, he would only ride Lop Ear or Horse.

After lunch, the rains started. Looking up above the sky, Cormac commented, "Very funny. Ha-ha! You wait until I get my saddle nice and clean and then you rain on it."

But as long as he was doing it, God was making no halfway job of it. It started right off with large drops, and quickly turned into a downpour, severely lashing the countryside. There would be no skullduggin' goin' on in this storm.

Cookie put up a tarp over his kitchen and kept two pots of coffee going constantly. "Looks like we got us a real gulley washer, Mack," he said.

The occasional lightning flashes out of the rain-whipped darkness were making the herd restless; everyone was in the saddle. The punchers talked to the herd and sang to them and hollered friendly insults at each other about how bad their voices were and kept making friendly sounds in general to keep the herd distracted from the weather.

Hearing the cowboy's voices was soothing to the herd; they knew they weren't alone. It was a long day and a longer night with each of the men in turn riding in for coffee or some of Cookie's sowbelly, beans, and cornbread or sourdough bread.

Cookie had proven to be every bit as good a cook on the trail as he was on the ranch and was also downright insightful. He had brought along some extra sugar and about midnight, produced a large tray of candy, a white creamy-soft concoction so sweet it made Cormac's teeth hurt.

"Cookie, you'll do. This is gonna cheer the boys up considerable. You're one in a million to think of it."

"Yeah, yeah," Cookie said, and waved off the compliment, but Cormac knew he appreciated hearing it. Along with a cup of hot coffee that tasted so strong Cormac wondered if the cup would dissolve, that candy went down right easy, and it made him think of home for a moment. Bits and pieces came back to him clearly:

He was ten years old. "Cormac wash your feet before going to bed, you've been running barefoot all day." . . . "You've torn the knees out of that pair of pants so many times, there's nothing left to patch." . . . "Cormie, fill the lamps please, before it gets dark, and take this catalog out to the toilet with you the next time you go." . . . "Cormie, please slop the hogs after dinner." . . . "Cormie, quit teasing your sister, or I'll have your father tan your hide." His pa never did that but once, and that was when he caught Cormac trying to shave with his straight razor when he was five years old. Cormac had gotten tanned good for that one.

Cormac confiscated a couple of extra pieces of candy for Lop Ear and Horse.

"What home?" he mused to himself as he made them each kneel for it. "You don't have one anymore."

The North Star was high when the rain passed and the clouds cleared. Cormac rode out on Lop Ear with Horse trotting alongside. He instructed Red to let the boys, other than those on guard, sleep a couple hours before getting on the trail. The dawn was taking its own sweet time about comin', and they would be tired today, but so would the herd; there wouldn't be many brushers and runners on this day. Mostly it would be a day of plodding forward, likely only making eight or ten miles, but that would be eight or ten miles farther than they had been.

CHAPTER 15

———— ◆·◆ ————

Cormac and company had covered about five miles when they topped a hill about an hour before dawn and caught sight of a fire in the distance. It appeared to be near the top of a hill about two or three valleys ahead. Cormac reckoned he had found his rustlers, most likely on their way to collect his herd.

"We'll have to see about that, guys," he said. Lop Ear's ears perked up.

"That's all right," Cormac told him. "You go on back to sleep. I'll wake you up when we get there." Lop Ear snorted. Cormac figured that was horse talk for "very funny."

Dropping down off a hill very nearly brought him to grief and smack-dab into the middle of a bunch of Indians. He pulled up behind a large mesquite bush right quick. Below, there were several trees, each serving as a tie pole for hastily thrown up lean-to's of canvas, hides, and blankets. There was just enough light to make out their ponies in a makeshift corral with a lot of sleeping bodies strewn about. A wild guess told Cormac there was in the neighborhood of thirty to forty horses with a rider for each: not a neighborhood he cared to visit. The absence of teepees meant no women or children; this was no group out sightseeing. This was a war party out raiding and no place that Mrs. Lynch's little tater picker, Cormie, needed to be.

"Quiet, guys," he whispered, and reined Lop Ear back around the hill.

There had been talk by the Rangers of Lakata Loma, a young buck leading a small group of other malcontents that had broken from their tribe of Lakota Sioux up in the Dakota Territory and who were marauding south, raiding, raping, and killing all they could find.

That many warriors would require much food. The Indians were adept at living off the land, hunting and fishing as needed, but that many of them in one group would make survival a struggle in unpopulated areas where they couldn't steal cattle or horses to supplement their hunting efforts. A herd of cattle that could be hidden in some out of the way canyon would be just what the doctor ordered, a home base from which the Indians could branch out.

An idea began to form; where before he had one problem, now there were two. Well, just maybe, with a little luck, they could solve each other, but he would have to get a move on. Cormac heeled Lop Ear to a slow trot. Sound would travel very easily in the early-morning silence, but the thick grass, soft from fresh rain, muffled most of the sound, allowing him to up the speed to a canter, then to a gallop. Lop Ear and Horse were happy at the chance to stretch their legs.

They skirted the valley and came quietly up on the other side, behind a clump of bushes looking down on the Indian camp. The bushes weren't big enough to hide Lop Ear and Horse standing up, so they had to lie down, and Cormac warned them to be silent. GERT slipped easily out of the scabbard, and he checked the load.

It was getting light and there was movement beginning in the camp below. Cormac crawled through the bushes to the Indian side and found a surprisingly dry place to lie. The branches above had grown and twisted together to form something of a roof. He squirmed down into the ground, making indentations for his elbows. Looking down GERT's sight, he judged the distance to be about two hundred yards. GERT could handle that without breaking a sweat.

What with the rain and all, the Indians also must have had a late night and were waking up slowly. GERT could help them with that. If they had any coffee, they weren't goin' to get any on this fine morning. That should start their day off for them and make them about as grouchy as an ole she-bear with a toothache.

Cormac figured to put a bullet or two smack-dab into the middle of them to get their attention and then run like the devil, although Lakata Loma would make a fine target, if he could identify him. With some luck, Cormac just might put a stop to his senseless killin'. His pa's belief of giving the other fellow a fair chance came to mind.

Sorry, Pa, he thought. *Some folks deserve no more than they give.* Lakata Loma gave no one a fair chance. There was no reason at all, that Cormac could see, for him to be treated any differently. The sound of a grumpy camp waking up from a bad night floated up the hill in the placid air: grumbling voices and sharp retorts in an Indian tongue, the sounds of wooden tree branches being broken for fires came from several locations around the camp along with the "clunks" of clay pots, the horses stirring, and a couple of stallions trying to keep their respective mares under control.

Cormac's long glass was bringing them up close, and his attention was drawn to a brave stepping out from under a low hung tarp of some kind, wearing only a loincloth, moccasins, brightly colored face paint, and a feather in his hair. The Indian looked around as he stretched; it was Kahatama! Cormac looked again. It was! It really was Kahatama! Their medicine man really could bring back the dead. Well, damn. That was a lot to believe, but there he was.

Cormac watched as he slipped an arrow quiver over his shoulder. Picking up a longbow and a rifle, the Indian strode forcefully toward a larger fire that had been started in the center of camp; other Indians moved aside to allow him passage. Kahatama glanced up the hill to where Cormac was hiding, and through the glass, Cormac was looking directly into the same eyes that had gotten so big when Cormac's knife surged into the Indian heart . . . Kahatama! . . . What the hell? Cormac just couldn't accept that. He almost dropped his long-glass. He looked again. Did the Indian know he was there? Kahatama appeared to be looking directly at him. If he fired, would the Indian strike him down with a bolt of lightning?

Well, damn! What Abraham had been telling him about the strong medicine of Black Hill's medicine men bringing back the dead was more than legend. Cormac would never have believed it. Cormac followed him with his long glass. This couldn't be right. This just could not be. The long knife of Cormac's pa had gone under the ribs and directly into the redskin's heart. Cormac was sure of it, but yet here he was, bold as brass.

Cormac put the glass away before picking up GERT. Once he pulled the trigger, he was goin' to have to skedaddle in a hurry. He lined up her sights on Kahatama's head. This just did not make any kind of believable sense. But this time Cormac would make damn sure that Injun was dead. GERT would put a bullet hole through the center of his head big enough to drive a wagon through. Let's see their damned medicine man fix that.

About to pass a tree, Kahatama turned to it and raised his loincloth to do what most people do first thing of a morning. When nature calls, one answers. Nature was calling to him, and if he was going to offer Cormac such a fine, still target, Cormac was not one to refuse it. It would make it easier to put the bullet exactly where he wanted.

It seemed more than a little humorous, actually, an undignified manner in which to die for someone who, Cormac was sure, would want to leave this world in the midst of battle, snarling and snapping and slaying enemies with each hand: being remembered as a ferocious warrior. Instead, he would die with his hand holding his . . . the voice of Cormac's pa interrupted his amusement.

"When you get your sights on the target, pull the trigger before something ruins the shot." Cormac remembered being told exactly that when, fascinated by its beauty, he had held on a deer longer than necessary.

"Okay, okay," he answered softly. He lined up the sight dead center on the Indian's head, and then dropped it to the base of the skull. The downhill slope would raise it back up to the middle of the head.

Cormac had not understood when his pa had been explaining the influences involved in shooting downhill. To Cormac, the shot should be some amount above the target point to allow for droppage, not below, but every time he tried it his way, he missed. First inhaling softly, Cormac's gentle exhalation matched the slowly increasing pressure of his finger. Cormac hesitated as the Indian began to turn.

Kahatama was making decorations on the ground, for Christ's sake. Apparently no man can resist that temptation from time to time. Well, as long as he was going to turn around, Cormac could wait. Which direction the target was facing mattered not to Cormac, but if the Indian wanted to turn around for a frontal shot, so be it. He must have had a lot of something to drink before going to bed. However; he was having a good time decorating while he continued turning, bringing his face around and neatly into sight line. After perfectly centering GERT's sights on the center of the forehead, Cormac dropped them to the Indian's mouth.

He appreciated the humor of the situation. This big, bad, ferocious, and terrible savage that so enjoyed raiding, burning, killing, and raping—a mushroom of smoke and fire belched from the bore as GERT carried out the final disposition of a vicious human being. The authoritative voice of death echoed off the surrounding hills as her bullet went exactly where she had been aimed, just like his pa had promised, right through the head. All the stand-up went out of Kahatama.

He collapsed on the spot with a hole through his head big enough to easily slide an arrow through with a pulpy mass of flesh and brain matter protruding from the cavity on the backside of his head.

Now let's see some Injun magic bring him back, thought Cormac.

His decorating project and his terrorizing, raping days were over. This time nobody was bringing back that son of a bitch! Cormac took time to once again examine the scene with his long glass. He had to be positive, absolutely positive. Even at that range, it was easy to see the blood and gore spread across the ground. GERT had done her job very well.

"Okay, guys, get up," he called to Horse and Lop Ear, springing out in front of the bush so the Indians could see from where the shots were coming. Cormac quickly scattered three bullets from the long barreled Colt in the direction of the camp, taking no time to aim. Pistols were no good at that range anyway. With enough elevation, he could get the bullet there, but he couldn't hit anything. And even if it were possible, two or three Indians more or less would make absolutely no difference in anything he could see, especially if they managed to get their red-skinned hands on him. With Lop Ear's help, he had hopes of avoiding that. He and Horse were going to have to hurry a bit, though; there was already a bunch of Indians mad as hornets running for the horses.

Cormac jumped his foot into the stirrup, spinning him around while his other foot was still clearing the big gray's hindquarters. "Let's hightail it outta here guys, we got company comin'."

Indians were already boilin' outta the encampment. Cormac pointed Lop Ear in the direction of the rustler's camp and turned him loose.

The big Arabian sensed the urgency and poured it on. The muscles in his hindquarters exploded, and Cormac had to grab the saddle horn to stay aboard. By the time he got both feet in the stirrups and his backside in the saddle, Lop Ear and Horse were settling into their task. Cormac tucked his face into the long mane, urging him on.

"Show 'em your stuff, big guy, let's go!"

Lop Ear's stride quickly smoothed out, and they went up and down the hills, just hittin' the high spots with Horse matching him stride for stride.

Reloading GERT on the run was challenging, but Cormac got it done and had her back in her scabbard and the six shot Smith & Wesson in his hand when they exploded over the hill and into the rustler's camp with the Indians hot on their trail. Lop Ear being Lop Ear, Cormac had to intentionally slow him down some to keep the Indians from giving up, keep them in the race. He called Horse back to stay with them.

The rustlers were in for a rude awakening. *Come on boys, wake up and join the fun.*

Lop Ear and Horse blew through the camp and out the other side, knocking over most of their kitchen equipment on the way, along with a couple of rustlers who managed to get to their feet in front of them. The horses showed no interest in slowing down.

"WHAT THE HELL?"

Cormac heard the voice behind him and looked back over his shoulder as they cleared the camp and dodged into the trees on the other side. The Indians were just bursting over the hill; the rustlers were awake and reacting to the situation.

Running hard, they cleared the trees and sped up the backing hill, stopping only briefly at the crest to look back. It was a melee. Indians were still pouring into camp, getting pulled from or jumping off their horses, guns were going off, white-and-red skinned bodies were entangling on the ground with knives and tomahawks flashing in the just-rising morning sun.

Generally, rustlers were sneaky cowards getting their strength from numbers while Indians, on the other hand, were born, bred, and trained for combat. From the age of five, their life is spent in training to become skilled, fearless horsemen, and hand-to-hand fighters; they look for any opportunity to count coup and prove their manhood.

Now, nearly equal in numbers and thrown together with no opportunity for stealth and planning, it was a deadly free-for-all. There would be no winner here; both sides would take heavy casualties. Cormac's money was on the Indians. Then, with Kahatama out of the way—if he stayed dead, that is—and their ranks cut by eighty or ninety percent, what was left of them would more'n likely go home to lick their wounds. Any rustlers lucky enough to walk away would wander off, get drunk, and wonder what the hell had happened.

"Good job, old-timer," Cormac told Lop Ear while patting his neck. "Thank you. All in all, not a bad morning's work. Now let's get us the hell out of here." A bullet whirred passed his head like an angry bee as they turned to leave. It might have been an accident, a rogue bullet searching for a target, but more'n likely, it was a message from a rustler or Indian expressing his gratitude for an exciting morning.

"By my count, that makes it twenty-nine hundred and forty-one head," said Jake Bartlow, the cattle buyer in Dodge City the bosses wanted Cormac to speak with.

"I don't know how you got through. A large group of rustlers has been hitting the herds hard and killing most of the hands. There has also been talk of a large bunch of heathen Indians headed this way. I'm mighty glad you made it through; it's been slim pickin's around here lately."

"I don't know," Cormac answered innocently. "We didn't see anything of them. We just kinda moseyed through without any trouble. We stopped a few times to let the herd graze and a couple times just to lay around for a few days, and then once when Cookie wanted to stay in camp and make a batch of candy, and man can he make candy. It's soft and white and so sweet it'll make your teeth hurt."

"Don't listen to him, he's full of malarkey," spoke up Red with a smile and a nod in Cormac's direction. "They were both out there. Mack here just sorta introduced them to each other then held us in a valley for a couple of days waitin' for the dust to settle. After that, we just rolled right on through without a hitch. He just don't like talking about the Indian, it spooks him."

Jake Bartlow smiled and shook his head. "Now that's a story I think I'd like to hear," Jake said to Cormac. "How about you head your boys over to the Daisy Lil's, and after you and I settle up, I'll buy the first round of drinks and you can tell me what happened."

"Numbers don't always work right for me," Cormac told him, wiping his hatband. "But one of my boys is a real whiz with them. If it's all right with you, let me get him to help me out."

Jake smiled. "Of course it's all right. Meet me at my office in ten minutes?"

"That's not necessary. There he is now." The kid was sitting on the fence with Oley. Cormac waved him over, and Jake waited for him.

"The going rate is eleven dollars a head, and we counted twenty-nine hundred and forty-one head. That should come to . . ." He paused to work the numbers on his paper. The kid spoke up. "Thirty-two thousand, three hundred and fifty-one dollars."

Surprised, Jake looked up and smiled, then finished his paper calculations.

"Well, I'll be a monkey's uncle if he isn't right on the money. Dang, I wished I could do that; it would come in almighty handy."

Then, to Cormac, "I suppose you'll want enough in cash to pay your men and the rest in script." It was more a statement than a question.

"Yes, sir. But we gotta talk some about that number. You already said there's been a shortage of beef lately because of the rustlers, and that there herd is in fine shape. We brought 'em

through slow and easy over rich grassland and gave them plenty of time for grazin'. They're in top condition. I think fifteen dollars a head would be more fittin'."

Jake looked at him for a long minute, and then burst out with a grin.

"Hell! You're right; they are in prime condition. You did a hell of job. Anyone who can do what you did deserves top dollar. I'll consider it a bonus for getting rid of the rustlers and the Indians."

He held out his hand. "You got yourself a deal." Turning to the kid, "What's it come to now, kid?"

"Forty-four thousand, one hundred and fifteen dollars," the kid answered matter-of-factly.

Jake stared at him, shaking his head. "I never seen the like. I've heard of it, but this is my first time see'n it. That's amazing." He paused briefly to turn to Cormac. "I'm not even going to check his figures. Let's go over to the bank and take care of business, then go get that drink. I'm dying to hear what happened out there, and what's spooky about it."

"How 'bout I meet you there in about ten minutes? I want to leave my horses at the livery and get them some new shoes while we're here. I noticed this morning they had both lost a couple of nails."

After making the necessary arrangements for his horses, Cormac proceeded to the bank where he completed the deal and drew twenty dollars for each man, having the banker hold the balance of their monies until they were ready to leave town. Cow towns attract a lot of sharpies, and he didn't want the boys relieved of the money they had worked so hard for while they were kicking up their heels. Jake smiled his approval.

Daisy Lil's was one of seven saloons dotting the main street of Dodge City. The polished mahogany bar with a full-length

brass foot-rail paralleling one wall was longer than most, but the rest was standard bar furnishings with an abundance of spittoons and as many chairs and tables as would fit. Some were card tables and, of course, there was a gambling wheel.

They all looked cared for, but well used: signs of a high-volume business. The walls were bare and undecorated unlike the Saloon With No Name. The only door, other than the entrance, was located near the far end of the bar, leading to the outhouse.

It was late afternoon, and the place was filling up. They selected a table in the far back corner away from the bar and Jake ordered them a couple of drinks and a round for the men. When the drinks came, Jake told the bartender to leave the bottle. Although he sometimes liked a shot of good whiskey, when he had his druthers, Cormac's first choice was beer. Cormac told him the story of the cowboys, fast horses, and rustlers with Jake stopping him from time to time for more details.

"Well, if that don't beat all," he said when Cormac had finished. "That took a lot of guts to play it that way. Tell me about shooting the Indian. I'd of liked to have seen that, and that gun. What did you say you call it?"

"GERT. She was my pa's rifle, and he called her GERT, so I do, too. So, where you shipping the herd to?"

"No, no! No changing the subject. You've avoided telling me about how the Indian spooks you. What's the deal?"

Cormac hesitated.

"Come on. Out with it."

Cormac took a deep breath. "It's just unnatural . . . strange. I don't believe it, but I don't know how not to."

"Well, get it out here on the table and let's look at it."

Cormac took another deep breath and another drink. "Okay, here it is. I already killed this Indian once before. I sunk my pa's

knife, this knife . . ." Cormac pulled his pa's big knife out of its sheath and put it on the table. "We were in a knife fight, up in Wyoming, and I stuck that knife up under his ribs and into his heart. He was dead. He had to be dead. Another Indian took the body away draped over a horse. Before that, I had met a couple of mountain men fresh out of the Black Hills who told me the Black Hills are the religious center of the Indians and have special powers, and that there is a medicine man there believin' he can bring a person back from the dead, but I didn't believe it for a minute. But maybe I'm wrong."

He hesitated, and poured another drink for the both of them.

"I had been told the Indian doing the raiding down here was a Sioux named Lakata Loma, but I saw him clear as could be with my long glass. It was a Sioux alright, but his name is Kahatama. He's the one I killed once already. I guess the medicine man's medicine is strong."

"No," said Jake Barlow. "I think I can solve this for you. Now that you mention it, I do remember hearing the name before. It was Lakata Loma. I've never heard the name Kahatama, but I have heard that Lakata Loma is part of a set of triplets and has two brothers up in Wyoming Territory the spitting image of himself and all just as ornery. I have no idea what happened to the other one, or if he's still alive. In fact, this is the first I've heard anything about them in years. I've never known of any other Indian triplets, and only one set of twins. They were women that drove the buck-Indians nuts. They thought pretending to be each other was great fun, until they secretly swapped husbands one too many times and got caught. Both of the husbands got them together and beat the fire out of them so badly they no longer looked alike, and that ended that. But you got him, you say? Good. But do the Indians up north know that it was you that got the other one?"

"Oh, yeah. They know," Cormac answered as he turned his chair sideways to the table. "Up there they call me Two Horse because of . . . well, you saw my horses. They're better than most."

"Well, my young friend, you better ride light in the saddle when you're in Indian Territory. If you killed one twin in Wyoming and the other in Texas, you're big medicine now. It's gonna be a badge of honor to wear your scalp on their belt. And gettin' your horses would just be icing on the cake. They're gonna want you real bad; they'll have their eye out for you. In fact, to let it be known that they have your scalp and to be seen riding around on one of your horses could very well become a top priority. Indians are big on honor and counting coup. In some ways, they are like children playing a game and keeping score.

"Completing any act of danger is counted and recorded with a notch on their coup stick. Even just to touch you and escape unharmed would count, and the more coup they count, the more eagle feathers they get to wear. But riding your horse with your scalp tied firmly on their belt would be the greatest and longest lasting coup of all. Some of their young bucks may even go out looking for you. So I'm deadly serious. You watch yourself."

Cormac sighed. "The mountain men said something very similar. But I'm not worried. As fearsome as they believe me to be, if I see any of them around, I'll just jump up and yell boogitty, boogitty, boogitty! They'll all just naturally run right away."

"You laugh, but the more fearsome you are, the more of a challenge you become. It's like a game to them, an act of manhood to show who is the most brave, who has the best story to tell around the campfires, whose squaw has the best stories to tell about her man, who the squaws find the most impressive." Jake Bartlow paused. "You know," he laughed, "other than the killing part, I guess they really ain't that much different than us, are they?"

Cormac sighed. The drunk at the bar made up his mind.

Well, it was about time. He had been trying to talk himself into trouble since he walked in and seen Cormac. He had finally succeeded. While Cormac had been telling the story, he had kept an eye on a couple of toughs who had bellied up to the bar. Most bars have a mean drunk or two, and at first, these two had appeared no different than any others. One of them, a tall thin galoot wearing two guns, had been leaning close and speaking low to his compadre from time to time, and shooting glances at Cormac. His friend had given the appearance of not wanting to hear what he had to say.

While turning his chair in preparation for the inevitable, Cormac had loosened the Smith & Wesson in his holster and double-checked that the thongs were off his guns while watching skinny out of the corner of his eye, waiting for him to make up his mind. He finally talked himself into it. He turned and started across the saloon toward Cormac. As he rounded the table next to them, Cormac made as if to leave and stood up.

"Whatever happens next is my fight," he told a surprised Jake, who was in the middle of a sentence when Cormac stood up. "This kind of thing happens from time to time." As skinny skirted the poker game in progress and slid a chair out of his way, he came up with his gun in the process; it was quite a nice move. Then, he disappointed Cormac by speaking.

"My partner tells me that he knows who you are, and says I should stay away from your gun. He says it's almighty sudden. Well, you don't look almighty sudden to me."

Would-be-toughs never learn. They can talk, or they can shoot; they always have to talk. They think that as soon as they point their gun at somebody, that somebody is just naturally going to shake with fear and do whatever they're told. They don't believe anyone would ever attempt to draw while being covered by a gun.

What they don't realize is that if the person they are pointing their gun at chooses to react negatively, it takes time for the
would-be shooter's brain to realize it, then it takes time for it to
send a message to the finger telling it to fire; it takes still more
time for the finger to react to the command. From past experience, Cormac tended to believe that when someone was pointing a gun at him, they intended to shoot him, saving him all
that thinking time.

The drunk's shirt was held closed by oversize black buttons
with the thread holding the third button from the top needing
attention. It was stretched and about to break. Just as the drunk
was saying how Cormac didn't look almighty sudden to him,
he was cocking his gun and bringing it to bear on Cormac, and
Cormac nailed the button down with a .44 caliber bullet.

A look of shock twisted the tough's face. "I didn't think . . ."
he got out before he collapsed.

Well, what in the hell did he think? He admitted that his
friend had told him Cormac was quick and still the drunk just
had to try him. Cormac shifted his eyes to the drinker still at
the bar. The drinker held up both hands to show Cormac they
were empty and shook his head.

"I tried to tell him," he said. "He wouldn't listen."

Cormac holstered his gun and turned to a wide-eyed Jake
Bartlow.

"I didn't even see you draw," Jake mumbled, a look of something between amazement and fear on his face, "and I was
watching you." Cormac was familiar with that look. He had
seen it before. He didn't respond; he just left.

––––––––––

Cormac walked out into the street. It was a street just like a
street in any other western town, with a boardwalk on each

side and overhangs from the buildings to protect would-be customers from the rain during the season. At opposing ends of the street were a church and a stable. Cormac had spent the last few weeks on one horse or another, and stretching his legs felt good. He elected to stroll down and check on Lop Ear and Horse.

They were there, in neighboring stalls, right where he had left them, both standing lazily on three legs, munching contentedly on mouthfuls of hay. He admired their lines, thinking how lucky his pa had been at having Lop Ear given to him. Cormac hadn't done so badly himself when he chose the grulla. She stood only a bit smaller than Lop Ear, well muscled without being bulky, graceful without being delicate, and she was built for speed and endurance with plenty of both. Anywhere they happened to be became a beautiful picture of which he never tired. Lop Ear turned his big head to greet him with a friendly nicker.

"Hey, old-timer," Cormac answered.

Cormac started into the stall and then hesitated. Horse had turned his head around to look back beside Lop Ear's for a good look-see. With them standing side by side with their heads almost touching, their expressive eyes looked like they were trying to tell him something, and it occurred to him that he had noticed it before, but never really thought about it.

They looked like relatives. They had the same conformation: the high-held, graceful, long slender necks and legs, high-set ears, and broad foreheads with small muzzles. He had previously noticed how they both stepped proudly and carried their tails high, yet his pa had been told Lop Ear was bred from some Arab country, and Cormac recognized Horse's slightly smaller mustang lines. Maybe a hand or hand and a half smaller than Lop Ear, her features were just kind of a watered-down version of Lop Ear.

Cormac wondered if it was possible that one of Lop Ear's ancestors got loose somewhere along the line and ended up in the same band of mustangs as Horse's sire or dam. He slid into the stall beside Lop Ear.

The big gray nuzzled his nose against Cormac's chest friendly like, searching for the piece of apple or carrot he would sometimes bring them and found one of the pieces of carrot in Cormac's shirt pocket that he had gotten at Daisy Lil's.

Not wanting to be left out, Horse stuck her head over the stall and, with her nose in the center of his back, gave him a shove. Cormac fell forward against Lop Ear's head. Lop Ear snorted and pushed Cormac back to Horse. Horse thought this to be great fun and shoved him back to Lop Ear. Cormac sidestepped to avoid Lop Ear's return. "Very funny, guys," he said. "That was really cute." They appeared to be pleased with themselves.

Cormac gave them each their piece of carrot, scratching the knots on their heads while they munched. Leaning his face against the face of first one and then the other while he petted and talked to them, they shared the same air and smelled each other's breath and both appeared to enjoy the closeness of the association, as did he. He looked back and forth between them, into their eyes.

While they were crunching their last crunch, he went and got the hostler's currycomb. Returning to the stalls, he found both horses looking at him, waiting expectantly; they both loved the comb, and their skin would sometimes shiver from the feel. The grulla blew and Cormac blew back. "Okay, girl. You win. You first."

He had finished Horse and was out of sight in the corner of the stall working on a tangle in Lop Ear's mane when two riders entered the stable.

"He's still up in Colorado," one was saying, "working for Lambert. He got word to me to round up any men I can find and go help take over the L-Bar N. I got eight men waiting at the old Carob place out north of town, with you and me, that makes ten; that should do it. We'll leave first thing in the morning and pick the others up on the way out. Lambert is going to wait for us to get there before he moves in on them. He wants more manpower."

One of their horses blew, and Cormac quickly put a hand over Lop Ear and Horse's noses to keep them quite.

"Lambert's already started moving in on it, scaring off the riders, rustling the stock, diverting the water, and anything else he can think of. Now they're surrounding it to keep anyone from going off and finding help, but they need more guns."

Cormac could hear their saddle leather squeaking as they dismounted and began unsaddling and stalling their horses. The hostler must have been out getting supper; it was that time of day.

"I wintered there about five years ago," the voice continued. "It was the Circle T then, but now it's owned by a mighty tough lady who's harder to run off than Lambert thought. It's the largest spread in that part of the country, but the previous owner got in the way of a bullet and got himself killed, and his only son's got no guts. He couldn't handle the hands, and they started rustlin' the stock. It was fast turning into a rawhide outfit until this lady bought it up and changed the name to the L-Bar N.

"Coldwell says this little gal has more than enough guts to go around, although from what he says, I shouldn't say little. He says she's 'bout as tall as he is. He told me that the first day she rode in the gate she called them all together and upset their apple cart by giving them their walkin' papers. She was holding a Colt revolvin' shotgun at the time," he said with a laugh. "All those guys went out of there with their tails between their legs for getting run off by a woman. That was three years ago, and she's already turned the place around."

Cormac again cautioned Lop Ear and Horse to silence with his hands still cupped over their muzzles. Not wanting to attract attention, he stood very still, listening to the sound of them forking hay into the mangers. The other rider spoke up.

"If she was tough enough to turn the place around, what made Lambert think she would be easy to run off?"

"Coldwell and me was talkin' about that. He can't figure that out either, but he thinks Lambert would have gone after it anyway; he wants revenge for her firing him and making him look bad. He was one of the hands that she put the run on, and he was fit to be tied. And he wants the ranch; it's the best spread around. And I think he wants the woman. Even Coldwell thinks he's got his cap set for her, too. He says this Nayle lady is a real looker, an Irish gal . . . tall and mighty shapely with fire red hair.

What? What did he say? Nayle lady? Red hair? Irish? Lainey? Owning a cattle spread in Colorado? How in the world was that even possible? The L-Bar N . . . LN . . . Lainey Nayle? There couldn't be another woman answering to that description: tall, good-looking, Irish, redheaded, and named Nayle? Lainey was definitely a looker, tall, and most definitely shapely. But . . . what the hell?

All grown up, she was probably downright beautiful. He remembered her of a morning, standing straight and tall in her cotton gown and robe, smiling at him over her shoulder from the stove through her mussed, tumbled-down, long red hair. She had a graceful nose sprinkled lightly with freckles, and green eyes that sparkled when she smiled, an amazingly white-teethed smile guaranteed to sit any man back on his haunches. Then he remembered the fierce hatred in those beautiful green eyes. *Damn it, damn it, damn it!*

How did she come to own a spread in Colorado? There was a question looking for an answer, and what happened to the Schwartzes? Well, how she got there was not of any particular importance, nor was her not being able to stand the sight of him. She was there, and she needed help. Cormac Lynch would just have to go see about that.

He would love to see her again, but could he handle it? Or the withering look that would be in her eyes? Or the words she would say? If she even spoke to him. Maybe he could find out what was going on, take care of it, and leave without her learning it was him, and without having to meet her face to face.

"Hey, who the hell are you?" asked the rider closest to him when he stepped out of the stall. "What's the idea of eavesdropping on our conversation? You could have said something to let us know you were there."

Both men stepped out of the stalls, hands close to their guns, expecting trouble and not sure what to do about him.

"I would appreciate it if you boys would just re-saddle your horses and take a little ride with me," Cormac told them.

The newcomers looked at each other.

"What the hell are you talking about, and why would we go anywhere with you? We just got here. We ain't riding anywhere tonight. We're going to get a good supper and have a few drinks. And I'll ask you just one more time, who are you?"

Cormac ignored the question.

"You are absolutely right; I did overhear your conversation. And I don't believe you should be going up to Colorado to help outnumber some lady who just wants to be left alone to run her ranch."

They looked at each other again, then grabbed for their guns.

Cormac was still wearing both guns as well as the one in his waist that he had been carrying since starting the drive, so he just naturally pulled the two holstered six-guns out, cocked them, and pointed them so each of the men was looking into a bore. They were faster than most, their guns had just cleared their holsters. They decided pulling their guns might not have been as much of a good idea as they had originally thought it to be and froze dead still. Their skin lightened a couple of shades, and one got a sudden case of religion.

"Jesus!" he exclaimed.

"I do not believe he's going to help you, friend," Cormac told him. "Now, just finish taking your guns out of your holsters and drop them carefully into that pile of hay beside you."

"Who the hell are you? Everybody knows what Holliday looks like, and Tomlinson from Texas is just a little guy, but as far as that goes, I doubt if even they can get into action that quick, and I've never heard of anyone who looks like you so who the hell are you?"

"Who I am is nothing you need fret about. I'm just an old tater picker. Now, let's all get saddled up and go for a ride."

"Look, mister, I don't know who you are or what you intend to do here, but we mean you no harm."

"No, of course you don't. You were just taking out your guns to clean them . . . here in the stable. Now, if either of those guns come up any higher, my thumbs are going to slip right off these hammers in fright." Their guns, that had been slowly rising, stopped rising. Cormac put a smile on his face and took it off again.

"I won't tell you again. Throw your guns in the hay . . . carefully. We wouldn't want one of them to go off and accidentally shoot somebody, now would we?"

They did as instructed, and then, also as instructed, re-saddled their horses and Lop Ear and put the pack back on Horse. Their horses were not happy about leaving again so soon and registered their disappointment by resisting leaving the stable, but a couple slaps with Cormac's reins on their backsides convinced them of the folly of that idea. With comments that "he couldn't get away with this," they rode quietly out of the stable, Horse trotting behind.

So now they got me being faster than Doc Holliday, huh? Cormac shook his head. *Not hardly . . . but I'm goin' to have to quit lookin' in the mirror. I'm liable to scare myself plumb to death.*

CHAPTER 16

The kid, being too young to be in the saloon, was leaning against an overhang post out in front. Cormac instructed him to have Jake direct the banker to release the men's money when they were ready to leave town, send his to the First National Bank in Denver, and the rest to the Ocean 3 along with word that he was quittin'.

The old Carob Place turned out to be a dilapidated barn and aging cabin with eight horses tied behind it, apparently to shield them from the sight of approaching riders, but the only approach to the cabin was by passing over the hill in front of it, which gave all visitors a bird's-eye view of the entire spread, including the rear of the cabin and any horses tied there. Well, he never did hear anyone say bad guys were smart guys.

Cormac and his two new friends left their horses tied to a bush about forty yards from the cabin, and after cautioning his companions about what he would do if they made any noise,

Cormac escorted them to the front door and motioned them to go in first. As they unlatched the door, he gave them a hard shove, crashing them into the room and knocking over the table, and then stepped in behind with a gun in each hand. As they had said, there were eight people waiting: two were lying on bunks, one sitting on a stool in the corner by the stove, one making coffee, and four sitting at the table, two of which had crashed into a pile on the floor, along with the table.

The bad guy on the stool had his gun apart for cleaning, and the two on the bunks had hung theirs on the bedpost. The coffeemaker threw the pot at him and went for his gun, as did the two that had been sitting at the table and had managed to get to their feet as it crashed. Cormac sidestepped the coffee pot and shot its thrower first; he got the other two as they cleared leather; one with each gun, like in the dime novel about the two-gun kid. Maybe he should write a book, and call it *The Two-Gun Kid*, *The Two-Gun Dakota Kid*, *The Dakota Two-Gun Kid* . . . Aah! . . . Maybe he shouldn't.

Three were down and were going to stay down; unlike the storybook gunmen, Cormac didn't waste time intentionally wounding or trying to shoot guns out of people's hands. That's nonsense. If somebody needs shootin', they need shootin'; do it and get it over with and don't leave that person around to shoot you later.

With three down, that left seven. Slowly and carefully, they all got to their feet with their hands in the air, except John. On the ride from town, the one doing all the talking had been called John. Now, John, still clinging to the idea that Cormac couldn't get away with this, untangled himself from the other arms and legs in the pile and came up with a gun concealed behind him. He should have kept it behind him; when he started to point it at Cormac, Cormac shot him. And then there were six.

As the sound of gunfire died, he swung his guns at the closest two, cocking them as he turned. It had the desired effect.

"Wait, mister, please!" the closer of the two exclaimed. "For God's sake, man! I don't even know who you are!"

Cormac had not intended to shoot them unless they did something foolish, but he had to get their attention. Now he had it.

Making a show of slowly taking a deep breath and exhaling, Cormac looked around the room, also slowly, bringing his eyes back to the two still under his guns. The room was thick with silence and gunsmoke. He just as slowly lowered his guns slightly, still cocked.

Cormac gave it a slow five count, then said, "You're right. You don't know me. Okay. I won't shoot anyone else right now, if you'll do as I tell you."

There were nods of agreement from all around the room.

"One at a time, carefully take off your guns and put them in the corner by the stove."

Apparently, they had become believers, for they did as they were told. When all were disarmed, he directed them to sit on the floor at the other end of the cabin.

"I'm going to give you boys a chance to not get killed." He paused, and then added, "Today." They looked at him expectantly while he slowly looked at each of them in turn, doing his best to look ferocious. He seemed to be doing everything slowly, but it was working, so what the hell . . . never fold a winning hand.

"I heard tell from John there, that you were all going up to Colorado to help run some lady off her ranch. Now I just don't believe that to be a good idea. I don't believe that's something you ought be doin'. What I think you ought be doing is staying as far away from Colorado as you can. I believe the air in Colorado would be very unhealthful for you. Would any of you care to disagree with that idea?"

There was a lot of head shaking: so far, so good.

"Do you fellas suppose if I let you go, you can manage to stay away from Colorado?"

Six heads were nodding. Cormac looked at each of them again, slowly, of course.

"All right then. I'm not going to shoot anybody else, but let's us make sure we understand each other. I'm going to ride up that way, and y'all better be somewheres else. If I run into any of you anywhere in Colorado, I'll shoot on sight, no questions asked. In town or out on the range, it won't matter a lick. I'm just going to haul off with this big old Army Colt and start banging away. I may end up in prison or getting hanged for it, but that won't matter none, you'll still be dead. Any questions?"

There weren't.

An empty burlap gunnysack on the floor by the woodpile was handy, so he filled it with their guns and gathered their rifles, all the while keeping a close eye for any shenanigans. He needn't have worried; they were being good little boys and girl. Girl? He looked again. Darned if one wasn't. It hadn't consciously registered in his mind, but even the oversize loose shirt couldn't completely hide the fact that one was most definitely a girl.

An average-sized woman of about twenty with average looks, not unappealing, wearing a fringed loose buckskin shirt, neither tall, nor short, nor attractive, nor repelling. Cormac had heard that girls sometimes rode with outlaw gangs wanting to be equals, or getting paid for their pleasures, but this was his first experience with it. It took him by surprise.

He motioned at her with his Colt. "Who are you?"

"What do you care?"

The Colt clicked as Cormac eared back the hammer.

"Okay, okay, Martha Jane Cannary Burke, from Missoura

by way of Montana." She wasn't frightened, just commonsensi-cal. Her voice was even and pleasant enough.

That's who he had thought she was. Cormac had just recently heard about her, and something about her description was famil-iar. He smiled at her. "Are you riding with this bunch?"

"Not now. I was plannin' on it; I had the invitation. But I didn't know what the job was. Johnny there on the floor just said it was in Colorado, and since I was kinda partial to him and never been up to Colorado, I decided it was a good chance to go see it. I heard they got themselves some real mountains up there, and I didn't have anything else more excitin' to do in Deadwood, what with Bill Hickok bein' dead and all. But now you told us what's goin' on, I'll pass. Who might you be?"

"Mack Lynch. You can call me Mack."

"Damn!" The one who said he didn't know who Cormac was did then. "You mean to tell me I been in a shoot-out with Mack Lynch and lived?"

Cormac turned his head slowly to look at the speaker. He was having a little fun with the being-slow idea.

"Well now, you weren't really in the shoot-out, and you didn't have a gun in your hand, did you? . . . And, I haven't left yet, have I?"

The man swallowed hard and shook his head.

Cormac continued. "I'm going to trust that y'all understand me," he said as he put the sack down to get a better grip. "I'm going to run off your horses, but they probably won't go far. With a little walkin' you should be able to round up most of them, and the walkin' will give you time to think about what I told you. I'll leave your guns about a mile up the road."

With the rifles under his arm, totin' the gunnysack full of hardware while keeping them covered was quite a trick, but Cormac pulled it off and made it to the door.

He glared at each of them in turn one more time for effect, and then put on what he hoped was a threatening face.

"Remember," he said gruffly before he closed the door. "Don't be damn fools! Stay out of Colorado!" Would he shoot them if he saw them? Who the hell knew? It would depend on the circumstances . . . he might.

"Good day, Martha Jane Cannary Burke from Missoura by way of Montana," he said to her with a smile as he tipped his hat with one gun-filled hand and backed out of the door. Her face lit up, and she returned the smile.

"Good day to you, sir," she called. With a smile to brighten her face, a young Calamity Jane was more than a little attractive.

Stopping that bunch would buy some time to get there. Lambert was waiting for someone to come that wasn't coming, but he wouldn't wait forever. Now Cormac had to get there. He pointed Lop Ear's nose northwest and urged him up to an all-day-runnin', ground-eatin' kinda lope. Dodge City would just have to get along without Cormac Lynch and company.

––––––––––

Alternating between Lop Ear and Horse, they made good time. They had covered approximately two hundred and fifty miles in four days with few stops but to change horses. He stocked up on supplies in Roosterville; a town started, like many others, by accident, he learned from an old man chair-sittin' on the walk in front of the barbershop.

"It was named," the old man had said, in a raspy voice, "after its founder—a man answering to the name of Rooster. You want to hear about it?"

"You bet I do, old-timer," Cormac answered, wanting to learn about the area and about what was going on there.

On the way to the meeting at the old Carob Place, John had

told him that the L-Bar N was northwest of Roosterville and
another traveler, with whom he shared his smoking tobacco,
had given him directions on how to get to Roosterville. Now
he needed information, and anything he could learn would be
helpful. He still held the idea of sneaking in and taking care of
whoever was giving Lainey a bad time and then getting gone
again without having to face her.

The old man's face brightened; he hadn't expected that. He'd
been expectant of Cormac walking on by, as most folks probably did, but Cormac was wishful of learning about the area,
and this old man was wishful of someone with whom to talk.

"Well, sir," he began happily, wriggling himself a little deeper
into his chair, getting more comfortable. Cormac smiled. The
old man reminded him a little of his pa sittin' around the cracker
barrel in the general store in town with some of his friends,
getting wound up to tell one of his stories. This was lookin' like
it might take a while. Pushing his hat back on his head, Cormac
stepped around an old dog sleeping in the sun, and into the
street, seating himself on the edge of the walk and leaning back
against a post that was supporting the roof. The dog opened his
eyes and looked at Cormac, made a feeble attempt to wag his
tail, thought better of it, and went back to sleep.

"Well, sir," the old man began, "story goes that, after wandering
for a lot of years, this Rooster fella camped late one night on the
east bank of the Sweet River, which by the way, gets its name for
the taste of the water where it originally runs out of the ground way
up on that mountain, there. It's crisp, cold, and almighty pure."

The old man stretched a crooked arm and pointed at a peak
rising in the mountain range, taller than those surrounding it.
The motion pulled up his sleeve, exposing two bullet scars. There
was probably a story for that, too, but Cormac didn't want to
pry. If the old man wanted him to know about it, he'd tell him.

"When Rooster got up the next morning, he had been over-whelmed by the natural beauty surrounding him—that's what it says in the town history book the barber is writin'. He used to work for a newspaper back east somewhere and writes real pretty. I've read it and heard it read so many times, I practically know the whole thing by heart."

Yep, this was going to take a while. Cormac took out his bag of makin's and rolled a quirlie with one hand while reaching for a match with the other. Striking the wooden match on the wood of the walkway, he lit it while his eyes caught sight of an adver-tisement in the barbershop window behind the old man.

The sign displayed a picture of a little white round tag on a yellow string dangling from a white bag of Bull Durham smoking tobacco with a package of cigarette papers glued to its side just like his, sticking partially out of a cowhand's shirt pocket just like his, with the message proudly stating the nickel treat to be the "Cheapest Luxury in the World."

Not far wrong, Cormac thought as he exhaled the smoke from his first drag. *Not far wrong.*

"According to Curly's book," the old man was saying, "it had been in the fall with the mountains rising majestically in the distance, the lower portion of which was still covered with Golden Rod flowers and Aspen trees with their wind-sculpted peaks hidden under a new snowy blanket. Grassy slopes and millions of tall pine trees were filling the expanse between them and the Sweet River. Rooster had never seen a sight more beau-tiful and decided right then and there his wandering days were over. After many years of searching, without knowing what he had been searching for, he had finally found it. He set himself up a camp and began building a cabin. Before he had it finished, some other folks traveling through bought the hindquarter of a fresh-killed deer and some jerky from him, along with some wild onions." The old man paused to spit a tobacco stream at a lizard that had just crawled out from under the porch to lie in the sun. He missed close.

"The location," the old man went on, "turned out to be on a well-used route, and Rooster began selling and trading meat, onions, and some nuts from a tree he had found to others. After trading for some seeds and books—books that he later traded for a plowshare—he planted a garden, and it wasn't long till his cabin had a sign in front that read ROOSTER'S TRADING POST— GOOD EATIN AVAILABLE.

"It seems he had learned to cook some during his knockin'-around years. A passing blacksmith looking for a home opened a shop nearby and, within a month, they had been joined by a whiskey maker from Kentucky selling whiskey from the back of his wagon while he set up a still and began building a saloon.

"One by one," the old man rattled on, "others stayed, and the community grew happily until rowdy travelers became more frequent, and folks agreed they needed a peace keeper. They got together and decided to formally become a town and start paying taxes to give them the money to hire a Sheriff. It was suggested by the saloon keeper, voted on, and approved, that the name should be Roosterville."

As if to punctuate his sentence, he spit again at the lizard; this time his effort met with success. Unexcited, the lizard looked around, moved a couple feet farther away, did a couple push-ups, and went back to sleep. The old man refused the drink that Cormac offered him, and after thanking him for the story, Cormac went into the saloon to see if he could pick up any helpful information. The old man's story had been interesting, but held nothing of any use.

Slowly, Cormac sipped a couple of drinks to give him time to pick up more information; hopefully, he would hear something that would apply to Lainey. Local watering holes were a melting pot of information; people coming together generated conversations on most goings-on in any locality. Much of the talk was of no importance to anyone not living in the area: someone should fix the hole in the road coming into town, the sheriff was getting too lazy to be effective, the weather was sure nice for this time of the year, and Tammie Jenkins got caught trying to steal a piece of candy from the store. But his time turned out to be well spent when he overheard that a gunfighter named J.B. Sanderson had been seen riding through town and was guessed to be on his way to do something for Lambert. "Lambert" was said with a sneer.

Cormac stayed the night in Roosterville, and while riding away at sun-up the next morning, found it easy to see what had enticed them all to stay. It was quite a sight with the mountains and all, but there were many such beautiful sights in this part of the country. He still couldn't figure how Lainey ended up here, but she had located well, other than for Lambert and Sanderson, and Cormac Lynch figured to do something about them.

———————

The sun was just peaking over the horizon when Lainey Nayle walked out onto the front porch of the L-Bar with her morning coffee and stood looking around in a melancholy mood. It was such a beautiful ranch. A great deal of the surrounding mountainsides were blanketed with the brilliancy, radiance, and splendor of Colorado aspens and golden rod that bloomed from spring until Indian summer. The first snow of the year would cause the golden rod to wither and die, returning to the soil that had given them birth, only to repeat the brilliant display again the following spring.

Several streams coming out of the mountains wandered irregularly across the ranch, most being tributaries of the Sweet River, providing a natural irrigation system for the lush grasslands. The mountains provided barriers on the sides and rear that kept the cattle from roaming, leaving only the front of the ranch needing watching and herding, which could be done very efficiently with only a few hands.

She thought about the events that had transpired to put her here after all she'd been through, losing her parents, being kidnapped, and then rescued by Cormie.

Lainey sighed and shook her head. If only she had not reacted so stupidly when Cormac had rescued the girl, he might well be standing with her right now, and they would not be having the problem with Lambert. A smile warmed her face as she remembered pretending to be too weak to stop him from kissing her while wrestling in the snowbank, and getting herself naked and ready for bed and realizing Cormie was using a mirror to peek under the blanket dividing the room they had shared.

How very slowly she had unfolded her nightgown and unbuttoned the neck, taking time to brush off several pieces of nonexistent lint, and she remembered holding it and her arms high above her head to let the gown settle ever so slowly downward around her body. And she remembered a wagon ride to town when she had pretended to fall asleep with her head on his shoulder and the deep feelings that had ensued. And, she remembered sadly moping around for weeks after he had left.

When they had woken up and found him gone, Mr. and Mrs. Schwartz had sadly followed his wishes and registered the farm into Lainey's and their names. Two years later, they had been attacked by a pack of rabid coyotes while working in the fields. They ran as fast as they could but both the Schwartzes were bitten before climbing the only tree in the valley. The tree under which four crosses still stood. The disease had taken the life of Mrs. Schwartz within three weeks, and that of her husband three days later. And so Lainey had lost her second set of parents.

"This is how Cormie must have felt," she had thought, "all alone with his insides sick and empty."

Knowing nothing else to do, she had taken on what most would have considered a hopeless project for a lone, twenty-one-year-old woman: working the farm. She accepted that she could not do all that the three of them had been doing and mentally partitioned the farm into two fields: corn and flax.

Rising daily before dawn to milk the cows by lantern light, feeding the chickens, fetching the eggs, and slopping and feeding the hogs before breakfast, she worked in the fields until dark, and then took care of the evening chores, including the second milking of cows anxious with overfilled udders, once again by lantern light. It was hard, and she was tired all the time, but she managed, all the while with a gun tucked in a special pocket she had sewn into her dresses. She had remembered Cormac's story of losing his family because his mother refused to carry a gun.

Only once did Lainey think using her pistol was going to become necessary: when a drunken cowboy passing by was proving himself too amorous and insistent. When he was ignoring her requests to leave, Lainey began acting increasingly fidgety, frequently checking the road from town until the cowboy finally noticed and irritatingly asked her why.

"Well," she answered, acting timidly with her head down at first, and then glancing again at the road. "My brothers were due back from town an hour ago, and I don't want them to get in trouble again. The last time they came home and found me with a man, they beat him so badly they had to take him to town in the wagon for the doctor to fix up, and the sheriff put them in jail for three days."

Bemoaning his luck, the cowboy took a quick look in the direction of town, got back on his horse, and was probably in Texas by nightfall. Then, the skies opened and rain began to fall.

Large slow drops at first, then faster and heavier with even larger drops, continuing day and night for three days, then slowing to a drizzle for another two with a short spell of large hard driving hail in the center. Between them, the rain and hail flattened most of the crops and washed out the others. The creek, running fast and muddy, had for a time turned into a rampaging river and overflowed its banks with fast moving rapids that flooded many acres of the land, painting a fresh coat of rich alluvial soil over much of the countryside.

It was God's way, it seemed, of saying that no matter what piddley humans did, or how they partitioned off the world with their silly little barbed-wire fences, he was still in charge and would take charge whenever he felt the need. When the deluge had ended, Lainey had ridden out to survey the damage and found it to be total. The year's crops and all of her hard work were gone.

Stopping to eat her lunch beside a still-rampaging Red Stone Creek, a tributary of the Cheyenne River, she had climbed atop a large uprooted log that had been driven up onto the bank by the extreme force of the water. Taking advantage of having no work to do, she had eaten slowly, enjoying the warmth of the sun following the days of rain and cloud-covered skies. She remembered idly watching an oddly shaped dark stone a little larger than her fist being tumbled, little by little, into a cluster of rocks by a narrow, yet strong, eddy. Other river rocks were being easily and mercilessly tumbled and tossed about; this one was resisting, being rolled only inch-by-inch. "Stubborn little guy," she remembered thinking. It had reminded her fondly of Cormac. Her curiosity had gotten the better of her, and she retrieved it, surprised by its weight.

Returning to her lunch, she had set the rock on the tree to free her hands, which she needed to push herself back atop the trunk. In doing so, the rock had been jostled and rolled off and fallen, striking a broken and jagged branch on the way down, scratching the black surface and exposing it to be a solid gold nugget.

What Lainey knew about gold was absolutely nothing; she doubted her find. Holding the nugget in her hand and looking at what she knew it to be, she doubted it. This kind of thing happened to other folks, not to Lainey Nayle. She wished Cormie were there to share it with. If there was one, were there more? She worked her way about five miles upstream, finding no others. The first mile downstream, however, was much more productive, Lainey found three more, all of equal size, and then no more. She had walked another five miles fruitlessly before giving it up. She theorized that a large piece of gold, if such it was instead of the fool's gold she had heard of, had torn off from a main deposit only to break into smaller pieces and tumble downstream.

Travelers heading into the hills searching for gold had said that it was very heavy, soft, and easily scratched, and any nuggets found in a stream would most likely be rounded and bull nosed from the rolling. These fit the description to a tee, but still she doubted.

Escorted by Sheriff Woodrow's son, she had found the assay offices in Omaha and Cheyenne both to be temporarily closed, making it necessary to sell the nuggets in Denver. Uneventfully, the train had gotten them there safer and more quickly than riding a horse all that way, and her "little rocks" totaled fifteen point seven two pounds at one hundred and fifty dollars an ounce, totaling thirty-eight thousand dollars. She had very nearly fainted.

Catastrophes notwithstanding, she had enjoyed her life and experiences, but had no desire to be a farmer for the rest of it, although she might have felt differently had Cormie still been there. She remembered wishing he had been there to share in her good fortune. While in Denver, she had overheard two ranchers discussing plans to go in together and buy the Circle T ranch because it was such a beautiful and well-placed spread and neither could afford to buy it alone.

Within the hour, she had rented a horse, gotten directions, and was on her way to see the ranch. The Circle T lived up to its billing. It was a pretty ranch on a plateau in a large valley of the foothills of the Rocky Mountains north and east of Boulder, with plenty of water, and it had been well maintained, but, the seller warned, the hands were rustling the cattle and had killed his father.

The next morning found her waiting in front of the bank for it to open. Before dinnertime, having arranged to meet the seller there, she had negotiated herself a twenty-five thousand acre ranch for a dollar an acre, registered it and changed the name to the L-Bar N, and by suppertime had put the run on the crooked hands.

The next day, she had hired a foreman to teach her ranching, and had him hire a new crew. Now here she was, standing on the porch of the best ranch in Eastern Colorado—her porch— again wishing Cormie was there to share the good fortune.

After he had left, she had had occasional suitors, but none of any interest. She had gone riding with one a few times and on a picnic with a couple of others. All had been pleasant times, but men other than Cormie had just never provided any romantic interest, and somehow she knew that wherever he was, even though she had hurt him badly, the bond they shared was strong and would not break. The fingers holding her coffee mug were white from the pressure she was applying and some blood had dripped onto the porch from the other hand that had curled hard into a fist, digging her fingernails, unfelt, into her palm. It had to be that way. It just had to.

Interrupting Lainey Nayle's thoughts, her foreman walked out of the bunkhouse and across the yard to her. She wondered about their first meeting; what infinitesimally small event had transpired, starting the chain of events prompting him to enter the general store at the exact moment she had been leaving it, causing them to bump into each other when they had first met? She had liked him immediately.

He had never told her that he had been coming to look for her and had refused to work for Lambert after learning he was making plans to take over her ranch. He had wanted no part of the plan and had decided to help her if she would hire him.

The storekeeper had already told her that the best foreman around for her would be Shank Williams, if she could get him. That he was a tough, honest man with a fast gun, which he used judiciously. According to the storekeeper, Shank was a man of his word, no matter what.

"Good morning, Shank." Lainey smiled warmly.

Her green eyes sparkled, and her smile lit up her face. Shank looked up at her with the rising sun behind her, outlining her shape and glowingly reflecting through her red hair. *Lord, you outdid yourself on this one,* he thought.

"Good morning, Miss Nayle." He smiled back. "It looks like we got us the beginnings of a beautiful day."

She looked around silently one more time at the blue sky over the surrounding hills and at the distant snow-capped mountains.

"That we do, that we do," Lainey answered in her best Irish accent. Then, speaking in her normal, soft Irish lilt, "Let me get you some coffee, and you can tell me what happened in the pass last night. I heard gunfire."

After they had gotten settled on the porch chairs, he tasted his coffee and found it hot, black, and strong. She knew how to make coffee that a man could enjoy, and that surprised Shank not in the least. He seriously doubted there was anything Lainey Nayle didn't do well.

"After we finished moving the herd up closer to the buildings where we can better keep an eye on them, I sent Lem to try to get through the pass. I remembered an old trail that, to my knowledge, hasn't been used in years. I was hopin' Lambert didn't know about it and even if he did, would think it too far out of the way and wouldn't have it covered. Lem is more Injun than some Injuns; I was hopin' he could Injun through and go to Denver for help.

"It almost worked. He was nearly through when he stepped on a loose rock and fell. He said there were at least two, and maybe three, men hiding in the rocks that opened fire, but it was cloudy and too dark to see; they didn't hit anything. Lem was smart enough not to shoot back and let them see where he was. Instead, he just slipped out and came home."

Lainey nodded her approval. "How are we doing on ammunition? Most of the things in my vegetable garden are ripe; I think we have enough food for two or three weeks, and after that we can kill some beef, but I'm worried about the ammunition."

Shank had also been worrying some about that himself, but before he could answer Lainey jumped up.

"What is that, Shank?" She was pointing toward the twin peaks they had just been discussing.

Shank looked where she was pointing.

"What, Miss Nayle? I don't see anything."

"There is something moving out there, at the top of the alluvial fan, directly below Kater point."

Shank was still at a loss, and then he began to see small movement. "It looks like a single rider, ma'am, coming fast."

Stepping to the door, Lainey picked up the Winchester that had been leaning just inside and jacked a cartridge into the chamber as she turned to meet the possible threat. Shank smiled slightly. Standing tall and straight in the center of the porch, her attention focused on the fast approaching rider, she held the rifle with a familiar ease in the ready position, her body turned slightly for a quick and smooth rise of the rifle to her cheek, her face a study of strength and confidence: a western woman . . . and what a woman, he thought, strong and ready to take on whatever came at her, neither asking for, nor giving any quarter.

She was not a beautiful woman who happened to be strong. She was a strong, competent woman who just happened to be beautiful and, unlike most attractive women that Shank had known, she made little of it. She neither used it to her advantage nor acted coquettishly, nor pretended to be unaware of the fact. That she was prepared to take a part in their defense was comforting and no surprise. She wasn't just a boss that sent the hands into danger while keeping herself safely cooped up. He had heard the story of how she, with no help from others, had kicked the renegades off the ranch when she first took it over, but wasn't sure what to think of the story. He had since become a believer.

Shank recognized the odd shape of the rider's hat.

"It's okay, Miss Nayle. That's Candy."

Nearly fifty years old, Candy wore the dubious distinction of being the oldest rider on the ranch. All rawhide and wang leather, he was stringy tough. Other than Shank, he was always the first up in the morning and the last to give it up at night; he did more work than most. He had never met anyone who knew more about cattle than he did, but he kept that piece of information under his hat. He had heard that wisdom comes with age; one of the wisest things he had come to know was that no one wanted to hear about how smart he was.

Candy Johnson slid his horse to a stop in front of Lainey and Shank and took no time for greetings.

"I think Lambert is getting ready to blow up the pass! I've heard of a new explosive that comes in sticks for easy usin', and I saw three of his men riding up the trail with some boxes marked DYNAMITE tied to a packhorse."

"That son of—" Shank cut himself off. "Sorry, ma'am, if they blow the pass, it'll stop up the Sweet for sure. The lion's share of our water comes out of that ole river.

"They have a big lead on us; I doubt we can get there in time, but we can try. And we can sure as hell thin their ranks a little if we can catch them coming down." He bounded off the porch. "Get yourself another horse, Candy. I'll roust the men."

———————

Well up the side of a rough and ragged mountain on the other side of a gulch, Cormac Lynch could see a secluded out-of-the-way shelf upon which appeared to be a good spot for a camp. It would be about a twenty-minute ride away from one of the overlooks he could see in the distance above the L-Bar, as it was being called according to a helpful traveler, that was remote enough to reduce the possibility of being accidentally discovered, yet close enough to the L-Bar to be handy. He could see a small cave offering protection from the rain, and a large flat rock-shelf with a small clearing supplying a stream and plenty of deadfall wood for fires about ten or twelve feet below.

The sky was clouding up and mountain storms were to be taken seriously. He had heard that the air surrounding the lightning strikes at this elevation could fairly sizzle with enough electricity to make a person's hair stand on end. The surrounding area was thick with pine trees that would disseminate the smoke of a small campfire.

"Looks perfect. What more could we want?" Cormac asked the grulla and Lop Ear. Horse snorted.

"Okay, that settles it," Cormac told her. "We'll go there."

Although the campsite was only a few hundred feet away as the crow flies, it looked to be about a mile around the gulch to get to it. On the way, he was forced to duck behind some huge boulders to avoid a group of riders. He dismounted and held the muzzles of both horses to keep them quiet as the riders went by. There were two boxes he recognized tied on a packhorse. They were boxes of a new explosive called dynamite that he had seen used in the mine.

Shaky, unstable, and extremely dangerous, Nitro-Glycerin had been the only choice of an explosive available until just recently when somebody invented the much more controllable dynamite that could be lit with a fuse, but it still packed one heck of a punch. Cormac wouldn't have cared to have any of it tied behind his saddle. One of the riders was telling the others that stopping up the Sweet River would take care of most of the water for the L-Bar.

"We'll just see about that," Cormac said.

In the direction they were riding, he had seen a pass from which a river flowed that figured to be their destination. When the riders had passed, he selected a course that would get him there first. Riding Horse, they slid down some slopes the other riders couldn't with a packhorse full of dynamite. Once on flat ground, he turned her and Lop Ear loose and let them run. When the riders rode into the pass, he had been looking down at them over GERT's sights from across the river. When they had reached a clearing providing him a straight shot, GERT reached out and said hello to the dynamite.

CHAPTER 17

On the way to the bunkhouse, Shank slid to a stop as an explosion echoed across the ranch, loud even at a distance.

"Damn! That son of a . . ."

"Bitch!" Lainey finished for him. "He is deliberately stopping up the Sweet!"

"Anyone who would cut off range water is lower than a snake's belly," complained Candy.

Shank started again for the bunkhouse. "Let's go see how bad it is. Maybe we can open it up again."

There was no need to roust the men. The explosion had taken care of that. They were already streaming out the door, asking each other what the hell that was.

As Shank, Candy, and the four others Shank had chosen approached the pass, Shank could see the jagged formations still intact. They had expected to see a large, gaping hole from the explosion, but it wasn't there. There was no visible change.

Following the still-flowing Sweet River, they advanced slowly, guns in hand.

Cautiously rounding some boulders into a clearing, they pulled up in surprise, taking in the signs of the explosion. A small but recent slide filled one corner, and a few large boulders appeared to have been recently relocated from a higher elevation. The center of the clearing was a gruesome scene with various pieces and leftovers of men and horses strewn around.

The six looked around in silence. Even the horses sensed something and stood quietly. The only sound was of flies already beginning to gather on the bits of flesh. With a few hours of hot sunshine, the stench would be unbearable.

"What do you suppose happened, Shank?" Candy finally got out.

"Something must have set off the dynamite before they were ready, and I'm rightly curious about what. The rest of you stay put," Shank told the others. "Candy and me'll have a look around and see if we can piece out what went wrong."

Taking different directions, Candy Johnson and Shank Williams slowly outlined the clearing, meeting on the other side, and then without speaking, rode back through the center.

Shank was the first to speak.

"The horse tracks lead right to the center of the clearing where the explosion happened. There are no boot prints, so something set it off while they were still mounted."

Candy nodded his agreement, and then added, "From what I've heard, dynamite doesn't just go off. Something had to of fired it, and the only thing that makes sense from what little I know is a bullet, but from where, and from who? None of us were up here."

"I come to the same conclusion and been studyin' on that. It couldn't have been from close up without the shooter getting caught in the blast. The rocks around here are too steep to climb, and that only leaves above the trees on the other side of the Sweet with a straight-line shot. What do you make of it, Candy?"

"My thoughts exactly. Wanna go look?"

"I'd give a pretty penny to know who fired that shot. Maybe we can find something that will tell us."

The nearest crossing was outside the pass, where the current was still fast, but passable. One of the horses was reluctant about crossing and needed a few slaps from Candy's reins for encouragement.

Coming up to the thick stand of trees across the river from where the explosion had shaken the mountains, Shank told the riders, "Spread out and look for tracks. The shooter would have had to come through here to get to a place with a straight shot into the clearing. Go slow and don't miss anything."

It was Candy who found an old Indian footpath with fresh boot prints leading up into the rocks behind the trees. Too steep for a horse, Shank and Candy followed the recent tracks up the mountain on foot, stopping many times to catch their breaths.

"Man!" exclaimed a breathless Shank. "This guy must be part mountain goat. Look how far up we are, and there still isn't a shot to the clearing."

Another ten minutes' climb brought them out on a small rock shelf. Candy was the first up and stopped before going onto it.

"There it is." He pointed to a footprint. "And there is a perfect boulder to rest a rifle on, but that would be one hell of a shot. Look how far it is down there. This angle would make for a lot of drop, and drop shoots are tricky. This boy can shoot."

"Well, this says we're right, there was a shooter. And, going by the size of these tracks we been followin', he's a big man. And he has to be in good condition to have climbed up that path. I was watching and seen no tracks where he stopped to rest like we did; but who in the world would it be? All of our men are accounted for."

"I don't know, Shank. Someone with a score to settle, I'd guess; but if he's working against Lambert, I'd like to shake his hand and buy him a drink or ten."

Shank nodded. "Now, let's see if we can get down from here without breaking our fool necks."

Lainey was worried. It had been on her first supply run to town when she had met Lambert at the general store. She remembered him to be one of the Circle T riders that she had fired. He was a wide man with wide shoulders over a massive chest. His arms were thick muscled and long, hanging lower than most. Cruel and wide-set eyes had glared out at her from an unshaven round, monkey-looking face.

When there was no one else within hearing distance, he had made a crude suggestion to her. She had responded the way she always did whenever something like that happened—she ignored it and walked away with no reaction, response, or acknowledgment that it had even taken place. In anger, Lambert had thrown down the items he had been carrying and stomped out of the store.

That Lambert was prepared to kill, he had already proven: three times. Two of her riders had been shot and killed trying to get to Denver. A third had been lassoed and drug to death when he was caught while searching for strays. A fourth had been severely beaten and released with a message that if she didn't want all of her men to end up the same way, she should pack up and leave.

The men wouldn't hear of it. When Farley had been so badly beaten, Lainey had only just barely managed to keep Shank from going after Lambert. She briefly regretted that decision, but had she allowed it, she felt certain that he could not have gotten through Lambert's men without getting himself killed.

"Ma'am, you don't strike me as one to cut and run when times get tough," Shank told her emphatically when she had called a meeting on the porch with all of the men to tell them she would rather leave than get anymore of them killed. "Well, we ain't either." The men all strongly agreed. Looking around at the other riders for their approval, he said, "We ride for you, ma'am. There's not a man amongst us that will stand for you being harmed or your spread taken from you, and we'll listen to no more such foolishness."

To a man, they each voiced their agreement. She had nodded and mumbled thank you and gone inside, not wanting them to see the emotion running down her cheeks.

Now she was afraid Lambert might win. Her men were doing the best they could, but they were outnumbered. They needed to get help desperately, but there was no way to leave the ranch other than the front or back range or the Southern pass, and all were being watched. The ranch buildings had been centrally built for convenience of operation, not for defense. Being out in the open made it impossible to approach without being seen, however defending it against a straight-out attack from a large group of invaders would be difficult, if not impossible.

She remembered a cabin she had seen in a mountain alcove while on one of her rides. Lainey loved to ride early in the morning when the sun was just climbing the horizon. On one such ride, she had rounded a rocky corner and found a long-abandoned cabin tucked back behind a small stand of trees. It would have gone unnoticed by a casual passerby. Maybe it would be better to abandon the ranch buildings and move the men there; it would be more easily defended.

Her men were all either on patrol or with Shank but for the

two who had been instructed to remain with her. She called to them to bring the big wagon up to the porch and help her load it. They would leave immediately upon Shank's return.

While Lainey Nayle was loading the wagon, Burnell Lambert was nearing the pass to survey the damage done by his men. He turned his horse quickly behind a boulder pile in time to watch the group of L-Bar riders coming out of the trees. He was puzzled as to what they might have been doing on that side of the river; he was also puzzled as to why there was still a river. The explosion should have stopped it up. Obviously, something had gone wrong, but what could have possibly happened? Blowing up the side of a mountain was not complicated, just stack a bunch of dynamite against it, light the fuse, and run like the devil.

He watched Shank and his riders go by. His horse sent a whinnied hello at the other horses, but the sound was masked by the noise of the river. The rapids were less than in the pass, but still substantial.

Lambert was embittered over most everything since being thrown off the L-Bar. He hated Lainey Nayle for doing it to him and making him look bad, and he hated Shank for not joining him.

"He thinks he is so righteous," he thought, "but I'll take care of him before this is over."

Shank had a fast gun, but so did he. It was just that he didn't advertise it and few knew about it. When someone needed killing, he did it away from the eyes of others, preferably from ambush; but just as easily face to face. He practiced drawing regularly in private and had become surprisingly quick.

After Shank had turned him down, Burnell Lambert had brought in J.B. Sanderson when his efforts to locate Mackle had failed. Mackle had been his first choice, but nobody had known how to reach him, and rumors placed him somewhere in Texas. Sanderson was said to have shot seventeen people. Lambert had seen one of the shootings and knew himself to be faster. Sanderson would never learn Lambert hadn't the money to pay him; Lambert would kill him after he had gained control of the L-Bar. Lambert couldn't help smiling—when he took the L-Bar, he would also take the woman. She wouldn't ignore him again.

After the men had passed, Lambert rode up to the clearing but stopped at the edge; the stench was horrible. This is where the explosion had taken place, but why? What had set it off? He wet his bandana with water from his canteen and tied it over his nose and mouth. Stopping frequently to re-wet it, Lambert searched the clearing for clues as to what had happened, coming to the same conclusion as Shank Williams and Candy Johnson. Someone had shot into the dynamite, and the only place from where a shot like that could have been made was high above the trees on the other side of the river.

That must have been what Shank and his men had been doing. Somehow, they must have realized what was about to happen and placed a man on the mountain where he could get a clean shot at the clearing. He stared up at the peak. It must have been Shank, or maybe Candy Johnson, up there with the rifle. Lambert doubted anyone else could have made that shot.

With the help of the two hands, Lainey was just finishing loading the wagon when Shank and the other men rode up to the house. Shank Williams agreed that it was a good plan and told the men to make themselves bedrolls. He knew of the cabin. The only other building up there was a small stable. He and the men rolled their bedrolls out onto the ground as soon as they arrived.

The next day was uneventful, and Lainey breathed a little

easier. It was tempting to think that something had happened to Lambert and that it was all over. Maybe he had been killed in the explosion, but in her heart she knew better. She wondered, too, about who had fired the shot that had set off the explosion. She would like to thank him, whatever his reason had been.

The small kitchen area of the cabin was too constricting, and Lainey had taken to cooking outside over a campfire using Dutch ovens. After breakfast, Shank had gone with the men to check on the stock and returned to tell Lainey what he had been thinking about. He and Lainey sat down on a blanket for another cup of coffee under a tree handy to the site.

Shank opened the conversation. "I still can't get a handle on who fired the dynamite. I would sure like the chance to tell him thank you. But I wonder if somehow we have a friend working for Lambert. How else would he have known about it in time to be just at the right place to make that shot when they got there?"

"I have thought and thought about that and couldn't come up with anything," answered Lainey. "Your idea is the only one that makes sense. We haven't had the chance to get word out to anybody, but I would sure like to meet him, too. I'd cook him a dinner that would make his eyes bug out."

"You know," Shank said thoughtfully, "I doubt that Lambert was caught in the explosion. We just ain't that lucky. I don't think he would have gone along to do it himself; he would have sent his flunkies to do the dirty work." He paused while Lainey refilled his coffee cup. Having her do for him was pleasurable. He had fantasized about her being his wife, but he was just a hand on her ranch, and he knew it was just a fantasy, nice to think about, but a fantasy, nonetheless. A man had a right to dream, and Lainey Nayle was certainly a dream worth having.

"We can't just let him continue to do whatever he wants to do, whenever he wants to do it," Shank went on. "I think we should take it to him, this sitting and waiting goes against the grain. It gives him time to plan."

Lainey brushed away a fly that was pestering her. "I was thinking along the same lines. What do you have in mind?"

"I believe we should start searching and see can we locate his base of operations. He has no ranch to work from; it's got to be someplace in the hills, and not too far away at that. My guess is somewhere to the Southeast, not more than a half-day's ride: probably closer. I think we should find where he is and take it to him."

"You can do that? After losing Ray and the others, we only have fourteen men plus yourself. We're spread pretty thin."

"That's why we have to do something now, before we lose more. Lambert has the advantage because he has us outnumbered and can pick and choose when and where to hit us. I think his plan is to cut us down one or two at a time until we don't have enough men left to protect the ranch, then he'll just move in and take over. Yesterday, I ran into a fella I used to be kind of friendly with who works for Lambert. He warned me that Lambert was going to bring in the Mackle gun."

"What's a Mackle gun?"

Shank smiled. "It's not a what, it's a who: a gun fighter named Mackle. He's said to be fast as hell, pardon me, ma'am. He's really quick, and they say whoever he points his gun at, dies."

"Oh, Lord," Lainey responded. "That's not good. Now that you mention it, I have heard of him once or twice. And I understand he has killed a lot of people."

"Well, to be fair, I've never heard of him killin' anyone who didn't need killin'. I think all he does is push back."

Lainey was sitting on a blanket on the ground and leaning back against a fallen tree with her legs extended. She slid one foot back, with a piece of rolled packing paper in her hand held in readiness above her knee. She had set a trap for the pesky fly.

If he fell for it and landed on her knee, he was a goner. Raising her knee had exposed a nicely turned ankle that had Shank failing in his attempt to ignore it.

"What do you mean, push back?" she asked, glancing at him. Shank averted his eyes quickly, hoping she hadn't noticed.

"Civilization is gradually comin'. It's the trend of things for everyone to live peaceful, non-violent lives. Everyone is supposed to follow the rules of society, be kind to your neighbor, and turn the other cheek, as the preachers are fond of saying. Even now, to city folk, fighting and violence are terrible things, to be avoided at all costs; that's the idea of civilization." Lainey smiled slightly when Shank paused to pour himself another cup of coffee, always the storyteller. With a motion of the coffee pot, Shank offered to refill her cup, but she declined with a shake of her head.

When he was once more comfortably seated, Shank continued. "This is all fine and dandy when everyone plays by the same rules. Having no violence in the world would be a nice thing, and someday it might happen, but in the meantime, somebody needs to take a stand against the people who don't follow the rules, them that have no regard for the rights of other's. Someone needs to show them that there are still people around that are simply not going to take it and will strike back. I think Mackle is one of those someones, another example would be Lynch. Instead of turning the other cheek, they both strike back . . . and strike back hard. But some feel that everyone has a price; maybe a lot of dollars might convince Mackle that we need killin'. If it does, God help us."

Lainey Nayle caught her breath when Shank said Lynch. *Was he talking about Cormie?* Were there any other Lynches?

Struggling to keep her voice steady, she said, "Tell me about this Lynch."

Shank glanced at her. Something in the way she said Lynch caught his attention.

"Mack Lynch . . . another fella who takes no nonsense from anyone. When he's pushed, I've heard he explodes all over whoever is doing the pushin'. From what I hear, he's about as fast as Mackle. Say, there's an idea. Lynch and Mackle, now there's a pair to reckon with. Even one of them is quite a few. Let's send for Lynch to come take care of Mackle."

Mack Lynch . . . Cormac Lynch. Shank was talking about Cormie. Cormie was fast all right—surefire, blistering fast. She had heard it said he could outdraw a lightning bolt. Lainey remembered Cormie saving her life by shooting a snake that was getting ready to strike at her. No, that was wrong, she realized, the snake had already begun its strike. If only they could get him to come—but that was never going to happen. She had taken care of that. It occurred to her that she was still holding her breath and let it go. Shank noticed and looked at her sharply.

"Are you alright, Miss Nayle?"

Lainey smiled. "Yes, Shank, I'm fine. Thank you."

"Anyway," Shank went on, watching her closely. "I was joking about getting Lynch to take care of Mackle. I've never heard of him hiring out his gun to anyone . . . of course, I've never heard that Mackle did, either, for that matter, until my friend told me Lambert was getting him. There's a first time for everything, and once they get to ridin' the owlhoot trail, who knows how far they will go."

Lainey looked at him sharply. "But you've never heard of Lynch doing that?"

Shank was surprised at her interest. "No. I don't think so," he answered, shaking his head. "Actually, I've never heard that of either of them. I was just using that as an example. Although, if they did, and if they ever did meet, I'd ride a hundred miles and pay money to see that shootout."

Shank finished his plan. "We have to hope Lambert doesn't get Mackle, and we need to deal with the situation as we know it. That's why I think it's time to take the fight to Lambert, not wait for him to control the circumstances."

"Do what you think best, Shank, I trust your judgment."

The fly landed on her knee.

"Ha!" Lainey exclaimed with satisfaction as she swatted it. "Got you!"

Shank got to his feet. "I'll take Candy and do some scouting around today, see what I can find out."

"Shouldn't you take more men?"

"No, I don't think so. Two can move less noticeably than four or five."

"Like I said, you do what you think best. By the time you get saddled up, I'll have some food for you to take along."

With amused affection, she watched his slightly bowed legs walk away. Sometimes, the legs of cowboys who had spent the greater part of their lives in the saddle took on the shape of the horses they had spent so many years wrapped around. She had noticed his eyes on her ankle. "I could do a lot worse," she thought briefly, but the thought died for lack of interest.

As she stood up to go into the house, Shank stopped and looked back with a chuckle. "I can't get away from that idea of a Mackle-Lynch shootout. That would sure be something."

"If Mackle has a lick of sense," Lainey answered emphatically over her shoulder as she went inside. "He'll stay just as far away from Lynch as he can get!"

"Now what the hell was that all about?" Shank wondered, watching the door close.

CHAPTER 18

After dispatching Lambert's men and their dynamite, Cormac Lynch returned to his previously chosen campsite. Closer inspection proved it to be sitting on a steep-sloped four-foot rise, but that wasn't insurmountable. It still looked good to him, but discovering a small moss-covered stone basin continually filled by a natural water seep hidden in the brush sealed the deal.

A rider on the trail had given him the location of the L-Bar N. "You can't miss the L-Bar," he said with a smile, pointing at one of the higher sections of mountains. "You just ride up that mountain in that direction until you see the prettiest sight you ever seen . . . then look around her. She's got the best ranch in Colorado."

Cormac had smiled at the reference to Lainey. She seemed to be creatin' quite a stir.

"But don't let her looks fool you none, pardner," the cowboy had added. "I worked for her for a short time when she first bought the ranch. When she gets her dander up, that's one tough lady."

Cormac knew all about that. When Lainey got her Irish up, she'd hunt grizzly bear with a willow switch . . . and if the grizzly had any sense, he'd run.

The lay of the land can best be learned from the shadows at different times of the day, and Cormac wanted to scout the area in the morning and at least part of it again in the afternoon. Once the shooting started, he needed to know the lay of the land. After getting camp set up the way he liked, he made up a survival bag with some flour, part of the little sugar he had left, and coffee in a bag along with extra cartridges for the Smith & Wesson and some bullets, cap and powder charges for the Colt, a pan and metal cup, and then as an afterthought, added a clean shirt that could serve as bandages along with an unopened bottle of whiskey. He stashed the bag in a safe place that he hoped would also be a dry place to leave the Colt's powder bags nearer the bottom of the mountain and the water seep. It would serve as his survival bag, if such became necessary. Living on sugar and flour with the help of wild nuts, berries, and onions would be uncomfortable, but survival isn't about comfort.

"Now, let's go forth and seek justice," Cormac told the horses, borrowing another line from the dime novel. The first order of the day was to have a look at the L-Bar, then learn the lay of the land and search out Lambert's location.

Looking down at the L-Bar from an overlooking mountain to the south, Cormac was impressed. Lainey had done very well; he was proud of her. He, on the other hand, had accomplished nothing. Located beautifully in a large valley that looked to be about twenty to twenty-five thousand acres, the ranch was guarded on three sides by mountains: an impressive spread with a tremendous amount of thick grazing grass naturally irrigated by God.

From above, several mountain streams coming from the Sweet River were easily visible wandering across the valley. There appeared to be another valley to the north that would provide some protection for the stock from the winter's north-winds and snow. It brought to mind Dakota winters with nothing between them and the North Pole but a barbed wire fence, and as his pa had been fond of sayin' when the winter winds were howling around the eaves, somebody must have left the gate open.

He spent the rest of that day and the better part of the next half-circling the flatland side of the L-Bar, searching for passes, streams, trails, or any other way of approach, but mostly getting to know the land and looking for tracks that might lead him to Lambert. On the second day, he heard gunfire, but it was too far off to determine the likely cause. Finding tracks turned out to be no problem; there were many. The problem was like in one of his pa's stories where a man had been searching in witch country for a particular witch, but she turned out to be a twin and one witch looked so much like the other witch, he couldn't tell which witch was which.

There was no way to tell the difference between the tracks of Lambert's men and those of L-Bar riders. Fresh tracks of five horses that had been moving toward the L-Bar turned abruptly and dug in. The horses were running east . . . why? The L-Bar was to the north. Shots fired from that direction answered his question. Cormac loosed the reins and clucked his tongue, and Lop Ear broke into a run.

There were more shots that led him a short distance up a trail into the mountains. They rounded a corner and stopped on a small plateau overlooking a box canyon. In the canyon, two punchers he took to be Lainey's riders were hunkered down in a cluster of boulders. Through the process of elimination, the attackers had to belong to Lambert and were spread out, fan-shaped, behind other boulders that had bounced down the side of the mountain about a gazillion years before. The L-Bar riders were sewn up tight. Well, maybe GERT could do a little unstitchin'.

He checked her load and crawled to the edge of the plateau, where he could fire from a prone position, and laid out a half dozen cartridges close to hand. She was a single shot, but the action was fast and easy to reload. His pa would have called the distance, "a fur' piece," but Cormac thought GERT could make up for the distance.

As his first target, he lined up on the man in position to be the most effective against the L-Bar riders and squeezed the trigger. He always made sure to pull the rifle stock tightly against his shoulder, but the kick was still impressive. GERT had quite a kick to her, GERT did.

He slid a new shell into the chamber as the first man slumped to the ground. A bullet from behind splayed rock chips across his face. Cormac had been so intent on following the sounds of the shots, that he had paid no attention to his own back trail. That's the kind of mistake men usually don't walk away from. There was no two ways about it, he had been lucky.

Before the sound of the shot died, he had let go of GERT, rolled to the left, coming out with his waist pistol on the roll: it would already be pointed downward toward his feet and in the right direction. Anyone following him would be close; there had been no time for the shooter to get above him. A second shot kicked up dust where Cormac's head had just been. The shooter had been over-confident and walked out onto the plateau before firing his first shot and was standing in plain view.

Cormac put two bullets into the center of the gunman's chest, and he quit shooting at Cormac. Actually, he quit doing anything at all.

Cormac rolled back to the edge of the plateau to resume the original chore and found the situation had changed. The man he shot was still dead, but the other four were trying to leave, and Lainey's men were making it difficult. Two of the attackers managed to get mounted, but one of them was immediately shot out of the saddle for his effort. One got away, giving Cormac someone to follow.

He crawled away from the ledge before getting to his feet; those L-Bar boys could shoot, and although it was unlikely their rifles had the power to reach him—he was above them—he thought it prudent to not test that theory. Prudent. *How do you like that word, Mother?*

To give Lop Ear a break, Cormac changed the saddle to Horse and then backtracked to find a way down to the floor that didn't expose him to fire from Lainey's men, if they were still there. The tracks of the escaping rider weren't hard to find. He was riding hard and straight to put as much distance as possible behind him as quickly as possible. Cormac let Horse choose a comfortable pace and followed at a lope.

About a mile farther, the tracks became erratic and wavering: the trail of a horse being guided by a rider swaying back and forth in the saddle, pulling the reins as he did so. A short distance later, there was blood on the ground. The tracks led into an arroyo and Horse stopped short, almost stepping on the body of the man he had been following. He was just a kid, not more than nineteen years old. Cormac shook his head. Too bad, but he should have been more selective of the company he kept. Cormac stepped down to confirm what he already knew . . . the boy was dead. Like he said, those L-Bar boys could shoot. Lainey had hired well, but they sure played hob with his plans to follow the trail back to Lambert. They surely did.

Until they were all accounted for, Lainey Nayle always waited nervously for her men to return. She hated that every time they rode out they were riding into danger for her. She did not understand the mentality of criminals; why could people not just live in harmony? Why were there always people wanting to take what belonged to others, or force their wants on others? Both her real parents and her adopted parents were hard working and God fearing; they would never have even considered taking something that did not belong to them.

The West was still in a state of growth, and civilization was sporadic with settlers and developers still very much responsible for setting and enforcing the law. But someday, laws would be spelled out and equally enforced across the country. Citizens would be able to live in peace without fear: renegades and gangs would no longer be allowed to exist. Shank was right. Until that day, she had to accept the fact that people such as herself must have the courage to stand up for what was right; that meant relying on men such as Shank and Candy and the others.

Lainey was nervous and could not remain inside. She was sitting on the small porch when Shank and Candy rode up just after dusk. Relieved, she stood up, eagerly waiting for their report. She was impatient when they stopped to discuss something. Then, taking Shank's horse, Candy rode toward the stable and Shank walked the rest of the way to where she was standing.

"Hi, Miss Nayle," he said, stepping up beside her. "How are you?"

"The question is how are you? I was beginning to worry about the two of you. Did you learn anything today?"

"Not as much as I would have liked. We found a lot of tracks from riders scouting us. I think they're waiting for something before making a final assault, more men maybe. We had a bit of a problem around mid-day, but got out of it with the help of some mystery man."

"Mystery man?"

Shank removed the metal cup from the hook on the side of the water bucket that was sitting on the porch awaiting anyone with a thirst. He took a little water in the cup, swiveled a few times to rinse it out, threw the rinse water into the dirt, and took a full cup more. Rinsing his mouth, he spit into the same dirt and then drank. Lainey waited impatiently without speaking. His pauses for effect had bothered her at first, but she had become accustomed to them. He returned the cup to its hook and pulled the sack of Bull Durham from his shirt pocket and began to build a smoke.

"We was comin' down out of Saddle Pass when we got jumped by five riders comin' from the south. There was no place for us to go but into the box canyon. We made it to the rocks, but they had us pinned for fair. They spread out, and unless they done somethin' stupid, it was just a matter of time. We had been there maybe about twenty minutes and had just about decided to try a run through the middle of them. It sounded better than being sitting ducks and getting picked off one at a time. We was just gettin' ready to make a try for the horses when someone up on the plateau fired what sounded to be a small canon. He nailed one of our attackers."

Shank struck a wooden match on the porch upright and lit his smoke.

"There were some more shots from up there, but I don't think they were meant for us. I think someone snuck up on whoever fired that first shot. The last four made a run for their horses, and me'n Candy got two before they made it and one more just as he got mounted. One got away, but Candy thinks he got lead into him before he was out of range. I don't think he was goin' far. We would have looked for him, but we had just been sprung from one trap and had no desire to maybe find another.

He went on. "We did go up on the plateau though, and found where someone had sprawled out on his belly to shoot. We found his toe marks and where his elbows dug in: he's a big guy. The guy that blew up the dynamite was also a big man, probably the same man, from the looks of things. I looked over the edge, and that was one heck of a shot, and that's a heck of a rifle he's got there. From the imprint of it in the dirt, it looks to be nearly as long as one of them Tennessee Long Rifles. I've heard it said that according to Davy Crockett, with a Tennessee Long Rifle, he could shoot a wart off a Tennessee mountain frog from his front porch in Washington, and I don't believe he's got a thing on our boy right here, whoever he is.

"There was an imprint where he dropped the rifle and rolled over to shoot his ambusher with a six-gun from his waist belt. It would have been the fastest as it was already pointed in the right direction. Whoever snuck up on him learned the hard way not to do that again; he was still there with two bullet holes in his chest close enough together to cover with half of a playing card."

Lainey didn't know what to make of it.

"Who do you think it was, Shank?"

"Like I said, it must have been whoever it was that blew up the dynamite. It's the only thing that makes sense, but I have no idea who that might be, Miss Nayle. We haven't been able to get out of this valley to tell anyone our predicament; I doubt anyone else but Lambert's men know what's happenin'—I don't even know anyone who can shoot like that. I'm a fair hand with a rifle, and Candy's a real wizard, but I doubt either of us could have made that shot even with that rifle . . . or the shot in the pass, as far as that goes. Our rifles won't even shoot that far. I've heard of a new rifle called a Henry that's said to do some extraordinary shootin'. Maybe he has one of them."

They talked about it a little longer while Lainey fixed some supper for them and Candy. She had fed the other hands earlier, but had been too nervous to eat herself. They voiced various scenarios over fresh-butchered beef and thick gravy poured over fresh bread, but no explanations were apparent.

After eating, they walked outside and knocked it around some more while Shank and Candy smoked before turning in. Shank's tobacco of choice was his beloved Bull Durham; Candy, on the other hand, preferred foul-smelling cigars. They called it a night in agreement that whoever had fired the shot was more than welcome.

———————

Cormac Lynch returned to camp and gave Horse and Lop Ear a thorough rubdown before frying up some bacon to eat along with the last of the biscuits he had picked up at a cafe in Roosterville, washing it all down with three cups of coffee and using the last biscuit to sop up the bacon grease in the pan. Not wanting to sleep in the cave, he fashioned his ground cloth into a lean-to for some protection in case of rain and turned in. There had been a few thunderheads rolling out of the mountains before nightfall. He was betting on rain.

He awoke to find himself unhappily correct; low clouds were keeping the clear blue sky hidden, and rain clouds in the distance were dumping large amounts of water on the side of the next mountain and probably had been doing so most of the night. Before stirring up the coals from the night before, Cormac stacked a goodly amount of firewood in the cave away from the rain, and only then did he give the coals some attention. After stirring them up, he added a few pieces of wood, being rewarded with enough flame to heat the leftover coffee and fry up another bunch of bacon.

Once up and in the saddle, the range that he had yet to check looked to be coverable in a few hours. He rode Lop Ear, and as always, Horse fell in behind. Most of the remaining area had been covered by mid-day. Along the way, Cormac collected a promising lunch consisting of some nuts and a hatful of blue-berries.

They rode down off a craggy bluff to see a grassy shelf over-looking the L-Bar below.

"What do you think, Lop Ear? That grass look good enough for lunch? If you don't think so, let me know." Lop Ear had no response. "Okay, I'll take that as your approval, so be it."

Cormac dismounted and walked to the edge to look down on the ranch. Yep, Lainey had certainly done well for herself. How in the world she had parlayed a two-bit farm—after seeing the size of most ranches, Cormac had to reluctantly admit that with only thirty acres under the plow, their farm had been a two-bit operation—into a full-sized working ranch was beyond his figurin', but he was glad for her.

From out of a stand of birch trees below rode a large group of riders that split into two, one heading toward the L-Bar and one toward the Sweet River Pass with two boxes tied to a pack-horse. Lambert didn't give up easy; he was bound and deter-mined to dynamite that pass.

Behind him, a gun cocked and a voice said, "You hadn't oughta be . . ." This was one of the situations for which Cormac had practiced. Whoever was behind him now most probably thought the click of the hammer would make him stand still;

or, if he anticipated any response at all on Cormac's part, would probably expect him to show partiality to a right-hand draw as would most. That being the case, if he were to react at all, it would be expected that he spin to the left, crouch, and draw. However, at the first click of the hammer, Cormac immediately threw himself head first into a dive to the right, drawing and cocking his pistol while twisting in the air to face the gunman behind him.

". . . sneakin' up on Miss Nayle that way," the voice was saying.

Cormac's gun was coming up on the speaker's chest, his thumb beginning to slide off the hammer when he heard the part about Miss Nayle. He barely managed to stay the shot and let his gun continue upward, unfired, as he slid to a stop in the dirt.

The jaws of the two men facing him had dropped, their eyes staring at Cormac with a peculiar look on their faces. They said nothing, watching him as he got to his feet, holstered his gun, and dusted off his jeans.

"You oughtened be sneakin' up behind folks either; a man could get kinda dead that way."

"We didn't," replied the bowlegged man with a gun in his hand. The second man had been pulling his gun, but stopped midway. "We was here first. We heard you comin' and slipped behind those rocks to see who you was. Who are you anyway? And what are you doing here?"

"I mean you no harm," Cormac answered, starting toward Lop Ear. "I have to leave right now."

"If you take one more step without answering my questions, I'm going to put a bullet in you."

"No, you're not. If you were going to shoot me, you would've already done it. Anyway, if you was the type that goes around shooting people just for the hell of it, you wouldn't be working for the L-Bar. I take it you do ride for the L-Bar. There are some riders below headed to blow up the pass again. I stopped that once, but I've got it to do again."

He swung up on Lop Ear.

"So you're the one," the man said, stuffing his pistol back into its holster. "You're right; we do ride for the L-Bar. We'll get our horses and ride with you."

"No! I think there are others sneakin' up on the ranch. I'm glad you're here. I was plannin' to go after them, but I've seen you boys shoot and you'll do; two of you can protect her better than one of me. So I'll deal with the dynamite, you two go protect the redhead."

Pulling his hat down tight, Cormac loosened the reins, clucked his tongue twice, and they shot out of there like a bullet. There was an old Indian trail of sorts paralleling the riders; he took it, but since he had to travel the same distance as those he needed to catch, in addition to getting down the mountain to their level, it was going to be a horse race to get to them before they got to the pass. Once into the pass, they would be impossible to stop. He couldn't hope to get to the vantage point he previously had in time to stop them. He had to catch them while they were still in the flat lands.

Lop Ear had his work cut out for him, and Cormac gave him his head to let him do it. Horse was close behind. Cormac would not have bet a dollar to a doughnut on which of the two was the faster. Their speed was something that needed to be experienced to appreciate. He was thoroughly familiar with it; he had experienced it many times, and it never ceased to amaze him. There was running, and then there was running.

Somehow, Lop Ear seemed to sense the urgency, almost as if he knew he was running for Lainey, and today he was doing some plain and fancy running. This time it was belly-whomping, muscle-stretching, and flat-out, mile-eating running. He settled low to the ground with a singular drive and focus. They rounded corners, jumped dead logs and gullies, clambered over a recent small landslide, and cleared a couple of mountain streams, each at least ten or twelve feet wide with Horse replicating his every jump.

Cormac leaned far forward in the saddle for better balance and to reduce wind resistance. His hat was blown back as always and hanging by the neck cord with tree branches smacking his face, his eyes tearing and blurring from the speed. He could feel the bunching-up of the powerful muscles and the following explosive release catapulting them over whatever obstacle arose. Cormac could only hang on and shift his weight when needed to help on the jumps.

Cormac wondered about an Arab country that could produce such a horse, but Horse's Mustang heritage kept her right in there. Both horses soon became white with sweat. When the trail reached a point even with the entrance to the pass, it turned downward; the threesome turned with it, sliding and bouncing and scraping down the side of the mountain, eventually coming out through a small stand of trees at the bottom that masked their arrival onto the valley floor. The riders with the dynamite were coming from Cormac's right, an equal distance from the pass entrance that was on his left. Like an inverted *V*, the riders on the right side, Cormac on the left, they would come together at the entrance to the pass.

The three of them were out of the trees and halfway across the flat land separating them before they were seen and the riders started galloping for the pass. Lop Ear was beginning to falter. Horse had covered the same distance at the same speed but without carrying any weight. Cormac crammed a handful of cartridges from the saddlebag into his pockets and his third gun into his waist belt. Motioning Horse up beside them, he made the jump onto her back. Without even a bridle, he was now riding bareback, normally not a problem; this time, however, Horse was covered in sweat. He had to grab a handful of mane to keep from sliding off the other side.

He could count six of them and see he was correct about it being dynamite tied on the packhorse. Although they began firing before they were in range, he held his fire until he was close enough to do some good. An occasional bullet whistled passed his head a little too close for comfort but most weren't anywhere near.

Shooting a pistol from the back of a running horse was a chancy thing at best; only an unusually high amount of luck would score a hit from that distance. Cormac was hoping they were not lucky folks. In fact, it was his intention to make them just the opposite, although it was looking like he was going to need a bucketful his own self.

He could feel Horse beginning to weaken. "Hang on, girl," he screamed against the wind. "We're almost there."

And then they were. When they were less than fifty feet away he began firing. Being so close, he had to be careful not to hit the explosives. He felt a jolt high in his chest followed quickly by another to his shoulder. He emptied two saddles before hitting the middle of them. Then Horse ran one down, and Cormac shot another in the face, and something hit him in the back, hard.

The man Horse ran down got to his feet and fired as Cormac spun Horse toward him. Cormac felt a blow from the front, and at the same time, one from the back before he shot the man point blank. Something hit Cormac on the side of the head, and he began to get dizzy and sick to his stomach. He jammed a gun into the ribs of a closing rider and pulled the trigger. His legs seemed to be giving out on him; it was getting hard to squeeze them tight enough to stay on top of a spinning, sweating Horse. He wheeled her around to face the last rider and found him sitting dead still on his mount off to one side, pointing his rifle at Cormac, but not firing. His positioning seemed to be saying that if Cormac wouldn't shoot him, he would return the favor. That was fine with Cormac. He figured he probably already had enough holes in him to do him for a while anyway.

The situation somehow seemed familiar, but Cormac had no time to think about it right then. He was going to have to trust somebody . . . he was beginning to feel mighty strange, and the world was going all topsy-turvy. Squeezing Horse for all he was worth, he caught up the reins of the dynamite laden packhorse and led it to the rider, asking him to please take it to Lainey Nayle at the L-Bar and rode away. He hoped the rider could be trusted; he had no choice. Cormac Lynch was not goin' to make it, and that's just all there was to it.

———————

It was dark when Shank returned to the cabin. Lainey Nayle watched him ride into the makeshift corral and went out to greet him.

"Where's Candy? Did you lose him someplace?" Lainey immediately regretted her choice of words when she saw the look on Shank's face.

"Oh, God no!" she said, before he could respond. "What happened?"

Shank knew that Candy was one of her favorites and hated what he had to tell her.

"That's exactly what happened, ma'am. I lost him." Shank finished unsaddling his horse and poured some oats into its feed bag before he continued. He sighed disgustedly as he leaned against a fence post and began building a smoke.

"We met a stranger who told us he thought some of Lambert's men might be headed this way, and we were hightailin' for home when we spotted them in front of us. We took a shortcut Candy knew about and managed to get in front of them, trying to get home in time to set up a trap for them. There were ten or twelve of them and only two of us. They spotted us, and then it was a horse race. We made it to some fallen trees where they couldn't get behind us. Me'n Candy make a pretty darn good pair; we did better than hold our own. He was right handy with that rifle of his.

"We got four or five of them good'n solid and dusted a couple more. They finally gave it up as a bad job and lit out for parts unknown, but Candy had already taken a hard belly hit. He said if he was going to die, he wanted to die on the L-Bar. He said I should bring him home. We was on the other side of the Sweet, and it was runnin' full and then some, musta been some rain up in the mountains."

Shank took a long pull from a whiskey bottle he removed from one of the saddlebags that he had hung on a rail and lit his quirlie. Lainey was sick to hear what was coming.

"There was no safe place to cross without riding ten miles out of our way; I knew Candy didn't have much time left. I tied his feet under his horse's belly and his hands to the saddle horn, and we started across. We had damn near made it when a large tree came out of nowhere and hit them broadside. We didn't even see it coming. They didn't have a chance, Miss Nayle. Both him and the horse went under and never surfaced again. I followed the river until it got too dark to see, and I had to give it up. I did the best I could, Miss Nayle. I surely did."

Lainey could hear in his voice and see he was close to breaking

down. He and Candy had been partners for years, even before
she came: when she had hired Shank, she also got Candy. She
put her hand on his arm.

"I know you did, Shank. Don't blame yourself. You did the
best that anyone could have done. At least he got his wish. He
got to die on the L-Bar." She took his hand. "Come on up to
the house. I'll fix you something to eat, and you can tell me
about the stranger. You look half starved."

"Yes, ma'am, I reckon I am. We lost the saddlebag with those
sandwiches you packed for us while crossing the Sweet this
morning. Do you mind if I bring this bottle with me?"

Lainey smiled. "Of course not. In fact, that bottle looks like
its seen better days. I think I have a larger one in the cupboard . . . that I keep for medicinal purposes," she added.

"Medicinal purposes . . . yes, ma'am." Shank smiled weakly.
The whiskey was working its magic.

She had put aside some leftovers from dinner: a large steak
and a bowl of beans and gravy with the last couple inches from
a loaf of fresh bread. Shank fell to eating with a single-mindedness
that left no room for other thought.

When Shank had finished, Lainey took away the bottle that
he had been drawing from to wash down the steak and set a cup
of fresh coffee in front of him that had been brewing while he
was eating.

"Try this on for size. I'll give your bottle back to you later.
Tell me about the stranger."

Shank watched forlornly as the bottle disappeared into a
cupboard, but he knew she was right; the words were already
getting tangled up in his mouth.

"I don't understand all I know about it. Candy and me found
this high point south of here in the area I told you I wanted to
look at. It overlooked the whole valley. We could see for mileses."

Lainey smiled at his mis-pluralization.

"We was about to leave when we heard a couple of horses coming down the trail from up above; we pulled our horses behind some boulders until we could see who it was.

"It was a big guy riding a large gray horse with a grulla trotting behind. We threw down on him to find out who he was. I wanted to know if he was one of Lambert's crew or maybe the one who pulled me and Candy out of that box canyon." Shank hesitated, remembering the situation as it had played out. A chill ran through his body. "I think we damn near died for it."

He paused again, and then went on. "He had dismounted and was standing looking down at the L-Bar, thinking real hard on somethin', and me'n Candy slipped out from the rocks behind him without him hearing us." Shank paused yet again. Lainey Nayle could see he was struggling to get it out, not from the liquor, but from whatever had transpired. She waited quietly until he was ready to continue.

"He was looking down at the L-Bar," Shank repeated. "I cocked my gun to get his attention and told him that he shouldn't oughta be sneakin' up like that on Miss Nayle. I swear that's when we almost died. I've never seen a man move that fast in my whole life, especially a big man. He wore two guns but most people draw right so I figured if he drew, he would pivot around on his left foot to face us, and pointed my gun where his chest would come around to.

"Instead, at the sound of my gun cocking, he threw himself to the right into a head-first dive, twisting like a cat going through the air. Twisting to face us, drawing his gun and cocking it while he was still in the air. I heard it click. And it was pointed right at my middle."

Shank shivered again, as if he was cold, but it was a warm night. "Let me say that again. While in the air, he twisted to face us, drew his gun, cocked it, found me, and lined it up dead center on my chest. I was too shocked at his speed to react . . . you just don't expect a man that size to move that fast. I just stood there with my face hangin' out, staring at him. I'd bet that man could outdraw a rattlesnake.

"While my gun was still pointin' in the wrong direction, where I had expected him to be, his was coming to bear on me; but for some reason, he didn't fire. If he would have, there is not a single doubt in my mind that I would not still be alive to be telling you about it. Now, I been thinking about it; I think what stopped him was hearing your name. It's the only thing that makes any sense. In the middle of getting his gun lined up on me, he heard your name and called it off."

"My name?" Lainey puzzled. "Why my name? What makes you say that? How in the world could my name stop somebody from shooting if they believed themselves to be in danger?"

Shank shook his head and shrugged his shoulders. "Don't know, ma'am. Been chewin' on that all day, but I think that's what did it."

"Because, when he left, he took off outta there like a bat outta hell, that horse of his is really something, but before he left . . . Oh yeah, I almost forgot. He was the one who stopped Lambert from dynamiting the pass. He said there were some riders below with dynamite heading for the pass that he had to stop again. When I offered me'n Candy to ride with him, he said no. He said he would take care of them. He said he thought there were other riders sneakin' up on the L-Bar that he had been going to go after but since we were there, he would go after the dynamite, and we should just get home and protect the redhead. Also, he said I wasn't the kind of guy to go around shootin' people without a reason or I wouldn't be workin' for the L-Bar, so obviously he knows you. And why else would he be helping us? That made twice; three times if he stopped the second try on the pass, and I ain't heard no explosion."

After Shank had turned in, there were no thoughts of sleep in Lainey's mind. Who in the world could be out there trying to help her to save the L-Bar? It had to be someone she knew. His comment about her red hair proved that, but who could he be? There had been a few suitors, but none that had generated any serious thoughts. There had been one with whom she had struck up a friendship while on the stagecoach coming west, but he was a small man and certainly not the type to do battle for her. She went to sleep and dreamt of a faceless rider following her everywhere and shooting anyone who came near her.

CHAPTER 19

＊━━◆━━＊

After turning the dynamite over to a stranger he hoped was trustworthy, Cormac Lynch grabbed two handfuls of mane and pointed the horses in the general direction of camp, hoping they would remember the way. Horse and Lop Ear were plodding along side by side; plodding was a good way for them to cool down.

Horse was covered in white sweat and Cormac was having a devil of a time trying not to slide off. He figured to have a better chance of staying aboard if he got himself into Lop Ear's saddle. Every movement shot pain through him. Somehow, he managed to get from one horse to the other, but it took a lot out of him, and there wasn't much left in there to begin with. And whatever there was seemed to be running down his legs, soaking his socks. He was probably going to have to buy a new pair of boots. He pulled Lop Ear to a halt. If he was to have any chance, he had to stop losing so much blood. Cormac was so very tired. To just slip to the ground and rest awhile was very tempting, but if he did, he knew he would never get up.

Getting his belt off was difficult, getting his shirt off, a nightmare. The most blood seemed to be coming from a hole in his upper chest near his shoulder and from one of the holes in his back. A bullet must have gone into the front and kept right on going out the other side. He got his belt strapped around both before tearing his shirt in half and stuffing part of it under his belt to stop the leak in his chest, with the other half, he managed to plug the exit wound in his back. Cormac was bleeding from some other places, too, but not as badly, and he couldn't do anything about them anyway. Offering up a silent prayer, he nudged Lop Ear to resume his plodding. They had covered many miles together, the two of them . . . the two of them and Horse. Most of the miles had been with his legs wrapped around Lop Ear. The three of them had gotten to know each other well, and Lop Ear knew that Cormac was in trouble. His gait seemed to have gotten smoother.

Then they were stopped. Slowly it registered through the fog in Cormac's mind that they were stopped, and Lop Ear's muscles were tensed and trembling. With much effort, Cormac pulled himself out of his stupor and looked around. There was nothing unusual that he could see. Then all hell broke loose. The wild roar of a mountain lion, attracted by the smell of blood, woke him up for real, and something hurtled at him from the side of the mountain.

Lop Ear saved him. He bolted and Cormac lost his grip on the saddle horn. Falling backward, narrowly missed by the lion, Cormac hit the ground in a jarring, bone-shaking smash and heard himself scream from the pain. Instinct and adrenaline took over. Cormac reached for his gun as he rolled to meet the lion, but his hand came up empty. He had not hooked the thong, and had lost one of his guns when he fell. Upon hitting the ground, the lion spun and charged back at him. Cormac yanked out his belt gun and pulled the trigger . . . the hammer clicked on an empty chamber.

The lion hit him, and together they rolled across the ground with the lion trying to shake free of the gun jammed into his throat. Cormac pulled his pa's knife, which he always wore on his belt, and began stabbing the lion as they rolled. It appeared to have no effect. The lion's front legs were around Cormac, his claws trying to dig at Cormac's back.

The mountain lion was on top of Cormac when they quit rolling. Frantically, Cormac felt for a rock to use as a club but instead found the lost gun. He prayed there was a least one load left in it and jammed it against the lion's head and pulled the trigger. It only clicked. Cormac knew he was a goner. He had once before wished to have died, when his family had been killed; now it was going to happen.

The shrill trumpeting of two wild horses suddenly cut through the air, and Horse's white-blazed face dove into his limited view around the lion's head, wild-eyed, teeth bared, and her ears flat against her head. Her mouth clamped down on the lion's neck as she reared up on her hind legs taking the lion with her. Backing away from Cormac and shaking the lion from side to side until the skin tore, she flung the lion through the air.

It had only touched the dirt when Lop Ear's rear hooves kicked it once again into the air toward Horse, spinning to align her powerful back legs for the death blow. The lion was cata-pulted yet again into the air and hit the dirt dead and limp an instant before Lop Ear's front hooves crushed its skull, and the two horses continued to alternate blows, until, their fury spent, they backed off trembling, shaking their heads, blowing and prancing: using up the excess adrenaline-induced energy.

Cormac Lynch fell back and lay there, looking upward into the heavens, fighting for each breath, the panic and fear ever so slowly leaving him, and his breathing slowing to normal. He became aware of the stars, each one so bright and so close. He found himself wondering how many days' ride away they were. The mountains of Colorado were higher than the plains of Dakota, making the stars appear closer. Becky would have loved the sight of the sky so completely filled with stars.

Many summer nights she had drug him with her up the hill behind the house from which flowed the artesian well. There, they would lie on their backs for hours talking and pointing out shapes in the stars.

They must be hypnotic—that same calmness and peace grew gently and softly. It was a blessing to feel the pain seep away and a great sense of comfort and contentment take its place. The feeling steadily overwhelmed and wrapped around him like the blanket his mother had made for him. He clearly remembered climbing into a chilly bed on a cold night, shivering and enjoying the pleasantness of the light but warm goose down quilt beginning to replace the coldness with warmth and contentment. Now, the feeling was so complete, Cormac doubted he could have moved a muscle should he have wanted to, which he didn't.

He allowed his eyes to close so as to relax and allow the feeling to roll through him. Something seemed to be materializing out of a strange and far distant brightness and floating toward him . . . somehow Cormac knew it was something good. Something he wanted to see. He waited anxiously for its approach, realizing as it neared that it was separating into three individual shapes, which were beginning to look familiar. He wanted them to come more quickly. He wanted to join with them. So this was death? It wasn't so bad. He was ready.

He could not remember ever feeling so completely contented

and fulfilled. The closest to it that came to mind was lying in bed at night back on the farm after a long day's work and hearing the soft breathing of Lainey sleeping on the other side of the blanket . . . *Lainey!* . . . *Lainey!* . . . *My God!* . . . *Lainey!* He had to keep moving; he couldn't die now!

All he had accomplished so far was to postpone the dynamiting of Sweet River Pass. That wouldn't stop Lambert. He would just keep on trying until he was successful.

Cormac tried to move and failed, and tried again—again he failed. He couldn't move; nothing worked. There was just no more there. He was empty. He willed his fingers to move, but they refused. He tried to open his eyes and couldn't. He had tried as hard as he could; he was all in. But he couldn't quit on her. He couldn't abandon Lainey when she needed him.

That's why he had come, because she needed him. Now, in order to help her, he needed her; he needed her strength. He had always had the ability to concentrate and focus when he was trying to read or study and something else was going on in the room. He needed that now more than ever before. With strong singularity of purpose, he forced himself to concentrate on a memory of her.

With tremendous effort, he strived to block out everything but Lainey. He blocked out his panic. He blocked out his weakness. He blocked out his surroundings. Lainey, with her so-bright white teeth smiling at him through the red hair hanging over her shoulder: always beautiful. Lainey Colleen Nayle at her very best, and Lainey Colleen Nayle's best was simply incomparable.

But that was no good. That wouldn't do it. He needed her anger. He needed her Irish up. He needed her rage. When truly enraged, the fierceness of her fury was a hurricane out of control, and that's exactly what he needed now.

Again he could see her face. She was mad. She was angry. He had pushed her too far. He had teased her too much. He had laughed at her too long, and she was furious! Her face was changing, he could see the softness becoming hard and her cheeks flush. He concentrated harder, blotting out all that was not Lainey.

Her freckles became pronounced and her ears inflamed. He could see the strength of her savagely bitter fury taking control: her lips tightened, her brow furrowed.

The numbness locking his muscles was striving to invade and overpower his mind; he had to resist it. Focusing all the strength he could muster, he held on to the image locked in his mind and fought back the terrible numbness. Again he attempted to move, and the pain flooded through him, replacing the peace and comfort, and all three figures disappeared. It was sad to see them leave; they had been somehow familiar. Cormac was confident that he would have been able to recognize them had they only come a little closer.

The pain was excruciating, but it was a feeling, cutting through the numbness, and he heard someone in the distance groaning.

Lainey's eyes were flashing their warning, her freckles standing out, her lips were moving, out of a face full of anger she was screaming at him, targeting him with her fury.

His eyes opened into slits and his fingers trembled. The groaner turned out to be him. He had to move. . . . He had to get to his feet.

She was wearing her favorite green cotton dress, her hair falling loosely around her face. She was grabbing up a pan from the cupboard, preparing to throw it at him. He could see her face twist and that eye squint, taking aim, and then she let fly. The force of the throw sent the pan flying hard and fast toward him, spinning, turning, and twisting through the air.

Sweat beaded his forehead, his face grimaced; he gritted his teeth, and strained upward to his knees, reaching out for something—anything. He desperately needed something on which to support himself, concentrating with every bit of strength he had remaining, he remembered.

He was ducking, but not fast enough, the pan was glancing off his head as it passed, denting itself on the stone fireplace and bouncing and clanging across the floor.

Cormac's hands clutched a cottonwood tree and managed to get one foot underneath him.

"Cormac Lorton Lynch! Damn you, Cormac Lynch! You get out of this house right this instant," Lainey was screaming at him at the top of her lungs!

Somehow, he managed to pull himself to his feet.

The morning sun streaming in the window was lighting up her red hair and the beauty and thrill of her anger. He remembered his laughter mocking her, enraging her anger; she was grabbing up the heavy cast-iron skillet from off the stove with both hands and running after him, chasing him furiously out of the door with it held high. If she caught him, she was goin' to lay him out cold!

Eyes shut, grimacing, gritting his teeth, and groaning loudly, he was swaying; his arms wrapped tightly around the tree and holding on for dear life, for Lainey's life. He was swaying. He was swaying, but he was standing, waiting for the dizziness and nausea to pass.

She would have used it, too, if she coulda caught him.

Cormac realized that, in spite of it all, he was smilin'. That girl was pure somethin', she was . . . pure somethin'. He had to keep her safe. He couldn't let her down.

Recognizing the rock face from which the lion had attacked, he knew his stash wasn't far, now if he could only get there. Don't try. . . . Do! With no strength to waste, he ignored the lost gun in favor of trying to get to his stash. Staggering and crawling, he weakly recovered his gun that had been in the lion's mouth, and by leaning heavily on a boulder, struggled again to his feet, but he was too weak to walk, and he fell. He crawled a few feet and collapsed, only managing to get to his hands and knees and continue a few more feet before collapsing again.

Determined, he again forced his mind to focus on Lainey. Lainey was in trouble! Lainey needed help! Lainey needed him! He had to take care of Lainey! If he collapsed, he would stay there forever. He had to continue drawing strength from Lainey . . . protect Lainey!

First, he had to get to his emergency supplies. Unfortunately, to keep them from being found by animals, he had hidden them on a ledge five feet above the trail and covered them with rocks. Crawling, falling, and scrambling agonizingly slowly, his only strength coming from adrenaline, he got up the hill. One of the factors in choosing this location had been a water seep that kept a small natural stone basin filled. He inch-wormed over to it and stuck his face in the water. He needed rest badly, but the holes in him needed to be cleaned and plugged first.

Cormac could just reach the sack. Dragging it to him took long; building the small fire longer. Filling the little pan with water, he placed it in the middle of the fire and, while it was heating, put coffee makin's in the metal cup and set it beside the pan. He needed coffee almost as much as he needed sleep. The best he could tell, he had gotten some deep gouges and scratches and taken six hits, two passed through the flesh at different locations around the edges of his upper body, going in the front and out the back, or vice versa, one through the meaty portion of his right side and one solidly through his left shoulder.

It was good that the bullets were gone, bad that they had opened another hole on the way out. One of the hits must have been a .44 caliber slug, maybe an Army Colt such as his own, that went in small but flattened out to leave an exit hole in his back feeling, to his searching fingers, to be the size of Texas, but fortunately, apparently only taking small bits of flesh with it. Most of the flesh felt like it had mushroomed out like a dough-nut around the hole, leaving it available to be pushed back into its original position.

Two bullets, however, were still inside, and Cormac had to get them out or risk lead poisoning. Luckily, they were smaller than the .44, possibly a .38 and one of the cartridge-type bullets used by the Smith & Wesson similar to his own.

The easy wounds, such as those on his legs that bled a lot but really only grazed the surface, he washed and patched first: a three-inch shallow graze above his left ear reminding him of the earlier wound he had taken when his family was killed, another deeper groove on the right side of his neck from which he bled like a stuck pig, and three minor scratches. One of the bullets remaining inside had rotated during flight and had entered his body sideways, penetrating only about a half inch and stopping when it hit a rib, making removal relatively easy. However, the other was deep in his left shoulder and would require a more serious operation. A solemn sounding word: operation. He was going to operate on himself.

"This is goin' to be great fun," Cormac said to himself as he prepared for the operation. "Real easy to get out . . . sure."

After pouring a hefty amount of whiskey in the coffee, he drank it first, then, after another good belt for courage, splashed some on the knife blade, and went to work. Biting on a piece of wood to keep from screaming and attracting unwanted com-pany, he dug, passing out from the pain, reawakening to dig some more and passing out again, repeating the process over and over several times until both bullets were out. He finished up by rinsing the wounds one last time with whiskey and packing them with whiskey-soaked clean moss from the water seep as he had been told was done by Indians.

All in all, dying would have been easier, all of these holes in him were downright incommodious, and he was not even finished. He had sterilized the large wound in his back and pushed all of the protruding flesh back inside but it had yet to be cauterized as he had seen done to a man wounded in a mining accident. Cormac had placed the blade of his pa's knife in the fire, and it was heating.

"It's me again, God; this is the best I can do," he said weakly, looking up into the sky. "The rest is up to you, but I'm asking you to help me help Lainey . . . *please*. She's a really good person, and she's in trouble she doesn't deserve."

With that, Cormac removed the knife from the fire, clamped down his teeth on a fresh stick, hesitated, took a deep breath, and in a sudden move, slapped the side of the knife flat against the wound for the few seconds that he could take before passing out.

Lainey Nayle had eventually fallen asleep only to be re-awakened by the sound of horses coming in on the hard-packed trail toward the cabin. At first surprised that they were being allowed to get so close, Lainey remembered that Shank had quite a few drinks before turning in, and the others, who had been out patrolling, had gotten in late.

Lainey hurriedly put on her robe and grabbed a pistol from the shelf on the way to the door, through which she stepped quickly and then to the side into the shadows as the riders neared the porch. Shank's voice cried out to the other hands to wake them, and Lainey could hear feet running toward the house when the horses had come to a stop.

"Hello the house," the rider called urgently out of the darkness. "Hello the house!"

Lainey's voice was calm, and she let them hear the hammer of her pistol clicking into firing position.

"What do you want?"

It turned out to be one rider and one packhorse. Shank and her men surrounded the rider and pulled him to the ground before he had a chance to answer.

"Miss Nayle," Shank asked, "can we get a light on so we can see what we got here?"

The rider spoke up. "It's Miss Nayle I need to talk to!"

"There will be plenty of time for that after we have a look at you," Shank replied, pushing him through the door. Lainey touched a match to the wick of the coal oil lamp, placed the glass chimney around it, and adjusted the wick to halt the black soot rolling up into the air. Holding the lamp above her head so as not to blind herself, she turned, allowing the light to illuminate the prisoner.

What she saw was a man of about her own age in normal cowhand attire, most likely clean shaven normally but now sporting what looked to be a two-day growth of beard. He didn't look like a mean man, although his physique said he probably could be if riled. He wasn't riled, and Lainey realized that he also wasn't frightened. He was wisely not resisting, apparently just waiting for the chance to tell whatever it was that he had come to tell them. Could this be her hero? No. He was full-sized, but could not be described as a big man.

"Let him loose, Shank. He doesn't appear to be dangerous. I see you have his gun. Let us all sit down and find out what he has to say. In fact, the fire has burned down, but I'll bet the coffee sitting beside it is still hot. Since it doesn't appear we are going to get anymore sleep tonight, let's pour ourselves some to drink while we are listening to whatever this gentleman has come to tell us."

"But, Miss Nayle," the prisoner began.

"Just wait a minute, please. Whatever it is that you have come to tell us, I am reasonably certain, can wait a couple more minutes."

When all were holding steaming coffee cups, he asked, "Now?"

"Now would be fine," Lainey answered, still in her robe, looking over her shoulder and smiling at him through some tumbled-down hair. She could have asked him to ride through hell in a hand basket, and he would have gone searching for a basket.

"Well?" Lainey asked when he hesitated, trying to restart his brain.

"Uhh . . . uh . . . Well, I . . . I used to ride for Lambert. My name is Bert Tayman, and I think you need to know what happened this afternoon, ma'am."

A murmur of surprised anger made its way across the room.

"Wait, please," he said with his opened hands held palms out in the traditional signal to stop. "Hear me out please. I said I used to work for Lambert. I just quit. I would like to change sides, if you will have me . . . and I need to tell you that Mackle is bad hurt."

Lainey's hand stopped with her coffee halfway to her mouth and the murmuring ceased at the mention of the name. The silence in the room was a thickness hanging heavy in the air. He had their attention.

After a second to get her breath, Lainey asked, "What about Mackle, and why do I need to know about him?"

"I was surprised to see him riding for you, ma'am, but as long as he is, I won't ride against him."

"What do you mean, riding for me? I have heard of Mackle, but I have never met the man, and he certainly does not work for me."

"Well, he was this afternoon, ma'am, when he stopped us from blowing up the pass."

Shank exploded, "That was Mackle? The big guy on a big gray horse?"

"Well, he was on a grulla when he came at us out of nowhere, but there was a big gray trying hard to keep up. Both horses were covered in sweat. Since the gray was wearing the saddle, and Mackle was riding the grulla bareback, I'm guessing that he rode them two horses near to death to catch us and had probably swapped horses just before he attacked."

The chill spread through Shank again as he realized how close he really had come to meeting his maker earlier in the day: the Mackle gun had been zeroed in right on his chest. But why had Mackle stopped short of shooting him? Was it Miss Nayle's name, as he suspected?

"How do you know it was Mackle?" Shank asked.

"I first met him some time ago. . . . Three other fellows, along with myself, were over in Dakota Territory branding some cattle that didn't quite belong to us, when he rode out of an arroyo and accidentally into the middle of our camp. He was willing to just ride on—said he wasn't interested in other people's problems anymore. Then the men I was with said they were going to kill him. I tried to talk them out of it, but they weren't listening to me; so he just ups with this big ole scattergun and changed their minds.

"Then, he swapped the scattergun for a strange-looking old rifle that looked about a mile long and scared up a jackrabbit with it. After it was running, he dropped it with one shot, just to show us he could. Then, he made us herd them cattle back to their owners and told us that he would bring up the rear and if any of us tried to run off, he said he would shoot us out of the saddle.

"Well, I tricked him and got out of range and rode off into some trees, but just as I was entering the trees, I looked back and there he was, looking at me over the sights of that ole rifle. I knew I hadn't fooled anyone but myself. If he would've pulled the trigger, that big ole rifle would have just reached right out and knocked me right out of the saddle just like he said.

"Later, when I began hearing stories about Mackle and his description, I realized that that was who he had been, and that I had not only seen the Mackle gun; I had been under it, and lived. I doubt there are many people who can say that. To realize it was a strange feeling."

Shank knew exactly what he was talking about. "So why are you here?"

"Lambert heard that a spread east of here had gotten hold of some dynamite to clear some land. He had some of the boys go steal a bunch of it. He had tried to blow up the pass once before but somehow you found out about it and stopped him. This time there was six of us with two cases of dynamite strapped to a packhorse, and we were just about to enter the pass, when he rode right into the middle of us with both guns blazing: one man against six. We saw him coming in time to start firing, but he was riding too fast to be much of a target. His horse ran straight into Jackson, knocking him and his horse upside down. Then he was in the middle of us: spinning and shooting and getting shot . . . a bunch of times.

"He got all the others before turning to me. I had recognized him and wasn't shooting. When he turned to me, I was sitting still, holding my rifle sighted on him just as he had on me. I hoped he would know I wasn't going to shoot at him. I guess he did because his gun started up at me, and then stopped. There had been six of us, like I said, and he got all but me, and could have gotten me, but instead he just holstered his guns and grabbed up the reins of the packhorse carrying the dynamite and brought it to me.

"For some reason, he trusted me. He held out the reins and asked me if I would please take it to Lainey Nayle at the L-Bar, said he didn't believe he could make it. I said I would. He said 'Thanks pardner,' and rode off with that big ole lop-eared gray horse following, but he sure took some heavy hits. There was blood all over him. There were bloody holes in his pants and his shirt, and there was blood running down the side of his face, and I could see more running down a doodad he was wearing around his neck, and a steady stream dripping off his boot."

"What kind of doodad?" Shank wanted to know, curiously.

The ex–Lambert rider thought about it a moment, then answered, "The blood made it hard to make out, but I think it was an arrowhead on a cord of some kind."

There it was! "Oh my God!" Lainey exclaimed, jumping to her feet and knocking over the table and everything on it: the coffee, the dishes, the checkerboard, the bean can of cigarette butts, a knife and whetstone, and the people unlucky enough to have been sitting on the other side of the table from her.

In that stark instant, it all came together. What, in the back of her mind, she had been thinking and praying for but dared not let herself think about or even believe possible. *Cormie was here!* Somehow he had learned she was in trouble and had come. . . . *He was here!* . . . Heaven help those who got in his way . . . they were on a shortcut to hell.

It was the arrowhead that did it . . . she remembered giving it to him. In that stark instant, all of the images of what she was being told fell into place.

The big ole scattergun . . . Cormie had used a shotgun on the men who killed his family.

The rabbit-shot with a funny old rifle . . . Cormie had taught her to shoot on a funny old rifle he called GERT.

Shank had said the stranger was rattlesnake fast. . . . Cormie had saved her life by shooting the head off a striking rattler.

And now, this man says Mackle rode off on a grulla horse with a lop-eared gray following him. . . . Cormie had left home on Lop Ear and had taken the outlaw's grulla horse with him.

Mackle—Mac L—Mack Lynch—Cormac Lynch: Mackle and Cormie were one and the same. *And he was here, Cormie was here!* Cormie was the one who had been fighting for her, and now he was somewhere out there in the darkness—badly wounded and probably dying.

Those bastards may have killed him! And if they have, by God they won't be far behind.

"I want every man jack of you in the saddle within five minutes and out searching for him until he's found!" she screamed. "And don't come back until he is!" She spoke with fury in her voice while running for the door. When she reached it, she spun and looked back.

Shank Williams was momentarily frozen speechless from the instantaneous mutation her face had undergone in those brief seconds. Flushed, brittle, and full of hatred, her ears were bright red with fire in her eyes and her face was filled with an intense Irish fury he would have never believed possible. She repeated her mandate vehemently, the soft Irish lilt transformed into the angry, guttural Irish brogue of her father rolling strong and powerful from her tongue: *"And don't any of you be showin' your faces around here again without him!"*

Lainey grabbed the gun belt and rifle hanging by the door, and still in her robe and night clothes, bolted out the door, galloping wildly into the night on the Lambert rider's horse, in total disregard of Shank William's frantic calls to stop.

CHAPTER 20

Cormac Lynch was floating down a river on a log with broken and jagged branches gouging him in several places; the pain was horrendous, his body on fire, and someone was throwing water on him. The log was about to go over a waterfall, and there were voices drifting up from below.

Presently, he realized it was just a dream. He was nauseous and wet with sweat, he had a fever, and his head was being pounded by a double-jack sledgehammer with every heartbeat. He was getting wetter and hearing voices. He tried to ignore both unsuccessfully.

"Let me go back to sleep," he begged softly. "Please, I'm all wrung out."

Rain was falling on him and his mountain. Later, it would get heavier. Right now there was urgency to the voices—something needed doing.

"Go away," Cormac mumbled. "I'm done in."

But the voices continued, the volume rising and falling, punctuated by an occasional sound of wood cracking. Reluctantly, his groggy mind was drug out of the peaceful darkness. The voices were real, but he had no idea where they were coming from, where he was, or why was he lying in the rain.

His head was throbbing fiercely with every heartbeat, there was a violent pain in his shoulder and back, and his legs hurt like hell. He started to turn to relieve the pain in his back, and then became aware of where he was. He was lying on a rock with most parts of his body screaming in agony. He stopped the yell that had begun in his throat before it escaped his mouth. He still didn't know where the voices were coming from, but he didn't think it wise to make noise until he had found out.

A little at a time, he moved his body to find out what parts of him were still working and was happy that everything was functioning, horribly painfully, but functioning. The cold rain was reviving him, and feeling awful-mighty good on his fever. The voices coming from somewhere below were becoming clearer. Laboriously suppressing the moans, Cormac drug himself to the edge of his shelf. It was dark, and someone had built a fire on the flat some ten feet below, protected enough from the rain by a heavy growth of tree overhangs that caught most of the diagonally falling rain.

"You're going to sign this paper eventually; you might as well do it now and save yourself the pain."

Another crack punctuated the words. The crack turned out to be a slap, and the voice turned out to belong to a monkey-faced man with arms to match. Cormac Lynch had found Lambert, and the victim turned out to be a woman who had fallen to the edge of the firelight.

"Come on, get up. I didn't hit you that hard." The monkey took a drink from a whiskey bottle, and then continued. "I want to thank you for riding out to us like you did. It was damn foolish of you to be out alone, but it certainly saved me a lot of trouble, especially the way you're dressed and all, but who the hell did you think you was anyway, riding into this camp full of men like a crazed woman?

"Yeah, I know you rode one of us down and got three more before your gun went empty, but you caught us by surprise, lady. We never thought about a woman being able to shoot like that. And Cotton'll probably die by morning, that'll make it five. But we got you now, and you're not going anywhere. I intended to have you and your ranch, and I still will. But if you cooperate, I'll let you live as my wife, and we'll fix up the ranch even better than it is now. If not, after you sign the deed over to me, I'll have you right here, then turn you over to the men." He took another drink from the bottle.

"There ain't gonna be much left of you when they're done. They're pretty mad that you managed to kill some of their friends, so when they're done with you, we'll just plant you right here under a couple tons of rocks and tell everyone you went away. Nobody will believe us, but there won't be anything they can to do about it. And without you, we'll be able to handle your men."

The woman began to move, and Cormac knew without seeing the red hair that it was Lainey. He had found Lambert; now all that was necessary was to put a bullet through him, and Cormac could rest in peace.

Lambert pulled Lainey to her feet. There was blood coming from her nose, and even in the poor firelight Cormac could see bruises. She was only wearing some kind of nightgown, and it was torn at the top. Lainey Nayle was standing straight and proud, staring Lambert in the eyes and refusing to respond, and it was making Lambert furious.

"You wouldn't talk to me in town, and you think you're too damned good to talk to me now, but you will. And I'm going to enjoy every minute of it. By the time I get done with you, you'll do and say a lot of things you never thought you would."

The fury and rage of losing his family and what had happened to his mother and Becky that he had thought forgotten roared through him!

No . . . No! God damn, no! Not again! This was not going to happen to Lainey!

He yanked out the Colt. He was goin' to put a lot of great big holes in that son of a bitch, and the .44 Colt was just the thing to do it.

Then Cormac Lynch waged his greatest battle ever—to keep control of his mind. It was in him to blast Lambert the hell off the face of the earth, but that wouldn't get Lainey anything but dead. There were others that had to be accounted for. Cormac willed himself to act rationally. Quietly, he reloaded his guns. In his haste, he fumbled and dropped some of the cartridges, removed more from the packages, and tried again.

Having counted seven men around the fire, Cormac was wishin' mighty hard he had his third gun, but wishin' wasn't going to make it happen. He had left one with the lion. Holding the guns under his arm to muffle the sound, one at a time he cocked them both and worked himself into a sitting position on the edge of his rock shelf.

Lambert was still hitting Lainey from time to time, detailing exactly what he was going to do to her.

Like hell he was!

Cormac was going to see about that in short order. Cormac upped his guns to begin firing when another voice came from an area away from the fire, which had previously gone unnoticed by him. It was the first that he had realized there was such an area out of his vision and that there was at least one somebody there, maybe more.

That complicated matters. He dared not start shooting from where he was if he couldn't see everyone; there would certainly be a gunfight. Lainey might get killed. Cormac couldn't run, probably couldn't even walk, but he could sure as hell fall—and he could shoot. And if he could stay on his feet just fifteen seconds, he should be able to see all areas and get the job done. He looked up at the sky and said silently, "God, just help me stay on my feet long enough to get her out of this, please. Then I'm all yours," after which he added, "if you want me."

He probably didn't.

Cormac took a deep breath and, with the .44 Colt in his left hand and a .44 Smith & Wesson in the right, he slid off the edge of the shelf, firing twice on the way down.

Something had drawn Lainey's attention. She looked up just as he jumped. "No, don't!" she cried.

One of his bullets caught a man by the fire; the other bullet, which he had earmarked for Lambert, missed. Lambert was fast, Cormac would give him that, no slowpoke he. At the warning, Lambert had stepped to the side, two guns materializing in his hands while Cormac was still falling.

As Cormac landed, something slammed him backward against the stone wall supporting the above-shelf, and he heard Lainey scream. He brought both guns to bear on Lambert, wanting desperately to empty them both into him, but he dared not. He couldn't spare that many bullets. There were others to deal with; he would have to place his shots precisely, but he could sure as hell make sure that cold-blooded bastard died. Cormac fired both guns at the same time, one bullet going into Lambert's center chest, the other between his eyes. The force knocked him backward into the darkness.

The others were getting into action so there was no time to be selective. It was just pick a target and fire. Cormac had only twelve bullets to begin with and had used four of them getting two men. He knew where his bullets had gone and knew both to be dead.

Disappointingly, there had been three out of his sight. Sanderson was one of them. He went down as easy as any other. That left eight and Cormac figured he had maybe seven bullets left. If he never missed and hit every one of seven shots, which was a tall order, he would still come up one short. He felt more blows, but the wall held him upright, and he was able to keep firing. Lainey had gotten her hands on a gun from somewhere and was working it as fast as she could. Ah, they made a pair to draw to, Lainey and he did; they made a pair to draw to. Too bad they could never be togeth—

CHAPTER 21

The voices were back, this time with no sound of urgency in them. A man and a woman were speaking softly.

"I don't understand what has kept him alive this long; he was leaking like a sieve." The woman was speaking in a whisper. "He had been clawed by some kind of animal and had six wounds bandaged that he must have gotten while taking the dynamite away from them. Two of them looked like he had dug bullets out himself, and one of them he cauterized himself. He took seven more when he jumped off the ledge. God had to have been on his side; none of them hit any bones or anything critical." She paused. "I'll never forget the mixture of fear and happiness I felt to look up and see him coming off that rock."

"I bet that was somethin'," the man answered. "I would have paid money to see that. There was an outlaw not too long back named Cole Younger got himself eleven bullets put into him. Him and his gang tried to rob a small-town bank in Minnesota, and the townsfolk shot the stuffin's out of 'em. He lived to tell about it though, and to get sentenced to life in prison."

Apparently, Cormac wasn't dead, but he had no idea of how he came to be wherever it was that he was. The bed he was in was very soft and comfortable, as was the pillow under his head, much the same as the down pillow his mother had made him for his eighth Christmas, a match for the down-filled blanket she had given him the year before. Unmoving, he listened to the conversation. The last time he remembered moving had not been a pleasant experience. He was not anxious to try again.

His eyes were working fine though; they verified what his ears had been telling him. That soft Irish lilt could only belong to Lainey. She was talking to the bowlegged fellow who had tried to get the drop on him. Cormac must have been unconscious for several days as the bruises on her face were mostly healed and barely noticeable. He had been right: all grown up, with the flickering light of the fireplace playing softly across her face and the red highlights in her hair, she was magnificent. But that didn't do her justice. His mind struggled for a description that would. He regretted not having studied harder and learned more words. The only words that came to mind were from a theatre poster he had seen in Denver: stunningly magnificent. In his own words: dynamite-blowin' beautiful. No . . . Lainey Colleen Nayle was another example of God's finest work: exquisite perfection.

Sven had said his girl was so beautiful it hurt his eyes to look at her. That was most certainly not the case with Lainey. Cormac's eyes were not bothering him one little bit. He would have been more than happy just to lie there looking at her forever. It occurred to him that he felt good—contented. Like the man called Rooster in the old-timer's story, Cormac's years of wandering had been a continuous search for what he had not known he was searching for, and, like Rooster, he had found it: feisty, redheaded, and Irish, Lainey Nayle. He was through wandering, and there was not one damned thing wrong with him. The other women he had met but couldn't get interested in before just weren't Lainey.

The man's voice took on an accusing tone. "But none of that would have happened at all if you wouldn't have lit out in such an all-fired damned hurry," he said angrily.

Obviously, he cared for her, and then Cormac realized the tone in their voices said they cared for each other. Well and good . . . Well and good. At least she had found somebody. Cormac tried to be happy for her—it didn't take.

His feelings of contentment had been short-lived. He remembered how she was going to look at him when she realized he was awake; she had seen him kill more people. The coldness and hatred would again be in her eyes, her wrath would take control of her face, and venom would overwhelm her sweet Irish lilt.

For the first and only time in Cormac's life, he felt fear. He couldn't deal with her hatred and wished Lambert would have been a better shot. She couldn't know he was awake. Quickly, he closed his eyes before the tears escaped.

When he again came to, the light coming in the partially open door illuminated and created shadows on the lavender curtains and the picture on the wall. This was definitely a lady's room, most likely Lainey's. Cormac remembered that she had liked lavender. He was in her bed. Without success, he tried to remember how he had come to be there.

The last he remembered was jumping off the rock shelf, the sulphuric, acrid smell of gunpowder, and straining to see through the smoke. He had to get out of there. He had been shucked out of his clothes and the only thing he had on was the bottom half of his long underwear with one leg missing. It must have been cut off to treat a wound. Cormac did not even want to know how he had gotten that way.

His clothes had been washed, neatly folded, and stacked on the dresser; his boots were sitting on the floor looking clean and well oiled. He remembered one getting soaked with blood and thinking it would be ruined. Somebody had spent a great deal of time on them. It took a few minutes, but he got to his clothes and with one hand or the other on the dresser for support, managed to get them on. The shirt wasn't his and fit him before he had it all the way on, but it would do.

The window opened silently. With his stomach sickening from the effort, Cormac stumbled and fell his way over the sill and to the ground, sitting in the dirt and leaning back against the house, waiting for the nausea to pass. It took a while.

When it had, he gritted his teeth against the pain and staggered to his feet. There was something warm running down his side. He put his hand inside his shirt and it came out dark in the moonlight: most likely blood. Well, at least he had some left.

It would stop after he got up on Lop Ear and let him do the walking. Then Cormac remembered the mountain lion. Damn! Lop Ear and Horse were probably halfway back to Dakota by now. He forced himself erect once more and started slowly across the yard to the barn. There would be some horse there; it didn't matter whose. He could turn it loose after he found Lop Ear and Horse, and it would eventually find its way home.

In reality, after they had calmed down, they would most likely have returned to camp and were probably waiting there for him. He didn't doubt that wherever they were, they would be together.

He thought he was doing pretty well, until he realized that he was facedown in the dirt. He struggled to his knees and was trying to get to his feet again when the door burst open and Lainey rushed out.

"What in the Holy God damned hell do you think you're doing?" she called bitterly and explosively.

There it was: all the anger and rage he wanted so badly to escape. He wanted desperately to not be face to face with her. Cormac had never lost sleep worrying about what people thought of him, other than for Lainey.

She rushed to him and fell to her knees on the ground facing him and held his shoulders to keep him upright. The moonlight was bright, and he was surprised to see tears on her cheeks. Lainey was crying? With Lambert out of the way and the bow-legged fella to care for her, Cormac thought her life was once again in order.

"I'm sorry," he said meekly, placing the first two fingers of his left hand on her lips, trying to stop her before she could say the words that were going to destroy him. "Please . . . I'm sorry. I was trying to leave so you wouldn't have to deal with me again, honest. So you could just enjoy your life here on the L-Bar N, your Lainey Nayle ranch. I just couldn't handle the thought of hearing the anger in your voice and seeing that hatred in your eyes again," he said, shaking his head, "not from you, Lainey."

Lainey removed his fingers and stared at him for a very long moment without speaking, processing what he had told her. Then her face got all twisted up, her lips started quivering, and more tears began flowing. Slowly shaking her head, she caught a ragged breath and murmured incredulously, "You ninny . . . you sweet, wonderful ninny. You came all the way here from wherever you came from, knowing you were putting your life on the line, and nearly lost it fighting for me, all the while believing that I hated you? My God!" she said, still shaking her head sadly. "My God! I am so sorry!"

She put her arms around him and began bawling, actually bawling, her face tucked deeply into his neck. Dumbfounded was another word from the book that he could never imagine anyone using, but here he was, totally dumbfounded. He never had been able to throw a noose around the thoughts in a woman's head.

Presently, her sobs subsided. Taking his hands in hers, she sat back on her heels and looked at him. Now that he was no longer trying to move, he had regained a little strength and was able to sit up on his own. She let go of his hands and used her apron to wipe her eyes. For a long moment, she just looked at him in silence, and then her eyes fell to the arrowhead hanging around his neck and again welled up with tears. She reached for the arrowhead she had given him so long ago.

Holding it in her two hands, she said softly, "I have always prayed for the opportunity to tell you how sorry I was for the way I acted. I've never had any interest in anyone else since the sleigh ride when I pretended to sleep on your shoulder. The L-Bar N does not stand for Lainey Nayle; it stands for Lynch and Nayle. The ranch is half yours. Your name is on the title right along with mine. It's only because of you that I have it. It's only because of you that I am even still alive. For as long as I can remember, whenever I have been in danger, somehow you have always been there.

"My dream has always been that someday you would ride through that front gate, and we would take the Bar out of the brand. I have always loved you, and have never been able to imagine you with anyone but me, and I certainly never wanted to be with anyone but you and never have been. I cried when I found the will in your pocket which proves that all the time you were gone, you were thinking of me, too."

She paused to wipe her eyes again, and then looked straight

into his. "Now, Mr. Cormac Lorton Lynch, I have waited so very long, and I would really like it, right here and right now, if you would wrap your arms around me. That is, if I am right . . . if you feel about me the same way as I feel about you . . . and if you have the strength."

He did, and he had.

As he held her, a horse nickered in the darkness, quickly echoed by another, and Cormac could make out Lop Ear and Horse in the darkness, watching them with their heads over the top rail of the corral, as close to him as they could get. As the shadowy figure of a bowlegged cowboy walked past the corral gate, it swung open and Lop Ear and Horse trotted out to stand over Cormac.

His world was complete. He looked up into the heavens to say thank you and found a full moon smiling brightly down upon them. His mother, Pa, and Becky; and Connor and Jasmine Nayle came strongly to mind. He winked. He would have sworn they winked back.

"Look up," Cormac Lynch told Lainey. "Your family and mine are all giving their approval."

The soft glow of the moon reflected from the tears on her upturned face as she looked into the sky for a long and silent moment and then into Cormac's eyes and smiled.

"I know," she said softly, happily snuggling her face gently against his chest, "I know."

AFTERWORD

———◆———

Martha Jane Cannary Burke, "Calamity Jane," born May 1, 1852, was both famous and infamous. She bragged she had been able to cuss like a man at thirteen, and as the oldest of six children, took over as head of the family in 1867 at fifteen when her father died. In her own accounting, she joined General George Custer as a scout and Indian fighter at eighteen, was excellent with guns, drove mule teams, prospected for gold, and fell in love with Wild Bill Hickock. When she died at age fifty-one in 1903, she was buried next to him in Deadwood, South Dakota.

She is said to have worked as a dishwasher, cook, waitress, dance-hall girl, nurse, ox-team driver, scout, Indian fighter, occasional prostitute, and trick-shot artist in Buffalo Bill's Wild West Show. Although fictitious, this meeting with Cormac Lynch is time and situation appropriate and could have been possible.

———

Cole Younger, known to have ridden with Quantrill's Raiders in the Civil War and later, as an outlaw, with his two brothers, Jim and Bob, along with Jesse James, was referred to by Shank Williams in *The Black Hills* as having taken eleven bullets and lived to be sentenced to life in prison.

In actuality, it was reported in an article published by *Return to St. Louis Civil War* that he was interviewed while in prison November 7, 1880. In the article, Cole Younger was quoted as saying, "I have been wounded altogether twenty times, eleven of these wounds were received at Northfield. Jim was wounded four times at Northfield, and six times in all. Bob was never wounded until the pursuit in Minnesota, where he was struck three times."

The Sweet River used in *The Black Hills* is a fictitious river located approximately thirty miles northeast of the Cache La Poudre River in Larimer County, northwest of Fort Collins, Colorado, an area which impressed me greatly with its beauty when I traveled through as a teenager.

The Lynch farm was fictitiously located on the Red Stone Creek, which is about fifty miles northeast of Pierre, South Dakota, my birthplace; about two hundred miles east of the Black Hills, the stomping grounds of Wild Bill Hickok, Calamity Jane, and Crazy Horse; and just a few miles northwest of Highmore, South Dakota, where I lived for a time on a farm, shot at my first rabbit at seven years old—missed—went to a country school, and watched a prairie fire burn many thousands of acres and very nearly myself, a friend, and his mother before being heroically rescued by my father, Earl C. Thompson, who drove fearlessly through a blazing wall of fire.